BP

#12

Charlotte,

It's hard to believe the little town of Indigo is now my home. I hope you'll be able to meet my fiancée, Loretta, and her daughter, Zara, before long. There are still days when I ask myself how I can be so lucky, but I know that despite my past, you wish me well.

These days everybody around Indigo is gearing up for the big Cajun music festival. It should raise enough funds to restore the little opera house to its original condition. Music acts are coming from all over Louisiana, plus a few home-grown performers that would surprise you with their talent. Indigo's no cultural backwater, at least not when it comes to Cajun culture. Too bad the owner decided to show up right now. The guy's Acadian, but has little interest in his family's legacy and is making noises about selling the place. That's got all the members of the preservation committee riled. But with people like Marjolaine Savoy to save the opera house, I have a feeling this guy won't stand a chance. Come down for a visit, Charlotte, and with Marjo's help, I'll show you why the history of this little bayou town is worth celebrating.

Luc

D0684784

Dear Reader,

I have only had the pleasure of visiting Louisiana once. It was one of those parts of the country that is so unique you can't help but love it. I planned a research trip down there for this book, but Hurricane Rita blew into town the day I was supposed to go, wreaking even more devastation on an area already badly hit. In the true spirit of Louisiana, though, the residents are bringing their cities and towns back to life, a little at a time.

My research was completed with the help of many wonderful Louisiana residents: historian Jack Belsom, director of collections at the Louisiana State Museum Greg Lambousy and museum historian Karen T. Leathem, Ph.D., as well as the State Library of Louisiana expert Marc Wellman and the members of the Louisiana State Historical Society. I wish I could have included all the great material they gave me.

History is such a rich teacher. I hope that as you read this book, you are inspired, as I was, to learn more about the people who founded this country and gave each area its own unique flair. This country, and our world, is not just a melting pot—it's a really good bowl of gumbo.

Shirley

SHIRLEY JUMP
The Legacy

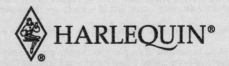

TORONTO • NEW YORK • LONDON
AMSTERDAM • PARIS • SYDNEY • HAMBURG
STOCKHOLM • ATHENS • TOKYO • MILAN • MADRID
PRAGUE • WARSAW • BUDAPEST • AUCKLAND

To all the wonderful people in Louisiana who helped me with the research for this book, proving the spirit of community is alive and well in the bayou.

And also to my brother, Frank, whose loving spirit and generous heart are an example for us all.

ISBN-13: 978-0-373-38949-0
ISBN-10:   0-373-38949-3

THE LEGACY

Copyright © 2006 by Harlequin Books S.A.

Shirley Kawa-Jump is acknowledged as the author of this work.

www.eHarlequin.com

Printed in U.S.A.

Shirley Jump can't sing, dance or clap along to "Kumbaya" so she opted for the only career that doesn't require natural rhythm—writing. She sold her first book to Silhouette in 2001 and now writes books about love, family and food—the three most important things in her life (order is reversible, depending on the day)—using that English degree everyone said would be useless. Though she's thrilled to see her books in stores around the world, Shirley mostly writes because it gives her an excuse to avoid cleaning the toilets and helps feed her shoe-shopping habit.

CHAPTER ONE

ALL PAUL CLERMONT WANTED to do was to conduct his business, rid himself of one unwanted family inheritance and then get out of the heat and humidity of Indigo, Louisiana.

He'd been doing exactly that—until a woman he'd never met screeched into the driveway in a spray of gravel. She'd jumped out of her car and planted herself between him and the real estate agent who held a For Sale sign. "You can't sell this building," the other woman said.

"I'm the owner," he explained. "I can sell it if I want to."

The tall, lean brunette parked her fists on her hips. She was an attractive woman, with a long, neat French braid running down her back. A few stray tendrils wisped around her face, tickling at the soft pink of her cheeks.

She was beautiful—if he ignored the look of annoyance on her face. "All these months, we've been trying to contact you. *Now* you show up to sell the place?"

He quirked a grin at her to show her he wasn't evil incarnate. His ex-wife, however, might disagree. "I'm making a business decision, nothing more. And I think Sandra here—" he thumbed in the direction of the agent who stood mute and frozen in place, holding the sign "—has no issue with me selling this place. Why do you?"

The temper in the brunette's vibrant blue eyes simmered steadily. "Because I care about this building, unlike you."

The blasted Louisiana heat had soaked Paul clear through, even though it was October. If there was a god of humidity, this place would be his headquarters. Paul had been in Louisiana for a few days, doing a follow-up story on hurricane recovery efforts, and had decided to stop by to finally see the property his family had bragged about for years. Clearly, none of them had paid a visit here recently, at least not in this century.

"If you like this place so much," he said, "buy it yourself. Now, if you'll excuse me, I'd like to get this…this *thing*—" he waved at the dilapidated building beside them "—listed."

"It is not a thing," she said. "It's a *legacy.*"

Paul took in a deep breath to calm himself. At the same time, a small chunk of siding fell from the wall—more proof the place wasn't worth the land it sat on—and tumbled to the ground, landing in a jumble of vines and weeds.

The rest of the plantings were, he had to admit, well-tended, as if someone had been working on the grounds but hadn't yet tackled that particular section. Window boxes beneath the tall, elaborate front windows were filled with blooming flowers, and small, carefully trimmed shrubs bordered two sides of the building's exterior.

The opera house had been beautiful once, that was clear. The two-story building had been designed in an imposing Greek Revival style, with tall, arched windows that framed carved double doors large enough for Goliath.

A wrought-iron balcony formed an impressive presence. Paul glanced up, following the lines of a magnificent cupola, which looked freshly restored, along with the roof.

He considered taking out his camera again. His gaze drifted over the opera house, seeing it with his photographer's eye—rather than that of a jaded owner—and for a brief moment the place inspired a feeling of magic, and a direct link to the past.

But then, as he looked closer, he saw the flaws. The peeling white paint, a split window frame, the torn curtains inside.

It was a gorgeous building—that was falling apart at the seams.

He'd taken a few shots of it when he'd first arrived, intrigued by the intricacies of the design, the elegant air amid such a rustic setting. But that was all he wanted, a picture or two that he might be able to sell to his editor down the road, or to some architectural magazine.

As he looked at this "family legacy," Paul figured his uncle Neil, who'd died two months ago, had either a mean sense of humor or a vision problem. The opera house had been passed down through a long line of Valois generations, going eventually to Uncle Neil and now Paul.

After all these years, however, the building defined decrepit, reminding him of Miss Haversham's crazy house in Dickens's *Great Expectations.*

"Why sell it?" the woman asked him. "All you have to do is own it. Amelie Valois's will appointed Indigo as its caretaker. We'll go on doing what we do, and you go on back to whatever it is you do." She paused. "Unless you want to sell it to the town?"

"Is Indigo willing to pay enough to recoup my investment? I just paid off a very much overdue tax bill on this property."

"Considering the town's limited tax base, we could offer," she hesitated, "a dollar."

Paul snorted. "A *dollar?* That doesn't even pay for the gas it took me to get here." He turned back to Sandra. "Where do I sign?"

"Sandra, talk him out of this," the woman said. "You know what the opera house means to the town."

The agent's face went as pale as the white sign she held. She couldn't be a day over twenty, and he suspected she wasn't used to being caught in the crossfire of a verbal brawl over an MLS listing. "Perhaps...you want to come back later?" she squeaked.

"Do you even know what this building is?" the woman asked.

Her again. With the agent about as useful as a stone, Paul had no choice but to deal with the spitfire. He sighed. "The Indigo Opera House. And also a mess."

She let out a gust of frustration that Paul would swear was tinged with smoke. "It's a cultural icon. You can *not* put it up for sale."

"Are you deaf as a haddock?" he demanded. "Because I've already told you that I can, and I am."

Sandra was quaking in her black flats. "Mr. Clermont, you really should hear Marjo out. She's got a point. And, uh, in all honesty, I think Marjo would kill me if I put this For Sale sign up."

So her name was Marjo. It had a nice ring to it, but it came attached to a woman who did, as Sandra had pointed out, look ready to commit a homicide right here on the wide steps—with him outlined in chalk. "All right, Miss—"

"Savoy. Marjolaine Savoy."

"Miss Savoy," he corrected, "I'll hear you out." He flung out his wrist and glanced at the beaten watch that had survived several near-death experiences in his travels. "You've got three minutes."

Although she looked as if she'd rather let out one hell of a high-pitched scream, Marjo bit her tongue, sucked in a breath and eyed him squarely. "The Indigo Opera House was built by Alexandre Valois for his wife just before the Civil War and has been an integral part of this town for centuries. You can't sell it. Indigo is counting on reopening it for the music festival at the end of the month. If you had read *any* of the letters we have been sending you, you'd know all this."

He didn't bother telling her that he was so rarely home in Nova Scotia that sending him mail was a waste of time. Or that his uncle Neil had been bedridden in the last few months of his iife, and probably not up to corresponding with this woman or her committee. He'd heard stories about the opera house over the years, but given the way his Cape Breton family tended to exaggerate at family get-togethers, he'd figured it was more myth than fact. If there was one thing Capers were good at, it was concocting a tale tall enough to rival Paul Bunyan.

When Paul had learned of his inheritance, he'd initially ignored it, intending to deal with it when he had time. That time had never come. One assignment after another had kept him out of Canada more than he was in it.

Then a past-due tax bill had arrived, and after a brief investigation, Paul learned that Uncle Neil had squandered the Valois inheritance on bad stocks and left the property as a negative investment for Paul. The unexpected blow to his wallet had been enough to send him down here between assignments to get rid of the property before he put another dime into it.

Paul wiped his palms together. "I just want to let it become someone else's problem."

Her gaze narrowed. "Aren't you a descendant of Amelie Valois?"

"Yes."

"Then this—" she swept her palm in the direction of the fixer-upper "—is *your* legacy, too."

"Lady, I don't do legacies. I don't put down roots. I don't get to know the neighbors. And I don't renovate opera houses just because some uncle I've seen maybe five times in my life saw fit to dump this thing in my lap." He gave her another grin, then tipped an invisible hat in Sandra's direction. "And since you seem so damned determined to get in my way, I'll have to finish this real estate business later."

"You will not—"

He took a step toward her. If they hadn't been so filled with frustration, her deep blue eyes would stop a man in his tracks. They were the kind that would have intrigued him, had him wondering what thoughts were hidden behind them—on any other day but this one. "Maybe this building is important to you, but it's not worth a damn thing to me. I *will* sell it and you won't stop me."

Then he turned on his heel and walked back to his rental car. He heard her muttering unflattering comparisons between him and several species of four-legged animals.

If Marjolaine Savoy was on Indigo's welcome committee, it was no wonder the town's human population was lower than its alligator one.

HER MOTHER'S Pfaltzgraff had never taken such a beating. Marjo had come home from the confrontation in front of the opera house and started cleaning. She took out her frustrations on the dishes, seeing Paul Clermont's face in every soap bubble. She tried to scrub his image off the dinner plates, but he stubbornly refused to go.

"Are you okay, Marjo?" A soft hand on her shoulder, and instantly her temper subsided.

She turned to look into the sweet, trusting eyes of her younger brother. "Yes, Gabriel, I am. Just a little frustrated today, that's all."

He looked at the dishes and the sloshed water all over the countertop. "Did you have hard-to-clean plates?"

It took her a second to make the connection. "Oh, no, no. Just a bad day overall."

"Poor Marjo." Gabriel reached out and pulled her into a hug, a tight, nearly smothering embrace that pressed her face into the crook of his shoulder. When had her brother gotten so tall? He'd always seemed little to her, as if he'd never passed the age where he needed her to walk him to the bus, to be sure he had his lunch money, his math book.

Despite the years that had passed, one thing hadn't changed: the protective love of the brother who had relied on her ever since their parents had died. To others, his embraces might seem needy, but she understood them.

When Gabriel loved someone, he loved fiercely,

with no judgments, no boundaries. Marjo thanked God once again for his calming, accepting presence.

When he finally let go, she looked up at him and smiled. "You're the best, Gabriel. You always know exactly what I need."

"You feel better?" His sea-green eyes were still shadowed by concern.

She nodded. "I do."

"Good." A bright smile broke across his face. "Can I have some peanut butter?"

Marjo laughed and made him a sandwich, which he happily took out to the front porch to eat, sitting in the rocker and pushing off from time to time, rocking in the easy breeze. Gabriel was like that, so concerned, so ready to help, and then just as quickly content with a couple pieces of bread, some peanut butter and a cushy seat on the old wooden porch.

After the death of their parents in a car accident, she had been left to care for then five-year-old Gabriel, whose IQ was now around seventy. Because he was at the high end of the mental disability scale, the doctors had said Gabriel would be able to live on his own someday, needing only minimal assistance from Marjo in doing things like filling out loan and job applications, making big decisions.

But Gabriel was sweet and trusting, often too much so. Over the years there had been cruel children who had taken advantage of his mild nature. He'd also been the kind of kid who would run after a butterfly in the middle of his own birthday party, or who would forget his shoes and be halfway to school before he noticed.

Stepping into the role of Gabriel's caretaker had been a no-brainer, really, even though Marjo had been nineteen, in her second year of college and on the cusp of starting her own life.

Gabriel had needed her, needed someone who loved him, understood him and could make sure he avoided the potholes and speed bumps in life.

So she was there.

She watched him munch away, without a care in the world, and again felt the heaviness of the day descend upon her shoulders. Damn that Paul Clermont. There was no way he was going to sell the opera house, not when the restoration committee was on the verge of restoring it to its former glory.

The CajunFest was a mere two weeks away. Local businesses were counting on the festival to draw in people from all over the area, particularly the ones who often overlooked Indigo in favor of the more touristy St. Martinville and New Iberia. The bean counters on the festival committee were talking thousands of visitors during the course of the day, and the money spent would mean a financial windfall for Indigo.

She and the other members of the committee had worked so hard, for so long, trying to preserve this corner of Indigo's past. Up until now, the Valois family had abided by a loophole in Amelie's will that allowed the town to use the opera house as they saw fit, in order to ensure the property remained an active part of the community. Previous Valois descendents had been cooperative, if a little distant. According to Hugh Prejean, the expert in all things historical in Indigo, no Valois heir had stepped foot on the property in years.

Until now.

She couldn't imagine that. If this building had been part of her family, she would have fought long and hard to maintain its beauty, its place in the community. Didn't Paul Clermont see how important family—and family history—was?

Maybe he'd been orphaned as a small child, left to the wolves because of his disagreeable nature. Marjo chided herself. Surely he hadn't been left to the wolves—

He'd simply been raised to think like one.

Either way, she would fight him if he went forward with his plan to sell the opera house. Restoring that building was the cornerstone of all she, and the committee, wanted to see happen in Indigo. If the opera house regained its former glory, it could help Indigo bring in some much-needed income and give the committee enough money, down the road, to buy it from Paul Clermont for a fair price, thereby ensuring its future.

The opera house meant so much to this town, to its people. There was no way Marjo was going to let some outsider take that away from the bayou she loved.

If it killed her, she was going to prove to Paul

Clermont that the opera house was a worthy legacy, one that deserved his continued ownership.

And if he wanted to pick up a paintbrush and attack the siding, well, she'd cheer him on. And if he didn't, she'd come up with another plan.

That frustrating and handsome but cocky Canadian wasn't going to take away the one element that made Indigo special.

CHAPTER TWO

"HEY, MARJO! You home?" Her best friend, Cally, gave a quick rap on the screen door, then let herself in after giving Gabriel a quick hello. He returned the greeting, jammed the last couple bites of his sandwich into his mouth and clambered down the stairs, shouting to Marjo that he was going out.

With Darcy, his girlfriend, Marjo supposed. She went to the door to call after her brother, to remind him to be home early, but he was already gone. Gabriel had met Darcy in high school, and found a kindred spirit in the girl who was much like him, only a bit more independent. Darcy lived on her own, held down a part-time job and was attending beauty school. In the year they'd been dating, she'd inspired Gabriel to want the same level of independence, regardless of whether he was ready for it. Marjo still had to remind him to eat, to turn off the stove. Despite what Darcy or Gabriel thought, she knew her brother wasn't yet ready to make that leap.

Marjo sighed and shook her head. Lately she felt she was losing that battle.

Despite the hot October day, Cally looked cool and fresh. Maybe it was her blond hair or her easy, friendly manner, but she never seemed bothered by anything, especially not the heat. "I heard you had a showdown at the OK Opera House." She mock-fired two pistols with her hands.

Marjo laughed. "Word travels fast."

"*Chérie,* dis is de bayou," she said, affecting her best Louisiana accent. "You can't sneeze around here without half de town t'inkin' you're dyin' of typhoid five minutes later."

Marjo laughed. "True."

"So tell me, is this hunk who owns the opera house as gorgeous as half the female population of Indigo made him sound?"

"He's not attractive at all." Marjo turned her face away, busy pouring them each a glass of iced tea.

"Liar." She followed Marjo out of the kitchen and into the front room, where the tall multipaned mullion windows faced the porch and the picturesque view of the deep, lush and vibrant bayou.

Marjo paused at the window for a moment. A hundred years ago her great-grandfather had built this little cottage. But when his son, her grandfather, had started Savoy Funeral Home, the Savoy families had moved into the spacious apartment upstairs, to be ready at a moment's notice for a family in grief. Marjo and Gabriel's father, Timothy, had been the second generation to run the funeral home, which had come to be known as a place that catered to traditional Cajun values and traditions.

But when Timothy Savoy had brought his Atlanta-born bride to Indigo, Elaine had refused to use the funeral parlor as a home. She'd never spent a night there. The day they returned from their honeymoon, the newlywed Savoys had moved into the cottage.

Timothy, smitten until the day he died, had indulged his wife, especially in her love for gardening. Every year, moonflowers wrapped their evening beauty around the porch posts, up a lantern pole installed when Marjo was three, and around virtually anything that stood still. Camellias of all colors burst brightly among shrubbery and indigenous plantings. For every season, there was a bloom—Violet Wood Sorrell for spring, Summer Snapdragons, Camellia Sasanqua for the fall. Elaine Savoy had carved out a pretty little oasis in this corner of the bayou. But despite her garden, Marjo's mother had never been happy here.

Perhaps if her mother had put down roots in the community instead of in the ground, Marjo thought, she might have smiled more and cried less.

Marjo turned away from the window and took a seat in Grandmother Savoy's rocking chair, one of a thousand family pieces that made up the cottage's decor. Cally sank into the embroidered armchair beside her.

"So what did this guy do that was so bad?" Cally asked.

"Tried to put the opera house on the market as if it was a painting that didn't fit with his new sofa."

"And that's a bad thing because…?" Cally asked. "I mean, wouldn't a new buyer keep it running?"

"Not necessarily," Marjo said. "Remember Dewey's Country Store, that little mom-and-pop place in New Iberia? Some developer came in and snatched that up. Thought he could turn a frog into a mink coat."

"I remember that. I don't know anyone who shops at that fancy deli. Next they'll be bringing in some uppity coffee shop to try to convince us a six-dollar cup of coffee is a good idea."

"Exactly," Marjo said. "Which is why I don't want Paul Clermont selling the opera house. We've raised a good chunk of the money we need to finish the restoration and get it opened again. But we're a long way from being able to buy it. None of the Valois heirs before him stood in our way. They were happy to see the space being used instead of going to waste. But now that Sophie's moved the antique shop into Maude's cottage, the opera house is just sitting there, not bringing in income—or anything else."

"Yeah, but the new location has really helped business for Past Perfect," Cally said. "Sophie's on cloud nine, even if she is being pulled in three directions at once, between commuting to Houston, the shop and her pregnancy."

"Not to mention keeping her new husband happy," Marjo added. "Despite all those commitments, she's been a big bonus to the restoration and the CajunFest committees. Her fund-raising experience helped us bring in some outside support for the festival. But then she got so busy, she needed to find some way to cut back. I told her the committee would be fine, that she should just see to her new family."

"You don't have to take the whole thing on your shoulders, Marjo," Cally chided. "And before you argue with me, you and I both know that's what you tend to do."

"I've got the committee."

Cally's pursed lips said she disagreed, but she didn't say anything further.

"Either way, Paul Clermont can't just sell the opera house to become some office building or boutique." Marjo rocked back in the chair. "I can't let the opera house disappear, Cally. It may not be part of my family, but it's a part of Indigo. And we need to preserve our history."

There were days when it seemed Indigo, and its past, was all Marjo had left of her family. Tante Julia lived in a nursing home in New Iberia. Marjo had a bachelor uncle who had moved to Lafayette, but in Indigo, there were no Savoys besides her and Gabriel. But it was more than that. After her parents had died, the people of Indigo had become her family, wrapping their sheltering arms around young Marjo. They'd been there whenever she needed them to help her raise Gabriel and continue the family funeral home business. They'd helped her get used to the adult shoes thrust on her at a young age.

"Maybe it's time to move forward, Marjo, instead of looking back." Cally's voice was soft, tinged with care. Marjo knew her friend meant more than just the opera house. The past year had been one of standing still for Marjo, when she knew she should be moving forward. It had seemed so much easier to embrace the status quo than add another element into an already precariously balanced life.

"Sometimes keeping the past around reminds you of what's important," Marjo countered, running a palm along the arm of the rocker. "My mother loved that opera house."

"She did? I never knew that. Did she sing?"

"No, but she loved music. She was from the city, born into a monied family, and she always missed that life. Whenever she went to a performance at the opera house—back then, there was the occasional musical by a local church, things like that—she felt like she had stepped back in time. For just a moment she could return to her old life and leave the bayou behind. She loved my father, but she hated Indigo."

"Why didn't they ever move? Was it because the family business was here?"

"Partly," Marjo said. "But mainly because my mother couldn't go back to what she had left. The minute she married a Cajun, her family cut her off— financially, physically and emotionally. It's funny that a hundred and fifty or so years after Alexandre and Amelie, a family would still sever blood ties because their daughter had married a man they found unsuitable."

"You never saw your grandparents?"

Marjo shrugged. "I don't think they even know Gabriel and I exist, assuming they're still alive."

"And you haven't wanted to contact them?"

Marjo glanced out the window at the bayou she loved so much. "My family is here."

Cally reached over and gave Marjo's hand a quick squeeze. "And look at the bonuses you get—we're just as dysfunctional as some real families."

Marjo laughed. "Anyway, that's why all this is so important to me. And for a lot of people in Indigo, restoring the opera house is like a sign of hope, I guess. It's a way for the town to grow and prosper, yet still preserve our links to the past."

Cally nodded, sipping at her iced tea. "You have a point. When Luc Carter came in and turned La Petite Maison into a successful bed-and-breakfast, he brought a little bit of hope to the bayou. Not to mention some very good-looking visitors."

Marjo laughed. "I think you'd be happier if the bed-and-breakfast only catered to Chippendales dancers."

"Hey, I'm all for supporting the performing arts."

Marjo sobered. "Well, I just want to support this community. I look around me and I see the Cajuns getting swept up into pop culture, trading their heritage and customs for cool jeans and fast food. We need to protect what we have left, for the future. For our kids."

"Speaking of that," Cally said, "when are you going to find yourself a man and have a few of those? Babies, I mean."

"You know I can't do that," Marjo said quietly. Yet, even as she spoke, a little voice inside her reminded her that she was thirty-five and her clock wouldn't be ticking forever. She turned and looked out the window. "I can't start a family, not as long as Gabriel needs me. He's not ready for life on his own, and I'm afraid that if I pushed him out too soon, he'd see it as me abandoning him."

Cally leaned forward and touched her friend's hand, her palm soft against Marjo's. "You need to have your life, too. Gabriel is nearly grown up."

"I will. Someday."

Cally bit her lip, but didn't say anything. It was a familiar argument, particularly since Marjo had ended her engagement to Kerry Tidwell last year. Kerry had made it clear he didn't want the package deal of Marjo and Gabriel.

Marjo had decided then and there that until Gabriel was mature enough to live on his own, her love life could wait. Her younger brother was more important than any man who might come along with a ring.

Despite her best intentions, though, the pain of Kerry's betrayal still stung. All along, she'd thought he'd loved Gabriel. Until she realized he'd been talking to group homes and assisted-living communities, and planned to ship Gabriel off as soon as Marjo had said "I do."

Cally kept trying to convince Marjo to let Gabriel go out on his own more, to loosen the proverbial apron strings. But no one knew Gabriel like his sister did. He wouldn't make it on his own. He was too fragile, too gentle, to survive the world out there.

And if that meant she needed to put her own goals on hold for a while, so be it.

Marjo rose and crossed to the ivy plant that hung in the window. She plucked a few dead leaves from the neglected greenery. "Right now, all I'm worried about is getting Paul Clermont to go back to wherever he came from and leave me and the opera house alone."

"Well," Cally said, turning her glass, watching the ice dance, "maybe you should try another tactic. Like, get to know him better."

"Get to know him better?" Marjo spun around. "Yeah, I'll try that—with a twelve-gauge in my hands."

"Hey!" Cally put her hands up. "I'm a lawyer, remember? Don't be plotting a felony in front of me."

Marjo laughed. "I wouldn't *really* do that. It's just that that man is like a nest of yellow jackets kicked up by some overeager teenager with a Weedwacker. He drives me nuts."

Cally waved a finger at her. "Now, be nice, Marjo. You know the old saying—and you also know it wouldn't be an old saying if it weren't true. So if I were you, I'd try catching this fly with some honey. Add a little Savoy sweetener, get him to come around to your ideas about the opera house."

Marjo considered the idea. "You mean, get him to see why the opera house is so important?"

"Yeah."

"I don't know. He doesn't strike me as the sentimental type."

Cally gave her a grin. "Then use your feminine wiles. If there's one thing that can turn a man from alligator to teddy bear, it's a pretty woman with a smile."

CHAPTER THREE

ONE MORE DAY, Paul figured, and he'd have that property listed. All he had to do was to find a Realtor who wasn't afraid of Marjo Savoy.

Given the limited population of Indigo, he'd probably have to go all the way to Lafayette or Baton Rouge to do that. Regardless of what that woman had said, he had no intentions of hanging on to the family money pit.

He would divest himself of the property, just as he had divested himself of nearly everything else that held other people down—his marriage, his furniture, his house—and then be on his way back to Egypt or Africa or wherever *World* magazine chose to send him. Living, as he always had, the life of a nomad.

He was thirty-seven, and that was exactly the life he'd always wanted.

He'd learned, after watching his father work himself half to death in mining jobs that he hated, that life was far too short to spend it killing yourself to pay bills. Paul's mother had stayed in Cape Breton, as rooted to the place as a hundred-year-old tree. Renault Clermont had left his family time and again, crossing Canada to search for work that would keep food on the table.

If Paul had to choose one word to describe his childhood, it would be frenetic. His father gone for long periods of time, his mother retreating to her room. Only when the raucous Clermont relatives arrived, ushering in kitchen parties that lasted into the wee hours, was the house filled with laughter, drinking and fiddling.

No matter that jobs were scarce and half the families were on pogey, collecting government assistance, the musical gatherings took place. Then the relatives would leave and all would fall deathly quiet, his mother unable to deal with the children, the reality of her life.

In many ways, his childhood home seemed much like Indigo—insular, set in its ways. Paul wanted to *experience* his life, to live it, not to look back at seventy-two with regret.

Renault Clermont was a good man, but he'd had the spirit sucked out of him by the daily grind of the mines. It had killed his dreams, dampened his zest for life and made him bitter.

Paul refused to live like that. Today, or any day.

He'd been driving on the River Road, which ran along the bayou, pausing from time to time to take pictures of the oddly barren yet also lush landscape. It was as if death and life had gone to war here, then declared a truce.

When he saw the sign for La Petite Maison, a two-hundred-year-old raised cottage that had been recently converted into a bed-and-breakfast, he decided to have a look. La Petite Maison, like many homes in Indigo, had been built from native cypress wood and was two stories with wraparound verandas.

The sun was already too high in the sky to capture the nuances of the building. But maybe later, once the sun began its daily downward journey, he'd have time to take a few shots. He really wanted to find a way to capture the cozy, retreat-like setting of the little building.

Cozy or not, it was, he suspected, the only lodging option he had in a town as small as Indigo.

Paul parked the rental car in the designated area and strode over to the wide gallery porch. As soon as he walked through the front door, he noticed the stone floor, the brick walls and the friendly face behind a front desk.

He had just handed his credit card over to Luc Carter, the B and B's owner, when an old man, dressed in jeans and a red T-shirt, ambled over to him. "I'm Doc Landry," he said. "Resident grouch."

Paul chuckled and introduced himself.

"I hear you're the Valois heir who tangled with Marjo today," the old man said.

Paul arched a brow. "Talk about news spreading like wildfire."

"Well, hell, boy, you got all the marks of front-page news. You're an outsider *and* you caused a commotion. We haven't had this much excitement in town since Skeeter Thibedaux hooked his big toe at the fishing derby. Won his weight class, too, Skeeter did." He laughed again, then shook his finger at Paul. "That Marjo Savoy, she's harder to handle than a twelve-foot gator during mating season. You better watch out."

"I'll be fine." Paul scrawled his name across the receipt, then filled out the register. Luc gave him a grin. Apparently he'd heard about the incident, too.

"That's what they all think," Doc Landry said. "Marjo isn't one of those women who take no for an answer. No sirree. She's like a tick on a hound when she gets her mind wrapped around something."

"I'm a stubborn man myself."

"That's what I thought—till I met my Celeste." The old man chuckled, then grabbed a pipe out of the back pocket of his jeans and headed toward the back veranda. Even from where Paul stood, he could see the dark bayou waters making their sluggish journey past the property.

He grabbed his bag and slung it over his shoulder. The rugged, roomy backpack had served him well in deserts, rain forests and dirt huts. A dozen interior compartments protected his camera equipment, yet left enough room for a couple days' worth of clothes and a twelve-inch iBook. After years of carrying the same pack, he'd gotten used to the fifty or so pounds on his shoulder, along with the flexibility of just one bag.

Paul crossed the lobby and headed up the stairs, but before he could reach the top, his cell phone started to ring. If he was lucky, it was Joe, his editor at *World,* calling with some hot assignment that would give Paul an excuse to leave this whole opera house mess behind. "Hello?"

"Paul?" His sister Faye's voice, always a welcome sound. "Where the heck are you? I can barely hear you."

"Stuck in the swamp. Or, rather, what looks like a swamp." Entering his room, he shut the door behind him. "I'm in Indigo, Louisiana."

"What on earth are you doing there?"

"Remember that piece of property Uncle Neil left me?" It was a rhetorical question, since his sister had been at the reading of the will. She'd inherited a bunch of furniture and he'd been stuck with a monument. "God only knows why he did, considering I can count on one hand the number of times I've seen him over the years."

"He *was* the hermit type," Faye conceded. "Gee, who does that remind me of?"

Paul was a nomad, not a hermit. Two totally different creatures. Sort of. "Anyway, I'm down here to sell that opera house he left me. After that, I'm planning on heading to Tibet for a spec piece for the *New Yorker.*"

"I thought you didn't have to do that one until November."

Damn Faye's memory. "I thought I'd go a little

early. Rack up some brownie points with the new senior editor."

His sister sighed. "Are you ever coming home?"

"I don't have a home. I gave it to Diane in the divorce, remember?"

"You know perfectly well what I mean," she said, the younger-sister annoyance still in her voice. "I mean here. Cape Breton. Paul, I haven't seen you in months."

"I'll be back."

"When? You blow in and out like a storm. No warning, no hanging around. John and I love having you stay here, as long as you're doing it because you want to see your family, not because we're a convenient flophouse."

"Faye, you know that with my job—"

"Yeah, yeah." She inhaled a breath, and in the background, he could hear her baby start to cry, a little girl he'd only seen in photos. "You know…" she said, pausing as an idea took root, something Paul could almost hear across the phone line. "I think you should hold on to the opera house. Don't you remember all those stories the aunts would tell us about the Valois ancestors? That place is practically part of the family. It might be neat—"

"We never had a real family, Faye. Hell, Dad was gone so much he was more of a stranger than a father. And Mom—" He left off the rest of the sentence. Faye had lived the story. Their mother, too overwhelmed by her nearly single-parent role, had spent her days with soap operas and wine, leaving Paul to raise Faye.

Paul could only thank God that Faye had turned out better than he had. At least Faye had settled down, married a good man and was, as far as Paul was concerned, a nominee for Mom of the Year, the way she doted on her baby. "Besides, I don't see the point in keeping something that's only going to cost me in taxes and upkeep."

"This opera house could be the beginning of a life, Paul, a real one. Something you hold on to for more than five minutes. After that, you can work your way up to a couple kids and a dog."

"Nah, I'll just borrow yours."

"The point is to start *something*, Paul," she went on, ignoring his attempts to deflect the conversation with a joke. "*Now*, before you're too old and you look back and realize you're all alone." Her voice softened with concern. "You can't wander the world forever."

"I was married once."

"So was half of Hollywood. I think you just barely beat the stars in longevity."

He scowled. His marriage had lasted a good year and a half. He'd tried, she'd tried, but in the end, meshing the life of a constant traveler with that of a homebody simply hadn't worked. Diane had been a good woman, but not the right woman. Theirs had been an impetuous youthful mistake, one he regretted, if only because Diane had been caught in the crossfire. "I'm fine the way I am. And might I remind you, I'm also older than you. So I don't need a lecture."

"Yes you do, at least until you give me some nieces and nephews to spoil." She laughed.

He tossed the backpack on his bed. "You never give up, do you?"

"Not when it comes to my brother, no," Faye assured him. "So please, just for me, reconsider selling."

The cell phone crackled and static filled the line for a few seconds. "I'm starting to lose you, Faye— I'll call you later," Paul said, making no promises about legacies and especially none about producing nieces and nephews.

Faye, he knew, was only speaking out of love. She just didn't understand. He wasn't the kind of man who could put down roots and stay long enough to watch them grow into trees. He'd seen so many Capers do that, refusing to leave their island home. They stayed, even as jobs dried up, futures were lost. To Paul, that kind of stubbornness equaled foolishness. He had left home as soon as he'd finished high school. Since that day, he'd been on the road, unattached. And he was happy that way.

Which was exactly why he didn't need to own a piece of property in a sweaty, swampy town he never planned on visiting again.

Within two minutes he had himself unpacked. His cell phone and laptop were connected to their respective chargers, his toothbrush was on the bathroom counter and his bag sat on the floor of the closet, right by the door. He liked to be able to grab and go, with no worries about leaving something forgotten in a drawer.

When he was done, he put the current thriller he was reading on the nightstand and lay down on the four-poster. Immediately his body sank into the featherbed. The mattress was as close to sleeping on a cloud as a man could get. A little slice of heaven in the hot room. Paul unlaced his shoes then kicked them off. They landed on the floor with a hard thud.

Even with the French doors open to the veranda, the room was still warm, the breeze more of a whisper than a real wind. Still, he had to admit, the room was nice. An antique light fixture, made up of several tulip-shaped glass shades. The walls were white, the trim and floorboard wood-dark. The quilt—something he thought might be called a coverlet—was white, the pillows pink. Two small antique reproduction chairs flanked a dresser, complete with an ornate mirror and water pitcher. If he closed his eyes, he could easily believe he had stepped back in time, at least a hundred years.

There was a knock at his door, followed quickly by another more insistent one. Paul got up to see who it was. There were none of those security peepholes in this building, which had to be nearly as old as the opera house. He pulled open the door, hoping whoever it was would go away fast.

Marjo Savoy.

He groaned. Not again.

"Doc Landry downstairs was right," Paul said.

"Right? About what?"

"You *are* as persistent as a tick on a hound dog."

He saw her bite back a retort, then suck in a breath. "I'm here to make peace."

"Peace, eh?" He arched a brow.

"Well, sort of. I want to ask you to dinner."

For a second, the idea of going to dinner with the fiery Marjo intrigued him, but then he realized she wasn't here to ask him on a date. "So you can introduce me to the local gumbo, or sell me on the idea of keeping the opera house? Sorry. Not interested."

She parked a fist on her hips. "You're a photographer, right? For *World* magazine?"

"How do you know that?"

"Nothing stays a secret in the bayou. Soon as Slim Broussard's wife saw a car she didn't recognize driving around town, she was working the phone chain, finding out who you were."

"Well, I won't be here long enough to make the society pages, I assure you."

She didn't listen. "In your job, what do you take pictures of?"

The question caught him off guard. "People, mostly. I've done pieces on a reindeer herder tribe in Siberia, an Incan mummy, modern-day pirates."

"Stories, you mean."

"Yeah."

"Then meet me at the Blue Moon Diner at five o'clock and I'll tell you a story that will change your mind about leaving."

He put up a hand. "I really—"

"*I'll* be there. And if you're not, I'll find you. Doc Landry forgot to mention that I also have the tracking ability of a hound dog." She tossed him a grin, then left, leaving Paul wondering what the hell had just transpired.

And how a woman like that could run roughshod over him so easily.

CHAPTER FOUR

FIVE O'CLOCK came and went. Five-fifteen. Five-twenty. The waitress at the Blue Moon Diner finally stopped asking Marjo if she wanted to order and left her alone, except for the occasional ice-water refill. Marjo waited, patiently—well, as patiently as she could, considering she wasn't sure she possessed the patience gene—for Paul Clermont to show.

Earlier that Sunday afternoon she'd gone to work at the funeral home. There'd been no appointments, no funerals in progress, so she'd had a few minutes to get some work done and to also go online. She'd typed Paul Clermont's name into Google, trying to find out who she was up against. Marjo was a woman who liked to be prepared, who wanted to know the odds—so she could beat them.

What she'd seen had impressed her. Paul Clermont's photos were more than just visual records. He captured the spirit—maybe even the soul—of his subjects. She felt as if she were part of his pictures, in the wilds of New Zealand, the refugee camps of Africa, the Appalachians of West Virginia. Surely the man who had photographed a rare albino gorilla in the Congo and a hidden pyramid chamber in Egypt could have some understanding of the historical importance of the Indigo Opera House.

And if he couldn't, well, she'd have to tie him up and keep him hostage in her back bedroom until he did.

At five twenty-five, Paul entered the Blue Moon, looking so darn handsome she had to hate him on principle. He paused a moment in the doorway, framed by the setting October sun, which burnished his dark hair with gold. He had the broad shoulders and narrow waist that were mandatory requirements for any hero.

A man who was determined to upset her best plans shouldn't look that good. He should be Quasimodo's twin, so that she wouldn't feel her heart skip a beat whenever she looked at him.

Her gaze caught his, and for a second she forgot the purpose for this meeting. How long had it been since she'd gone out on a date? Been attracted to someone to the point where she had trouble remembering her own name?

As he approached, a charge detonated inside her gut. *Mon Dieu,* her own body was staging a mutiny. The trouble was, her mind wasn't sending out any complaints.

She'd never met a man quite like him. Most of the men around Indigo had been worn down by the hard work that living in the bayou demanded—the shrimping, the fishing, the constant worrying about keeping up with the bills and keeping ahead of the water, which seemed to slip in and erode more of the land along the bayou every year.

Marjo wanted to preserve every inch of Indigo, cast it in bronze and show the world this special, incredible place.

For that, she needed Paul Clermont's cooperation. She silenced her hormones and crossed her hands on the table in her getting-down-to-business position.

"I'm sorry I'm late," he said, stopping beside the table. He had one hand behind his back, and when he brought it forward, she saw he was holding a bright bouquet of camellias. "And I'm sorry for being disagreeable earlier."

A flush of surprise filled her as she accepted the bouquet, marveling over the rich color of a pair of Kramer's Supreme variety, the pale hues of a Pink Perfection, as well as a couple High Fragrance varieties, which added a sweet scent to the bunched flowers. She inhaled, a grin spreading across her face, even as she tried to ignore how the flowers had made her anger at him melt away. "You're forgiven."

"Good." He smiled, too, and slid into the seat across from her.

She fingered one of the silky blooms. "Did someone tell you these are my favorites?"

"No, it was a wild guess. Apparently a few things do stay secret in the bayou."

She laughed, then breathed in a second whiff of

the blooms. "My mother planted these all around our house," Marjo said softly. "I love camellias because they remind me of her." Unexpected tears rushed to her eyes. She blinked them away. Why was she getting so emotional now?

"Did she die?" Paul asked, his voice quiet and gentle.

Marjo nodded, still touching the velvety petals of the flower. "In a car accident, with my father, when I was nineteen."

"I'm sorry," he said, and she had no doubt he was being sincere.

"Thank you." She cleared her throat, ridding it of a sudden sentimental lump. "Anyway, let's get down to business."

"I do have an excuse for being late, by the way," Paul said. "I started taking pictures of La Petite Maison, because the light at this time of day was too good to pass up, and I lost track of time. And again, I'm sorry to keep you waiting."

"Is that an occupational hazard?" she teased, the flowers having lightened her mood considerably.

"It is. And a real problem when the last ferry has already left or you missed your plane out of Zimbabwe." The smile on his face was far too attractive. It was the kind of smile that asked a woman to open up, to trust him, to take this beyond a simple conversation. For a moment she considered doing just that, forgetting her reason for being here and just talking to him as a woman talked to a man.

A little selfish indulgence.

The waitress came over and deposited a menu in front of him, but he didn't open it.

Marjo suppressed the attraction building inside her. "Aren't you going to order?"

"Are you sure you won't have them poison my food? A little salmonella for the enemy?"

"I hadn't thought of that." She laughed. "Maybe next time."

He arched a brow. "Remind me never to let you cook for me."

The words whispered an innuendo, a hint of them spending more time together, and a need that had gone unanswered for too long now made itself known.

An image came to mind of Paul Clermont in her bed, his long, lean body curling around hers.

She'd been alone for such a long time, playing the role of mother, head of the household, business owner, but not woman. And definitely not a woman who put her own needs high on the priority list. What would it be like to do that? Just for one night?

Whoa, that wasn't why she was here. She grabbed the other menu and read the day's specials again, even though she'd figured out ten minutes ago what she wanted to eat.

"What do you recommend?" Paul asked.

"Well, if you're adventurous, there's the alligator special." She gestured toward the stuffed alligator head hanging over the lunch counter, then laughed at the face he made. "If you're more traditional, Estelle makes the best gumbo and turtle soup in the world. It's her specialty." She lowered her voice and cupped a hand around her mouth, knowing how easily even a whisper could travel in this town. "It's even better than my tante Julia's, but don't tell anyone I told you so."

"Your secret is safe with me." He smiled at her, and the electrical charges she'd felt before ratcheted up, increasing her appetite for something other than the Blue Moon's Sunday night special.

When their waitress returned with two icy glasses of tea, Paul took her suggestion and ordered the soup. Marjo opted for the same. Once they were alone again, she tucked the flowers into the space beside her, then began. "I promised you a story."

"About the opera house?"

"No, I don't think I'll tell that one now," she said, changing her plan. Although he seemed interested, she was afraid that if she told him the opera house's history today, it would still be too easy for him to walk away. Rather, she wanted to foster in him the same love for Indigo that she had, starting with the story that had long ago ignited her own curiosity. "Instead, I want to tell you about La Petite Maison."

"The bed-and-breakfast?"

She nodded. "Their histories are intertwined, like most everything around here. The land was owned by Alexandre Valois and was just one of many properties he built in Indigo in the early 1800s." She paused as the waitress deposited the generous bowls of soup in front of them. "Alexandre had a manservant who worked for him, a man by the name of Charles Baptiste. Charles was loyal to the core and had been with Alexandre since he was a baby. From what I've read in Alexandre's papers, it was clear Charles would have done anything for the boy he'd pretty much raised into a man. Alexandre's parents were distant, more the type that had children to carry on the family name, but little else."

"There are still people that do that—leave the raising of their kids to someone else," Paul said, giving Marjo the feeling that perhaps his childhood had been less than ideal.

She left that issue alone. "Shortly before Alexandre got married, Charles fell ill. So ill, he became bedridden and couldn't serve Alexandre anymore."

"And in those days, there was no such thing as disability pay."

"No, but Alexandre was committed to the people around him. He built the cottage, which later became La Petite Maison, for Charles and his wife and children."

"That's pretty generous. It's a gorgeous property."

Marjo smiled. "It still pales in comparison with the plantation house Alexandre built for his wife, but that's another story. Alexandre chose that remote location because Charles was a private man, and Alexandre knew that his friend would want to be away from the lack of privacy in Indigo. Charles was afraid people might alienate him because they thought his illness was contagious or had been some twisted punishment from God. Alexandre spared no expense, even bringing in a doctor from France and housing him in one of the outbuildings."

"In short, he did everything he could for the man," Paul said.

Marjo nodded. "In the end, it wasn't enough. Charles died a year later, a long, slow, agonizing death. From what we've pieced together from the sketchy medical records left by the doctor, we think it might have been stomach cancer."

Paul shuddered. "Not a good way to go. He must have suffered."

"After Charles died, Alexandre told Charles's family they could stay in the house, and he would continue to pay them Charles's salary, even though his friend and the man he considered his true father was gone."

"A man who thought with his heart," Paul said, finding the meaning in her words, "not his wallet."

"Exactly." Marjo held up a finger, telling Paul the story was far from done. "But here's where it gets interesting."

Paul had his spoon halfway up to his mouth, then he paused. "There's more?"

"After her husband died, Charles's wife never spent another day in that house. She took the kids, whatever money was left, went to France and never returned." Marjo quirked a grin. "Oh, and she took one other person with her."

Paul leaned forward. "Who?"

"The French doctor. Apparently they'd grown *very* close over her husband's sickbed."

"Quite the grieving widow." He shook his head. "Makes me feel bad for Charles."

"It worked out okay. One of the maids who worked for Alexandre turned out to be Charles's mistress, and the child she'd had three years earlier was his. As loyal as Charles was, he apparently made excellent use of his time off."

Paul laughed. "This is all true?"

"Yeah. We pieced it together from birth records and letters. It was quite the scandal in those days, particularly when Charles's widow left with the doctor. But until the day he died, Alexandre stuck by Charles and defended his name. He paid for Charles's illegitimate child to be educated. The maid and the boy moved into the cottage and lived quite well."

"That puts the little bed-and-breakfast into a whole new light."

"That's why I told you that story instead of the one about the opera house. I want you to *see* the opera house first, like you did La Petite Maison, then hear its story."

"I have seen it."

"But not the way you saw La Petite Maison today. You told me you were so wrapped up in capturing that building on film that you forgot the time, forgot our meeting, forgot everything." She paused and took a sip of water, deciding this was as good a time as any to make her case, to finally get to the reason she'd invited Paul here. "Do me a favor. Spend more than a few minutes with the Indigo Opera House. I think you'll see it in a whole new light, too. And then you'll realize you can't possibly let it go."

"Don't you think a new owner would be more supportive of your plans? More involved?"

"Maybe. And maybe not. Besides, all you have to do is remain the owner. I'm sure the town can give you a break on the taxes. And the restoration committee will handle everything else. The same thing happened with Shadows-on-the-Teche, when the original owner's grandson decided to sponsor a revival of the buildings."

"It's not just about the tax bill. I don't *want* to own an opera house. To me, that wreck of a building is a tie. And I don't like ties."

"But you *can't* sell it," Marjo protested. "Not now. If you put it on the market, we'll be forced to stop the restoration. We're having enough problems getting funding since hurricanes Katrina and Rita. Tourism dried up for a long time, and people are afraid to invest in an area that has already suffered so much. The committee, and the town itself, won't support something that might end up being sold to some developer who will tear it down and put up a discount store in its place."

"Here? In the middle of nowhere? I think the chances of that happening are remote."

Did he have to take her literally? "Either way, the committee won't want to sink any more time or effort into something that might not be there in three months, or six. And you are a Valois, and to the committee, having a Valois on the deed is vital."

"Why? As far as I know, none of the Valois family has been down here in years. I wasn't even sure the place really existed, that it was just a family tale, until it popped up in my uncle Neil's will. An uncle I'd rarely seen, I might add, and who'd never shown up at a Sunday dinner to boast about this 'treasure.' To most people in the family, this place was a good story for Sunday dinners, nothing more."

"Your uncle remembered it," she said. "He was here once, in the early fifties. Though he never had the money we needed to restore it, I think he wanted to make sure the property stayed in the family."

Paul sat back in his chair. "My uncle was *here?* In Indigo?"

"I never met him, but Hugh, the town historian, told me Neil came into town long enough to pay a visit to the opera house. He didn't stay long. Hugh said he got the feeling Neil was the kind of man who liked to be alone."

"He was the family hermit. We rarely saw him."

"Either way, after his visit, he wrote to Hugh once in a while to see how the place was doing. For the last thirty years or so, a woman named Maude Picard rented the opera house and turned it into an antique store. She dealt with a lawyer in New Orleans, and when she died last January, we tried to contact Neil but never heard back."

"He was quite ill. Cancer."

"I'm sorry," she said with sincerity. She clasped her hands on her lap, praying she could get her message across to him. This moment might be the only one she had to convince Paul not to sell. "You need to understand something about Cajuns. If there's one thing that's important to the people of this area, it's their heritage. Their traditions. Their customs. The opera house is a part of that heritage." She lifted her hand and toyed with her spoon. "This area is…unique, just like I hear Nova Scotia is. It's filled with people who are fiercely protective of their heritage. We have our own dialect. Our own type of food. You won't find what we have here anywhere else in the world, and because of that, a lot of us are fighting to preserve our heritage."

"Even as the world around you changes." He spooned up some gumbo.

"Yes."

"Fine. Then I'll sell it to someone who promises to keep the building as it is. Maybe I'll even name it The Valois or something. That should make you happy and honor my uncle's wishes."

Again, he was trying to wash his hands of the building, as if it were bothersome dirt. "That's not enough," Marjo protested, ignoring her gumbo, which was quickly growing cold. "To keep it truly the Indigo Opera House, it has to be owned by a Valois, because they're the ones that founded it, and to people here, nothing can replace generations of ownership. If you knew the history—"

"I know enough. If there's one thing my uncles and aunts like to do, it's talk about where they came from. They rehash several hundred years of history and make it sound as if we were still trying to get out from under the English. Just because my relatives are like that doesn't mean I am. I like feeling disconnected—unattached to anyone or any thing. I live out of a backpack and I don't worry about being home for supper for anyone. I come and go as I please, and thankfully, I get paid to do that."

Marjo shook her head, unable to believe anyone would prefer to live their life free of family ties and roots, particularly someone who had grown up in an area so entrenched in its history. She'd always been such a part of this community and found it inconceivable that someone wouldn't have a place to call home, a place that surrounded you like a warm blanket on a chilly night. "To me, that's sad. What kind of life is that?"

"Depends on who's living it. I happen to think my life is perfect the way it is." He went back to his soup.

She glanced at his left hand. No wedding ring. She shouldn't be surprised, given what he'd just told her, but she was. Paul was tanned, fit and seemed to be a happy, successful man, the kind any woman in her right mind would want. Yet when Marjo looked in his blue eyes, she got a feeling—those same feelings her granny Lulu used to get about storms on the way—that Paul Clermont's life was not as perfect as he painted it. "Why don't you come out and take pictures of the opera house?"

"I already took a couple, in case I need them for the Realtor or maybe a piece down the road. I don't see the need for any more photos."

"If you see the inside, the amazing construction of those nineteenth-century craftsmen, I'm sure you'd think differently. I don't know anything about photography, but I know something about you, about your work. It's damned good." She clasped her hands together once again, before she went overboard. "I saw that series you did on the tribe in New Zealand. The Maori tribe who'd never seen an outsider before? Their culture was dying, because the very seclusion they sought had become a double-edged sword. You captured their story, but not in the captions. It was the pictures of their faces, their homes. And I have to admit, you did it really well."

He sat back, surprised. "You looked up my work?"

"Even out here in the sticks, we get Internet access. And some of us actually know how to use Google."

He grinned. "I'm flattered you looked my work up, and even more flattered that you liked it."

"Then please do this one thing," she said, sliding

her bowl to the side and reaching briefly for his hand. When she touched him, once again the contact ignited something inside her. She'd meant only to emphasize her point, but clearly something more than that had happened here.

"What?" he prompted.

She pulled her hand back. "Look at the Indigo Opera House as an assignment. As a way to capture someone's story. Maybe you could even get that magazine of yours to run a piece on it. That way, we all win."

"How do you see that?"

"I get the publicity I need to fund the rest of the restoration, as well as spread the message about the importance of preserving our Cajun heritage. And you'll undoubtedly end up with dozens of offers from rich philanthropists in New York or Hollywood who will invest in the property as a conversation piece." She had to choke out those last few words, but surely anyone who saw the opera house would love it as much as she did.

"I'll think about it," he conceded. "You've whet my appetite with the story of the bed-and-breakfast. Not enough to make me want to own a piece of Indigo, but enough that I want to see the rest of the opera house through my lens." Paul considered her words, his body still. "But only if you tell me one thing."

"What?"

"What's in it for you?" He leaned forward, and

his piercing blue eyes seemed to zero in on her, slipping past her defenses. "Because there's more to this for you than just fixing up some old building and making people remember a way of Cajun living that is disappearing faster than fog on a sunny day."

"I don't want anything more than that."

"As you say down here, that's a load of toad crap."

She laughed. "We say it a little less pretty than that."

"I'm with a lady," Paul said, tossing her one of those grins that he seemed to have in abundance. "A lady who has a secret. And until I find out what your story is, Marjolaine Savoy—"

The sound of her name slipping from his lips in that deep, intent tone made her heart skip a beat.

"—I'm not making any promises."

CHAPTER FIVE

THE NEXT MORNING Paul stood by the slow-moving Bayou Teche, his camera in hand. Centuries-old oak trees coated in moss stood like silent sentries over the water, their branches weighed down and reaching toward the bayou like the hair of Mother Nature herself. It was the kind of place where a man could fall completely off the map, lost in its lush wilderness.

Of course, the beauty around him included alligators lurking in the bayou, a thought that reminded Paul he needed to pay attention.

Through his camera lens, he sighted a brightly colored bird in a tree, then turned to frame a stand of dead oaks that looked like blackened ghosts. He didn't depress the shutter button, instead he simply observed the landscape through the narrowed, distant eye of the lens.

The bayou was, as Marjo had said, unlike any place he'd ever been before. It seemed to combine the desolation of the desert with the teeming life of the rain forest, and yet there was also an otherworldly feel to the place. Before him, a gnarled cypress reaching at least a hundred feet up to the sky as an elegant red-shouldered hawk circled overhead, watching, always watching, for prey.

Last night's dinner with Marjo had been enjoyable, even if the two of them butted heads more often than they agreed. If he could just get her to accept his plans for the opera house, maybe he could leave this place.

"What's that?"

Paul turned around, lowering his camera as he did. A boy, well, a young man, stood behind him, eyeing the camera, a quizzical look on his face.

"A camera," Paul said.

"Does it make those instant pictures?"

It took Paul a second to understand the question because of the Cajun accent. "A Polaroid? No, not exactly. But it does let you see the pictures right away." Paul held out the camera, showing the young man the review screen.

"Is that a picture you just took?"

"No, just the scene from the viewfinder."

The young man's face scrunched up at that word, but then he nodded, apparently satisfied with Paul's answer. "I'm Gabriel," he said suddenly, thrusting out a hand. "I make twenty-two at my next birthday."

"Paul." They shook, Gabriel's hand pumping up and down.

"What are you doing in the bayou?"

"Well…" Paul paused, filtering the information. Gabriel seemed to be a little mentally challenged—

not much, but enough that Paul didn't think entering into the legalities of his ownership problem would be a good idea. Besides, the way word traveled around here, anything he said would likely end up in the weekly paper. "Selling some property."

"Why?"

Gabriel's face was guileless, truly curious. "Because I don't want to own it anymore."

"You don't want to live here?"

"It's not exactly the kind of property someone lives in," Paul replied, skipping the main question. He didn't want to live here, or anywhere.

"Oh." Gabriel considered this, shifting back and forth on his feet in an almost rocking movement. "Why can't ya?"

The words came out blended, like, "I-cancha."

"The building I own is the opera house," Paul said, figuring if he didn't say that straight-out, they'd be playing the why game for a while.

The boy's blue eyes brightened. "You own that? Wait till I tell Marjo. She's gonna want to meet you."

"I already met Marjo." And tangled with her twice, earning a spot on her permanent enemy list, a dish of gumbo notwithstanding.

"She's my sister." Another beaming smile.

"Oh," Paul said, surprised. It wasn't that he'd expected Marjo Savoy to exist in a vacuum, he just hadn't pictured her as part of a family. Her well-mannered brother didn't seem to have inherited an ounce of his older sister's disagreeable nature.

"You should keep it," Gabriel said. "The opera house, it's really important to people. I forget why, but I know it's really important."

"Well, I'm going to think about that," Paul said, deciding he would, indeed. Owning an opera house wasn't a hardship, as Marjo had said, and required little more than keeping his name on the deed. Still, the idea of being a landlord wrapped around him like a tentacle.

"Good!" Gabriel's wide smile risked becoming contagious. "You gonna take pictures of it?"

"Well, I hadn't—"

"I love pictures," Gabriel said. "Some of them make me sad, but some make me happy. Know what I mean?"

Paul nodded.

"You must like pictures a lot." Gabriel looked again at Paul's camera, longing clear in his eyes. "I wish I had a camera like that. Then, whenever I wanted to see something again, I could just look at the picture."

Paul smiled. He'd had the same wish as a child. How many times had he begged his parents for a camera? And then, when he'd finally received his first one for his twelfth birthday, he'd never been without a camera again. "Here, why don't you try this one on for size?" He carefully handed over the Nikon to Gabriel.

He took it from Paul, weighing the silver camera in both palms. "It's big. Heavy. Like a rock."

Paul chuckled. "Yeah, I guess it is."

"Can I take a picture?"

"Sure," Paul said. "But, first, let me show you how it works." He came around behind Gabriel, helping him lift the camera into position and sight the image of the bayou in the lens. Then he showed him how to flick the zoom in a little, perfecting the shot. "Now just push that button."

Gabriel looked back at Paul, hesitating only a second, before returning his gaze to the camera and doing as Paul suggested. The image imprinted on the digital card inside, then an instant later, appeared on the screen. "I did it!"

His joy was evident, the pride in his eyes like a beacon. For the first time in a long time, Paul remembered exactly why he'd gone into this job. "Yeah, you did. And you did a great job."

"Thanks," Gabriel said. With two hands, he passed the camera back to Paul. "Wish I could keep the picture. Put it on my wall. So my room, it's like the bayou, too."

"Well, the picture stays in the camera because it's a digital image, not a real image," Paul explained. "I have to hook it up to my iBook with a USB cable, then download the file and—"

He could see he'd already lost Gabriel in explaining the technicalities. "Maybe I'll get it printed out for you," Paul said, then immediately chastised himself for making a promise he might not be able to keep. Although he would consider retaining ownership of the opera house, in the end he knew he would probably list the property as originally planned and get back to his life.

"What are you doing?"

What was with this woman? She was always coming up behind him. Paul wheeled around to face Marjolaine Savoy.

"This is getting to be a bad habit," he said, giving her a grin. As he spoke, he was struck by the strength in her vibrant blue eyes, the long, tight braid that seemed to beg someone to undo it and the soft curves that filled a spaghetti-strap sundress. Okay, so maybe he didn't mind her coming up behind him.

Clearly, the bayou didn't provide the only interesting views in Indigo.

"Paul's showing me how to be a picture taker." Gabriel held up the Nikon.

Marjo looked to Paul for confirmation. He gave her a short nod. "Gabriel here has quite an eye."

Her brother beamed. "Maybe…maybe I can get a job doing pictures. I'd like that better than working with Henry on the dead bodies."

"Maybe," Marjo said, not committing to anything. Gabriel had lots of enthusiasm but little follow-through. "Give Mr. Clermont his camera back and we can get on home."

"I want to take some pictures." Gabriel gave her that stubborn pout that meant he wasn't going to leave without a fight.

"Gabriel, we need to get home. I have to get to work. We have a wake tonight."

"I want to take some pictures," he insisted. "Paul said I could take a few of the bayou. Then I can go to work."

Marjo looked at Paul, wanting him to take her side so she could get Gabriel home and make her way over to the funeral home.

"Take one or two more, Gabriel, then do as your sister says." Paul turned to Marjo. "It'll only take a second."

Gabriel smiled again, then turned the camera on Paul, snapping the photo before Paul could voice a protest. Then her brother wheeled around and framed Marjo in the lens, depressing the button again.

"Gabriel," she repeated, her voice a warning.

Her younger brother let out a sigh, then reluctantly returned the camera to its owner. "Can we do it again?"

"Sure. Whenever your sister says it's okay." Paul sent a glance Marjo's way, and Gabriel turned his hopeful eyes on her. Two against one.

"All right," Marjo said. "But only if you've finished your chores and—"

Gabriel ran up and gave her a hug, his joy apparent in the tight squeeze and big smile. "I will." Then he broke away just as quickly. "'Bye, Paul! I gotta go. See you soon!"

Gabriel dashed away, faster than Marjo had ever seen him move before.

"He's a great kid," Paul said. "So enthusiastic and friendly."

"Thanks." She lingered a moment longer, feeling she should say something else. A crazy thought. All she wanted to do was to put as much distance between herself and Paul Clermont as possible.

Dinner last night had actually been fun, when they weren't sparring like Tyson and Holyfield. Maybe the tension came from their opposing views on the opera house, but every time she looked at Paul Clermont, he ignited a spark inside her that she'd thought had long ago gone out. "Well, I have to get to work," she said, but her feet didn't move.

"Where do you work? There aren't very many businesses around here."

"The Savoy Funeral Home. If you follow the road through town and up to the left, you'll see it over by the church and the cemetery. It's been in my family forever." She shrugged. "Guess I just followed family tradition."

"Do you do the embalming?"

It was a natural question, and one she'd been asked a hundred times before. "Not so much now. I'm the funeral director so I do most of the planning and oversee the services. Henry Roy is our undertaker and he does the embalming. Gabriel helps him. I learned how to embalm, even did it for a while when I was younger, then I got my degree in funeral administration. I mean, it was the family business, we just grew up with it. It was natural to help out. I remember when Gabriel and I were little, we'd help dress the bodies."

"Wasn't that…upsetting?"

"It was at first," she admitted, and fell into step beside Paul as he began to walk along the edge of the water. "But, down here especially, you learn that death is simply part of life. There are a hundred different Cajun superstitions around death, but by and large, we see it simply as part of the cycle."

"Like the bayou," he said, pointing toward the olive-green water, teeming with life, yet edged by dead trees that hadn't been able to survive along the crowded banks. Together, life and death created a picture of beauty.

"Yes."

"So, was funeral work your life's ambition?"

"No, not even close," she said, laughing, enjoying this respite from a day that had been filled with the very detail work she hated. "When I was a kid, I had this crazy idea that I could be a singer. My mother took me to a professional teacher in Lafayette for years, and for a while, I performed locally."

"So why didn't you do it professionally?"

"It was just impractical. I had…" She glanced back in the direction that Gabriel had gone. "Responsibilities."

Paul looked at Marjo and saw the woman beside him with new eyes. Apparently there was a lot more to her than he had thought at first glance.

That didn't mean he was considering a truce,

maybe more of a ceasefire as they walked along the natural path that formed at the bayou's edge. It eventually led up to La Petite Maison. Occasionally, Paul would see an alligator skimming along the surface, showing little more than his eyes and looking like a log rather than a predator. "You were right, this place is different from anywhere else I've been."

"If you stay here too long, it'll grow on you," Marjo teased. "And if you stand in one place too long, the Spanish moss will grow on you, too." She smiled, the kind of smile that Paul knew would linger in his mind, stay with him all day. "I can't imagine living anywhere else."

This woman was the polar opposite of him, and yet even as he moved closer to her to avoid the low-hanging moss, he felt a rush of need for Marjo Savoy surge through him. He glanced over at her, wanting to run his fingers through that long, impossible hair, to trail a palm along the soft skin of her arms. It was almost painful to walk along beside her, pretending he wasn't acutely aware of her every breath.

"I can't imagine settling down anywhere, period," Paul said. "Although I did own a house, back when I was married, but that didn't last long."

"The home ownership or the marriage?"

"Both." When he didn't elaborate, Marjo let the subject drop.

They reached a thick stand of trees, which gave them two options: forge their way through the foliage so they could pick up the path on the other side, or go around the trees. Marjo turned around at the same time Paul did, and they ended up facing each other, inches apart. She stopped. He stopped. His eyes met hers, and desire sang along his veins, thudded in his heart, pounded in his brain.

Kiss her, his mind whispered. *Kiss her, before you remember all those reasons why you shouldn't.*

"Sorry," he said, not meaning it.

"No, I'm sorry. I wasn't looking where I was going and—"

"It's okay," Paul said, touching her lips with a fingertip.

She inhaled, parting her lips as she did, nearly kissing his finger. He watched her mouth open, intent and serious.

And then, in the space of an instant, he leaned down, brushing his lips lightly against hers in a touch so gentle it was more tease than anything else. He pulled back a centimeter or two, waiting for her to react.

She leaned forward, and her lips met his in a hot, frenzied kiss, the kind that came about on the spur of the moment, fueled by want and nothing else. Fire ignited nerve endings throughout his body, awakening a part of him that had slumbered for so long. Too long. For one amazing, senseless minute, she kissed him, seeming to melt into him as his palms cupped her face.

A bullfrog let out a loud, groaning belch, a stark reminder of where they were.

And why he was here.

Marjo jerked back. "That shouldn't have happened."

"You're right. I'm sorry. I just—" He cut off the sentence.

"I've really got to go," Marjo said, breathless, confused by her body's betrayal. Then, before she could do something really stupid like kiss him again, she turned on her heel and headed off to work.

The one benefit of working with dead people all day—it effectively killed all thoughts of romance.

CHAPTER SIX

ON MONDAY, Cally came by, dragging Marjo out of the funeral home long enough for a quick lunch at the Blue Moon. Cally knew Marjo well enough to know she'd forget to eat, buried in the paperwork on her desk. Once their food arrived, Cally cocked her head one way, then the other, studying Marjo from the opposite side of their booth. "Something's different about you today."

"Same as always." Marjo forked at her *boulettes de chevrettes*, but didn't take a bite.

"You don't lie very well, you know." Cally grinned. "And you have that stunned, can't-believe-I-did-that look about you. So…" Cally leaned closer. "What did you do?"

"I kissed Paul Clermont," Marjo whispered, knowing the Indigo gossip chain often started right here at the Blue Moon. "But it didn't mean anything."

"You kissed him!" Cally sat back, clearly shocked. "I don't blame you. He is totally hot."

Marjo agreed with Cally's assessment, but that

still didn't make it right to be fraternizing with the enemy.

"It was just a spur-of-the-moment thing," Marjo said. "And it's not going to happen again."

"Uh-huh. That's the same thing I say when I dip into a box of chocolates. I'm going to stop at one."

"Well, this time I will. Getting involved with that man will only confuse the issue. I have enough going on, what with the effort to renovate the opera house and the CajunFest happening there in a little under two weeks."

"Speaking of things you say won't happen again, are you going to sing at the festival?" Cally asked.

Marjo was surprised by the question. "Me? Why? We have lots of great local talent. Nobody needs me."

"That's a crock and you know it. Heck, half the town's been asking about you, wondering if you'll sing."

"It's been years since I stood on a stage."

"So? Just get up there, girlfriend, and use the gifts God gave you."

"I am. At the Savoy."

"Marjo," Cally said, reaching for the friend she'd had ever since the two of them had met in Mrs. Langley's kindergarten class, "when are you going to quit that funeral home and pursue what makes *you* happy?"

Marjo shook her head. "I'm thirty-five. I can't be going after some pipe dream."

"Now is the perfect time. Before you're ninety and can't remember the words to your own songs."

Marjo laughed. "Tante Julia can remember every person she ever came in contact with, along with the words to some songs that shouldn't be sung in mixed company."

Cally rolled her eyes. Before she'd entered the nursing home, Marjo's ninety-two-year-old aunt had been well known in Indigo for her compulsion to tell off-color stories at the worst possible time. Like during a wedding or a baby shower. Or, worst of all, at Tee Tim's funeral. "Tell me she's not performing at the festival."

"Only as a backup singer," Marjo joked.

"Seriously, Marjo, you should get up there. Show Indigo what you've got. You never know where it might lead. Like, out of this place."

The waitress slipped the bill onto the table. Marjo laid some money on top, then rose, her food still mostly untouched. Her appetite for it had deserted her. "I have to get back to work. The Dufrene family is coming in at one and I need to put together some information for them."

"Promise me you'll think about it? In between thoughts of kissing Paul Clermont again, of course." Cally winked.

"I'll think about singing. But not Paul Clermont."

"Uh-huh. That's what they all say." Cally gave her a grin.

After she left the diner and returned to work,

Marjo tried not to think about what Cally had said, or about kissing Paul Clermont, but it didn't work. No matter how busy she got, or how many times she straightened the furniture in the viewing rooms, both thoughts kept coming back, stubborn as thistle.

Particularly the one about kissing Paul.

What had gotten into her? How could she have risked upsetting the careful balance of her life? She had plans, plans that required she stick to a pre-scribed path if they were ever going to work out. Because Gabriel needed that security and there was no one to give it to him but her.

After work, she headed home, made supper for Gabriel and herself then set off for the restoration committee meeting at the Blue Moon Diner. Most of the usual members were already there, dining on sweets and coffee. At this rate, she might as well move into the back room in Willis and Estelle's little restaurant.

Marjo looked around. Sophie Boudreaux was absent, but that was expected. Exhaustion from trying to keep up with her job in Texas, manage the antique shop and help raise Alain's two children, combined with a pretty serious case of morning sickness, had forced Sophie to curtail her involve-ment with the committee. It was too bad, because Sophie's career as a professional fund-raiser made her a great resource person. Marjo scanned the rest of the group, and noted another important absence.

"Where's Hugh?" The elderly man was the greatest supporter of the restoration project, and the only one of the committee members, as sweet and helpful as they all were, who understood Marjo's driving need to preserve the town's heritage. Hugh Prejean was the opera house's champion, and she didn't feel right beginning the meeting without him.

"He might have gotten tied up with something at home," Jenny LaFleur said. "Although, I don't remember him ever bein' late before. He's like the Indigo rooster, up and at 'em before anyone else has even put the coffee in the pot."

Marjo glanced at the clock. Quarter after the hour. Jenny was right, Hugh was never late for anything. They'd often joked he'd be early for his own funeral.

Concern crossed the faces of the others in the room as Jenny's words sank in. Marjo felt a sense of foreboding in the pit of her stomach, but she pushed it away. Surely, Hugh would be here any second.

"Well, let's get to work," she said, pulling a file folder from her bag and handing out an agenda to everyone. "I'm sure Hugh will show up soon."

But as she started the meeting and listened to Loretta Castille update everyone on the VIP dinner planned for the night before the festival, she wasn't so sure even she believed that. Hugh was never late, never missed a meeting. For him not to be here was highly unusual.

"So what are we going to do about this man from Nova Scotia?" Doc Landry asked. His upcoming wedding to Celeste Robichaux had finally convinced him to retire. "I met him and he seems hell-bent on trying to sell the opera house. He doesn't give us the time of day for months, and then just thinks he can come on down here in a fancy rental car and sell the place out from under us?"

"I'm working on him," Marjo said. "He is, after all, one of the descendants of Amelie and Alexandre, so he technically has the right to do whatever he wants." Murmurs of dissent and frustration rippled through the room. "However, I'm hoping that if I can show him his family's history, and what a valuable piece of that history the opera house is, he'll agree to hold on to it and let us move forward."

"And what if he doesn't? A lot of people in this town are counting on the festival and the opera house." Doc Landry scowled. "Indigo's not exactly Boomtown."

"I say we string him up and serve him in the gumbo," Jacques Bergeron grumbled. "That'll put a dent in his engine."

Marjo didn't try to figure out Jacques's meaning. He had a habit of mixing his metaphors. When someone corrected him, he told them language was like soup—you could put in any old thing you wanted and still come out with something good.

"Let's talk about the CajunFest," Loretta interrupted, using, as always, her deft touch to soothe tempers and steer people back to the important issue. "Are we on track with all the participating businesses? I know we had a lot of interest from companies outside of Indigo, too."

"Yes," Jenny said, reading down her list. "We just got three more from New Iberia and five from other area towns. That should really add to the event. But…"

Jenny frowned, and Marjo felt that sense of dread again. The festival was so close; the last thing she needed was another disaster. It was bad enough that they were running out of time to finish the repairs on the opera house. "But what?"

"Alain just told me that two bands backed out. Seems the third member of the Possum Trio has a slipped disk and won't be out of the hospital in time to play, and the other band had an argument over wearing matching sequined vests, which led to a very dramatic breakup. The loss of those two leaves a big hole in the schedule."

"If there's one thing that's plentiful in Louisiana besides gators, it's musicians," Marjo said. "Don't worry, Jenny, I'm sure Alain will find someone else." The police chief, a fiddler in his spare time, had gladly taken on the task of coordinating all the musicians for the festival.

"Well, we were talking before you got here and we were thinking…" Jenny's voice trailed off and she looked to the others for support. "Maybe you could sing."

"Me?" Marjo squeaked. "But I—"

"Don't give me a but, Marjo. You can sing better than half the people in Louisiana. You have an incredible voice."

"Jenny, I don't think people want to hear me sing." How long had it been since she'd sung in public, other than church?

And then it hit her.

The last time she'd sung in public had been at an audition, the day of the accident that took both her parents' lives. The accident that had changed the course of her life, taking her away from her dreams of someday becoming a professional singer and into her role as Gabriel's guardian. She'd also stepped into her father's shoes at the Savoy Funeral Home, because it was what was expected.

"You're better than that Possum Trio," Jacques said, then let out a belch. "Sorry. This pecan pie is damned good."

"Well, we'll see." Marjo hedged. "I'm sure we'll find another musician and you won't need me at all."

"Uh-huh." Jenny clearly didn't believe her.

"On to the repairs," Marjo said, eager to change the subject. "We still have quite a lot of work left to do on the opera house." She looked at the list in front of her, now numbering twenty-plus items. "We have almost enough money to make basic plumbing and wiring upgrades, but nowhere near what we need to do a true historical restoration. How has the fund-raising been going?"

Luc Carter held up the latest balance sheet. "Another two hundred dollars came in since our last meeting." He shook his head, clearly as disappointed as Marjo.

Two hundred wasn't enough to pay the contractors to repaint the siding a historically accurate color. It wasn't enough to replaster the walls, replace the floor and fix the chairs.

Marjo looked at the resigned faces around her and wondered how she would ever generate enough momentum to keep this project going.

"We need to raise more money, if we have any hope of getting the opera house up to code so it can be used during the festival and for Loretta's VIP dinner the night before," Marjo said. "Anyone have any ideas?"

"Why don't we just hold the CajunFest at the Blue Moon or something? I'm sure Willis would let us use the parking lot." Renee Porter gave a shrug. "I don't think we're going to get the opera house done in time. We can hold the festival performances there next year, at our second CajunFest."

"Yeah, if that Canadian doesn't sell it out from under us," Doc Landry muttered.

"I won't let him," Marjo said.

Elsie Montrose looked up from her knitting long enough to lay a hand on Marjo's. "Maybe it's time to just let it go, Marjo dear. What use does Indigo have for opera, anyway? We're just a little bayou town."

If her own group was starting to bail on her, then Marjo needed to find another way to save the opera house, and fast, or the entire project would be lost, along with a vital part of Indigo's history.

There was one key to success, and it wasn't a

very cooperative one. Paul Clermont. Somehow she had to swing him over to her way of thinking. Maybe with a Valois heir behind the project, the rest of the group, the rest of the town, would be energized and the restoration would finally be completed.

As she left that night, concerns weighed heavily on her mind. Concern for Gabriel, who hadn't come home for dinner again tonight. Sometimes the boy wandered off into the bayou and got so wrapped up in watching the frogs and the turtles that he forgot the time. But lately he'd done it more and more often, which meant he was probably spending time with Darcy again.

But Marjo couldn't worry about that now. It seemed all her months of hard work on the opera house were going to come to naught. And she was concerned about Hugh. Perhaps he was ill or had fallen asleep early.

As she started walking back to her house, enjoying the night songs of the bayou creatures, she decided to stop by Hugh's to check on him. He lived alone and was one of those stubborn men who believed a few onions could solve any ill.

As she turned down the road to Hugh's place, she saw Paul Clermont approaching.

"Marjo," he said, coming up beside her. "What are you doing out on Indigo's streets so late?"

The image of the camellias he'd given her, sitting in a vase in the center of her kitchen table, came to mind, softening her as easily as they had when he'd put them in her hands. "I'm checking on a friend. Actually, he co-chairs the restoration committee with me. He didn't come to tonight's meeting and I'm a little worried about him."

"Do you want some company?" Paul asked.

She looked up at him, but in the darkness of evening and the small pool of light from the street-lamp, she couldn't tell if he was being sincere or just teasing her.

She opted for sincerity. "Actually, I would."

He pivoted, then fell into stride beside her, close enough that she could catch the scent of his woodsy cologne, feel the heat emanating from his body. "I'd like a little company tonight, too, and who better than a woman who would rather see me on another planet?"

She laughed. "You don't have to go that far. Another country is fine."

He returned the laughter. "Don't worry, I'm on my way to Tibet soon, for another assignment."

Right this second, the thought of jetting off to the Far East didn't hold the same excitement for Paul that it usually did. Maybe it was the clear night air, or maybe it was just the woman beside him, who drove him crazy and intrigued him in equal parts.

Marjo Savoy was the last person Paul had expected to run into on the streets of Indigo at this time of night. He'd been out for a moonlit walk, something he'd done more and more lately when he found himself unable to sleep.

"Funny how I keep running into you," she said.

"Yep, I keep showing up, like a bad penny."

"Or a hungry raccoon." She gave him a grin. "I will admit, you have a certain charm. I'm sure many women have fallen for it."

"But not you, right?"

"Sorry. It takes more than a quick wit and a nice smile to win me over."

"Oh, so you've noticed my smile?"

She rolled her eyes. "Only because you keep showing it off."

Truth be told, she had noticed his smile, and a heck of a lot more, particularly since that kiss. In fact, Paul Clermont had lingered in the back of her mind, his image teasing at her, tempting her to revisit unfinished business.

Business that didn't have one thing to do with the opera house.

Paul chuckled. "I'll try to be more dour around you then."

She laughed, a light, happy sound that for a second caught him off guard. Paul almost told a joke, just to hear her laugh again. But then he remembered their differences about the opera house, and knew kissing her again seemed like a mistake.

"Tell me about Indigo," he said.

"What do you want to know?"

"I hear you're the resident historian. Estelle at the diner told me you're so good, you'd clean house if there was ever a Louisiana *Jeopardy*."

"Actually, that title goes to Hugh Prejean. I've just heard so many of his stories, and worked with him going through old records, that I can tell you almost anything about Indigo."

"First question, fifty points. Where did the name come from?"

"That's an easy one. Indigo grew up around a plantation, like so many of the small towns around here. People moved where the jobs were, and there was an indigo plantation here. At the time, the dye was vital to the country. It's the blue in our flag, as well as the blue for half of the flags in the original thirteen states."

"That's pretty cool. Tell me more."

"It'll cost you," she said, grinning.

"How about a hundred points?" And a kiss, he wanted to say, but didn't. Even as his hand strayed near hers. Even as his mind replayed how she'd felt in his arms

"Indigo also became the color of Levi's jeans," Marjo went on, clearly not aware of what was running through Paul's mind. "Also, police uniforms, army and navy uniforms." She slowed her pace a little as she spoke. "Blue was the color of nearly everything back then, and the slaves who worked the plantations practically became blue themselves, both in spirit and in skin color. The songs they sang on the indigo plantation came to be known as the blues."

"And that music formed the foundation of much of

Louisiana's music," he said, putting together what little he did know about the area. "Jazz, R&B, everything."

She nodded. "It's amazing what impact one little plant can have on a community. A country."

"Same as the impact of one person, one building." His gaze slid toward hers. "Is that what you're trying to do, Marjo? Make a big impact with one building?"

"We're here," she said, avoiding his comment, and stopping in front of a small cottage home that Paul would swear had less square footage than some of the hotel rooms he'd stayed in over the years.

The house was bathed in darkness, blending into the inky night so it was almost invisible. "The lights are out."

Marjo hesitated on the sidewalk. "That's not a good sign. Hugh is a night owl. He's always staying up until three or four in the morning to finish a good book. He says there's not enough time to read everything he wants."

Paul chuckled. "A man after my own heart. No matter where I go, I always have a book with me."

"We better go in and check on him. He could be asleep but…"

"You doubt it."

"Yeah." Marjo pressed a hand to her stomach, as if trying to quell a bad feeling. Paul knew, because he had the same feeling in his own gut.

They made their way down the small stone walkway and up the stairs to the front porch. The old wood creaked beneath them, as if protesting the intrusion. Marjo rapped on the door, called Hugh's name. No response. She did it a second time, and still, only silence.

She moved to a small window, cupped a hand over her eyes and peered inside the house. "I see him. Oh, God. He's not moving."

"Probably just fell asleep in his chair," Paul said, but he didn't believe that. "We'll have to break in."

"This is Indigo. Most doors are unlocked, particularly if someone is home." Marjo took in a breath, then reached for the door handle. As she'd predicted, the door was unlocked and swung open with a squeak of the hinges. "Hugh?"

She and Paul entered the house and approached the old man. As they got closer, Paul could see Hugh was slumped over.

And sure as hell wasn't asleep.

CHAPTER SEVEN

MARJO GASPED, obviously drawing the same conclusion as he had. She put a hand over her mouth and stopped on the braided rag rug. "No, not Hugh."

Paul stepped forward, put his fingers on the elderly man's carotid. Nothing. Not even a flicker of life. His body was cool, edging toward stiff. "He's been dead for a while."

Marjo turned away, then seemed to center herself and turned back. The glimmer of grief and shock had been pushed aside as she took charge of the situation. "We'll have to call Alain, the coroner and Hugh's children," she said, checking off the necessary steps on her fingers. "When Hugh arrives at Savoy, I'll make sure he's taken care of the way he deserves."

She was handling this so well, Paul thought, even though he knew she must be used to this sort of thing. She was efficient, yet calm, going about her list of things to do quickly and easily.

In a few minutes, the calls had been made and the house was soon swarming with people and light. It wasn't until the coroner finally wheeled out Hugh's body that Marjo sank into a chair.

"You all right, Marjo?" A police officer came over to her. He was tall, about the same height as Paul, but the man had none of the stiffness about him of a regular police officer. Paul suspected the law operated with the same easy approach as the rest of Indigo.

"Yeah." She sighed. "I'm going to miss him."

"We all are. When you think of Indigo, Hugh's one of the first people that comes to mind."

She nodded. "He was a real champion for the historical society and the restoration committee. For all of Indigo, really." Then she seemed to recover, and glanced over at Paul. "Alain Boudreaux, this is Paul Clermont. He's a Valois descendent from Cape Breton. Alain is the police chief here."

Alain extended his hand and shook with Paul, a firm, honest grip. "Nice to meet you. Can't remember the last time we've had one of the Valois family members down here."

"I'm just here for a few days. Taking care of some business."

Marjo let out a cough.

"You know, I think I'm one of your distant relatives. Real distant, considering I'm from Alexandre's side of the family, about twenty-five times removed. My grandmother and mother are both Valois. Sometime, I'll have to introduce you."

Paul nodded, though he had no intention of being here long enough for a family reunion. "That'd be nice."

"If you're from Nova Scotia and a Valois, you *must* play the fiddle," Alain joked.

"I used to." He thought of those parties with his uncles. Fiddle dueling had been as common as the tall tales shared around the table. "It's been years since I picked one up, though."

A deputy came up and whispered something in Alain's ear. He nodded. "Well, if you're ever at Skeeter's, bring your fiddle, or you can borrow one of mine. The Indigo Boneshakers play there on Friday nights. Every once in a while, a local will fill in between sets. After a couple of beers, everyone sounds good." The two men chuckled. "Either way, I'd love to hear how they do it in Canada."

Paul didn't tell Alain that he fully intended to be back on the road in forty-eight hours at most. "I'll keep that in mind."

Alain said his goodbyes, then headed out to his car. Marjo said she'd take care of anything that needed to be locked up in Hugh's house.

She headed into the kitchen and turned on the hot water. "What are you doing?" Paul asked.

"The dishes. I…" She let out a long, tired breath. "I don't know what else to do."

He laid a comforting hand on her shoulder, the gesture meant to be friendly, yet he could feel that sense of connection all the same. "Then let me help."

She gave him a smile, the kind that tattooed itself on his memory because hell, if she smiled like that again, he'd gladly throw in a few loads of wash and break out the vacuum cleaner. He stood beside her as she washed and he dried, returning the dishes to the cabinet. As the bubbles multiplied and the pile of dirty dishes dwindled, something odd happened between them.

A truce of sorts began to form.

No, it was more than that. It was a moment that forged the beginnings of a bond. They'd just dealt with a difficult situation together.

"You said you and Hugh researched the town's history together. How did you get so interested in that?" Paul approached her with the same curiosity that had inspired many of the photo narratives he'd put together for *World*.

"He used to be my babysitter."

"Your babysitter?"

She laughed. "When I was a kid, my dad became friends with Hugh. They were in the same men's coffee club at St. Timothy's, and eventually the two struck up a friendship. My dad loved the history of this town, too, nearly as much as Hugh." She added some more soap to the water, then began washing again. "I was a little hard to handle as a kid—"

"I find that *so* hard to believe."

She splashed him with soapy water. "Hey. I wasn't that bad. I just…well, I hated to go to bed at night. Hugh had come by once for dinner, and I guess I latched on to him and made him tell me a story before I went to bed. Within five minutes, my dad said, I was out like a light. The whole plan eventually backfired, though, because as I got older, I became more interested in the stories Hugh would tell…and then not want to go to bed."

"Have you ever been anywhere else? Traveled outside of Indigo?"

"Not really, other than the occasional trip to Lafayette or New Orleans," Marjo said. "I've lived in the same place all my life. I love Indigo."

"How do you know you love it if you've never lived anywhere else?" He thought of his family, who had struggled financially because they'd never wanted to leave the place they loved.

"I can't imagine anywhere else on earth that could make me as happy as the bayou does."

"But haven't you ever been curious to see the rest of the world?"

She shrugged, and Paul got the feeling that Marjo Savoy hadn't always wanted to stay in Indigo. "Once, I guess. Back when I thought I was going to be the next Mariah Carey, with a definite touch of the bayou."

What couldn't this woman do? She could handle a dead body with calm, had, from what he'd heard around town, spearheaded a historical revival in Indigo and was Gabriel's primary caretaker, something that must have had its challenges over the years. "You never told me the other day. What *do* you sing? Or rather, what did you sing?"

She rinsed the bowl she held before answering. "Do you really want to know? Or are you planning on signing me up for the next American Idol competition to get me out of the way?"

He laughed. "I hadn't thought of that one. If I get desperate, maybe I'll give them a call."

She made a face and he laughed again.

"Seriously, Marjo, I do want to know. I don't think I've ever met anyone like you."

"Me? I'm as ordinary as they come."

The cozy kitchen, the heavy warmth still hanging in the air and the quiet, mournful songs of the night animals seemed to intensify the moment. "You're definitely not ordinary, Marjolaine."

When he said her name, his voice a song all its own, a thrill went through Marjo, skating along her nerve endings. Had anyone ever said her name quite like that? For a moment she forgot what she was doing, forgot about Hugh, the restoration committee, the opera house. Forgot everything but the way her name had seemed to roll off his tongue.

"Sing for me, Marjo," Paul said, his voice low. "Please."

She opened her mouth to protest, to argue that there were dishes to be done, and a home to get back to, but instead, what came out were the first few notes of "*Le Pays des Etrangers.*"

The French words, which she'd memorized years ago, came easily to her, carried on the soft melody, telling a story about another country, another world.

When a smile crossed Paul's face, she continued with the tune, her voice increasing in volume as the song took root inside her.

How long had it been since she'd sung? Too long, clearly, because with every note, a remembered joy began to enrich her spirit.

"I've never heard that song sung quite like that before," he said when she finished.

Heat filled her face. "I'm out of practice and—"

He put up a finger, shushing her. "I meant, I've heard that song a hundred times and never has it made me feel that way."

She pulled back, surprised. "Feel how?"

"Almost…homesick, which is crazy, because since leaving Cape Breton, I've never looked back." He paused for a moment, then shook his head, as if that was all he wanted to say on the subject. "Anyway, that was beautiful. No, not just beautiful. *Incredible.* Why aren't you singing professionally?"

She turned back to the dishes, taking an inordinate amount of interest in the way the sponge plunged in and out of a glass, as if cleaning Hugh's dishes was the most important thing in the world. "There's a thousand reasons. Number one being that most people don't make it in the music business."

"Most people don't have your voice."

She dismissed the comment. "I'd have a better chance of being struck by lightning and winning the lottery the same day. In other words, one in a gazillion."

"Isn't that what life is about? Taking chances?"

She put the last glass into the dish drainer and grabbed an extra towel off the counter to dry her hands. "Maybe for someone like you, but not for me."

"Someone like me?"

"You don't have any responsibilities. No children. No house, no mortgage. I have bills, Paul, and a brother who depends on me. I can't run off with a half-baked dream just because I think I'm the next American Idol. I have to deal in reality, not impossibilities." She tossed the towel onto the counter, then crossed into the living room, straightening pillows and blankets that didn't need straightening.

He followed her, taking an afghan from her hands before she could fold it again. "I'm sorry. It's not my place to tell you how to live your life."

The apology caught her off guard, making her feel vulnerable. She stopped tidying, and suddenly just wanted out of the house, away from this man who should be the enemy, but who seemed to keep turning the tables on her. "We're finished here. Thanks for your help."

He looked as if he might say something, but instead followed her out as they left the house, this time locking the door behind them. Marjo paused on the sidewalk. "Thank you for coming with me and for all your help." Her words were businesslike, her tone cool. She turned on her heel and started down the sidewalk.

Paul fell into place beside her. "That's it? You're just dismissing me?"

"I have to get home. Gabriel—"

"Wait," Paul said softly. He caught her gaze. A beat passed between them. Another. "Tell me, Marjo, are you still that hard to get into bed?"

Right this second, she'd be as easy as he wanted, especially when he looked at her like that, with those deep blue eyes that seemed to see into her soul. After the preview she'd had earlier today, she could only imagine how good he'd be if they went beyond kissing.

"I'm too old for a babysitter now."

"I'm not talking about babysitting." Then, before either of them could think twice, he leaned down and kissed her.

No, not just kissed her. He played a song on her lips, started the tune carrying to a concert. She hesitated only a second, then found herself moving into his arms, lifting her head and giving him a melody of her own.

He was good, very good, sending her hormones dancing and her mind traveling down a path that involved doing something with Paul Clermont that didn't involve running him out of town.

As his kiss deepened, she thought of taking him home, inviting him into a bedroom that had had one occupant for far too long. He reached up, tangling his fingers in her hair. Desire snaked through her veins, singing its siren call.

She jerked back to her senses and out of his arms. "I—I can't do this."

"Because of our disagreement about the opera house?"

"For that and a hundred other reasons," she said, running a hand through her hair, as if by doing so she could erase the feel of his hands. "But mostly because I have other priorities right now."

"Other priorities besides yourself?" he said. "You can't put a building or a festival or even your brother ahead of you all the time, Marjo."

"Says the man who has perfected the art of severing ties," she retorted. "Until you commit yourself to something besides yourself, Paul Clermont, don't tell me what to do." She took a step away, then pivoted back. "And definitely don't kiss me again."

He grinned. "What if you kiss me first?"

She hurried down the sidewalk, not answering him. Because as much as she wanted to tell Paul that there was about a blizzard's chance in the bayou of that happening, she knew one thing for certain—

She'd be lying.

CHAPTER EIGHT

THE NEXT MORNING, the scent of brewing coffee and the brightness of the sun streaming through his windows finally roused Paul a little after nine. He rolled over, glanced at the clock then looked at it again.

The numbers nine-zero-seven gleamed back at him from the digital display. He flicked out his wrist and focused his bleary gaze on his watch. Yep, same time there.

He hadn't slept past 5:00 a.m. in years. A decade maybe. Ever since he'd taken his first picture for pay, Paul had been out of bed before the roosters crowed, intent on getting the story. He prided himself on being the first on the scene, the last to leave.

He got dressed and went downstairs for a late breakfast. The buffet in the breakfast room was generous for a B and B. Beignets, pain perdu, bacon, fresh country eggs, toast, home-cooked preserves in every flavor from fig to watermelon, café au lait, juice…everything he could have imagined on a Louisiana table. Paul selected a little of everything, his plate filled to overflowing by the time he sat down.

A few minutes later, Luc Carter, who owned the bed-and-breakfast, stopped by his table to ask him if he was enjoying his stay. "I am, thank you," Paul replied.

Luc gestured toward the opposite chair, then sat when Paul nodded. "Did you know you've stirred up quite the controversy around here?"

"With the opera house?" Paul grinned. "Yes, Marjo made it clear that I'm not the most popular guy around."

"Marjo means well, but she's a little…intense when she believes in something."

"Just a little." Would she be that intense in bed? Paul wondered. A part of his mind went down that path, imagining Marjo in his bed, showing him just how intense she could be.

Luc chuckled. "Actually, I came by to put my two cents in. While you're considering your options with the opera house, I want to tell you how important it is to Indigo that this CajunFest happens. Indigo is not exactly a hotbed of tourists, and being a small business owner engaged to a small business owner, I know what an impact this festival can make."

"I'm not standing in the way of the festival. I just don't need to own an opera house. To me, it's like buying a helicopter for a dog."

"I understand. Before I moved here, I used to be the kind of man that didn't hang on to much." He looked up at the pixie-ish woman with spiky strawberry-blond hair who was bringing in a basket of fresh bread. "But eventually you find something—someone—you'll do anything to hold on to."

Luc smiled as he watched the woman cross the room. Clearly, she was his fiancée. She turned, caught him looking and exchanged a private smile with him. It was obvious to Paul that the B and B owner had found something very special.

Paul had never experienced that feeling, not really, despite all his travels and all the people he had photographed. He'd married Diane on an impulse, thinking that marrying her would curb his wanderlust and give him everything he'd missed out on in his childhood.

But if anything, marriage had done the opposite. Although he had seen that look before between dozens of couples, he'd never gotten any closer to it than through the lens of his camera.

"Well, I'll leave you to your breakfast." Luc gave the table a pat, then rose. "You let me know if there's anything I can do to make your stay better."

The friendliness of the people here astounded Paul. It was as if Indigo was a giant family and every visitor the prodigal son. Everyone from the owner of the general store to the gas station attendant who'd filled his tank had offered a smile and a kind word.

Paul finished his meal, then headed out into the warm sunshine, his camera bag, as always, slung over his shoulder. For some reason, the urge to leave town at first light had dissipated. Maybe the slow-moving bayou had affected him. Everything seemed to move at a different pace here—the river, the people, the meals. People even talked slower here, as if they had all the time in the world.

He stepped onto the veranda, a cup of coffee in his hand, and stretched the kinks out of his back.

"Hey, Paul!"

He turned to see Gabriel sitting on the bottom step, as if he'd been waiting all morning for Paul to appear. Given the excited gleam in the young man's eyes, Paul wasn't so sure that was far from the truth.

"Hey, Gabriel. How are you?"

"Good." He beamed. "I have a little time before I have to go to work, and I was thinking…" He rose, shifted from foot to foot. "I mean, hoping…"

"You want to take some pictures with me today?"

Gabriel's face instantly brightened. "Sure!" He sobered just as quickly. "Only…if you don't mind. Marjo said you like to be like a black bear, stay by yourself and all."

Marjo was right. On any other day, Paul was a one-man show, making his way through cities, forests and war zones. He'd never liked the encumbrance of a reporter or another photographer, preferring to work on his own.

But today the thought of company was appealing. Clearly, he *had* slept too long, because he was getting soft. Sentimental.

"I don't mind you coming along," he said to Gabriel. "In fact, I have a spare camera in my bag.

You can use it, take your own pictures, and later, we can compare notes."

Gabriel gave him a quizzical look. "How can we compare notes if we're taking pictures?"

Paul laughed. "You have a point."

The two of them made their way down toward the bayou, walking in the direction of Indigo. From time to time, Paul stopped. He'd train his camera on a gnarled cypress or a small rowboat tied along the banks. As he snapped a cormorant standing in the shallow waters along the edge, an alligator slipped into the water, silent and deadly. Paul took a photo just as the animal came into the frame, capturing what he saw as the true essence of the bayou. Beauty and danger, tangled together as surely as the twisted branches of cypress.

He looked over at Gabriel, who was mirroring Paul's actions, being selective about his shots, looking through the viewfinder before judging if a picture was worth taking. "Can I see what you've got so far?" Paul asked, coming up beside Gabriel.

"Sure." Gabriel handed over the camera without hesitation. Paul liked Gabriel. He was a simple soul, whose trust and openness were rare in most people.

Paul flicked on the review button, then scrolled through the photos Gabriel had taken. A close-up of a delicate flower, a bird in a tree, a mole poking his head out of the ground. "This one's really good, Gabriel," Paul said, holding it up so Gabriel could see, too. "I love the composition in this photograph, the way you blended the light and the dark of the water and the land. It's fabulous. And this one—" he pushed the button again "—is great. Look how you zoomed in on this bird just enough to make him the focal point, yet left enough negative space so that he really stands out against the bayou. It's a spoonbill, isn't it?"

Gabriel nodded. "Yeah, it is. But what's composition and zoom?"

Paul explained the terms as he reviewed the photos, using Gabriel's pictures as a kind of show and tell.

He hadn't exaggerated. Gabriel had gotten a wonderful shot of the pink-and-white bird as it stood on one leg in shallow water, its long flat bill and dark eyes turned in their direction. "You're really good at this, especially for a beginner," Paul said again.

Gabriel beamed with pride. "Do you think I can get a job?"

"Yeah, I think you might." He rarely said that, all too aware of the danger of encouraging someone to pursue a career path they weren't equipped to handle. But in Gabriel, he saw something, as if the young man's gentle spirit imprinted itself into his photographs. He placed the camera back into Gabriel's hands, closing the boy's palms over it. "You keep this."

It took a long second for the words to sink in, but as they did, Paul watched the light in Gabriel's eyes turn from misunderstanding to astonishment. "I can really keep this?"

Paul nodded.

"I can take my own pictures?"

Paul nodded again.

"And I can keep them, forever?"

"Sure," Paul said. "If you want to print them out, you can e-mail them to me, no matter where I am, and I'll get them done for you."

Gabriel's smile grew wider. He turned and wrapped Paul in a hug so tight, for a second Paul couldn't breathe. "You're a good man," Gabriel said, patting Paul on the back.

When Gabriel stepped back, Paul had to clear his throat a couple of times before he could speak. No one had ever said those words to him before, and to hear them coming out of Gabriel's mouth had double the impact. "Thank you," he said at last.

Gabriel smiled again, this time a softer, secret smile, the same one Paul had seen on Luc earlier today. "I want to take a picture of my girlfriend. Darcy." He cupped a hand over his mouth and whispered, "We're gonna get married someday."

"You have a girlfriend, eh?" Jeez, was every man in Indigo involved in a relationship except for him? Maybe it was the kind of place where people came in two-by-two, like a Louisianan version of Noah's ark.

"I should have known I'd find you here."

Paul turned and saw Marjo striding down the grassy lawn toward them. She was dressed in a long white dress with a thousand tiny, enticing buttons running down the front. With her long dark hair loose around her face and those devastatingly clear blue eyes, she looked very much like an angel.

When she saw him, a smile flitted across her face and something powerful lurched in Paul's heart. He found himself smiling back, enjoying for a second that same special, private moment that Luc had shared with his fiancée in the dining room of La Petite Maison. Just as quickly it was gone. Paul caught himself and went back to business mode. He wasn't staying here, and it would be crazy to give the impression there was a relationship building between them.

"Paul gave me a camera!" Gabriel said, running up to meet his sister, showing her the digital camera and explaining how it worked. Clearly, Gabriel had paid more attention to Paul's words than he'd expected. Gabriel scrolled through the photos he'd taken, showing his sister the images he'd captured.

"Wonderful, really wonderful," Marjo said, laying a loving hand on her brother's shoulder. "But it's time to quit now. You need to get over to Savoy and help Henry. We have Hugh's wake tonight."

Gabriel frowned. "I'm gonna miss Hugh."

"Me, too." Marjo gave him a quick hug, then sent him on his way. Gabriel turned back every few feet and waved at Paul as he made his way up the lawn.

"I have to go, too," Marjo said. But she didn't move.

"Don't leave," Paul said, reaching for her, meaning only to have her stay a moment to enjoy the scenery. But when he touched her, a deep longing roared through him. "Just for a little while."

"Okay," she said, relenting, and he wondered if she had felt the same connection he did. "But only for a little while. I have to get back to work. I have…" Her voice trailed off.

"Hugh's wake?"

"Oh, yeah, that." A flush filled her cheeks.

"Do you need help with anything? Dishes? Pillow fluffing?" He grinned.

What was he doing? This was the exact opposite of what he wanted. Why was he still here, anyway? Did he think he'd settle down, get married, have a couple kids?

Of course not. He wasn't going to repeat the mistakes of his parents, or the ones he'd made in his first marriage. Or the ones he saw among fellow Cape Bretoners, so firmly cemented to their community that they gave up their dreams to stay.

Paul had a job that required distance—literally and figuratively. Bringing a relationship into that life would be unfair to Marjo.

But maybe, just for a little while, he could relax his no-involvement rule. Relax, in general. During the last few assignments, a weariness had come over him every time he got on a plane, coupled with a sense of déjà vu, as if he'd already done this, shot that.

Which was crazy, because the one thing Paul

prided himself on was never doing the same story twice. In every shot, in every assignment, he sought uniqueness, a perspective that had never been done before, and in doing so, he had been well rewarded by *World*.

What he needed was a story. One good story that could jump-start his passion for his job again, and he didn't think it was going to be his upcoming assignment in Tibet.

He glanced at Marjo and an idea formed in his mind. Maybe…that story was here already. "Tell me about the opera house and Alexandre Valois."

"Do you really want to know?"

"I've been thinking. You were right. I should be looking at this as an assignment. If it's the kind of thing *World* runs, I'll see if my editor is interested in a piece on Indigo."

The light in her eyes, so bright five seconds ago, dimmed a bit. What had he said? Wasn't that what she wanted? Publicity for her cause?

"A win-win," Marjo said, echoing her earlier words.

He nodded. "I'd like to see the opera house, on the inside. Will you show it to me? Please?" he added, a teasing note in his voice.

The soft smile, the one that he liked the best of all her smiles, slipped across her lips. "Yes, but later, because I really do have to get to work." She turned to go back up the grassy slope.

"Marjo!"

She turned back.

"What time is the wake?" Paul asked. "I'd like to come by and pay my respects to Hugh."

"Come by anytime tonight. Hugh will be there." Another, quicker smile. "And so will I."

Paul didn't know if it was because of his bloodline link to this place, but as Marjo walked away, Paul was shocked to feel a keen sense of loss—

And, at the thought of seeing her again, an even stronger sense of anticipation.

CHAPTER NINE

"You really outdid yourself this time, Marjo," Cally said, crossing the room with Marjo. "Hugh looks great."

The room where Hugh Prejean's wake was being held was the largest in the Savoy Funeral Home and furnished in a French Provincial style. Marjo was glad she'd chosen it. Judging by the number of visitors and the multiple floral arrangements, she'd needed the space. Hugh's daughter and two sons had flown in from opposite ends of the country. Marjo had met with them earlier, and they had expressed their gratitude for the way Savoy had handled Hugh's arrangements. Hugh's niece, Amelia Prejean, who lived in Indigo and helped run the antique shop, Past Perfect, had been out of town on vacation and was flying in the following day.

"Henry gets all the credit," Marjo told Cally. "He insisted on doing it right for Hugh." She let out a sigh. "I don't know what's going to happen to all our plans for Indigo without Hugh around. He was the one who got people excited about the restoration and the town's revival."

"You worry too much. Everything will work out fine." Cally gave her a final pat on the shoulder, then crossed the room to greet Jenny LaFleur.

Marjo made her way through the room, doing what she always did—ensuring perfection. She straightened floral arrangements, made sure tissue boxes were full, greeted people who had come to pay their respects. She paused from time to time, glancing over at Hugh. She wished he could still be here, supporting the town, the bayou, that he'd loved so much. He would be missed for his wit, his intelligence and, most of all, his passion for this tiny town and its history.

Gabriel stayed on the sidelines, uncomfortable with this part of the funeral business. He could help Henry with the bodies, but there was something about the wake and funeral that Gabriel couldn't handle. Perhaps it was the finality. Or perhaps it was the memory of his parents lying in this very room when he was seven.

Gabriel rarely attended the viewings, but today he'd insisted on coming, out of respect for Hugh, who had always been so kind and patient with him. Nevertheless, Gabriel had yet to move away from the wall and come into the room.

Just as Marjo was moving toward him to make sure Gabriel was okay, a young blond woman came up beside Gabriel and slipped her hand into his.

Darcy.

Marjo liked the girl well enough, but worried Gabriel was seeing too much of her. They'd been inseparable since graduation and saw each other before and after work and every weekend. Marjo had thought the relationship would cool with the arrival of fall, when Darcy started her beauty school course in New Iberia, but instead it had seemed to heat up. She made a mental note to speak to Gabriel again. He was far too young and immature to be "falling in love" or tying himself up with one girl.

It had been just the two of them for so long, Marjo and Gabriel, their own little micro-family. She simply couldn't imagine a day where she'd walk into the house and not see her brother.

Jenny came up and laid a hand on Marjo's shoulder. "It's a real shame about Hugh."

"It is. He was such a big part of this town." She looked over at Hugh again. He seemed so peaceful, she could almost believe he was sleeping. His children stood in the receiving line, visibly shaken by the loss of their father. "I think we should look at the CajunFest as a way to honor his memory. He was so excited about the reopening of the opera house and—"

"Actually, I wanted to talk to you about that," Jenny cut in.

"About what?"

"The CajunFest and…" Jenny paused. "Well, the future of the opera house."

"We're moving forward as planned," Marjo replied. "It's what Hugh would have wanted."

"The committee has been talking, and we think…" Jenny took in a deep breath, and Marjo felt sure she knew what was coming. "Well, we think maybe we should stop trying to stand in the way of the Clermont guy and let him sell it," Jenny said. "Maybe some business will snatch it up and bring money to Indigo that way. The festival will still happen, of course, but we've been thinking we should just give up the idea of using the opera house during the festival."

"*Sell it?* For what? So it can become some hardware store or clothing boutique?" Marjo noticed people looking at her and lowered her voice. "Are you serious?"

"Listen, Marjo, it's not about the opera house or you or anything. I hate to even bring it up, especially here. But time is ticking away and nothing's happening. The festival is supposed to happen in ten days and we have nothing ready in the opera house. We need to retreat to Plan B."

"Plan B?" When had there been another option? She couldn't believe the committee would desert Hugh's dream of reviving the opera house.

"The committee feels that without Hugh, there's no way the rest of the town will continue to back this project," Jenny explained. "We still don't have all the money we need, and people are tired of being asked to contribute. Sophie's campaign raised a lot of money, but funding a restoration is costly and a much bigger task than we expected. Besides, what's the point in raising all this money if Paul Clermont sells the place? It's not that we don't love Indigo, it's…well, we're a small town—a village, really. We don't have a big pool to draw from for any additional funds and support, and we don't have the resources to go after outside donors. I know you're passionate about this project, Marjo, but you, well, you're only one person, and you're so busy with this—"Jenny swept her hand to indicate the funeral home "—and Gabriel. You can't do it all."

Marjo wanted to argue, to tell Jenny that yes, this could still work, that they could get the opera house back to its former beauty, but then she saw the resignation in the other woman's eyes and knew arguing would be pointless. Marjo had lost the battle before she'd even known there was one. "Let's talk about it tomorrow," she said. "We'll call a meeting and figure out where to go from here."

Jenny gave her a soft, indulgent smile, one that said the cause was already lost. "Okay."

Marjo watched Jenny walk away. She knew that the committee members didn't mean her any harm. There wasn't a malicious bone in the group. They were just being smart business people. And as much as Marjo hated to admit it, they were right.

The numbers for the opera house were daunting—there were too many expenses involved in restoration and not enough money to cover them. The committee had hoped the festival would bring in the rest of the money, but if it didn't, even Marjo had to admit that it would be near impossible to reignite their enthusiasm, especially with Hugh gone.

They had tried, Lord knew they had. Hugh had always said not to worry, that someday the Indigo ship would come in and everything would be fine.

He just hadn't predicted that the crew would mutiny.

For Marjo, the fight was far from over. If she had to do it alone, she would somehow find a way to fund the restoration and get the opera house up and running as a viable business, thus keeping Alexandre and Amelie's memories alive and giving a much-needed boost to the town.

And to hedge her bets, she'd keep praying for that ship. Although at this point she figured she needed the *Queen Mary II*.

"You're here awfully late."

She turned around to see Paul Clermont, dressed in a navy-blue suit, with a white shirt and navy-striped tie. He looked more handsome than any man she'd ever known. Given the khaki shorts and white shirts he normally wore, she was willing to bet the suit was new, bought solely for this event. She was touched that he'd done that. "The wake's just getting started."

"Just getting started?" He glanced at his wristwatch. "But it's after ten. Aren't most wakes from two to five and seven to nine or some such thing?"

"In the rest of the world, yes, but here in Indigo, we do things a bit different." As she talked, she made her way through the room, making sure everything was tidy. "Up until World War II, there was a custom of all-night wakes in this area. A family member, or several, would stay with the body all night. It dates back to the days of grave robbers. Someone always sat with the body until it was in the ground. There are still a few Indigo residents who want that option for their loved ones."

"I've seen some tribes on the other side of the world where people did that, too," Paul said. "I think it's a nice custom, bringing the town together to honor someone who has died."

"Well, if there's one thing people like in Indigo, it's tradition," she said, moving to tuck a wayward mum back into an arrangement. "That's why the funeral home is still here. People like being buried in the cemetery behind St. Timothy's Church, they like knowing the family's all going to be together, that the priest who married them will also be the one to give them a proper goodbye."

Paul nodded. "What you said earlier about Indigo is right. I've noticed when I've walked around town that this place is like a whole other planet, as if God carved out this little corner without a mold."

Marjo smiled. "That's a really nice way of putting it."

He moved closer to her, making room for Louella Purcell. The older woman lumbered past him, the feather on her wide-brimmed black hat bobbing along and her little dog, JoJo, trying to squirm out of her tight grip.

"I noticed something else, too," Paul went on when Louella had passed them. "The pictures Gabriel took captured different elements of Indigo than mine did. He saw details that were important to him. A chair on a veranda, a baby bird in a tree. When you look at his pictures, you see the town through his eyes."

"And if I looked at your photos," she said, moving closer still as the room filled up, "would I see it through your eyes?"

"Those were shot through the vision *you* gave me," he said, his voice low and soft.

"Me?"

"The story you told about La Petite Maison, the passion you have for this place—it's all impacted the way I now see this place."

She considered Paul for a long time, the conversation with Jenny still fresh in her mind. Maybe…maybe there was a possibility she could get Paul to support the opera house, to see it the way she did. "Are you doing anything tomorrow?"

"No, not at the moment." He grinned. "Why? Do you have plans for me?"

She winked. "Nothing nefarious, I promise."

"Pity."

The way he said that made her wish she did, indeed, have some other purpose in mind. "Meet me at the opera house at ten. I did promise to show it to you."

She was called away by Henry to answer the phone, but as Marjo left Paul, she felt more buoyant about the future than she had in weeks. If it was the last thing she did, she would bring Paul Clermont around to her side.

And then, maybe, she could win back the support of the rest of the town. Of the two, she suspected Paul was the harder sell.

Maybe Cally was right. It was time to get out a little honey.

WHEN PAUL GOT BACK to his room at La Petite Maison, he saw the green light on his cell phone flashing, telling him he had a message. He unhooked the phone from the charger, then took it outside on the veranda to enjoy the cool evening breeze.

Frogs croaked somewhere in the bayou, crickets chirped, night birds sang their songs. It was the melody of Indigo, and it was oddly peaceful.

When he connected with his voice mail, he heard the deep bass of Joe, his editor, barking into the machine. "Hey, Paul, I've got one you're going to like. Right in your own backyard, too."

Indigo?

He quickly realized that wasn't the place Joe meant.

"There's this group of fishermen in Nova Scotia," the message continued. "Survived a near sinking and a hell of a storm. Sort of like *The Perfect Storm,* but with a happier ending." Joe chuckled. "Anyway, I want you to get up there ASAP and get me some photos of the guys, the boat, for next month's issue. They've avoided the media, wouldn't even take the money from the *Enquirer* for a shoot, but I know *you* can get their story. Hell, you could pull a story out of roadkill. Besides, this one's got human interest written all over it. Might even get you one of those awards." His editor laughed, then hung up.

There it was, the out he had wanted. But for the first time since Paul had picked up a camera, he didn't want to rush out on assignment. He wanted to stay right here, snap another picture of a cypress or an alligator, take a few minutes to show Gabriel how to make the most of every shot, help him find the story in each picture.

And most of all, he wanted to show Marjo a bit of his world.

Hell, who was he kidding? He wanted to show Marjo more than that. He wanted to spend time with her, this spitfire woman who pushed all the wrong buttons and yet still managed to intrigue him as no one ever had before.

She was fire and ice, both strong and distant, full of a passion that lurked beneath that all-business exterior.

For the first time since his divorce, he found himself considering a relationship, something that lasted longer than the few days of a photo assignment. That was *not* a good sign—it was the kind of thinking that had a man tossing away a damned good career for a dream that didn't exist.

He knew that far too well from watching his parents' marriage disintegrate because of the lengthy separations and his mother's growing despondency. Each time his father came home to visit, he had grown more bitter and distant.

Paul's mother had retreated from a life that wasn't what she'd envisioned, either, leaving the two adult Clermonts more like roommates than spouses whenever Renault was home. Paul had once thought he could live a different life with Diane, but after a month of marriage, he'd realized he'd walked into the very trap he'd been trying to avoid. He and Diane had very different expectations of life, and that had only led to unhappiness.

Which was exactly why he should leave Indigo now and forget about any kind of relationship between him and Marjo Savoy.

He stared at the phone, replayed the message from Joe a second time, figuring that hearing it again might make it sound more exciting. It didn't.

His finger hesitated over the send button. He should call Joe, tell the editor of *World* he'd be out of here on the first plane. It was time to move on, to put this place behind him, as he had so many places before.

Paul stood on the veranda a long time, holding the phone and telling himself to do the right thing.

The problem was, he didn't know what that was anymore.

This place had gotten to him. Or maybe it was just a little indigestion from the gumbo and turtle soup.

CHAPTER TEN

PAUL DIDN'T WANT TO keep Marjo waiting for him this time, and he arrived at the opera house a few minutes before ten.

A minute later Marjo pulled up and got out of her little blue Honda. Immediately, he was struck by how amazing she looked, and all his well-laid plans from last night evaporated.

Her hair was down again, unfettered by her usual braid. Had she done this for him? Or because she didn't have an elastic handy?

His male ego hoped that was the reason.

"Good morning," he said as she approached. "You look incredible. You don't look at all like you spent the entire night at a wake."

"Thanks." She smiled. "I've got a couple of hours until Hugh's funeral. Are you ready to see the opera house?"

He held up his camera. "Absolutely."

She withdrew a set of keys from her pocket, inserted one into the lock on the carved door then pushed. It opened with a creak.

Not a good sign, Paul decided, for his ancestral "treasure."

Marjo led him inside the darkened lobby, then flicked a nearby light switch, bathing the space in a warm glow. The lobby had been used as the retail space for the antique shop and was separated from the auditorium by large double doors. Marjo opened the doors now and beckoned Paul inside, turning on another light.

A long central aisle ran between rows of velvet seats up to a spacious stage, and to either side, staircases rose to an upper level. Wall sconces and chandeliers washed the interior with gold, illuminating the pale floral wallpaper and the high windows.

"This is…incredible," Paul said. He pointed to the private boxes bracketing the stage. "Look at the intricate woodwork."

"Alexandre spared no expense."

"It shows." He raised his camera and sighted the carving, then the curve of the ceiling, the scars in the wood.

Marjo led him up the stairs and began to tell him the story as she'd promised. "This area was settled in the late 1700s. Growing up in Nova Scotia, I'm sure you know how the Acadians came to live here."

He had heard the tale at least a hundred times at family gatherings. Heritage was an important part of life in Cape Breton, too. But Paul, who had wanted to be anywhere but in Nova Scotia, had never really paid attention to those family stories. "Tell me anyway. I'd like to hear your version." In her sweet, lilting voice, the details, he was sure, would be far more interesting than when he'd been five and his grandfather had been reciting family history lessons.

"The French set up colonies here, starting in the 1600s, and also in Acadia, now the Maritime provinces of Canada."

He grinned. "Oh, yes. The Acadian history is something every schoolchild learns."

Her hand trailed lightly along the wood railing as she climbed the narrow staircase. "Later, when Napoleon claimed Louisiana, the people who settled here were known as the French Creoles. However, in the 1750s, after the British won Acadia from the French as a prize for settling a war, the British marched in and claimed Acadia for themselves. They told the Acadians to either swear allegiance to the British crown or face forcible eviction."

"Many ended up shipped out on boats and forced into indentured servitude in places like the West Indies," Paul said.

Marjo nodded. "*Le grand dérangement* was a horrible time in our history. Many came to Louisiana, settling in this area. Lafayette became the unofficial capital, because more French settled there than anywhere else." They had reached the top of the staircase. "Alexandre Valois was a French Creole and the grandson of wealthy parents, who had a distant bloodline to the French monarchy. The Valois family started out with an indigo plantation—"

"But switched to sugarcane," Paul interjected. "Because someone in the family had been successful with it."

Marjo nodded. "Alexandre's mother. So, you do know some of this story?"

"Some. Although my family is descended from Amelie, not Alexandre, my sister did some research into both family lines on her computer."

"Well, stop me if I repeat anything," she said.

"No, please, go on. It sounds so much better coming from you than my relatives. And, I admit, I never really listened much to these stories."

"In those days, marriages were often still arranged, particularly to enhance the family wealth and protect the Creole heritage, which was seen as more pure than that of the Acadians, who'd settled here nearly a century earlier. Alexandre's family wanted him to marry a wealthy second cousin, a fellow Creole." She paused by a painting hung on the wall, a severe portrait of an older couple and their young, twenty-something son. "Here they are," she said. "It's one of the only portraits we have left of the Valois family."

Paul studied it, seeking…he wasn't sure what, in their painted eyes. Like many portraits of that day, the Valois family wasn't smiling, but in Alexandre's countenance, Paul detected a rebellious streak. It was the way his lips curved a little more on one side

than the other, and in the glint in his eye. "But Alexandre wanted someone else." He turned to Marjo.
When she gave him a questioning look, he went on.
"I read my Shakespeare in college. It wouldn't be a
good story if it didn't have some element of tragedy,
now would it? Besides," Paul said, gesturing to
Alexandre's portrait, "he looks like a man who
wouldn't want to be told what to do."

She laughed again. "That part's true."

Paul studied the portrait again, then he lifted his
camera and snapped an image. "Did he marry her?"

"Amelie was an Acadian, so to Alexandre's
parents, she didn't have the true blood they wanted
for their son, nor the royal connection. Ironically, her
parents felt the same about him. Both sets of parents
were interested in protecting the bloodline, so they
couldn't see the love Alexandre and Amelie had for
each other. But the couple ran off and got married
anyway. Their parents grudgingly accepted the
marriage, and for quite a while, Alexandre and
Amelie were happy. But when she couldn't have
children, Amelie grew more and more despondent
about the one thing missing from their perfect life."

Paul thought of that and how it mimicked his own
childhood.

"What happened next?" Paul asked.

"Alexandre was concerned about his wife," Marjo
said, leading him along the upper level. Below, he
saw the stage, the worn, ripped seats, the space that
had once been beautiful. "Alexandre realized that

because she was so devastated about her inability to have a child, she had stopped singing. Amelie was a gifted singer."

He raised an eyebrow. "Like someone else I know?"

Marjo ignored his comment, but her cheeks flushed. "Alexandre built the opera house as a gift for his wife to inspire her to sing again. He wrote in his letters how her voice could charm angels and how her singing had captured his heart when they met. To inspire her, he paid Adelina Patti, a famous opera singer, to stop here during her tour of Louisiana and give a performance during the 1860 to 1861 season."

"Wow. She was quite famous in her day, from what I've heard. I have an aunt who loved opera."

"It was quite the coup for the opera house. Alexandre also hired a music teacher from New Orleans to help retrain Amelie's voice. Soon she was giving concerts in this very opera house, along with other local musicians and traveling groups. Of course, the whole thing was an embarrassment to Alexandre's parents."

Paul quirked a grin. "Not something the wife of their son should be doing."

"Still, it worked out wonderfully and the opera house was very successful for several years." Marjo pointed across the balcony at the gilded boxes on either side of the stage that Paul had noticed earlier. Narrow staircases led up to these private seats.

"Those were built for Alexandre's parents, who wouldn't deign to sit with the common folk," Marjo said, affecting a suitably upper-crust attitude. "Not that it mattered. Josephine Valois rarely attended any of Amelie's performances, and when she did, she made such a drama of it that it seemed the queen herself had descended on the opera house."

Paul pulled the strobe flash from his backpack, attached it to the Nikon then took a photo of the small gilded chairs on the private balconies. For just a second as he looked through his viewfinder, he could actually see Josephine Valois, regal and prim, showing no emotion while she watched her daughter-in-law perform.

"My family never talked about this," Paul said. "My father traveled a lot, and worked out of province. When he was home, he was sleeping. My mother…was distant. I don't even know if they knew these stories. If they did, they never shared them."

He shrugged. A lump had formed in his throat and he swallowed it away. Paul had dealt with this, and despite it all, he and Faye had turned out all right. He looked around the auditorium, so silent now. "What happened to Alexandre?"

"The Civil War." Marjo took in a breath, her eyes filling with a sadness. "Alexandre believed in fighting for his beloved Indigo, so he enlisted, much to the heartbreak of his wife. With Alexandre gone, Amelie couldn't stop the Union soldiers from taking over the plantation house for barracks and the opera house as a military hospital. They moved into the cottage, La Petite Maison, with Charles's mistress and her child. If you'd thought Josephine was embarrassed by the opera house, this was even more humiliating. I don't think she ever forgave Amelie, as if one woman could have prevented an army from changing their lives or the war that ate up nearly all their wealth."

Paul's camera hung from the shoulder strap, unused. He stood there in the auditorium, wrapped in the story and Marjo's soft, heartfelt delivery. He wanted to know more, to hear that it had ended well, because these people were becoming as real as the carved railing sloping down the aisle. "Did Alexandre come home from the war?" As he asked the question, a distant memory told him there was no happy ending to this story.

Marjo shook her head. "He died in a Yankee prison camp, from a fever, or maybe just exhaustion. In their grief, Alexandre's family cut Amelie off, blaming her infertility for the loss of their son, their bloodline. Amelie's brothers died, her sister lost her husband, too, and I think all of them lost their spirit."

"How tragic. So much loss in one family."

"It was too much for her. To be so young and to lose the love of her life. Though she owned the opera house, which Alexandre had left to her, Amelie couldn't bear to look at it anymore. It was no longer her dream, not without her beloved Alexandre. She sold the plantation house, but couldn't part with the opera house, even though she needed the money. So she returned to Nova Scotia, where her family had gone after the war wiped them out financially."

"And eventually that led to me and my sister, a few generations later."

"Not a bad bloodline after all, huh?" Marjo said, giving him a smile. She led him back along the balcony toward the staircase. "Amelie would return from time to time to visit Alexandre's grave behind St. Timothy's, to see the opera house and wander the grounds, as if she could connect with him by being here. People said they always knew when Amelie had been here because they'd find a single camellia on the stage the next morning."

"Your favorite flower."

"My mother's, actually," Marjo said, her voice so quiet, Paul had to strain to hear her. "She heard the stories about Alexandre and Amelie, and planted camellias all around our little house, ordering varieties from around the world. She was quite the romantic."

"And you inherited that trait?" Paul grinned.

She laughed. "I'm as far from a romantic as you can get. I just like the way camellias look."

"Uh-huh," he said, leaving it at that. He suspected Marjo, who had fought long and hard to be sure Alexandre and Amelie's story wasn't forgotten, was more of a romantic than she realized. "Did Amelie ever remarry?"

"No." Marjo let out a sigh, then took his hand and led him further along the balcony, past the staircase, to another portrait. This one was of a woman alone. She had that same secret smile that Paul had seen on Luc's face and Alain's. Clearly, this beautiful woman was Amelie Valois.

"It was so tragic," Marjo said. "From the painting we have of her—" she indicated the portrait in front of them "—and from her letters, it was clear she was a beautiful woman, inside and out. But losing Alexandre broke her heart. When she died, she asked to be buried beside him. They're together now, in the Valois vault in the cemetery behind St. Timothy's Church."

"She *is* beautiful," he agreed. As he looked at the portrait, into Amelie's blue eyes, eyes that had been passed down for generations, a deep sadness filled him. For Alexandre, for Amelie, for the children they'd never had.

He shook his head. He wasn't a sentimental guy. These were people he'd never met before, people who had loved each other a hundred and fifty years ago. Being upset because some long-ago aunt had been widowed young was crazy.

Paul followed Marjo down the stairs and back to the lobby. "And to keep the opera house in the family, Amelie's will decreed that the opera house was to be passed down to the firstborn niece or nephew in each generation." That's where he came in.

Marjo nodded. "Amelie wanted to make sure the opera house stayed within her family, so it went first to her sister's son, then to his brother's daughter…and then, eventually, to you. The remains of Amelie's estate were used to pay for the taxes and some upkeep."

"Until my uncle squandered it on bad stocks."

"Well, he must have cared about the opera house because he came down here to see it. From what Hugh told me, your uncle was very interested in the history of the place and actually thought of living here."

"How did you pay for the upkeep after he stopped sending the inheritance money?"

"For a time, the opera house became an antique shop. It didn't make a lot of money, but it kept up with some of the bills. The business end was handled by a lawyer in New Orleans."

Paul arched a brow and looked around the place. "Antique shop?"

"Yes, in the lobby area. Earlier this year, it was relocated to Maude Picard's cottage. It's owned by Alain's wife, Sophie, and Hugh's niece, Amelia, runs it."

Paul scanned the room again. "I never could have pictured Sticklys and Chippendales in this building."

Marjo leaned against the concession stand and gave him a smile. "Sometimes you find treasures where you least expect them."

"Is that the case with you?"

The tease in her gaze disappeared and she

wrapped her arms around her chest, creating a distance between them. "Not me. I'm a 'what you see is what you get' girl."

"I doubt that." Paul waited until she turned back to look at him again, her blue eyes filled with such spirit and strength. Had he ever seen eyes quite that beautiful before? They drew him in over and over again. "There's definitely more to you than meets the eye."

"I have to get to work." But she didn't move. She kept her gaze on his, their heartbeats locking in rhythm. "I, uh, have Hugh's funeral in a little while. I can leave you to finish taking pictures or—"

"Stay a minute longer. Please." He reached out and touched her hair, pushing back a stray tendril then allowed his hand to linger. He wanted to touch more of her, so much more, but for now, this would do.

She hesitated a fraction of a minute, then relented. "Okay."

He released her, then inspiration struck. He dug into his backpack for his portable strobe and attached the light to the camera. A flick of the zoom and he captured a railing, a newel post, the corner of a frame. A flick in the other direction and his camera caught the blend of golds and crimson, the wood and plaster.

Beneath his feet, wide wooden planks still bore the scars from Yankee boots. There was both architectural elegance and a link to the past in this little building.

Unfortunately, the years of neglect were also evident in the peeling paint, the chipped wood and the missing tiles. Although it wouldn't take too much to make the building ready for public use, restoring it with historical accuracy would be much more time-consuming and costly.

"You're having the CajunFest here...when?" Paul asked.

"A little under two weeks. The festival will be held outdoors, but we were counting on using the opera house for some of the performances."

He let out a low whistle. No wonder she'd been so panicked when he'd tried to put it up for sale. "But there's so much to be done." He lowered his camera and turned around, taking in the small lobby that extended across the width of the building. It was definitely in need of a facelift.

Marjo sighed. "There's not enough funding for anything beyond the most pressing repairs. And as of yesterday, there's no more Indigo Opera House Restoration Committee."

He turned back to face her. "What?" Had the committee given up on the opera house?

She lovingly trailed a hand along the edge of the display case. "With Hugh gone, the group decided that the restoration was too monumental a task. To do this right, we need to be historically authentic, and the committee is afraid we'll never raise the rest of the money we need. They decided—" she took in a breath "—to give up on it."

"And what do you think?" he asked.

Marjo bit her lip, then sighed. "Even I can see when I'm beaten. I may love this town and this opera house, but Jenny was right. One woman can't do it all. So…" Her shoulders sagged. "Mr. Clermont, you have my support in selling it."

He stared at her, mute. Of all the things he had expected Marjolaine Savoy to say today, that hadn't even made the list. In her eyes, he could see what it was costing her to admit defeat, and for a moment he wanted to reach out, pull her into his arms and make it all go away. "But how can you give up?"

"Don't argue with me." Her smile was bittersweet. "I'm giving you what you wanted."

"I've talked to Luc Carter. I know how important this CajunFest is to Indigo, to its economy. If you allow the public to see this part of Bayou Teche history, it can only help everyone."

She put the keys into his hand and closed his palm over them. "It's yours. Do what you want with it."

"What I want, huh?" The metal was hard and cold against his fingers. He slid the keys into his pocket, then began to wander the lobby, running his hand over the woodwork. All these years, this little opera house had been part of his family's heritage….

A week ago, those words hadn't meant much to him. But now…

Paul raised the camera, squinting through the

viewfinder, snapping shot after shot. The digital numbers on the Nikon ratcheted up quickly. Ten, twenty, a hundred, two hundred, filling the memory with impressions.

As he moved around the room, a funny thing happened. The story of Alexandre and Amelie not only began to come alive, but became a part of him. The stories Marjo had told him took on a new meaning, as if finally being here, touching the wood-work, feeling the solid floor beneath his shoes, made these people real, rather than the stuff of legends.

And then there was Marjo, the fiery woman who fought hard for the things she believed in, for the people she loved. In every line of her body, every sparkle in her eyes, he saw the one thing he had been lacking for a very long time—

Passion.

He wanted that. Hell, he wanted her. Being here had, for the first time in months, maybe years, reig-nited something Paul thought had died inside him. And being around Marjo ignited even more.

Putting a For Sale sign on the opera house seemed like a betrayal of her, and his past.

"I'm not going to sell it," he said after a while, the idea taking shape in his head as the words emerged. He was jumping off a dock he had stood on all his life. "I want to keep it."

She blinked. "You want to…what?"

As soon as the decision was made, a surge of ex-citement rose in his chest, new images filling his mind now, ones that he would later capture with his camera. He was as swept up in this place as Marjo, as if her passion were contagious. "And I want to pay for the repairs, and down the road, the rest of the historical restoration. The performances for the Cajun-Fest will be held here, as planned."

"But…" Her jaw dropped and she shook her head. "How…? Why…?"

"One of the benefits of not having a mortgage means most of my pay over the years has gone into the bank," Paul said, knowing this was the right thing to do with that money, feeling it in his gut. He was enjoying the stunned look on Marjo's face. It felt good—damned good—to give her this. To give her town this. "I have quite a lot of savings built up, just sitting there, collecting dust. I'd like to use it to restore this place to what it used to be. It clearly meant a lot to my people—my family and others—over the years, and now, I guess…" he paused and gave her a grin "…it's starting to grow on me, too."

Marjo's eyes lit up as his meaning sank in. "But that will cost so much. Too much."

"I really want to do this."

"You mean it?"

"Yes." He'd do it again, just to see that look on her face. Hell, he'd buy and renovate half of Indigo if she'd smile like that again.

Something in his heart swelled as she hurried into his arms in an impetuous, joyous hug. "Thank you."

· "You're very welcome," he said, his voice rough,

the tension tightening in his gut. She rose up on her toes, and then—

Kissed him.

Her kiss was filled with exuberance, excitement, but those emotions quickly yielded to one that had little to do with the opera house. Heat rocketed through Paul. It felt as if a hundred years had passed between their last kiss and this one, as if he'd been away from her forever.

Paul lowered the camera, seeking blindly for the nearest flat surface to lay it on. As soon as his hands were free, he tangled them in her hair, in that long, dark, glorious hair, bringing her closer to him.

She curved into him, her breasts pressing against his chest. His hand roamed down the silky fabric of her dress, outlining curves, slipping down her back, over her hips.

Five seconds ago, they'd been talking about the distant past. Now, with Marjo against him, the Valois story, the opera house, all of it seemed a million miles away. On some other planet.

She let out a soft moan, her hands ranging over him, answering the thoughts of his body, as if she could read him. Her tongue dipped into his mouth, tasting and teasing, sending him down a crazy, fiery path.

He moved with her, backing Marjo up against the concession booth, the need for her pounding loud and insistently in his head, drowning out every other rational thought. Of their own accord, his hands slid between them, curving around the firm flesh of her breasts, causing her to dip her head and trail heated kisses along his neck, asking without words for more.

More would be a mistake. More was the kind of thing that went down a road Paul wasn't yet ready to travel. "Marjo," he said, struggling for sanity as she tempted him, "I—I think we better stop before we, uh, christen this place in a way the committee might not like."

"You're right," she said with obvious regret. She pulled back, dropped her head to his shoulder and inhaled. "That probably shouldn't have happened."

"It was a hell of a thank-you."

She laughed softly, a merry sound that echoed within the walls of the old building.

Paul caught her chin in his palm, then trailed a finger along her jaw. "I guess the opera house hasn't lost its magic."

A devilish gleam shimmered in her eyes. "Imagine what could happen when it's restored."

He grinned. "Maybe I should tip the contractors extra for a rush job."

Marjo laughed, and he couldn't help but think how great it was to see her so happy. "As long as we're done in time for the CajunFest, then I think that's a great plan."

"Oh, we'll be done in time," Paul said, twining a tendril of her hair around his fingers, then letting the silky tress slip through very, very slowly. "I'll make sure of it."

Anticipation pooled in his veins, a feeling he hadn't had in years. At the same time, an alarm went off, reminding him that he needed to pay attention.

He may be supporting his family history by preserving this little piece of it, but he had no intentions of repeating his father's mistakes. Doing that would be about as smart as skinny-dipping in the alligator-infested waters.

CHAPTER ELEVEN

MARJO PACED THE FLOOR of her kitchen later that night, circling the small room again and again. Every few seconds, she looked at her watch, but the time kept moving forward, and the front door had yet to open.

She poured a glass of Chardonnay and took it out to the veranda, settling into the rocking chair and allowing the quiet of Indigo to help still the nervous patter of her pulse. It wasn't just Gabriel coming home late that had set her heart on edge.

It was Paul Clermont.

She'd never expected that he would listen to the story of Alexandre and Amelie and be as moved as she had been when Hugh had first related it to her. Or that Paul would reverse course and opt to pay for the repairs on the opera house, giving them the gift of a true historical restoration.

Just when she thought she could predict his actions, he made a U-turn. And that set her off kilter, driving her back into his arms, even though she'd vowed she wouldn't get involved.

Not that a couple U-turns didn't have their perks. Every ounce of her body wanted to go back to the opera house, to pick up where they'd left off and to let him fill the lonely spaces in her heart and her bed.

She rose, pacing again. Inviting Paul into her bed, or anything else, was not an option. Gabriel needed more of her attention than ever, especially since he'd started coming in late, leaving work early, disappearing for hours on end. She was all he had, and if she deserted him—

She would never forget the look in his eyes the day she'd had to tell him their parents had died. Marjo never, ever wanted to see that heartbreak again.

Her life had been so wrapped up in Gabriel for so long, she couldn't imagine anything else. Besides, Gabriel wasn't equipped for life on his own, just because he'd taken a couple of home ec courses in high school and attended the life-skills class for kids with similar disabilities.

He needed someone to oversee the details. Because if there was one thing Gabriel rarely worried about, it was the minutiae of life.

Marjo headed back into the house, her wineglass still full, and got busy cleaning out a kitchen cabinet, because she knew if she didn't keep her hands occupied, her thoughts would undoubtedly wander toward the worst-case scenarios.

Finally, a little after eleven, she heard the squeak of the screen door. "Gabriel! Where have you been?"

"Out with Darcy." He laid the camera Paul had given him on the kitchen table, then crossed to the sink, poured himself a glass of water and leaned against the counter drinking it, as if nothing was wrong. As if he hadn't worried his sister half to death.

"Do you know what time it is?"

"Uh-huh."

"And why are you coming in so late?"

"Because I wanted to see Darcy. She's my girl-friend. We go out on dates."

That Marjo knew too well. Darcy was a nice girl, but things between Gabriel and her had become too serious, too fast. Marjo had tried to tell her brother that playing house wasn't the same as actually doing it—preparing meals, doing laundry, paying the bills.

Gabriel's mental handicap didn't preclude him from ever living on his own, with some help from Marjo to fill out applications, balance his check-book. And Darcy was already doing some of that, but still...

Was Darcy the best influence on Gabriel?

"You shouldn't be out this late, Gabriel. What if—"

"How old am I, Marjo?" he asked, cutting her off.

"Almost twenty-two, but I don't see what that has to do with anything."

"I'm old enough to make decisions. *By myself.*"

"Of course, Gabriel," she said, her voice soften-ing, knowing how much her little brother wanted to be an adult, and knowing, too, how the odds were stacked against him. "But you're young and…I just don't want you out on the roads this late." She didn't voice the hundred other worries she had, the concern that Gabriel wouldn't be able to handle himself if something went wrong. That he would panic, as he had last year when he'd cut his finger while slicing a tomato. Or the time a car accident had happened in front of his school and he'd run from the playground all the way home.

Doc Landry had told Marjo that Gabriel was a few years behind his peers, but he was going to catch up as adulthood helped level the playing field. Until then, her job was to protect him, finish raising him. And lately, he was making that very difficult.

In the last year or two, the relationship between her and Gabriel had edged toward confrontational. There'd been more arguments, less fun and, worst of all, a lack of the closeness the two of them had always had, that "us against the world" camaraderie. She couldn't blame him entirely. Her focus had been split, ever since Paul Clermont came to town.

There were responsibilities in her life, responsibilities that would still be there when Paul Clermont left town, and she couldn't afford to neglect him.

"Why were you out with Darcy so late?" she asked.

"Because I love her and she loves me." Gabriel stood straighter, taller. "In fact, I asked her to marry me."

"You did *what?*" Her voice was barely below a

scream. "You are *way* too young to get married. In fact, way too young to even think about it."

"No, I'm not, Marjo."

She shook her head. This marriage thing, like so many of Gabriel's "interests," would undoubtedly pass. When he was twelve, he'd wanted to be an artist one day, a musician the next. Surely the relationship with Darcy would cool any day now, the same as his passion for painting had.

"Marriage is a big step, Gabriel."

He scowled. "I know that."

"It's something you need to think about for a long time before you rush into anything, and from now on," Marjo said firmly, "I want you home at nine. You need your sleep."

"No, Marjo," Gabriel said. "I need my own life. You tell me not to take pictures, tell me when to go to work, when to come home. I can do all that. *By myself.*" He spun on his heel, then left the room.

Marjo sighed and sank into a chair, wishing she had a crystal ball, anything that would help her fix things with Gabriel and get her life back to the way it used to be. Lately, it seemed as if everything was changing.

Even her own emotions. She thought of Paul Clermont, of the kiss they'd exchanged in the opera house today. Of how it had done the one thing she'd resisted all year—changed the status quo. And yet, he'd told her he had no interest in settling in one place, reminding Marjo of her mother.

Elaine Savoy had never been happy here because she'd never really put down roots. Marjo *had* roots, and the last thing she wanted to do was to forget those just because some handsome guy from Canada swept her off her feet.

Clearly, it wasn't just things around her that needed to be set to rights. It was the feelings inside her.

As she listened to the sound of an angry Gabriel heading to bed and the slam of his door, she knew that only by ending any thoughts of a relationship with Paul Clermont could she refocus her priorities and find a way to get through to Gabriel.

Then everything could be the way it should be, before Paul had come to town.

The thought should have made her happy, but instead, she felt as dejected as the drooping pink camellias on her dining room table.

WHO'D HAVE THOUGHT anyone could make rolling a wall with paint look so damned sexy?

As Paul watched Marjo roll the sky-colored paint up and down the plywood that would create a backdrop for the opera house stage, his thoughts were definitely not on what kind of coverage the paint would give him for his dollar.

Her hair was back in the braid again today, but in a looser version, as if she'd rushed to style it this morning. The wispy tendrils whispering around her face made her look younger, more innocent. And most of all, more tempting.

She wore a cropped blue T-shirt that exposed her taut belly every time she reached for the top of the plywood with the roller, and her khaki shorts showed off absolutely amazing legs.

He'd called Joe earlier this morning and found out the fishermen back home in Nova Scotia had gone out on a quick trip to recoup some of the money they'd lost in the storm. That bought Paul some time before he had to leave, a couple of days at most. For the first time in his career, he wished it were two weeks instead of two days.

Paul quickly finished cutting in the base of the green bayou water for the Indigo landscape they were creating, then stepped back to admire their work—and Marjo. "You give painting a whole new meaning."

She laughed, exchanging her roller for a smaller brush dipped in green to create trees. "How do I do that?"

"By looking like that. You're much too distracting."

She glanced down at the sprinklings of paint on her shirt. "Do you want me to leave? I'd hate to keep you from your work."

He caught her hand before she could start working again, the movement causing a bit of paint to splatter on her nose. With one finger, he wiped it off, then caught her chin in his palm and looked down into her eyes. "No. Stay."

Her lips parted slightly, as if she wanted to say

something, or perhaps kiss him. Desire pounded in his head.

He leaned down, about to taste those sweet lips one more time, when someone hollered, "Lunch break!"

Aw, hell.

Marjo stepped back quickly, her face flushed. She turned away from him and put her roller onto the edge of the paint pan, then brushed her hands together, as if she was done with the job—and with him. "We better go eat. There's a lot left to accomplish today."

She was avoiding him. For the life of him, he couldn't figure out why. As far as he knew, nothing monumental had happened since her excitement yesterday at his financial support for the project. Nevertheless, a decided coolness had entered their relationship, as if she were purposely trying to keep them from becoming anything more than business partners.

In the lobby of the opera house, the members of the restoration committee chatted excitedly, buoyed into action by the financial windfall that gave them the funds they needed to complete the repairs in time for the festival. He had set aside enough funds to pay for the more painstaking historical restoration that would happen later.

The volunteers and contractors stood in line, waiting for bowls of gumbo from Willis and Estelle's diner, as well as sandwiches, pies and icy cold drinks. The hum of conversation carried throughout the room.

"Thanks for doing this," Luc Carter said, coming up beside Paul in the food line, which stretched around the entire perimeter of the lobby. "The whole town is behind the project now that you've stepped up to put some serious dollars for a full restoration. I, for one, really appreciate it. I mean, the town supported this project before, and there are a lot of businesses signed up and excited about the CajunFest, but today, the mood is different." He glanced around the room, clearly pleased. "I've never seen so many people out to help, *and* they're even more enthusiastic than before. It's like they've received a shot of confidence adrenaline. Indigo might have a revival yet."

"I can't take the credit," Paul replied. "It's Marjo. She showed me what a great place this was."

"Told you the tragic story of Alexandre and Amelie, didn't she?" Luc laughed. "That one got to me, too. I ended up volunteering for both the restoration committee and the CajunFest. She is one persuasive woman. And a hell of a storyteller."

"That she is," Paul said, accepting a bowl of soup from Estelle.

The owner of the Blue Moon Diner greeted him by name, then put an extra piece of bread on his plate, something he noticed she hadn't done for anyone else.

"Be sure you get enough, Mr. Clermont," Estelle said.

Paul glanced over at Luc, who had left the line to greet his fiancée, Loretta. The two of them were engaged in an intimate conversation and their love for each other was hard to miss. Something heavy sank in his gut. Something that felt a lot like envy.

After he had exited the food line, he placed his tray down on a table and took up his camera, wanting to capture a few more images of the people of Indigo working together. Luc and Loretta didn't seem to be the only couple in this town who were in love.

When Paul had married Diane, it had been a relationship based more on convenience and common interests than passion. She'd been in college, interning for a client who'd hired him for one of his first commercial photo shoots. For a while, he and Diane had talked about working together professionally. He'd figured her graphic design background meshed with his photography, like minds and all that. He'd proposed in record time, caught up in the idea of marriage more than anything else.

In the months that he and Diane were together, he had never seen her look at him the way Loretta looked at Luc. He'd never felt that overwhelming urge to see her, just to talk to her, touch her hair—

The way he did with Marjo.

Diane had been a great woman, just not the one who made him want to run home from work to be with her.

He scanned the room, hidden behind the Nikon, looking for the Cajun woman who had set off a firestorm in his gut. He finally sighted her, at the end of the food line, talking with her brother. Gabriel looked over, saw Paul and waved. He elbowed Marjo, who turned, her blue gaze direct and clear in his viewfinder. A smile appeared on her lips, then disappeared.

Did she feel this same intense firestorm that he did?

Or were they simply experiencing an infatuation that would end as soon as he left this place?

Either way, these were crazy thoughts. He must have inhaled too many paint fumes. But as he made his way over to one of the tables that had been set up in the lobby, he knew that wasn't the case.

Paul pushed the thoughts away. Regardless of what might be happening—or not—between him and Marjo Savoy, he had a job to get back to. A job that would send him far from Indigo.

He put his camera in his backpack, then took a seat at the table where he'd left his food. Immediately, several residents joined him, greeting him by name and making small talk about the weather and local news. Given their friendliness, it felt as if he'd lived here all his life. Even people he hadn't been introduced to treated him like one of their own.

Alain slid into the seat beside him. "See you've made some friends."

"I don't know half the people sitting at this table," Paul admitted under his breath. "Yet it feels like a family reunion. A lot like Cape Breton. This morning, before I could even get into my car, three people were offering me a ride over to the opera house."

Alain grinned. "A Cajun man will give you the hat off his head in August."

Paul looked around the room and decided that Alain was right. These people were like his family back home. Raucous uncles and food-bearing aunts included everyone in the party, blood relative or not.

Maybe he saw similarities to his home in this place because he wasn't here on assignment and hadn't kept a professional distance. He'd allowed himself to blend with the community.

Before he knew it, he'd be buying a raised cottage and tending to cypress trees in the backyard. Once before he'd fooled himself into thinking he was the kind of man who should put down roots.

And only a true fool made that same mistake twice.

"My wife felt bad she couldn't be here," Alain said. "She's been having a lot of trouble with her first trimester. Exhaustion, morning sickness. Doc Landry ordered her to spend some time in bed, but she's a stubborn woman. I practically had to take away her shoes to keep her home because she wanted to help so bad. Sophie's one determined woman."

"Sounds like Marjo," Paul said before he could stop himself.

"Do I detect a little something between you and our resident funeral director?"

"No," Paul replied. "I've just been working with her a lot on this project."

"Uh-huh." Alain gave him an I-don't-believe-you nod. "Hey, what are you doing tonight?"

"I don't have any plans." Marjo had been distant all day, making it clear there wasn't going to be a repeat of yesterday's kiss, which left a long evening stretching ahead of him, with just his camera and his laptop for company. A week ago, that would have been just fine, but lately he'd found himself craving company. Friendship.

It must be a case of bayou blues, Paul thought. A temporary state, gone as soon as Indigo was a dot on the horizon.

"Good," Alain said. "Come on by Skeeter's, the bar around the corner from the town hall. The Indigo Boneshakers have asked me to fill in for their fiddler tonight." Alain laughed. "Apparently he went a little overboard on some crawfish and beer last night and isn't up to playing anything but a porcelain bowl. They said they'd love a second fiddle, if I knew another player."

"I take it that's a hint?" Paul asked, grinning.

"Even better, a summons, from the chief of police at that."

"Sure," Paul agreed. "I'll be by. I can't join you, though. I don't have a fiddle with me."

"I'll bring you one of my extras after we get done here today, along with some of the music we're playing tonight. That'll give you a couple hours to practice. The Boneshakers have a CD they're planning on selling at the CajunFest. That'll be the

quickest way for you to get up to speed." Alain
leaned closer and gestured with his hunk of bread
toward Marjo, who had sat down two tables away
from him, with Cally and Gabriel. "And I think you
should get Marjo to come along, too. Half of Indigo
has been trying to talk her into singing in the Cajun-
Fest, including me. I'm in charge of booking all the
acts for that day, but she won't do it. She's as stubborn as an alligator waiting for a dove to fly into its
mouth."

Paul watched her, laughing at something Cally had
said, and wished she'd turn that smile on him. "I'll talk
to her, though I doubt I'll be much of an influence."
Hell, she clearly didn't even want to sit with him at
lunch. She'd maintained a friendly distance all day,
as if she regretted what had happened between them.

He turned from thoughts of Marjo and enjoyed
his lunch with Alain, comparing notes about fiddling
techniques. The rest of the day was much the same—
hard work but fun. The residents of Indigo pitched
in alongside the carpenters that Paul had hired, and
the lobby and the auditorium seemed to transform.
Chairs were repaired or replaced, wood was polished
to its original luster. The space sparkled and
gleamed.

Marjo continued to avoid Paul, choosing to work
as far away from him as she could.

He should have been pleased. He had, after all,
told himself a hundred times that he was leaving.
That he wanted no ties to this place. Once the opera

house repairs were well under way, he'd go. Another day, maybe two.

But when the crews knocked off for the day and he saw Marjo striding out the door, he forgot all those plans and ran after her, catching up to her on the outside steps. "Are you interested in hearing a really bad fiddler try to pretend he knows what he's doing?"

She laughed, and Paul realized he had missed the sound. "And that rusty fiddler, I take it, is you?"

He nodded. "Alain wants me to come down to Skeeter's tonight and play with the Indigo Boneshakers. Their regular fiddler is sick."

"I'm sure you'll do fine. Alain and his group are great guys." The words were polite but dismissive. Once again, Paul wondered what had made Marjo back away.

"Come with me," he said before he could stop himself. "It'll be nice to have a friendly face there. And…you could sing."

She shook her head before he finished the sentence, already rejecting the idea. "For one, I'm not singing in public. You're not the only one who's rusty." When she gave him a self-effacing smile, he had the distinct feeling she was only making an excuse. "And for another, I can't go tonight. I have work to do."

"You always say you have work to do." He leaned against one of the pillars and crossed his arms over his chest, waiting as two men lumbered down the stairs, making plans for a late-night catfishing trip. "Are you avoiding me?"

"No, not at all."

"Then prove it," he said, moving forward and reaching up to catch an escaped tendril of her hair. "Ah, Marjo, I've wanted to do that all day."

"Touch my hair?"

"No, this." He cupped her jaw with his hand and placed a kiss on her lips. A short, sweet kiss, nowhere near what he really wanted to do. "Meet me tonight. Please."

She watched him for a long, quiet moment, and in her eyes he saw the icy wall she'd erected that day melt, inch by inch, and give way to the simmering attraction between them. "Maybe." A flirty smile flitted across her face just before she turned away.

As he watched Marjo leave, Paul knew he'd forgotten one thing in his plan for a quick getaway. To leave his heart by the door, too.

CHAPTER TWELVE

MARJO ENTERED Skeeter's that night, caught up in the crowd that had gathered to hear the police chief show off his fiddling talent. In all her years of living in Indigo she'd never seen the bar this busy. Perhaps it was an extension of the upbeat mood in the opera house today, as if all of Indigo had been revitalized along with the opera house. She greeted a few people she knew, but lingered inside the door, Cally at her side.

Alain, the members of the Indigo Boneshakers and Paul were all up on the stage, tuning their instruments while a jukebox pumped a catchy zydeco tune through the sound system. From across the room, she saw Paul scan the crowd, then catch her eye, as if he'd been searching just for her. He smiled and a quiver rushed through her veins.

Oh, boy. There went her resolution not to get tangled up in a relationship, especially with a man like Paul Clermont, who made her forget her own name. "What am I doing here?" Marjo said.

"Watching a really hot guy play some music,"

Cally answered. "A really hot *single* guy, I might add."

"No, I mean, why am I getting involved with him? I don't have time or room for a relationship. I have other priorities."

"Priorities that exclude what's important to you?" Cally's eyes were filled with concern. "You deserve a life, too. It's been far too long since you've had one."

"I was engaged."

"That Kerry Tidwell had to be the biggest idiot this side of Bayou Teche for not seeing what a great catch you were. You and Gabriel." The band continued tuning up, and the hum of anticipation increased in the crowd.

"Which is exactly why I can't fall for Paul Clermont. What man wants to take on a buy-one-get-one-free relationship?"

"Gabriel and Paul get along just fine. I've seen them out by the bayou, taking pictures together. They looked like two peas in a pod. Why wouldn't you think that Paul would understand about Gabriel?"

Marjo sighed. She wanted to believe that, but couldn't risk it, not again. "Because Kerry did the same thing, at least in the beginning. He was great with Gabriel, took him fishing and everything. But when it came to getting married, he didn't want the bonus brother."

Two young women passed by on their way to the

bar. As they did, Marjo overheard the girls debating which fiddler was cuter—Alain or Paul. A flare of jealousy rose in her chest, which she immediately tamped down. She had no claims to Paul, his fiddle or anything else about him.

"Is that the only reason you and Kerry broke up?" Cally asked.

"Of course it was." But was that the truth? Or had it been a convenient excuse to avoid a marriage Marjo had never felt ready for?

"If you ask me, there's more to you running scared from relationships than just the Gabriel issue," Cally said, reading her mind.

"Hey, what about you? I don't see you settling down and having two-point-five kids."

Cally waved off that idea. "Before I'm ready for anything like that, you're going to need to call in Dr. Phil, Oprah *and* Jerry Springer. I'm a walking relationship disaster zone."

"I don't think we have to go that far. A little yellow caution tape should be enough."

Cally laughed. "Let's fix your life first, then we'll tackle mine."

"Mine doesn't need fixing. I have a life." She did, and she liked it just fine. This recent unrest would go away, as soon as she had some downtime.

"Marjo, nothing against the funeral home, but you spend your day with *dead people*."

Paul and Alain had picked up their fiddles and the group began to play in the tradition of Dennis

McGee, performing one of the tunes he'd recorded decades ago. The police dispatcher, Billy Paul Exeter, kept up the tempo with a set of drums decorated with the band's name and skeleton logo. People sitting at the tables clapped along and stomped their feet, clearly enjoying the show.

Marjo, though, didn't hear a note. From the second he started playing, the only thing she noticed was the deft fingers of Paul Clermont, working the fiddle.

"Well, maybe my love life is a little lacking," Marjo said to Cally, watching Paul move and feeling the same shiver of anticipation she'd felt every time she saw him. No matter what she'd just told herself, she wanted him again, wanted his kiss, wanted...more.

"Live dangerously, Marjo. Lay it on the table, tell him how you feel. And see where that takes you." Cally grinned. "Like into the bedroom."

"Tell him how I feel?"

"Oh, *please,*" Cally said. "You're half in love with him already. It's written all over your face, plain as the stars in the sky."

"I am not." Even as Marjo protested, her gut disagreed. She'd tried her best to avoid Paul, but even when she kept a physical distance between them, her mind was still focused on him. Thinking about what it would be like to kiss him again, to hear his laugh, to feel his touch.

To wake up in the morning and see him there, filling the space in her bed and her life.

"I should leave," Marjo said, turning toward the door.

Cally caught her before she could take a step. "No, you should stay and stop putting everyone in this entire damned town ahead of yourself."

"I do not." But this last protest was the weakest of all.

"Come on, let's go grab a beer and listen to these guys. And after *they* play, *you* go play with Paul." She winked at Marjo.

Marjo followed Cally, but only because she loved music and wanted to support the local group. Not for any other reason at all. But as she slid into a seat at a front-row table, she knew she was kidding herself.

She was soon caught up in the music, the magic of watching Paul send notes through the fiddle. He was good, much better than he'd said, and he had a way of fiddling and moving his hips, as if Elvis had gone Cajun. As far as Marjo was concerned, there wasn't a single other person on that stage.

At the end of their first set, Paul went up to Alain and whispered in his ear. Alain grinned and nodded, then grabbed the microphone. "Ladies and gentlemen, we have a very talented singer in our audience tonight, someone you all know. I'd like to ask Miss Marjolaine Savoy to come on up here and sing *Le Pays des Etrangers*."

"Oh, no. No, no *no*." Marjo put up her hands, warding off the idea. But Cally was already pushing her out of the chair, and the crowd gathered in

Skeeter's was cheering her on. Before she could think better of it, she was climbing the stairs to the stage and accepting the microphone from Alain.

It had been more than sixteen years since she'd held a microphone or sung in anything more public than a church pew. The metal felt strange in her hand, and yet, at the same time, like an old friend. Behind her, the band waited for her signal.

She took in a breath, faced the crowd and then closed her eyes. With a tremor in her voice, she sang the first few words of the song, then, as the band picked up her cue and added the melody, her voice gained in strength and confidence. She opened her eyes, and the song burst from her lungs like a bird held too long in a cage.

The notes sang through her heart, harmonized with the beat of her pulse, becoming one with her as always in the past. Joy soared inside her, as powerful as a tidal wave. Too soon, the song was done and the sound of applause shattered the quiet in the room.

"Another!" someone shouted.

"Come on, Marjo, one more!"

"Your audience wants a full performance," Paul whispered in her ear. "Don't disappoint them."

She turned and grinned at him. In his eyes, she saw a reflection of the same pride that had risen in her chest. He was happy for her, that was clear. "Do you think you can keep up with me?"

"I can handle anything you throw my way, Miss Savoy."

Marjo turned and whispered the name of a fast-paced zydeco tune to the band. Billy Paul nodded, then went at his drums with fervor. Marjo smile and danced a bit as the song took root, then she began to sing. Paul gave her a teasing look and moved up beside her, his body bending and swaying with the movements of his bow.

Three songs later, the band broke for a break. Alain thanked Paul for joining them and offered to buy him a beer. Marjo sent a wave Cally's way. Her friend had cozied up with Billy Paul in the corner, apparently deciding the love life advice applied to her, too.

What had happened on that stage had been magical. Wonderful. But it was also a huge mistake.

Singing onstage had only reminded her of the dream she'd long ago given up. But she couldn't run off and pursue an impossible dream.

She pushed on the door and exited Skeeter's before she could change her mind about staying. Singing another song, with Paul by her side.

"That was amazing." Paul said, catching up with her. "*You* were amazing. You got everyone dancing and really charged up the place."

She shrugged as if it was nothing, but, still, a tiny measure of pride grew in her chest. "It *was* fun."

Paul cupped his hand over his ear. "Is that you saying I was right?"

"Maybe," she conceded. "A little."

"Then does that mean I can walk you home?"

The gentlemanly question touched a soft place in her heart. Hadn't she just told Cally she wasn't going to pursue anything with this man?

Yes, she knew better, but for the first time in her life, she was tired of doing what was right, what was expected, what was better for all concerned. Instead, she decided to do what she used to do when she'd been younger and hadn't had all these worries crowding her shoulders like crows on a telephone line—she would go by the seat of her pants and take the opportunity that was walking right beside her. "Sure. I'd like it if you did."

The temperature had dropped a few degrees and she tugged her sweater tighter over her shoulders. Paul wrapped his arm around her waist, pulling her into his warmth. She thought of protesting, but it felt so good.

It was just one more sweet gesture. Cally was right.

Marjo *was* falling for Paul. And falling really hard.

They strolled along the street, not saying anything for a long while, just enjoying the subdued, ebony-cloaked version of Indigo. In that quiet, the attraction that had been simmering between them for days began to multiply.

What would it hurt to extend this moment? Paul would be leaving town soon. Off to Tibet or Timbuktu, leaving her with only a few memories. Why not add one more to the pile? One more kiss?

"Would you like to come in for a glass of wine?" she asked when they reached her house.

"I'd like that," he said. He followed her up the stairs, his hand in hers—when they had started holding hands, she didn't know, but wasn't about to let go—and then into the house and down the hall to the kitchen.

A single light burned over the kitchen sink, and the rest of the house was silent and dark, a sure sign that Gabriel was, once again, out with Darcy. Marjo pushed her worries aside. She could have a glass of wine with Paul and deal with everything else later. "Merlot? Or Chardonnay?"

"Surprise me."

She poured them two glasses of Chardonnay, then pivoted away from the counter.

"You drove me crazy up there on the stage," Paul said, taking a step forward.

"I thought it was my painting style that you appreciated," she teased, holding out the goblets toward him.

"Everything about you gets my attention." He took the two glasses of wine from her hands, placed them on the counter then took another step forward, bringing him centimeters away from her skin, her lips.

All she had to do was to lean forward a teeny bit and she would be in his arms again, taking what they had started in the opera house to the next level.

Her heart began to race, her pulse thundering in her head. She wanted him in a way that almost engulfed her.

She opened her mouth, but whatever witty thing she'd intended to say flitted away. "Paul…"

He didn't wait for an answer but leaned down and brushed his lips across hers, a tease of what was to come. "You drive me crazy," he said again, "absolutely crazy."

His kiss was slow at first, as if he was treasuring the moment, treasuring her. When she responded with a greater pressure, the tempo picked up, as the music had earlier, going from soft and soulful to fast and heated.

She wanted him, more than she'd ever wanted anyone. The desire nearly seared her with its intensity, the way it overpowered all rational thought.

"Paul," she murmured against his lips before clasping his neck and pulling him closer. She slid her tongue into his mouth, waltzing with his, driven by need, instinct. He groaned, hauling her against the hard planes of his chest, then slid his hands along her back, her hips, her buttocks, his touch both firm and gentle, making no secret of how she made him feel.

She grasped the edge of Paul's T-shirt and tugged it over his head, then tossed it to the side, not caring where it landed. Her palms explored his naked torso, the warmth and hardness of him intensifying the insistent want deep inside her.

His fingers slipped between them, and with fast, nimble movements, he undid the few buttons keeping her shirt together. Every one he opened sent another wave of anticipation surging through her. With tantalizing slowness, he spread apart the two panels of fabric, revealing the lacy pink bra she wore underneath to the golden light above the sink.

"You are…incredible, in every way," he murmured. Then he dipped his head and trailed kisses along the nape of her neck, down her throat, teasing along the crest of her cleavage.

She gasped and arched against him. "Paul," was all she could say, her words lost somewhere in the drumming of her pulse.

He slipped a finger under one of the silky pink straps, then slid it slowly to the side, taking his time, admiring her, stoking her to near fever pitch.

Marjo ran her fingers through his hair, inhaling the scent of him, memorizing the way he felt against her. He tasted every inch of her skin, and then, when she thought she could bear it no longer, he pushed the lace to one side. A draft of cool air raced along her breast, but before she could even gasp, he drew her nipple into his mouth, sending her soaring.

"Oh, oh, my," Marjo said, the words jerking out of her on a moan and a breath. "Paul, I—"

Outside, she heard the sound of tires on gravel. It took a long second before her mind made the connection, but when it did, she jerked away from Paul, clutching at her shirt and hurriedly rebuttoning it. "Gabriel. He's home."

"He has *really* bad timing," Paul said, grinning.

He released her, grabbed his shirt off the floor then slipped it back on. By the time Gabriel entered the house, she and Paul were at opposite ends of the kitchen table, sipping wine.

Marjo bit her lip when she noticed that Paul's shirt was on inside-out. She could only pray her brother didn't make the same observation.

"Hey, Paul," Gabriel said. "You here taking pictures?"

Paul slid a grin Marjo's way. "No, no pictures," Paul said. "Not tonight."

"I took some." Gabriel pulled the camera Paul had given him out of his backpack. "Wanna see?"

"Sure."

Paul and her brother started a discussion about focal points and composition. Marjo picked up her wineglass and headed out to the porch, taking a seat in the rocker. The warm Indigo night wrapped its familiar comforting blanket around her.

"Sorry about that," Paul said as he joined her a few minutes later. "I get talking about photography, and before you know it, hours have gone by."

"That's okay. I'm glad to see Gabriel having so much fun with the camera." Paul was obviously a good influence on her brother.

"He has an eye for it. He could apprentice under someone part-time and take some classes in photography. I think eventually he could make a good living at it."

Marjo didn't want Paul encouraging Gabriel to

run off on a whim. "He makes a good living already."

Paul started to speak, as if he was thinking of disagreeing, then stopped. "As long as he's happy."

Of course Gabriel was happy. If he wasn't, he would have said something to Marjo. Either way, she refused to entertain the thought of Gabriel becoming a photographer. He had a good job at the funeral home, one that would be there for as long as he needed it. She wasn't going to push him into a competitive field where he could suffer rejection.

Gabriel had had enough of that in his life, simply because he was different. She'd shielded him as much as she could, but there'd always be that one person who would say something that would put a chink in Gabriel's gentle spirit. Marjo knew from competing in singing competitions when she was younger just how easily a few mislaid comments could destroy someone's confidence.

"So, how did you learn to play the fiddle?" Marjo asked, opting for a change in subject.

"My dad taught me. It's pretty much a family tradition in Cape Breton. My uncles would come over on the weekends and create a party out of nothing more than a fiddle and a case of beer."

She finished her wine, then twirled the glass in her hands. "What's your family like?"

"Ordinary. Two parents, a younger sister named Faye, and me. My dad worked himself half to death for too many years, but now he's retired."

"That's it?"

He shrugged, then settled into the wooden chair beside hers. "Yeah."

He hadn't exactly opened up a door into his soul, yet he knew almost everything there was to know about her.

He'd kissed her, made his interest in her clear, but hadn't done anything that would take this relationship past the superficial.

Wasn't that what she'd wanted? Nothing long-term. Nothing that would take her from the roots she'd worked so hard to build for herself and Gabriel. If that was so, then why did Paul's reticence sting so badly?

"I forgot to tell you," Paul said, his hand slipping into hers. "There's one condition to my support of the opera house."

"A condition?"

"You sing at the festival."

"You can't force me to sing just so I get the opera house support."

"I can and I did. With the committee's approval, of course. In fact, it was a group idea. I spoke to Joan Bateman, who is writing the program." He grinned, clearly pleased with his plan. "You're already written into it, so there's no backing out."

"I can't sing—"

"Oh, yes, you can. You proved it tonight. You gave a hell of a performance, too."

"You don't understand," she said, rising and

crossing to the porch railing. "It's not that simple. I can't just start singing again."

"Why not?"

"I have *responsibilities,* Paul." Gabriel coming home late had been a clear reminder of where she should be directing her attentions. Paul wandered the earth with nothing more than a camera and a passport. He couldn't possibly understand her commitment to her brother, the family business, her need to stay on solid ground instead of grasping for clouds.

"You have an amazing voice. You shouldn't keep it hidden away in that funeral home."

"Don't talk to me about keeping things hidden away," she said, making an effort to keep from shouting because Gabriel was within earshot, inside the house. "You've barely told me more than three sentences about yourself since I met you."

"There's not much to tell."

She shook her head. "One thing I've learned in researching the histories of this town and the people who have lived here is that there is *always* a story to tell. Every one of us has a story."

"Not me. I gave you all there was. I'm divorced, I spend my days traveling all over the world, taking pictures and earning a living."

"That's it, huh?" She crossed the porch until she was close enough to see the reflection of the moon in his eyes. They seemed like deep, dark pools she could lose herself in. "Why did you get divorced?

Why did you sell your house? Why did you choose a job that makes you a nomad? Why—"

"Whoa, whoa," he said, getting up from his chair. "Somehow this got turned around into an argument about me, when all I wanted was for you to sing in the CajunFest."

"And I think you have no business telling me how to live my life when you are barely living your own."

He stepped back, and she could see that her words had hit their mark. Immediately she wanted to take them back, to seal up that mouth that often got her into trouble. There were definitely times when speaking her mind wasn't the best choice. "I'm sorry, Paul, I—"

"No, you're right." His voice went cold and hard, as rigid as his posture. "I don't have any business telling you what to do. Nor do I have any business owning something in this town. I don't know what I was thinking." He looked away for a second, as if deciding something, then turned back to her. "I will honor our deal and pay for the rest of the repairs on the opera house. But when that's done, I'll tell Sandra to find a buyer who will agree to honor the town's plans for the place—someone who has an appreciation for roots and legacies."

Then he turned on his heel and walked away.

CHAPTER THIRTEEN

THE NEXT MORNING Paul was packed and ready to go, as always, in less than a minute. He'd called the airline, arranged a flight to Nova Scotia, talked to Joe, his editor, and promised the pictures by the end of the week. Everything was set for him to leave Indigo.

To resume his life.

He crossed the room, exiting out the French doors and onto the veranda. The sun was just coming up over the bayou, turning the foliage from deep emerald to a bright, lively green. The golden light seemed to wash over the land, making it sparkle, as if it were a magic place.

He shook off the feeling, then turned and reentered his room. As soon as he got on the plane, this wistful feeling would stop. He'd slip back into work mode and everything would go back to exactly the way it had been. He'd be free again, which was exactly how he liked it. Even if a couple of nagging doubts persisted. Thoughts centered on a certain feisty brunette who expected more out of him than he ever had himself.

It was best to leave, before the idea of staying took hold of him again.

A knock sounded at his door, tentative at first, then firmer. He pulled the door open.

Marjo.

She wore her hair loose again and he was sure she hand never looked so beautiful.

Stay, his mind whispered. *Tell her you're not going anywhere.*

Ever again.

Before he could utter those words, he reminded himself he had a plane ticket. An assignment. A career to get back to.

"I came by to give something to you," Marjo said, handing him a thick manila folder.

"What is it?"

"Documents, tracing the history of the opera house. I thought you might want to know everything about the property. Before you sell it to the highest bidder." She turned on her heel and headed down the hall.

"Marjo, wait!" When she didn't stop, he hurried after her, catching up with her at the top of the staircase. He reached out and grabbed her arm. "Don't go, not yet."

"Why? You're leaving. It's all over town. Paul Clermont is getting on the first plane out of hell." Her eyes glimmered with sadness. "Why should I stay and delay the inevitable?"

"You don't understand. I'm leaving because I have a job, a photo assignment."

She gave him a short, polite nod. "Good luck with that. And if you're ever in the area again, do stop by."

That had to be the coldest goodbye Paul had ever received. Not that he didn't deserve it, but it sent a fist into his gut all the same.

"Marjo, I hate to leave things like this."

"Like what? Did you think a few kisses meant anything between us? How could they? We barely know each other. You're only doing what you said you were going to do. Moving on, severing all ties."

Put that way, it sounded like he was abandoning the town, abandoning her.

Indigo would be just fine without him, and he without it. But as he looked at Marjo, he had to wonder whether he was selling himself a bucket of rotten crawfish.

"Marjo, you don't understand. I know what it's like to tie yourself to a place so tight you cut off all other avenues. I watched my relatives work hard all their lives, only to see everything they owned wiped away in one bad fishing season. But they stayed in Cape Breton, thinking things would get better someday, when the only way out was to leave."

"You mean, run away."

"I'm not running away from anything." Yet, as the words left his mouth, he wondered how true that was. "You may think I'm deserting all of this, but I'm not. I'll be back." He gave her a grin, hoping to return to the camaraderie they'd had before, the easy connection that seemed to have disappeared. "I have to check on my investment."

She gave him a broad smile. "I appreciate what you've done for the opera house, and this town will be fine, regardless of who owns it. And so will I."

She was making it clear that there was no reason for him to come back. There was nothing waiting for him here.

The right thing to do—the only thing he could do—was to let her go and not look back.

"Then will you give Gabriel this?" he asked, taking a business card out of his wallet. He cleared his throat of the lump that had suddenly formed there. "If he ever wants to pursue photography, have him call me."

"*If* you talk to him," she said, "please don't encourage him to follow some foolish dream. I might not always be here to take care of him, and he needs to have a secure job. Besides, you know how these creative fields are, Paul. The criticism can be brutal. Gabriel has had enough of that already."

"I know that," Paul said. "I've been on the receiving end of a vicious critique more than once. But sometimes those things can make a person stronger instead of crushing them."

She shook her head. "Not Gabriel."

"And not you?"

"What's that supposed to mean?"

"Is that why you aren't singing?" he asked. "Because you don't want to be hurt?"

"Of course not." But she looked away from him. "I'm simply not a risk-taker. Nor do I want my brother to live that way."

"Oh, Marjo, don't be afraid of taking risks," he said.

She quirked an ironic grin. "I could say the same to you. Either way, thank you for the card and have a safe trip." She tucked his business card into the back pocket of her capris, then turned to head down the stairs. On the first step, she paused, and in that second, Paul willed her to turn around, to undo all of this, to demand he stay instead of letting him go as easily as a balloon string slipping through her fingers.

And then she did turn around, rose on her tiptoes and kissed him.

But her kiss lacked passion and tasted instead of goodbyes and bittersweet memories. Too quickly, she broke away from him. Her hand cupped his face for one brief second, and then she was gone.

MARJO DID THE ONLY THING she could do after leaving La Petite Maison and Paul Clermont.

She worked.

She did everything from organizing the old files at the Savoy Funeral Home to polishing the floor of the opera house. In the days after Paul had left town, she came home every night tired, sweaty and…miserable. What was it about that man? How could he have gotten under her skin in such a short time?

"Hey, Marjo!" Cally called, pulling into Marjo's driveway on Thursday night just as Marjo was climbing the porch steps, exhausted and ready for bed. "I thought you might need this." She held up a six-pack of light beer and joined Marjo on the porch.

Marjo sank into a chair and reached for the chilled bottle her friend proffered. "Thank you. You read my mind."

The heat wave had broken, leaving them with the moderate days and cool nights that were normal for October. It seemed as if the minute Paul Clermont left town last week, the heat stirred up by his presence had dissipated.

Cally sat beside her, twisted the top off her own bottle and took a drink before speaking. "So, are you trying out for the Toughwoman competition or what?"

Marjo laughed. "Maybe I am working a little too hard. But look at the benefits." She held up her right arm and flexed a bicep.

"I'm more worried about your cardio muscle."

"Cardio? I'm fine there." She patted her chest. "Breathing well, no murmurs or racing heartbeat."

"That's because there's no man around to make your heart beat faster."

"Well, there is that," Marjo admitted. She'd struggled all day to blot the memory of Paul Clermont from her mind. It didn't work. He remained there, as stubborn as a mule. "Look at the bright side. My nights are free again."

"Yeah, and what are doing with those free nights? Working until you run yourself into the ground. I don't think you're doing all this to help the opera house, but to get one good-looking Cape Breton man out of your system."

Marjo opened her mouth to protest, then realized she couldn't even lie to herself. "Yeah, I am. It's not working very well, though. Maybe I need a brain transplant."

Cally laughed. "Didn't you tell him how you felt before he left?"

"I was going to. I even went over to his room at La Petite Maison with this cool little speech all worked out. I had visual aids and everything." Cally raised her eyebrows. "No, not the kind of visual aids you're thinking of, though maybe those might have worked better. I took along the love letters of Alexandre and Amelie, thinking I could just casually mention how romantic the letters were, and that being at the opera house with him had ignited these feelings…"

"But?"

"But I didn't. Good thing, too, because he made it very clear that he was leaving. That Indigo, and me, were a temporary layover in his travels."

"Then he's an idiot, because in my opinion, you—and me—are the best catches in this entire bayou, and any man who can't see that doesn't deserve us." Cally clinked her bottle against Marjo's. "So there."

Marjo laughed. "You do know how to make me feel better."

"It's the beer talking. Makes me all self-righteous."

"Well, despite my deplorable love life, one that I don't need, I might add, I'm glad to see everything finally moving forward with the opera house. The CajunFest is all set to happen on Saturday."

The workers Paul had hired had been working all week. The plumbing updates were done, the chairs had been fixed and an air-conditioning system had been installed, which would provide a welcome respite for the festival-goers from the heat outside.

"And not a moment too soon. This town could use the boost." Cally spun the bottle between her hands. "What I'm worried about is afterward."

"Afterward? Far as I know, we don't have any other events planned."

"I meant, with you. This festival and the restoration have consumed all your spare time for months. What's going to happen when it's all over?"

The thought had occurred to Marjo, too. What would she do when all this was over, and she was left with a big hole in her life? She'd be alone again, with nothing to fill her days but the funeral home and Gabriel. "I'll still have my work at the funeral home."

"Is that what you want to do?"

What Marjo wanted hadn't been a consideration since she'd turned nineteen. Her life had been built around responsibilities. The business. Gabriel. "It's what my parents expected. What they needed me to do."

"No. They needed you to keep it open to provide an income for you and Gabriel. I'd say you've done your duty, Marjo. You've been there for sixteen years. They didn't say you had to run it forever or to make it your whole life." She leaned forward, elbows on her knees. From far off, a bullfrog let out his loud, belching song. "Do you think they'd be happy if they could see you so *un*happy?"

Marjo was ready to fire back an argument, to disagree with Cally as she had a hundred times before. But she hesitated and then shook her head. "No, they wouldn't."

"Then hire a funeral director and go work in the opera house. Make it a center for music once again. Sing your heart out every day, and find the happiness that you deserve, my friend." Cally reached out and grasped her hand, her palm cool against Marjo's. "It's *your* turn now."

"What about Gabriel?" Marjo worried her bottom lip. For so many years, that had been her number-one concern. *What about Gabriel?*

"He's getting older, in case you haven't noticed. He doesn't need you as much as you think. And besides, you don't have to sell the business—you just don't have to run it. Gabriel can work with Henry as long as he needs the job, and you can stop worrying so much."

Worry. It had become such a constant companion she couldn't imagine a life without it.

She allowed herself a moment to think about the audience in the bar a few nights earlier. When she'd gotten up on the stage and started singing, a butterfly had taken wing inside her chest.

For too long she'd suppressed that side of herself. But in Skeeter's, people had responded to her song, and the praise had reawakened her long-neglected desire to sing professionally. Not just sing occasionally with the Indigo Boneshakers, but to do it every day of her life.

"Maybe…" Marjo said, not making any promises, "I'll give it a shot. After the festival. And only on a part-time basis."

"Wow. You're agreeing with me?" Cally winked. "Must be the beer talking."

"Speaking of beer, this was a good idea." Marjo hoisted the her bottle in appreciation. "Thanks for this, and for being such a good friend."

"Aw, you'd do it for me. And you have, a hundred times over. You're the kind of friend who's there whenever someone needs you." Cally rose and gave her a quick hug. "Especially when someone has just had their heart stomped on by Remy Theriot. Remember when he dumped me last year, right in front of the Blue Moon? He tells me, and half of Indigo, that he'd only asked me out to bide his time until a better offer came along. Heck, I *was* the better offer. He was just too stupid to realize it."

Marjo opened her mouth to agree, but before she could speak, a car careened into the driveway. Anything moving that fast in the bayou meant one of two things: a lost and panicked out-of-towner or a life-and-death situation. Jenny leaped from the car, leaving the engine running. "Marjo! Come quick!"

Marjo was already halfway down the stairs, Cally close behind. "What happened?"

"The funeral home—it's on fire!"

CHAPTER FOURTEEN

BEFORE JENNY COULD finish her sentence, Marjo was in the car, her chest so constricted with worry she doubted she'd ever breathe normally again. Cally climbed in, too, then they took off down the road, Jenny's two-door Escort squealing around the curves.

The sky above the funeral home had turned blood-orange, as if the sun had descended on the bayou. For a heartbeat, Marjo told herself it wasn't fire. It was a sunset. Something, *anything* but her family's business going up in smoke.

But as Jenny stopped the car, Marjo knew. This was no sunset. No happy ending. It was devastation.

"Oh, my God," Cally said. "I can't believe this is happening."

Dancing, vibrant flames licked at the timber construction, climbed the pillars, crossed the roof. Once they'd engulfed the building, they leaped over to the sign, devouring one letter at a time as if erasing the Savoy Funeral Home.

Marjo was out of the car before Jenny put it in Park. She ran toward the scene, screaming, though she couldn't hear her own voice. Luc Carter caught her in his arms, holding her back. "There's nothing you can do, Marjo. It's gone."

"Gabriel! Henry!" The words were torn from her throat. She lunged forward again, but Luc held tight.

"They're okay," he said, repeating the words until they finally overrode her panic and sank into her mind. She looked up at him, waited for him to say the words one more time, in case she'd misheard. When he did, relief swamped her senses and she sagged against his chest. "They got out, Marjo. Don't worry."

She thanked God for that, and also that there'd been no loved ones inside the funeral home. It had been a slow week, which she now saw as a blessing.

Tears threatened but she brushed them away, trying to think, to determine the next step. For a moment she drew a blank, seeing nothing but the orange flames waving at her, taunting her.

Stop the fire. Save the building.

She pivoted, still secure in Luc's grasp, and saw dozens of Indigo residents dousing the flames with water. Chuck Bell, the head of the volunteer fire department, was heading up a bucket brigade and directing Indigo's sole fire truck into place on the other side. Alain was also there, helping to coordinate the effort, shouting orders and waving in the fire trucks from St. Martinville and New Iberia. His face was blackened from soot, his hair gray with ash.

"Where are they?" she asked Luc. "Where's Gabriel?"

"Doc Landry's looking after them. The new doc is way down the bayou, at the Landreaux place."

"Where did Doc Landry take my brother?" Marjo asked, needing to see Gabriel with her own eyes, to be sure he was okay. She couldn't lose him.

Luc pointed to the left. "They're over on the Melancons' porch, right next door."

Marjo broke away, crossing the divide between the two properties in seconds. Her throat, her lungs burned. She heard Cally call out to her, but she didn't stop.

Finally she stumbled up the steps, eyes watering, gaze darting wildly from one corner of the porch to the other. At first, she didn't see anyone, and panic clawed at her.

Then, a familiar shoe, a well-worn pair of jeans. Gabriel. Henry.

Henry was sitting up against the side of the house, his skin and clothes as black as a chimney, an oxygen mask clutched to his face. Gabriel had retreated into himself, standing against the edge of the porch railing, as far from the doctor and Henry as he could get. His arms were crossed tight over his chest, and he was rocking back and forth. He, too, was blackened, his hair a mess, his arms dark.

"Gabriel!" Marjo rushed to him, pulling her brother into a grateful hug. He smelled of wood and smoke, but most of all of home. "Are you okay?"

He nodded, stiff in her arms for one long moment before finally relaxing.

"That boy saved my life," Henry said, pulling off the oxygen mask. Doc Landry gave him a stern look, then gently pushed the mask back into place. "Came right in and dragged me out, he did."

"You didn't!"

Gabriel nodded again, clearly proud of himself. "I did. Ran right—"

"But you could have *died!*" Her voice rose in pitch as the possibilities flashed through her mind. "Don't ever do something that stupid again!"

The words were out before she could stop them, brought about by the rush of panic. Gabriel recoiled, as if she'd struck him. "You think I'm *stupid?*"

"No, no, Gabe. I—"

"I'm not stupid!" he shouted back. "You don't think I can make my own decisions. But I'm smart, Marjo. I am." He jerked out of her arms, then turned and ran down the steps.

The tears Marjo had held back earlier threatened again. She pressed the heels of her palms to her eyes and forced herself to remain where she was, instead of running after Gabriel.

Right now, she'd only be making a bad situation worse.

When Gabriel got like this, there was no arguing with him. He could be as stubborn as a weed. So she watched him go, helpless, her heart cracking.

"He's a brave boy," Henry said, grabbing for Marjo's hand. "Don't be so hard on him."

"He could have died. I can't lose him." She shook

her head, wiping at the tears in her eyes. "I just couldn't bear it."

"He's a grown man now, Marjo," Henry said, again lowering the oxygen mask and ignoring Doc Landry's glare. "You gotta trust him to know what to do."

"Run into a burning building? Henry, that's a lot different from just staying out too late with Darcy." Suddenly exhausted, Marjo sank to the porch floor beside the older man. He'd worked at the funeral home longer than she could remember and had always been a friend to the family. He'd been so patient, guiding and teaching Gabriel over the years. In fact, she considered Henry more of an uncle than an employee. She reached over and gave him a hug. "I'm glad you're all right. Really glad."

"Now there, Marjo," Henry said. "Don't you start crying or you'll make me cry too."

She laughed and pulled back, wiping at her eyes. "I'm not crying, I'm watering the flowers," she said, using the old joke they'd exchanged during especially emotional moments at the funeral home.

"Gabriel is gonna be just fine," Henry said, reading her mind. "He's got a good head on his shoulders."

In some ways, yes. Gabriel dressed to suit the weather, knew how to do laundry and dishes and had never crossed a street, even in quiet-as-a-tomb Indigo, without first looking both ways. But he also forgot to eat sometimes, or left the water running or lost his house key.

Henry patted her hand. "Don't worry so much."

"All I can do is worry." She leaned forward, peeking through the slats on the porch at the charred funeral home. The fire still seemed unreal.

But the funeral home was gone. Three generations of Savoy history, destroyed by flames in minutes. It was as if a part of herself had been ripped out. Memories flashed through her mind of her parents, Henry, Gabriel. Helping her dad after school, playing cards with Henry during downtime, planting flowers around the outside of the building with Gabriel. "Without Savoy," Marjo said, "I have to worry about putting food on my table. And yours."

"Me? I'm just fine. I've always been good about putting some of my paychecks aside, and now I've got enough that I can retire. I was thinking about doing it anyway. All I needed was a good kick in the rear."

She watched the fire trucks hose down the building, knowing there would be nothing left. "That's a hell of a kick in the rear."

Henry chuckled, then replaced the oxygen mask. "What about you?"

"I'll rebuild," she said, resolute, yet at the same time knowing it wouldn't be the same. "We'll get the Savoy up and running once the insurance money comes in. And get back to work." The prospect of doing that seemed daunting, and she wasn't sure she had the heart for it. It had to be the smoke, the shock that had her feeling more indigo blue than sunshine yellow.

"Take some advice from an old man who should have quit earlier to smell the roses," Henry said, his hand closing over hers. "Leave the Savoy behind. Let 'em put a gas station on that land if they want. And you go back to your singing."

"But Gabriel—"

"Will be fine if you quit trying to take such good care of him. The boy is ready to jump out of the nest, Marjo. Let him go."

But as Marjo bade Henry goodbye and went off in search of Gabriel, her doubts began to multiply. For a moment she wished Paul were here.

She searched up and down the streets of Indigo, but Gabriel was gone. She headed back to the funeral home and was immediately pulled into the welcoming embrace of the residents of Indigo, who surrounded the dying building, mourning the loss with her.

Her livelihood was gone, her brother wasn't speaking to her and the one man she'd started to care about had headed off to the far ends of the world to take photographs.

As Grandma Savoy would have said, things couldn't have gotten worse if she'd woken up to a spider in her gumbo.

CHAPTER FIFTEEN

IT TOOK TWO days for Paul to catch a break. The fishermen Joe had sent him to photograph were indeed wary of the media, even someone from their own province. He'd worked his way down the list of the men, trying to get any of them to share their story. It wasn't until he finally tracked down the last man, who was working the docks while his broken arm healed, that he got the piece his editor had sent him to find.

"You understand what it's like to be part of a crab boat?" Papoose, as he was called, because he'd been small enough to fit in the pocket of his mother's housecoat when he was born, settled his extra-large frame onto the captain's chair of the *Ocean Queen*. "It's not like no other job."

Growing up in the area, Paul was familiar with the shellfish industry. Men signed on for the life-threatening crab trips—the most dangerous job in the world, the experts said—because they had the potential to make a year's salary in a few days. "Is it because of the danger?" Paul asked. "The excitement?"

Papoose snorted, dug around in his shirt pocket and came up with a cigar stub. "Danger's always on the boat. Get your leg torn off by a rope, get yourself washed over by a storm. It's not the danger that makes crabbin' different. It's the men."

For the first time ever in an interview, Paul lowered his camera, even his notepad, and sat on the edge of the boat. "What do you mean?"

"Crabbers, they're all about takin' care of each other," Papoose said as he lit the cigar stub and puffed away. "Off the boat, they may hate each other, knock out some teeth in a bar over a woman, but put 'em on a wet deck in the middle of crab season, and you'll find one man jumpin' overboard to save another. When we're out there, we're family. Good, bad, ugly or wet. *Family.*" He gestured toward Paul with the cigar. "You gonna write any of this down with that fancy pen?"

Paul grabbed up his notepad and scribbled down his thoughts and the fisherman's words. He snapped a few pictures of Papoose, then sat again and listened as the man told a harrowing tale of a storm, a wave and a boat that nearly sank.

These men, he realized, worked harder than anyone he'd ever met. They worked in an industry that was fraught with danger, tight competition and an enemy larger than them—the sea.

His thoughts went to the bayou, to the determination of the people he had met in Indigo. In some ways, they were like the family on Papoose's crab boat. Only they were scrambling to hold on to a past that the present kept trying to absorb.

One thing Papoose had said to him remained long after the scent of the cigar had been washed from Paul's clothes. He'd asked Papoose if it was the money that kept him going back to the boats, the docks.

The man had thought for a long while, then shook his head. "When you find something that gives you family, you stick with it. I don't care who you are or where you find it. These guys, these boats, they're mine. And I'm coming back until I can't come back no more."

Now, in the dining room of his sister's house, Paul flipped through the slide show of images on his computer. He'd nabbed some really great photographs, the kind that would make his editor sing.

But for the first time since he'd gone into photography, the satisfaction of a job well done wasn't there. Every time he looked at the photos of the grizzled, tough fisherman, he saw instead images of cypress trees, Spanish moss and a stream that moved so slowly he'd have sworn it was standing still.

And in every frame, he was reminded of Marjo.

When you find something that gives you family, you stick with it.

He kept scrolling through the thumbnails of the digital camera's memory, through the pictures of Indigo, the opera house and then, near the end, the close-up of Marjo that Gabriel had taken that first day by the bayou.

He touched the screen with a finger, tracing the outline of her lips, curved up into a smile. Against the green of the bayou, her blue eyes were ten times more vibrant.

"It's good to see you," Faye said, coming up behind him. She wrapped her arms around him and gave him a tight, quick hug. In the background he could hear Lizzie, his newborn niece, cooing in the playpen in the living room.

A pang went through Paul's heart. He had missed Faye and her family more than he'd thought. All this living out of a backpack, crashing at a friend's house whenever he was in New York for a meeting with his editors, the constant grind of shoot after shoot, had finally taken its toll.

Either that or the days spent in Indigo had created a craving inside him for something more than what he already had. What that something was, he had no idea.

Paul rubbed at his neck. Whatever this feeling was, it was temporary. He'd go on to Tibet in a few days and be back to normal.

"Hey, who's this?" Faye asked, pointing at Marjo's picture.

"Someone I met in Indigo."

"Someone special?"

"Someone who lives in Louisiana, which is where I don't," he said, closing the subject.

"Yet," Faye said, grinning.

"Never. It's nice to be back here, Faye." After

he'd sold his house in the divorce, Paul had taken Faye up on her offer to move into her spare bedroom. He knew she'd offered because she wanted to take care of him, to help him nurse his broken heart.

But he hadn't needed Florence Nightingale. All he'd needed was a few assignments from *World,* along with some freelance corporate work, and he was gone again, happier by far when he was on a plane than when he was wandering Faye and John's four-bedroom Dutch Colonial.

Or at least it used to be that way. But when he'd walked into her house three days ago and inhaled the scent of fresh-baked bread, baby powder and something else he couldn't define, he'd felt an unfamiliar warmth spread through his chest.

"I'm glad I came," he added, meaning it, though at the same time reminding himself not to get too comfortable. "I needed to spend some time with my sister."

She arched a brow in surprise. "Is that you telling me I was right?"

He gave her a grin. "If I did, would you ever let me live it down?"

"Of course not, big brother." She gave him a light jab, then plopped into the seat beside him. As she did, her foot hit his backpack, sending the envelope Marjo had given him tumbling to the floor. "Hey, what's this?"

"I don't know. I never looked." He didn't tell Faye that he *couldn't* look. That merely opening the folder on the plane had caused him to miss that tiny spot in the bayou more than he'd expected.

So he'd left it in his bag, figuring once he was back in the old groove again, he would have enough distance between him and Indigo to flip through whatever it was Marjo had given him.

Yeah. Five days now, and he had yet to find that distance.

"Who's it from?" Faye asked.

"A friend."

A corner of Faye's mouth turned up. "I know that look. It's from that woman in the pictures, isn't it?" She danced the envelope back and forth, her blue eyes taunting. "Is it *love* letters?"

"Actually, yes, but they're not Marjo's. They're our aunt Amelie's."

"Our…" Faye's voice trailed off and she took a peek inside the envelope. "Holy cow, you're right. And you haven't read them?"

"Not yet."

"Are you kidding me? Paul, you have the will-power of an ox, I swear. How could you not look?" She withdrew the sheaf of letters, the paper fragile and tea-stained with age. "I'd be dying of curiosity."

"Which is why they're in my hands instead of yours. You can't even resist peeking at your Christmas presents." He gave her a good-natured grin.

"You aren't the least bit curious?" She read through the first few pages, skimming over the sentences. "Wow, Paul. This is incredible."

"I'm sure it is." He opened his e-mail program, intending to zap the proofs over to his editor.

Faye put a hand on his screen. "No, I mean really incredible. It's like opening a door to the past. Listen to this."

Faye began to read the letters, which were written in French. Although some of the expressions were new to Paul, he understood the sentiment, if not the exact translation.

"'My dearest Alexandre,

"'Mama has forbidden me from seeing you again, but she can't stop my heart from loving you. You have brought a sunshine to my days that I have never known before, a new song to my voice. Meeting you has changed everything—

"'*Everything*.

"'I wish to see you again. Soon. My darling, I can not wait for the sun to set, the moon to rise, for another day to pass so that I know I am closer to the day when we will meet again.

"'Until then, remember I am yours, always.

"'Amelie.'"

Faye looked up from the letter and Paul could swear he saw a tear glistening in her eye. "That's so sweet, don't you think?"

"Only a woman would think so—"

She swatted him. Hard. "You don't have a romantic bone in your body."

"I do, too."

"Oh, yeah? Then prove it." She thrust the sheaf of papers into his hands. "Read these."

"I don't—"

"You do, too, need to read them. For Pete's sake, Paul, you can't go through your life believing that happily-ever-after is only something that happens in Disney movies. You'll end up a hermit living in some ramshackle place in the middle of nowhere, wearing the same ratty sweater every day and muttering to yourself."

"Thanks for the vision of my future, my psychic friend."

She stuck her tongue out at him. "Read them. Or I'll stop feeding you."

"Hey, that's not playing fair," he called after her retreating figure. Faye was a damned good cook, something he'd forgotten in the time he'd been gone. Now that he'd been back at her house for a few days, he could already feel a tightening of his waistline from too many second helpings.

A second later he heard his sister in the nursery, cooing to the baby. He rose, taking the pile of papers with him, and crossed to the sunroom. Outside, fall was in full swing, the trees nearly bare now in the cool temperatures. This was a world away from the lush, humid bayou he'd left last week.

He settled into one of the padded wicker chairs, then started to read, working his way chronologically through the stack.

With each letter, he traced the story of Alexandre and Amelie, the same tale that Marjo had told him. Only, with the parchment-thin papers in his hands, the centuries-old ink fading on the pages, it all seemed so much more real.

Paul was a visual man, and this evidence of his ancestral roots suddenly drove home the reality of what Marjo had told him.

These people had lived. Loved. Died. And they'd left behind a building that had been passed down from one generation to another, because they'd believed in their family, in continuing the legacy they had started so many years ago.

And ended when it got to him.

Faye came into the sunroom and sat on the cushioned wicker sofa, the baby on her lap. She bounced the baby on one knee, which made Lizzie laugh and the slight wisp of blond curls on her head blow in the breeze. Faye gave Paul an expectant look. "Well?"

"Well what?" he said, feigning innocence.

"I'm making steak and potatoes for dinner," Faye said. "*Or* I could serve Alpo."

He chuckled. Knowing Faye, she *would* leave him a can of dog food on the counter. When they'd been kids, playing practical jokes on each other had been *de rigueur.* Paul held up the papers he'd just finished reading. "This is a hell of a story."

"In other words, I was right."

He gave her a grin. "Okay, you were right."

She leaned down and pressed a kiss to Lizzie's head, pausing a moment to inhale her baby scent. A sharp pain hit Paul in the chest—

Jealousy.

He wanted a little of that—that look, that contentment—for himself. He shook off the thoughts. All he needed to do was to get back to work and the feeling would go away.

Only, he had been back at work for a few days now, and if anything, he was more unhappy than before. Papoose's words nagged at him, intertwining with memories of Indigo and Marjo. Was the family Papoose had talked about possible for a man like him?

"Will you think about the rest?" Faye asked. "Settling down? Giving me some nieces and nephews to spoil ruthlessly? I still need to get back at you for that drum set you sent to Lizzie."

"One step at a time, sis. I read the letters. That was a start. It's not so easy for me, you know."

"Because you were the older one." Her gaze softened. "You went through more."

"There wasn't anything to go through, Faye. Dad worked all over Canada. Mom made her bedroom into a prison."

"Uh-huh." Faye crossed her arms over her chest. "And you don't think that might have skewed the way you look at marriage and family in any way?"

"Of course not." He paused. "Okay, maybe a bit."

"We didn't have the best example of marriage or

family life. The only time we had anything resembling a family was when the aunts and uncles came over, but that was temporary, and then it was closed doors and absent parenting all over again. You had to be the grown-up, when you weren't grown up yet yourself."

He thought of Marjo then, how she had been left to raise Gabriel on her own, only under more tragic circumstances. Was it possible that the two of them had the same skewed view of family and relationships? That each of them pushed away the very thing they craved?

And yet, Faye had turned out okay, ending up happily married. Perhaps there was some key he was missing, a key Faye had clearly found.

"Why do you always say things that make me think?" he said to his sister.

"Because that's my job as a woman," she teased. "So what are you going to do now?"

Paul looked out over the cold, fall landscape, nearly devoid of green, already hinting at the bitter white winter ahead. It wasn't the temperature he was worried about. It was something else that he was afraid was going to freeze if he didn't get back to Indigo.

He rose, leaving the packet of letters on the coffee table for Faye to read, too. "I'm going to tie up a few loose ends."

CHAPTER SIXTEEN

PAUL PUSHED the doorbell of the massive white Colonial he used to own, then waited, sure that when the door was opened, he'd be sent packing. And probably deserve it, too.

"Paul!" Diane's voce was friendly, not accusatory. He'd expected his ex-wife to react differently, but clearly, he hadn't known her as well as he'd thought. She opened the door wide, and waved him inside. "Come on in."

Diane looked nearly as young as she had the day they'd dissolved their marriage fifteen years ago. Her blond hair was a bit lighter and cut in a bob, her eyes had laugh lines that hadn't been there before, but otherwise, she hadn't changed much.

"How are you?" she asked.

"The same. More or less."

"Still a man of few words, I see." She gave him a good-natured grin as she led him down the hall and into the formal living room.

Once they were seated on the plush velvet sofas, Diane indicated a pile of *World* magazines on the end table. "I see your pictures from time to time. I even have a subscription."

"Really?" She had never taken that much interest in his career when they were married, mainly because the travel he did had become a bone of contention between them. "You surprise me."

"I guess I started it because I wanted to see what stole you from me," she said, toying with one of the magazines. "And after a while, I understood."

"Diane…"

"No, don't feel bad. I'm okay with it, really. And I understand now."

"You do?" He'd expected her to be unwelcoming, distant. After all, he'd been the one who had deserted her, and their marriage. He'd never have thought that she would understand why.

"It wasn't anything you had against me," she said. "It was simply that the call of the story was stronger than anything you felt for me and our marriage. We never talked about it." She sighed. "We never talked at all, and maybe if we had, it might have changed things. Or maybe we just weren't right for each other and were trying to shove square pegs into holes."

Diane was right. Always, it had been the story that had nagged at him whenever he'd been in this house. He'd felt as if he were only doing time until he could head off into the jungle or wherever the story was, camera in hand. "I never meant to hurt you. I should have been a better husband."

Diane rose, reached out and placed a hand over his. "It's okay. We were young and we rushed into things."

They had, indeed. He'd been looking, he supposed, for someone to care for him, after so many years of worrying about Faye and his parents.

"We should have talked," Paul said. "Actually, I should have."

Diane smiled. "It's not exactly one of your strong points. You can speak a novel's worth of words with your pictures, but when it comes to relationships, you just don't know how to articulate your feelings."

Was it the same for Marjo? Should he have opened up and shared his feelings with her?

"Are you happy now?" he asked his ex-wife. "Really happy?"

"Yes. Very." Diane's gaze went to a photograph that hung on the wall. It featured her and her husband, dressed in matching khaki pants and white shirts, smiling on the white sands of a Caribbean beach. A soft smile crossed her face as she looked at the photo—the same smile Paul had seen on Luc Carter's face whenever he looked at his fiancée. The same one he'd seen on Alain Boudreaux when the police chief talked about Sophie.

Paul envied them all. Although he was glad to see Diane so happy, a little part of him felt as if she had something he could never hope to experience.

"And," she added, pressing a hand to her abdomen, "we'll be having an addition to our family this spring."

"You're pregnant?"

She nodded, joy suffusing her face. "Due May first."

"That's wonderful, Diane." He meant it. She deserved to be happy.

"You could do the same, you know. Meet the right woman, settle down."

Paul rose from the sofa and crossed to the window, watching a trio of birds dipping into a wooden bird-feeder hanging from the old oak in the backyard. The yard was better tended than when he'd lived here. Shrubbery now ringed the old tree, with colorful, hardy mums circling the base. The sight made him think of Marjo's camellias. "I think I already have."

"Really?"

He turned back to her. "Anyway, I came by because I wanted to apologize. A long overdue apology."

"Apologize? For what?"

"For marrying you and then pretty much ruining your life."

"Oh, it wasn't so bad being married to you," she said. "I like to look at it as a…learning experience."

Paul chuckled. "That's an interesting perspective on divorce. Maybe you should go on *Dr. Phil.*"

Diane crossed the room and stood beside him. "When I married you, Paul, I did it because I wanted to get out of my parents' house. I thought putting a ring on my finger would make me grown up. But it didn't. All it did was push me into a role I wasn't ready for yet. You weren't the only one who made a bad choice." She took in a breath and for a moment watched the birds out the window. "From that experience, I learned a lot about what I *did* want out of life. After our divorce, I went back to college, finished my degree in communications and worked my way up in an ad agency. I learned who I was, way before I met Dave."

"I'm happy for you." The words were honest, true. He *was* happy for Diane, and wished his ex-wife nothing but the best.

"If you *have* found the right woman, Paul, you should go after her, and never let her go. And take my advice—leave your camera behind."

"Leave my camera…?"

"I think that's one of those things you're going to have to figure out for yourself, Paul."

As he left his ex-wife's house a few minutes later, Paul realized he had just closed one chapter of his life. It was time to start the next one.

Assuming, of course, that it wasn't too late.

WHEN PAUL GOT BACK to Faye's, he made a call to Joe. Then, as he logged on to the Internet with his laptop to book a flight, he found himself Googling Indigo and followed a link to a news story in New Iberia's online paper.

He read the small headline once. Twice. Dread filled him as he scanned the paragraphs below.

He didn't have to worry about being too late—he already was.

CHAPTER SEVENTEEN

MARJO SPENT the day after the fire picking through the rubble. She found a few photos, charred around the edges, a cushion from one of the armchairs, the pink fabric turned a sad, dark gray, a file cabinet that had remained oddly untouched while everything else in the office had disintegrated. Nearly the entire contents of the funeral home were either burned or so blackened and infused with the smell of smoke that they were unusable.

The parish fire chief had traced the source to a faulty wire in the wall. "Old buildings," he said, shaking his head. "Sometimes they just go."

But why this building? Why now? Her family had invested everything in the funeral home, and in an instant, it had been erased from the landscape of Indigo.

"Marjo, you okay?" Cally stepped carefully through the debris to reach Marjo's side.

The arrival of her best friend seemed to unlock something Marjo had barely kept hold of all morning. Tears spilled from her eyes, drizzled down her cheeks. "Yes." She paused. "No."

"Oh, sweetie, it'll be all right." Cally wrapped Marjo in a quick, tight hug. "I came by to see if you wanted some lunch. You really should take a break. After that, I'll stay and help you. I took the rest of the day off work."

It was past noon already? Marjo looked up at the sky. The sun was high above them, and she realized she'd skipped two meals.

"I'm not hungry. I'm just…lost." Marjo stared at the wasteland in front of her. The elegant, two-story building had been reduced to a pile of rubble a few feet high. Not a single wall remained, not the sign, not even the mailbox. Starting over seemed like an insurmountable task, one Marjo couldn't even consider at the moment. "I have no idea what to do. No plan. Nothing."

"That's okay." Cally laid a soothing hand on her shoulder. "Take some time off, think about things. There's no rush."

"But I don't *have* time," Marjo cried, scooping up a palmful of ashes and letting them sift through her fingers. The breeze caught them and carried them away. "The CajunFest is tomorrow, my life is a shambles, my job is toast—literally." She was too drained to even laugh at the irony of her words. "What the hell am I going to do?"

"Move forward."

Marjo jerked around at the familiar voice. Paul Clermont stood behind her, tall and handsome as ever, seeming more like a mirage than a miracle.

He had returned.

Cally gave her a knowing smile. "I'll catch up with you later." She winked, then headed back to her car.

"What are you doing here?" Marjo brushed the soot off her capris and hoped like heck that her hair wasn't a mess. Had she remembered to put on make-up today?

What did it matter? He was probably here to oversee the rest of the repairs on the opera house, or worse, to start the process to divest himself of the building.

She swallowed, then voiced the words she'd been dreading to hear. "Are you here to put the opera house on the market?"

"No." He took her hands in his, clearly not caring about the gray soot that covered her fingers. "I'm here for you."

Her heart thudded hard in her chest. "For me? Why?"

"I read about the funeral home on the Web in the New Iberia paper. I'm so sorry, Marjo." He glanced over the devastation and she could see in his eyes the same disbelief and sorrow she felt. "There's nothing left?"

She shook her head. "No."

"Are *you* okay? And Gabriel?"

"I'm okay, so is Gabriel. No one was hurt."

"Thank God." Paul studied her for a long moment, as if convincing himself that she was fine. "But I was already on my way down here for another reason."

"For what?" Hope sang in her chest, adding its melody to the hum of attraction still running through her.

"You, silly." He grinned, then traced the outline of her lips. "I'd rather be with you than in Tibet any day."

"Really?"

"You're a lot prettier and a whole lot more fun." He took her hand and helped her climb over the charred wood. "Come on. Let's get you home."

She went with him, silent as a wall, unable to think of a single thing to say. In the two days since the fire, she had felt numb, not really alive, but now her mind was a whirl of thoughts and feelings.

Paul helped her into his rental car, then a few minutes later pulled up in front of her house. He hurried around to her side before she could open the door, then took her hand and led her up the walk.

Never before, even when her parents died, had she felt this overwhelmed. It was as if those years of being the one who had to take charge had caught up with her, the final straw broken by the loss of the funeral home. Since the fire, Gabriel had been great, staying up with her until the wee hours of the morning last night. He'd fretted over her, made her tea, got her a blanket she didn't need and generally fussed over her like a mother hen.

This morning she'd handed him some money and told him to take Darcy to a gumbo cook-off in a neighboring town. Marjo didn't want him to see his sister crumpling like a piece of paper. She was supposed to be the strong one, to support her brother—not the other way around.

"Here, sit down," Paul said when they were inside. He led her to the small love seat that flanked the living room wall and she sank onto the soft cushions.

Paul knelt beside her, reached up and brushed the hair out of her face. "Are you okay?"

"Yes. Thirsty, from working out in the sun all day, but okay."

"Uh-huh. Sure you're okay." A smile crossed his lips. "You look dazed and dusty—"

"Sorry. I've been going through the rubble—"

He put a finger on her lips. "But still beautiful. You've had a hell of a time, Marjo. Let me take care of you."

She raised her eyes and met his gaze. "Take care of me?"

"That means you don't do a thing and someone else watches over you, catering to your every need. You've been caring for the entire world for too long." He brushed her cheek with his fingers.

When he moved to turn away, she grabbed his arm. "Don't go. Don't leave me."

He smiled. "I was just going to get you a glass of water."

"Stay," she whispered, rising to him and pulling him closer. The feel of him against her was like a healing balm. "Make me forget."

"Forget the fire?"

"Everything," Marjo said, then leaned forward, and quit thinking with her head. She kissed Paul Clermont with all the want that had built up over the past week as she waited, hoping he would come back to her.

He returned the kiss, his lips covering hers with a sweet passion that surprised Marjo. He cupped her jaw, then his hands dropped down over her shoulders to her waist, then up again to brush against her breasts.

When he did that, a volcano of need exploded within Marjo. It wasn't about forgetting the fire, the day, the stress of the past years; it was about this man and finally quenching her thirst for him.

"Oh, God, Marjo, I want you."

"I want you, too." To hell with waiting any longer, playing this game of seeing how far they could go without going over the edge. She took her shirt, tugged it over her head and tossed it into the corner of the room.

He smiled his surprise at her bold move, then cupped her breasts through the lace of her bra, his thumbs teasing her nipples. Marjo grabbed his shirt, fingers flying to undo the buttons, wanting only the feel of his skin against hers. She tossed it aside and slid her body against his, amazed by the warmth, the connection she felt.

"Let's go—" she sucked in a breath, fighting to concentrate, to make sense "—into my bedroom."

"Good idea," he said, casting a dubious glance at the hard cypress floor beneath them.

She laughed, then took his hand and led him from the living room. In the hall, he twirled her against him, unable to wait, his mouth once again hungrily devouring hers. She stepped back, pulling him with her until they hit the wall. With her firm against the plaster, his hands roamed the path up to her waist, over her breasts, sending her senses into overload.

She slipped her hands down his back, into the waistband of his pants, over his buttocks, squeezing the tight, firm flesh and pulling his pelvis toward hers, aching for him.

Paul yanked down her capris, then slid his palms up her smooth thighs, teasing the lacy edges of her panties. She stepped out of them, kicked the fabric to the side.

Fumbling, she reached for his belt, tugging it undone then freeing him from his khaki pants.

He hoisted her up, straddling her legs across his hips, and carried her into her bedroom, kicking open the door, then shutting it the same way.

They tumbled onto the bed together, ripping off their remaining clothes. Marjo slid her hand along his hard length, and he answered her by slipping two fingers inside her wet warmth. She arched against him, desire exploding within her. His thumb caressed while his fingers dipped in again and again until she knew she was going to die.

"Now, Paul," she gasped. "Now."

He slipped inside her and began to move, his strokes long and slow, building the fire between them.

Her hands grasped his buttocks, and she begged him without words to end this delightful agony. Intuitively understanding her need, he moved faster and brought his lips to her neck, whispering a kiss along her skin as they spiraled higher, their bodies melding in perfect harmony.

As the climax ebbed, Paul rolled to Marjo's side, tugging her to him. She curved perfectly into the space against his body. Never had she felt so secure, so safe—

So cared for.

Tears threatened, and try as she might to hold them back, one trickled down her cheek.

"Was I that bad?" Paul asked with a smile, whisking the tear away with the back of his hand.

She laughed. "No, no. It's not you. It's..." She took in a breath. "No one has ever taken care of me, not like that."

"A clear sign we need to do it again," he said, catching a second tear before it could drop off her lashes.

"I wouldn't want to get too used to it." What if his stay here was temporary? There was probably a return plane ticket in his wallet, and all of this would disappear as quickly as it had begun.

She knew how fast life could change. In a split second, everything could be gone, leaving nothing but a gaping hole in her heart.

Paul's face sobered. "That wouldn't be so bad, would it?"

No, it wouldn't, Marjo realized, not if it meant waking up next to this man every day. But, she still resisted saying the words.

Because she realized the man she'd just made love with was still, in many ways, a stranger. A man who may have shared his body with her.

But had yet to share his heart.

CHAPTER EIGHTEEN

INDIGO HAD BECOME a town transformed. People were bustling up and down the streets, circling the town square and the opera house, adding the finishing touches for the CajunFest.

Last night, Loretta's VIP dinner in the opera house lobby had been a huge hit. The food was great, catered primarily by Luc's cousin, a chef in New Orleans, and after all the paint and polish, the lobby and auditorium of the opera house looked much as they must have years ago. There was still work to be done, but the guests last night had been duly impressed. Marjo took that as a good—no, very good—sign of the opera house's future.

The morning had dawned sunny and slightly warm. Colorful booths crowded the grassy lawn like some exotic market. The scent of Loretta's tasty artisanal breads drifted through the air from her booth, along with the hum of musicians tuning up inside the opera house. The doors of the building were open, welcoming anyone who wanted to step into Indigo's past.

Marjo gave tours of the building in the morning, then helped the various acts on and off the stage, doing the introductions so Alain could coordinate security with his deputies and off-duty officers he'd called in from neighboring forces.

The busier Marjo stayed, the easier it was to push her worries about the funeral home and her future to the side. She also wasn't quite ready to deal with the incredible night she'd spent with Paul Clermont. As awesome as it had been, all it had done was muddy the waters, leaving her more confused than ever. Was this a fling? Or the start of something more?

And if it was, did she have room in her life for that right now? Was she willing to risk the safe, secure world she had created for herself and Gabriel for something that might not end in happily-ever-after?

Tomorrow, she'd deal with all that. Hadn't that philosophy worked for Scarlett O'Hara?

Okay, it hadn't, at least not with a happily-ever-after.

During the day, Jenny and other committee members had come up to Marjo, apologizing for wanting to pull the plug on the project. "You've worked a miracle," Jenny said. "Thank God you finally convinced Paul Clermont to back this."

Marjo wasn't so sure she'd convinced Paul of a darn thing. At least, not after last night. He'd left before she woke up, leaving a note on her pillow that said he had a special surprise for her today.

There wasn't a word of affection in the note. He'd simply scrawled his name at the bottom. What did that mean?

She pushed him out of her mind and made her way back up to the opera house stage. Nearly every seat was filled. She wasn't sure about numbers yet, but from what she'd seen of the crowds around town and here, the festival was going to be even more successful than they'd thought. Jenny had told her they'd sold hundreds of the vintage postcards Hugh had had printed before his death from different periods of Indigo's history.

Marjo slipped behind the thick curtains and peeked out. She saw plenty of happy faces, and many people had bags filled with purchases from the various booths. Sophie's idea of expanding the CajunFest to include businesses from neighboring towns had been a great idea and ensured wider media coverage. Already, there had been some buzz about future performances at the opera house.

The future of the opera house and the town, which Marjo and so many others had worked hard for, was finally coming to fruition.

"They'll be talking about this day at the Blue Moon for the next year," Alain said, coming up beside her. "I've never seen this many people in Indigo. We're practically a city."

Marjo laughed. "It is amazing, isn't it? I mean, the committee was hoping to hit twenty thousand attendees, but I don't think any of us really thought it would happen."

"You should see Luc. The man is in heaven. His bayou cruises are booked for today but people are making reservations like crazy. He's going to have to hire someone to help him and maybe even spring for another boat come spring."

"We have a party going on," Cally said, coming up to them. She swiveled her hips in a little dance. Cally was in charge of set design, moving the backgrounds and curtains for each act. Her clothes were a bit dusty, but the smile on her face said she was having fun.

Marjo laughed. "It does feel pretty festive, doesn't it?"

"Totally."

They waved Alain off as he headed over to check on the next act. Loretta's daughter Zara was just beginning her fiddle solo, and Alain was already beaming at his young student. Zara had really come around in the last few weeks, as if her mother's happiness with Luc had rubbed off on her daughter, too.

Cally touched Marjo's shoulder. "I just wanted to pop in with a quick hello before I find a seat to watch the Indigo Boneshakers. Billy Paul is playing and I'd hate to miss it."

"Things seem to be heating up between the two of you," Marjo said.

"Hey, he's a drummer." Cally winked. "You know I can't resist a man who knows how to use his sticks."

Marjo was still laughing as Cally left. The Indigo

Boneshakers were the next act, and once they were set up, Marjo headed out to the stage to introduce them. She glanced at the bio that had been printed in the program, then noticed the next act.

Paul Clermont and Alain Boudreaux. Fiddle duet.

Her heart skipped a beat. She'd been too busy today to see much more than a glimpse of Paul, and each time she had, he'd been in the company of one of the locals.

It seemed as if the man from Cape Breton had been unofficially adopted by the town. All Marjo had to do was to look to see why. His contribution had been like a shot of caffeine to a town that had almost given up on this festival, especially since Hugh's death.

Marjo finished her introduction, then returned to the wings of the stage, watching the Boneshakers get their show under way. In the back corner of the auditorium, a friend of the band's was selling copies of their newly created CD.

"There you are."

She turned and saw Paul standing a few feet away, a fiddle in his hand. He had on a light blue button-down shirt, open at the neck, exposing just a tease of the chest she had explored last night. His jeans hugged his hips, sending a shiver of desire through her. "Hi," she said.

"Hi, yourself." He grinned, the approval in his eyes making her glad she'd chosen a figure-flattering dark cranberry dress. "Are you thinking what I'm thinking?"

"That…and more," she said, one corner of her mouth turning up.

He chuckled. "Maybe we can, uh, get acquainted again, after my set."

"Are you sure you're up to the challenge?"

"Considering you nearly killed me last night, I might need to keep a defibrillator on the nightstand."

"Hey, the fourth time was all your idea."

"I can't help it." He took a step forward, his hand reaching up to cup her chin, thumb tracing along her lower lip. "You make me crazy. You have from the first day I met you."

"At least it's a better crazy now than it was that day."

"Much better," Paul murmured just before leaning down and kissing her.

Everything went still within her at his touch. When he pulled back and looked down at her, there was something in his eyes that was much deeper than the simple heat of attraction.

"Marjo, while I was in Cape Breton, I did a lot of thinking," he said. "I didn't just come back to Indigo to see you. I also came to tell you that I want you to be with me." He took her hands in his. "All the time."

For a second she thought he was proposing, then she realized the word marriage hadn't even skated along the edge of his sentence.

"I can't leave here." She gestured toward the stage. "I'm introducing all the acts."

"I meant after this is all over. I have to go to Tibet

to do a piece on an ancient temple that's been unearthed in a mountainside. I want you with me. I want you to see what I see when I travel the world. I want you to see what the world is like outside of Indigo."

"Tibet?" Marjo stepped back. "I can't go to Tibet."

"Why not? It would only be for a couple of weeks. When you come back, it'll probably be time to oversee the reconstruction of the funeral home. Besides, right now you're unemployed and madly in love with me." He grinned. "A win-win all around."

She didn't debate the madly-in-love part. She wasn't quite sure yet how she felt about Paul Clermont, except that whenever he was around she experienced a tightening in her chest and a sense of breathless anticipation that filled her whenever he wasn't around. "I may be unemployed, but I still have Gabriel. And there's plenty of other things to do before the rebuild starts—"

"Come with me, Marjo, and leave all that behind. For just a little while. After all this, you deserve a vacation."

The idea was tempting. It curled around her, urging her to say yes, to forget all those responsibilities for a few days. A week. A month. To finally put herself first, instead of an entire town. And Gabriel.

Over at La Petite Maison, her trusting brother was helping Luc with the boat tours. Probably waiting for the day to be over so that he and Marjo could go home, have dinner and maybe a cold glass of tea on the porch while they listened to the night sounds and debated the merits of vanilla ice cream over Rocky Road.

Who was she kidding? Marjo couldn't remember the last time they'd done that. It used to be a daily thing, but then, sometime in the last year, those evenings on the porch had stopped. Gabriel was out more often than he was in. Usually with Darcy.

It seemed as if she was losing her brother. Just the thought of him not being here left her feeling empty. At odds. If that was how she felt, how would it be for Gabriel if she went to Tibet?

"I want to go with you," Marjo said to Paul. "But there's still too much holding me here. Maybe in another year or—"

"Another year?" He frowned. "There's nothing holding you here, Marjo, except yourself."

"That's not true."

"No one in this town expects you to carry the burden by yourself. Just look around the festival, at the dozens of people who are working to give Indigo a new lease on life."

"I head up the committees. There'll be a lot of work once the festival is over. I need to coordinate all that."

"What happened when Hugh died? Life went on. The festival still happened." He studied her. "What are you so afraid of?"

"I'm not afraid of anything."

"You are, too. You're terrified to change your life.

To do anything more than sing at Skeeter's because you are too damned afraid to leave this town. Indigo isn't a home for you, it's a security blanket."

The words hit home, but Marjo refused to accept their truth. "How dare you say that?"

"Because I've seen it in my own family. My mother, too afraid to leave Cape Breton, yet at the same time too afraid to deal with life when my father wasn't there. My cousins, struggling for years, hoping next year's catch would be better and refusing to learn another trade because fishing was what they knew. They tied themselves to a world that had nothing to offer."

"Nothing except family."

"Family doesn't pay the bills, Marjo." He shook his head. "The place they loved became a trap."

"And you escaped that trap by traveling, is that what you're trying to tell me?"

"Yes. And so can you." Paul's expression filled with concern. "I want you with me, Marjo. I want to show you my world."

"Paul, I live here because it's my home. Not because it's some prison I want to escape. You don't understand."

"I understand all right." She couldn't mistake the hurt in his voice.

For a second she wanted to take it all back, to tell him yes, she'd go to Tibet, hop on the first plane out of here with him and never look back. But if she did, she'd be lying. As much as she wanted to, she truly couldn't leave.

She was needed here, to comfort the grieving, to give Gabriel a home and to help him navigate the waters ahead. She couldn't do any of those things from some mountainside in Tibet.

The music stopped and applause erupted from the audience, telling her that the Boneshakers were done with their set. Alain came striding up, his fiddle already in his hands. He clapped Paul on the back. "You ready?" He looked at Marjo. "Oh, I'm sorry. I'm not interrupting, am I?"

"No, you aren't interrupting anything," Paul said. "Nothing important at all." Then he walked over to Alain, and the second the Boneshakers exited the stage, Paul strode out, fiddle in hand, trailed by Alain. Paul didn't even wait for Marjo to introduce them before launching into the fiddle duet.

Just as well, she told herself. His offer had probably been brought about by lingering feelings from last night. Tomorrow, he'd change his mind.

But as she looked out over the audience and saw Sophie, Alain's very pregnant wife, beaming at her husband, Marjo's chest constricted. Sophie's love for Alain was evident in every inch of her face, in the protective hand she rested on her abdomen, as if the baby were included in this moment between them.

Envy raced through Marjo. She wanted that for herself, too. She always had, no matter what lies she had told herself so that she could get through the hard days after her parents died.

She glanced again at Paul. With just a few words, she would be closer to making that dream come true.

The problem was, she would be forced to choose—her brother over Paul. She'd had to make a similar choice once before, and had opted for Gabriel, as she always had.

Marjo turned away from the sight of Sophie and Alain. She was making the right decision, she was sure of it. If so, why did it drive such a painful wedge into her heart?

CHAPTER NINETEEN

As soon as Paul launched into his duet with Alain, he knew he'd been wrong to force Marjo to make such a big decision on the spur of the moment. He glanced over at her and he could see her fiery spirit in her eyes, her smile, the way she stood.

She deserved more than what she allowed herself. The problem was convincing her of that.

When the duet was over, the crowd applauded and cheered in appreciation, Paul glanced at the program that sat beside his sheet music. Beneath his and Alain's names, he saw that the following act had been crossed out, with the word canceled written beside it.

Marjolaine Savoy.

Before Marjo could come onto the stage and announce the next act, Paul took the mike in his hands. "Ladies and gentlemen, I'd like to introduce an incredible singer—Miss Marjo Savoy. Please give her a warm welcome."

From the sidelines, Marjo shot him the kind of look that could be considered a felony in certain states. He just grinned, laid down his fiddle then crossed the stage and grabbed her hand before she could back out again.

The audience clapped in anticipation. "I'm sorry for pushing you into a decision about traveling with me," Paul said. "You're right. You do have responsibilities here. A life."

She opened her mouth, closed it, speechless. From the audience, a couple of people called her name.

"Just give me this one song, and afterward, we'll figure out a way to make this relationship work. A way that works for both of us, whether you're here or I'm there. Just sing for me, Marjo, and we'll work it out."

"You're nuts." She shook her head, but he detected a lilting laughter in her voice.

"Yeah, maybe I am," he conceded. "But you are amazing, so please give this crowd—" he waved toward the audience, who were chanting her name by now "—what they want. And what you want. You *can* have it all, Marjo, if you try."

"One song," she said, making no promises about the rest.

Once she reached the center of the stage, Marjo froze, the panic clear in her eyes. But then, as soon as she grabbed the microphone, everything within her seemed to relax, as if she'd just come home at the end of a long day.

Paul picked up his fiddle, moved into place

behind her and started the song he had been practicing all last night. The same one she had sung a capella to him, and then again in Skeeter's. The song that had never left his mind since she'd granted him that private concert. He struck the first note, sure she was going to clam up just to spite him.

Instead, Marjo opened her mouth and began to sing. Not just sing—this time she created magic with her voice, captivating the audience with the French words, telling a story with only notes and inflection, bringing the old Cajun tune to life.

After she finished, the audience applauded wildly, then called for more. "Do you know *Quelle Etoile?*" she asked Paul.

He did, thankfully. He nodded, then started the new song with its story about which star to seek. Once again, she stepped in with perfect pitch and tone.

They did three more songs, a couple of Cajun waltzes and a fast-paced song about broken hearts, all at the urging of the audience. With each one, Paul saw a different side of Marjo emerge, like a butterfly that had finally been released from its cocoon. This was clearly what she was meant to do.

When she finished, the two of them hurried off the stage to make room for Heather Bateman. Marjo had told Paul that Heather, an accomplished classical violinist, had come to Indigo in the summer to convince her sister Joan to leave the small town. But Heather had fallen in love with Samuel Kane, an

Indigo carpenter, and hadn't left yet. The fiddle she lifted to her shoulder was a priceless antique that had been in Samuel's family for generations. As she started playing a Cajun tune, Paul caught sight of Samuel in the audience, love and pride radiating from his eyes.

Marjo stood in the wings of the stage, clearly exuberant about the performance she and Paul had just completed. "You were right."

"Wow. Twice in the space of two weeks you've said that. Are you sure you haven't just transplanted the real Marjo with a kinder, gentler version?"

She gave him a light jab. "Watch it, or I'll hit you again. Lower."

He grinned. "You wouldn't dare, because that would ruin all your fun, too."

Marjo blushed, but she had to admit Paul was right, and not just about protecting her interests. Singing in the opera house had fulfilled a lifelong dream of hers. She stood on her tiptoes and pressed a kiss to his mouth. "Thank you." For returning. For the unforgettable time in her bed last night. And for giving her an experience onstage that she would remember forever.

"Marjolaine Savoy?"

Marjo turned and saw a tall man in a black suit with thick white pinstripes. He was balding, and wore wire-rimmed glasses that were too wide for his face, giving him the appearance of a wise old owl. Maybe that was why he wore the trendy suit. "Yes? That's me."

"Dave Basie, with the Merit Agency in New York." He put out his hand, took Marjo's and gave it a firm shake. "I was very impressed."

For a second Marjo stood there, mouth agape. She recognized the name of the agency. Surely he wasn't here for her.

"We've got a lot of talent in our little town," she agreed. "The Indigo Boneshakers even put together a CD—"

"I was referring to you."

She heard the words, but they didn't process for a long second. "With *me?*"

"The other acts were impressive, I agree. And I'll recommend some of them to my colleagues. But you have a unique style and sound. Not quite traditional Cajun, but not middle America, either."

"I—I don't know what to say." She glanced over at Paul, who had a Cheshire cat smile on his face.

The agent grinned. "That's the easy part. Say you'll allow me to represent you and then we'll take your voice to the next level. Record deals, concert dates—"

She put up her hands to stop him. "I can't do all that. I can't leave here. I have a job, my brother."

He reached into the breast pocket of his suit, pulled out a monogrammed silver case. From it, he withdrew a business card, which he placed in her hand. She stared at it. A couple decades ago, this would have been the answer to all her dreams, to all she had trained for when she was young.

"I know, all this is a little overwhelming right now," he said. "Take my card and think about it. Call me when you make up your mind." He gave her a smile, then sent a nod Paul's way. "Thank you for bringing me down here. You were right, it *was* worth my time." Then he turned and left.

Holy cow. An agent. Here. Listening to her. And even more, *liking* what he heard.

"You did this?" she said to Paul.

He grinned. "Yep."

"But…why?"

He pulled her further into the recesses of the stage, where old sets and props lay stacked against the wall. "Because you have a wonderful talent, Marjo, and I really believe it's one you should share with the world."

"I appreciate that, Paul, but I just can't do anything right now. Maybe next year—"

"You need to do something now, Marjo." There was an urgency in Paul's voice.

"When Gabriel doesn't need me anymore, I can call that agent."

"Gabriel is grown up. You're the one who's afraid of letting go and moving forward." He shook his head, and a sadness filled his eyes that nearly killed her. "When you're ready to make room for something more than just a single appearance."

And then he turned and walked away, leaving her alone in the opera house that had once inspired romantic dreams in Marjo.

PAUL WALKED THROUGH the festival, trying a sample of Loretta's breads and her father's honey, sampling a new recipe from Willis's kitchen at the Blue Moon Diner and thanking Joan Bateman for writing the brochure. He also picked up a copy of her latest book, *Bayou Betrayal.* "I had no idea you wrote under the pseudonym Jules Burrell," he said. "I've read almost all his—your—books."

Joan winked. "It was a secret for a long time, but I have to admit, it's fun having people—especially fans—know who I am."

"Well, I'm glad for something new to read. I finished your last book yesterday and already need another crime mystery fix."

"Thank you. Hope you enjoy this one, too," she said as she signed the book and handed it over to him.

Everywhere he went at the festival, it seemed he ran into someone he knew. As he made his way down the main street of Indigo, he felt a heaviness descend over his heart. Leaving this place a second time— the final time—would be harder than he'd thought.

As much as he'd hoped otherwise, it was clear nothing was ever going to happen between him and Marjo. He couldn't will a relationship with her and she didn't want to make room in her life for one.

Staying would only prolong the inevitable. There was no way he could live here and see her every day, knowing they had no future.

He took his camera out of the bag that was per-

petually over his shoulder and snapped a few more
shots of Indigo. Eventually he wandered behind St.
Timothy's Church, slipping in and out among the
gravestones in the small cemetery behind the
building. Finally he came to the white marble vault
of the Valois family.

Alexandre and Amelie. Together in death, even if
they had been robbed of the long, happy life they'd
wanted. Paul touched the smooth marble.

They had been here. Lived in this place. Loved
each other.

Was staying in one place really so bad? What if
he kept traveling…and missed out on a love as deep
and everlasting as theirs had been?

He took a photo of the vault with the angel on top,
then the battery beeped a warning that it was getting
low. Time to quit. To leave Indigo and Marjolaine
Savoy. He tucked his camera back into his backpack,
then headed for his rental car.

He'd go back to the bed-and-breakfast and book
the first flight out, before he tried something really
stupid to get Marjo's attention—like propose.

CHAPTER TWENTY

MARJO MADE IT through the rest of the CajunFest by concentrating solely on the remaining events.

Sixteen years ago, she would have done anything to have heard an agent say he'd liked her performance and would have signed with him right then and there. At nineteen, Marjo Savoy had been willing to take a risk.

Something she couldn't afford at thirty-five.

And yet, she'd taken the biggest risk of all today. She had fallen in love with Paul Clermont.

What if she did go with him to Tibet? Or to other corners of the world? What if she signed with that agent, cut a record? What would happen to her brother? Her town? The comfortable quiet life that she had created?

Outside the perimeter of Indigo waited change. Something she'd avoided for years. The day her parents died, she'd also lost her sense of security. All the years since then, she'd spent trying to build that security for Gabriel, a bubble that would keep him from being hurt.

But the more she tried to do that, the more fragile that bubble became.

When the festival finally ended and the cleanup crew set to work, Marjo realized Paul hadn't returned, as she'd secretly hoped he would. Disappointment weighed down her steps.

What had she expected? She'd practically shoved him out the door herself. He was probably already gone, on a plane to the other side of the world.

As she walked toward her car, she ran into Luc Carter.

"It worked out great, didn't it?" he said. "The bayou boat cruises were a hit. I could have used Gabriel's help, but I don't blame him. There was a lot of fun to be found in town today."

Marjo glanced around at the vendors closing up their booths. "I can't believe we pulled it off."

"This festival has definitely put Indigo on the map."

Marjo nodded. "You haven't seen Paul around, have you?" she asked, trying to sound casual.

A knowing grin crossed Luc's face. "He went back to his room at La Petite Maison. I'm sure he hasn't left yet, if you want to catch him."

He hadn't left yet. There was still time. "Thanks," Marjo said, and with a quick wave headed for her car.

She didn't know what she'd say to Paul when she caught up with him, but she knew she didn't want to leave things the way they had at the opera house.

Marjo started the car and was just turning in the

direction of the bed-and-breakfast when a thought slammed into her.

Gabriel.

She'd been so focused on finding out where Paul was that Luc's words hadn't even registered. Gabriel hadn't shown up to help Luc. He hadn't been at the opera house, either.

Marjo whipped the car around and hurried toward home, pulling into the circular drive in front of the house, the tires squealing and spitting out the crushed seashells. She tried to think. When was the last time she'd seen Gabriel?

Oh, God. Yesterday afternoon, when she'd given him the money to go to the gumbo cook-off.

She'd been in such a rush to get to the opera house this morning, to be sure everything was in perfect shape, that she'd never even checked to make sure Gabriel got up and had breakfast.

She raced into the house and ran into Gabriel's room. His bed was neatly made, just as Marjo had left it the day before when she'd changed the linens.

She headed for the kitchen. The beignets she'd brought home for breakfast yesterday from Loretta's bakery—all six of them—were still sitting on the plate above the microwave.

"Gabriel!" she called, running into the living room.

On the mantel she spied a small envelope marked with her name. She tore it open, fumbling with the sheet of paper inside.

"Dear Marjo," Gabriel had written in his familiar looping handwriting. "Don't worry about me. Darcy and I are together. We'll be back on Saturday night. Love, Gabriel."

He was gone.

Worry constricted around her chest, squeezing out her breath. She dashed into the kitchen and started calling everyone in Indigo she could think of—Alain, Doc Landry, Henry, Luc and then, finally, the number she should have considered first.

Darcy's.

Darcy wasn't at her apartment, but her parents were home. It took about five seconds for Marjo and the St. Cyrs to put the pieces together.

Darcy's parents hadn't heard from her since yesterday, either, when she'd mentioned something about an appointment in Lafayette. Since Darcy lived alone, they hadn't thought much about it. But now, they were concerned, too. Marjo hung up and waited an agonizing twenty minutes for Darcy's father to go over to his daughter's apartment to discover she hadn't been home, not even to feed her cat, though she'd left two open cans of cat food on the kitchen floor.

Marjo hung up the phone after the second conversation, promising to call Darcy's parents if she heard anything at all. She called Alain again and told him everything she knew so far. Outside, rain began to fall, throwing her back sixteen years to another late night, another storm.

And a horrible outcome.

"Don't worry, Marjo," Alain said. "They probably got tied up at some museum or something. Lost track of time."

"Yeah," she said, but she didn't believe it. Gabriel wouldn't do that.

And yet, as she thought back, she realized that he might. In the last year he'd been stretching the boundaries more and more, a little at a time. There'd been times when he'd taken off for hours without a word. She'd thought it was a phase, but clearly, she'd been wrong.

There was a knock and she raced to answer it, flinging the door open. "Gab—"

Paul stood on the opposite side of the screen door, a bottle of wine in one hand and a loaf of Loretta's bread in the other. "I hated the way we ended things today. I thought we should talk. And what better way to do that than over a picnic?"

"A picnic? But it's dark and rainy—"

"And the perfect time to spread out a blanket and cozy up together."

She opened the door and let him in, needing his comforting presence. She took the wine and bread from him, laying the items on a nearby table.

"Marjo? Is something wrong?"

"Gabriel's missing." A sob left her throat. The worry that she'd managed to hold on to by keeping busy suddenly sprang free.

"Are you sure?"

She nodded, then started pacing again, unable to

stand still. "He left a note that said he'd be home tonight. I think he left yesterday afternoon. I didn't even notice. I was in such a hurry to leave this morning, and I should have checked on him, but—"

"Shh, shh," Paul said, crossing to her and taking her into his arms. "It's okay. We'll find him."

"What if we don't? What if he's been in a car accident or lost or…" She threw up her hands, unable to voice anything worse.

"Okay, let's start at the beginning," he said. "Where do you think he went?"

Marjo pulled away from Paul and crossed to the window, wishing, praying, for headlights to appear. "Out with Darcy. Maybe to Lafayette, because she told her parents she had an appointment there. They might have just gone to see the city. Gabriel loves cities. The busy-ness of them, the lights. But overnight? Where would he have stayed? How would he have found a hotel?"

"Does he have a cell phone?"

She shook her head. "He never needed one. He never leaves the bayou without me."

"Until now."

Guilt washed over her. If she hadn't been so tied up with the festival, the opera house and Paul, she would have been paying more attention to Gabriel, and this situation wouldn't have happened. She closed her eyes and wrapped her arms around her chest, then nodded. "Until now."

"Did you call the police?"

"Indigo's *and* Lafayette's. He's over twenty-one so there's nothing they can do. Legally, he can go wherever he wants."

"Then the best thing to do is just sit tight. He's with Darcy, so he should be okay."

She wheeled around. "How do you know that? Because you met Darcy once and took a few pictures with Gabriel? He's not like other boys. He will *not* be okay."

"Marjo, Gabriel isn't a boy anymore. He's a young—"

"Don't tell me about my brother. I know him better than you do."

"You probably do," he said, going to her and touching her arm gently. "But maybe he's a bit more grown-up than you think. He's probably able to handle everything just fine."

"And maybe you're completely wrong and I'm standing here, waiting, when I should be out looking for him. Just like last night when I was in bed with you, instead of thinking about where my brother was. I didn't pay attention, Paul. If something happens to him—" She reached for the hook by the door and grabbed her sweater and her car keys. "I can't stay here. I have to do something."

But before she could open the door, Gabriel walked in, with Darcy in tow. The two of them were laughing and chatting, but stopped when they saw Marjo's face.

"Gabriel! Where have you been?" Marjo shouted, rushing to him and checking him over, making sure he wasn't injured.

"Marjo, sit down."

She stepped back, startled by the strength in Gabriel's voice. "Okay," she said, taking a seat in the armchair.

Gabriel clasped Darcy's hand. The two of them exchanged a glance, then Gabriel nodded and turned back to his sister, taking in a breath as he did. "Darcy and I got married yesterday."

The words hung in the air for a long time, like a thundercloud. "You're...*married?*" she repeated. Even Paul looked stunned.

Gabriel nodded and held up his left hand, revealing a gold band that matched the one on Darcy's hand. "Yep."

"Gabriel, you can't just buy a couple of rings and call yourselves married. You need—"

"A preacher, a blood test and a license. We did all that. I know a lot, Marjo. I'm not stupid."

The word hit her like a slap, reminding her of the time she'd confronted him after the fire. "I didn't mean that, Gabriel. I don't think you're stupid."

"You never see me as a grown-up," he said, his frustration clear. "I'll be twenty-two next month, Marjo. I'm not a little boy."

"I know that," she soothed. "But getting married is a big step. Too big—"

"For someone like me?"

The pain in his eyes nearly broke her heart. Marjo wanted to take back every mean word said on a playground, every stare in a store, every person who had ever made Gabriel feel that he was different. "No, Gabe, not like that. I just want you to think first."

"I did think," he said. "I love Darcy, and she loves me. And now we're married."

"But you have to think about the rest, the other things that go along with such a huge step. Where are you going to live? Where are you going to work? What about children?"

"Darcy and I have that all figured out. We're going to live in her place and I'm gonna work at the funeral home, once it's built again. And I'm gonna look for a part-time job taking pictures." Gabriel beamed and pulled his new bride against his side.

"Everything's going to be fine, Marjo," Darcy said. "You'll see."

Marjo wanted to scream at them, to tell them there were a hundred other discussions that needed to be had before making such a choice. That it wasn't as simple as running off to a city and then settling into Darcy's one-bedroom. But it was clear Gabriel wasn't listening.

"Well, you send Darcy on home," Marjo said, crossing to the door, taking the situation in hand, as she had so many times before. "Tomorrow we'll go back into Lafayette and get this annulled."

"No!" The word exploded from Gabriel's lungs. "I will not. I love Darcy and I'm *married* to her. And

you can like that or not. I don't care." He spun around and was out the door before Marjo could stop him.

She rushed after him. "Gabriel!"

He turned back. "What?"

"I can't—" She felt a lump form in her throat. "I can't lose you."

"Oh, Marjo," Gabriel said, walking back and giving her one of his tight, all-encompassing hugs. He patted her back. "You'll never lose me. I'm gonna live right here in Indigo."

She pulled back and looked into his eyes. He *was* older, more mature. When had that happened? Why hadn't she noticed?

"Oh, Gabe, I'm sorry. I should have listened to you."

"That's okay, Marjo," he said, the forgiveness coming as easily as his smile.

And in that moment Marjo knew.

It was time to let him go.

"You're the best, Gabe," she said softly.

"No. I'm your brother."

She cupped his face, staring into eyes so like her own. "And you always will be. I love you."

One more boa constrictor hug, and then he was gone, promising to be at the funeral home tomorrow to help her finish sorting through the rubble.

As she watched him and Darcy leave, their happiness clear in the way they laughed and hurried to the car, Marjo had the distinct feeling that the more she tried to control, the further it all slipped out of her grasp.

CHAPTER TWENTY-ONE

WHEN MARJO CAME BACK inside the house, Paul met her at the door and led her over to one of the chairs, waiting until she'd sat down. She'd had a hell of a day, but he hoped he could make it better, make up for all that had gone wrong. He took her hands. "Gabriel will be fine, I'm sure."

She shook her head. "He's *married*, Paul. That's not fine at all. The funeral home is gone, which means his job is gone, too. How is he going to support her? How is he going to get by? For God's sake, I still make his sandwiches for him."

"Actually, I have something that will take care of one problem." Paul reached into his back pocket and withdrew a letter. He gave it to Marjo, then waited while she read it. Even he still couldn't believe the words on the paper.

"A book contract?" she said, looking up. "For you?"

"Yes, but we're going to include Gabriel's pictures, too. I did what I told you I would, and pitched a story on Indigo to my editor, telling him it would be really cool to see Indigo from two different perspectives, Gabriel's affectionate one and my more jaded view." He grinned. "Anyway, Joe loved the idea, but after looking at all the pictures, he said it deserved to go bigger than a few pages in the magazine."

"Bigger?"

"Bigger as in a hardcover, coffee table book." As he said the words, excitement built inside him again. "My editor called a friend of his in a publishing house and got me a meeting. The editor there had been bugging me for years to stay put long enough to put together a book. Soon as he saw this idea, he was hooked." Paul touched the paper in her hands. "He gave me this letter as proof of their interest, until we finish hammering out the contract. And, Marjo, I'm going to give Gabriel his portion of the advance. After all, without him, I'd only have half the story of Indigo."

"Does Gabriel know about this?"

Paul nodded. "I talked to him yesterday morning, when I first got back to town. I saw him on my way over to the funeral home to see you. He's excited, Marjo. This could mean a whole new path. He's still got a lot to learn and he knows that. He intends to apprentice for a few years, take some classes, work on his skills and at the same time, work at the funeral home once it's up and running again. But he has a dream, Marjo, a dream he's excited about."

"I'm happy for him," she said quietly. "I

really am. But…" Her voice trailed off and she turned away.

"I wanted to tell you a hundred times, especially last night and even more this morning." He trailed a finger along her lips, remembering the look on Gabriel's face when he'd told him about the contract. The boy had positively lit up with joy. "We were hoping to surprise you tonight, after the festival."

She glanced again at the letter, and he waited, sure she'd react with the same happiness as Gabriel. But as the silence stretched out and her posture grew more tense, Paul wasn't so sure.

"How could you?" Marjo slipped out of the chair and away from him. "How could you?" she asked again, shaking the letter.

"How could I what? All I did was talk to a publisher—"

"And fill his head with a dream that may never come true."

"Nothing is set in stone yet, but I don't see any problems."

Tears streamed down Marjo's face. "Do you know where I was when my parents died, Paul?" She didn't wait for him to answer. She crossed the room to the window and looked out at the camellias. "I was at an *audition*. I was supposed to come home that weekend from college, to watch Gabe while my parents went to a party. But at the last minute, I backed out and went to a goddamned audition instead, putting myself ahead of my family. Gabe got sick, the babysitter panicked and my parents rushed home to take care of him. But the road was wet and the tires were old and—" She shook her head, unable to finish the sentence.

"That wasn't your fault," Paul said. Marjo shook her head, not hearing him. He tipped her chin up with his hand. *"It wasn't your fault, Marjo."*

The words echoed in her mind, and though others had told her the same thing over the years, it was as if she really hadn't understood them until now.

It wasn't her fault.

It wasn't anyone's fault. It was just a tragic, terrible accident.

"You've done a wonderful job raising him," Paul went on. "He is one of the kindest, gentlest people I have ever met. He will always need you, but in a different way from when he was little. He's a man, a married man now. You can let go and he'll be okay."

"But—"

He gave her a grin. "There's always going to be a but, Marjo. The trick is learning not to think about them. It took me a hell of a long time to understand that." He took her hand and led her back to the sofa, lowering himself to his knees in front of her. "My parents had an awful marriage, and I never wanted to end up like them, my father gone all the time, looking for work, my mother holed up in her room until the day she died. Then I married Diane, and guess what? I was an awful husband. I didn't talk to her, didn't communicate. And I was gone. All the time."

"Why?"

He slid the backpack off his shoulder and onto the floor. "Because my camera became my way of talking. You said something to me one day about how I distanced myself from people. That I wouldn't open up. You were right. I've used a camera to keep me from ever looking head-on at life." He traced a finger along her jawline, seeing in her eyes that she had done the same thing, but for different reasons. "What's your wall, Marjo?"

"Paul, I can't do this. I can't—"

"For such a strong woman, you are damned stubborn." He smiled down at her. "What are you hiding behind?" he asked her softly.

Marjo was silent for a long while. At last she spoke, her voice so quiet he almost couldn't hear her.

"This town," she said. "I've poured my life into it because I thought I was giving back to the people who had helped Gabe and me after our parents died." She gave him a soft smile. "But you were right. In doing that, I guess I was really just avoiding dealing with everything."

"Because you were an instant mom and business owner and didn't have time to deal with anything else."

She thought about that for a second. "Yeah."

"Well, the town is fine, and your brother is a married man, and there's a Canadian on his knees in your house. Do you think you're ready to deal with a little change?"

She smiled, and he could see that a weight had been lifted from her shoulders. "Depends on why that Canadian is on his knees."

"I read the letters you gave me. And I visited Alexandre's and Amelie's grave."

"And?"

"Theirs was quite the love story. And it showed me that if I walk away from Indigo now, I'll be leaving behind not just part of my own history but one of the best things that ever happened to me. You."

"Me?" The word escaped her in a whisper.

He nodded. "I'm going to include Alexandre and Amelie's story in the book, but..." He took her hands in his. "I'd like *this* version—our version—to end differently."

"Differently?"

"I want to see Amelie's descendant get a happy ending. I think my family has had enough tragedy." He reached into his pocket and pulled out a small velvet box, then tipped back the lid to reveal a perfect round diamond. "Will you marry me, Marjolaine Savoy?"

"Marry you...now?" She looked at the ring, twinkling in the light. It was meant for her. Paul was meant for her. Maybe a happy ending was possible after all.

"Soon. When I got the book deal, I decided to take a leap of faith and quit the magazine."

"Quit? But you love that job."

"*Used* to love it. I found I love someone else much more. I don't want to risk that by being in Tibet when I could wake up next to you every day instead. I'd like to settle down here where my ancestors lived. In fact, I just bought a property here."

"But you already own the opera house."

"I don't think living in the opera house would be much fun," he teased. "I bought a piece of the land where the plantation house used to be. There's an outbuilding still left that someone tried to turn into a house a while ago."

"But that place has been abandoned for years. It's in terrible shape."

"Yep. Probably needs a lot of hard work. Know anyone who likes taking on hopeless causes?"

She grinned, unable to hold back her happiness another moment. He loved her as much as she loved him. "Maybe. Depends on what kind of incentive you're using for your workers."

He leaned forward and kissed her, a quick, heated taste of what was to come. Later tonight. Tomorrow. And all the days that followed. "How's that?"

"It's a start," she joked, knowing that she was going to love teasing him. Tempting him. "I warn you, I'm going to expect a heck of a bonus for all my hard work."

"Trust me, I'll be giving it to you. Several times over."

A thrill ran through Marjo. Living with Paul Clermont certainly wouldn't be boring.

She studied his face, seeing the love there. "You're really going to move into that old house?"

"No. *We're* really going to move into it." He took the ring out of the box and held it at the end of her ring finger, waiting for her to say the word. "I love you, Marjolaine, and I want to marry you."

Joy took flight in her heart, carrying her past the fears that she had let hold her back for so long. Too long. "I love you, too," she said, then took in a deep breath and slid her finger into the ring. Changing her life no longer seemed so scary, not with Paul beside her. It fit as if it had been made for her.

Maybe it had.

"There's one condition," she said, stopping him before he said anything else.

"What's that?"

"You never, ever put our opera house up for sale."

"As long as you keep making beautiful music," he said with a grin. Then he leaned forward, his lips meeting hers, and began a concert that Marjo hoped would last all night.

EPILOGUE

MARJOLAINE CLERMONT stood on the stage, waiting for the curtains to part, the lights to come up. From the sidelines of the completely restored opera house, her most loyal fans watched. Darcy and Gabriel were there, along with her beloved Paul and Amelie, their baby daughter.

Gabriel sent her a thumbs-up, and Amelie called out a "Ga-ga!" before a laughing Paul shushed her.

And then it was time. The heavy curtains parted and Marjo stepped forward into the spotlight, a spotlight she had grown used to in the year and a half since the first CajunFest. The instruments in the orchestra pit struck the first note, and in a moment she began to sing the songs her mother had played over and over again when Marjo had been a child.

As she sang, she scanned the audience. Only the first row or two were visible beneath the bright lights, but it was enough that she could see Cally holding hands with Billy Paul, who'd swept her off her feet and taken her to Vegas last month, finally corralling the marriage-shy Cally before she could change her mind.

The residents of Indigo were all here, or as many as the opera house could hold. The population of her beloved town was growing, and the sleepy bayou town had a new energy. Even the Robichaux family had come up from New Orleans. Celeste's daughters and their husbands flanked her and her new husband, Doc Landry.

Marjo sang until she thought her voice might give out, performing the same sets she had been practicing for weeks in a studio in Lafayette, getting ready to cut her first demo tape.

Ever since they'd married, she and Paul had made the travel part of their lives work, with a little ingenuity and a lot of laughs when they took Amelie along. Marjo had found she loved traveling, seeing parts of the world she'd never dreamed of visiting.

Paul's book, complete with Gabriel's pictures, had been a huge hit at this year's CajunFest. Gabriel had looked so proud as he'd autographed copies beside Paul.

The rebuilt funeral home was thriving. Marjo had lured Henry out of retirement long enough to set up the new business and train his son and wife to take over the day-to-day management. Although Gabriel still worked there, he'd also taken a part-time job in a camera shop in New Iberia, which helped him pay for photography classes. He and Darcy were happy, and often came over for dinner with Marjo and Paul.

Beside her husband sat his father, Renault Clermont. He had come down from Canada in

January and decided to stay for a while. Paul had worked hard to reach out to his father and get to know the man who had become a stranger to him.

As the last note left Marjo's throat, the thunder of applause began to grow, the sound so loud it shook the walls of the Indigo Opera House.

Marjo bowed, then, as she straightened, she let her gaze drift up to the balcony seats. For just a second, she thought she saw Amelie and Alexandre sitting there, beaming their approval that their legacy—of love, and of music—had been continued, its tune set to a new melody.

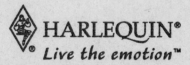

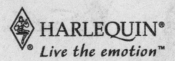

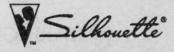

Harlequin Historicals®
Historical Romantic Adventure!

*From rugged lawmen and
valiant knights to defiant heiresses
and spirited frontierswomen,
Harlequin Historicals will
capture your imagination with
their dramatic scope, passion
and adventure.*

*Harlequin Historicals...
they're too good to miss!*

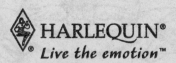

"I hope you'll let me explain, darling."

Alistair smiled persuasively. "I didn't know Fame Records was negotiating with you when I bought it —"

Ilona pushed him away. "Someone told me you always know exactly what you're doing. And I'm prepared, now, to believe that. It's too late to reverse any business dealings we might have, but in the future that's all it will be... business!"

Her words had stung. He walked to the door of her hospital room and looked back, his eyes dark with anger.

"If that's what you want, then so be it. But don't think I plan to disappear. I have every intention of staying around to safeguard my investment — so you'll just have to get used to seeing me every day, Loney, *darling*!"

Catch a Falling Star

Rena Young

Harlequin Books

TORONTO • NEW YORK • LONDON
AMSTERDAM • PARIS • SYDNEY • HAMBURG
STOCKHOLM • ATHENS • TOKYO • MILAN

Original hardcover edition published in 1984
by Mills & Boon Limited

ISBN 0-373-02670-6

Harlequin Romance first edition January 1985

CHAPTER ONE

HAD a stranger caught sight of the windblown figure sitting on a rock, gazing out to sea and strumming distractedly on her guitar, he would never for one moment believe that it was the well-known singer Ilona Craig. For Ilona, without her stage clothes and make-up, was a far cry from her public image. Without the glamour and glitter of the spotlight and dressed in shabby jeans and shirt, she looked like a typical college girl on holiday.

That was just the image she was trying to portray at the moment. Not that she disliked her fans—far from it. She was well known for her practice of answering her fan mail personally and for signing autographs anywhere and any time. But now she wanted a complete rest, and that meant seclusion and privacy. That was why she had been delighted when her mother's friend whom she called Aunt Mattie had offered her the use of her son Alistair's fishing shack on the coast of Spencer Gulf.

Mattie McLean, and her son Alistair, had been their next-door neighbours from the time Ilona was born until they had moved to Queensland just after she turned fifteen. Aunt Mattie had been the one to fly to Queensland and comfort her after the car smash that deprived her of both parents; and she was the one person Ilona could take her problems to and know that she would get good solid down-to-earth advice and comfort.

But Alistair was a different story. He was ten years older than she and had left home to travel just before she had moved away, and she had never seen him since.

All she knew of him was what Aunt Mattie had told her over the years. That had been the only hesitation that Ilona had before accepting the offer of the shack—what Alistair would think about someone using his premises without his permission. But Mattie had reassured her that he was away and not expected back for some weeks, so there was nothing to worry about and she could have her holiday in peace.

The shack was just what she had been looking for—miles from anywhere and secluded, with no chance of anyone finding her. The last six months had been very trying. With recording sessions and touring, Ilona was exhausted. Even her voice was tired. She refused to believe that there was anything else wrong with it and was sure that all she needed was a complete rest for it to come back to normal.

She had found that after singing for only a short time now, her voice would break and her throat become sore. None of the usual medications helped for more than a short while. But she refused to concede that there was anything drastically wrong and preferred to stick her head in the sand and opt for a good rest, much to the annoyance of her manager.

So she had packed her hire-car with groceries and the odd bottle of wine and escaped to the serenity of Spencer Gulf and the sea, with the idea of writing the songs she hadn't had time to put on paper for so long in preparation for her next album which was due to be recorded in a couple of months' time.

She'd been at the shack now for almost a week, and try as she might, her songs refused to come. Somewhere in the back of her mind was the niggling doubt that her throat problems were more than just tiredness. For her throat was still sore if she tried to sing aloud, and after a week of speaking to no one but herself, if it had just needed a rest, there should have been some signs of improvement. But there were none.

The gulls that had been quietly foraging among the rocks at Ilona's feet suddenly swept into the air together and wheeled and cawed in fright and indignation as the sound of a car engine broke the silence. Ilona looked up in surprise. Who could be coming here? The nearest neighbour was at least half a mile down the coast and no one came down this track unless they were lost or deliberately coming here.

She rose reluctantly from her perch and carrying her guitar by the neck went to see who was intruding on her privacy.

As she approached the shack, she saw a car parked behind her own. Her car had been garaged in the lean-to at the back of the shack, and the owner of the strange car seemed to know the place well, for he had found the small but overgrown entrance to the garage lane without any trouble and was now striding down to meet her, a look of undisguised fury on his otherwise handsome face.

Ilona took the opportunity to study him. He looked somehow familiar, and the thought crossed her mind that he might be someone in the music business who had managed to prise her whereabouts from her manager.

But she brushed the thought aside. He didn't look the type that she had come to recognise as part of her industry. His clothes were definitely too conservative for that and his russet-brown hair that shone red in the sun was far too carefully styled into a business type cut. Still, the thought that she knew him wouldn't go, and she looked more closely as he approached. He was tall, she could see, and definitely had a temper to match his hair, if the look on his bronzed face was any indication.

'Who the hell are you?' he shouted, as she approached.

Ilona was taken aback at his furious tone and under normal circumstances, would have retaliated in kind. But her throat was still sore, so she waited till he was completely within earshot before replying softly, 'I might ask you the same question. But I'm a lady, so I don't use that tone of voice to complete strangers.'

He pulled up with a jerk, obviously not expecting such a soft if barbed rejoinder. After a moment when he looked her up and down and seemed to come to some conclusion about her, he asked, 'May I know what you're doing here?'

'Well, if it's any of your business,' Ilona purred huskily, beginning to enjoy the encounter, 'I'm staying here for a few days.'

'Oh, are you? And who, might I ask, gave you permission? Or do you just go around breaking into places that take your fancy?'

'Do I look the type to go around breaking into strange places?' Ilona asked, her green eyes flashing with concealed enjoyment. He was arrogant, no doubt of that, she thought, and his temper was lurking just below the surface.

'It's hard to tell about the types who break in these days,' he grated, barely keeping the sting from his voice. 'Just because your jeans are clean it doesn't alter the fact that you have no right to be here,' he finished smugly, his brown eyes travelling across her well rounded hips in a way that left no doubt in Ilona's mind that his mind was on more than her clean jeans.

She had become used to sly remarks and innuendoes over the years and his hot eyes made no impression on her. She ignored them as she did with all the other men she had met who seemed to think that a singer was less than a lady.

'It just so happens,' she told him reasonably, 'that I have not only permission but a key. So you can mark down on your list that this place is quite safe and not being vandalised. I take it you are some sort of security person?'

His temper, carefully kept in check throughout their little confrontation, broke through. 'No, I damn well am not a security person, as you put it! I own this place, so you're trespassing, and since I neither gave you permission to use it, nor a key, it would seem you're not only a trespasser but a liar as well.'

Ilona's laughter stunned him to silence and his face set into lines of impotent fury. His hands clenched in rage, and Ilona choked back her laughter hurriedly when she realised that in his temper he might be tempted to hit her.

'You must be Alistair!' she choked. 'No wonder I've been thinking I knew you! Though I must admit you've changed a lot in the past ten years.'

The furious look left his face as quickly as it had come and one of bewilderment took its place. 'Do I know you?' he asked quietly. 'But I must,' he mused softly to himself. 'Otherwise,' he added aloud, 'how do you know me?' He looked at her carefully and Ilona flushed at his intense scrutiny.

'There was a time,' she told him, 'when I thought you would always remember me, and that I would never forget you. But times change, and so, it seems, do people. I'm Ilona—Ilona Craig,' she added, a little wistfully.

The look on his face was comical, and Ilona laughed again, choking back the laughter when his face clouded once more. This new Alistair was a man who definitely disliked being laughed at, she mused, and decided to keep the information in the back of her mind for later. Though why she should feel that there would be a later for them was a mystery to her.

'Well, well!' It seemed he was lost for words. 'You certainly have changed. I might have recognised you if you were dolled up for a record cover or a stage appearance,' he allowed. 'But, without your pigtails, you're certainly not the Ilona Craig I remember.'

A look of pleasure crossed Ilona's classic features, and a hint of rose tinged her high cheekbones. She was pleased, somehow, that he should have recognised her in her public image. 'So you would have recognised me on stage?' she asked. She was a little embarrassed, and didn't know why, and she tossed her mane of honey-blonde hair to cover her shyness. Her very obvious attempt at covering her dilemma appeared, she knew, coquettish, and she felt angry with herself for appearing so in front of him.

'Hey!' his voice cut through her reverie and the touch of his hand on her shoulder made her jump. 'What are we doing standing out here squabbling?' he asked goodhumouredly, all trace of his previous anger gone. 'If we're going to reminisce, we might as well do it in comfort inside.'

They strolled silently to the shack, both lost in thought of years ago.

Inside, the shack was primitive but comfortable. Water had been piped to the kitchenette sink from a rainwater tank, and remote as it was, it had electricity. But that was the only concession to civilisation that had been allowed. The whole cottage, for in many ways it was more than a shack, consisted of three rooms. Two bedrooms leading off the main room, which was a combination of kitchen, dining and living area. The only door to the outside led straight into this area and just outside it, under the window, was the 'shower', a canvas bucket affair with a shower nozzle attached which hung on the outside wall on a rusty nail, and had to be filled from the sink. The toilet facilities were even more primitive and necessitated a stroll through sand dunes and bush to a little house some yards from the main building. For safety's sake, a light had been strung on a long extension lead to it and could be switched on and off from inside, then stowed away with the shower and anything else pilferable when things were locked up.

Alistair took a seat at the table and watched with interest as Ilona began making coffee. 'I suppose Mattie gave you a key?' he enquired, with a smile. 'She's never done that before. Still, she's always telling me that you're like the daughter she never had. It's strange that we've always seemed to be in different places all these years.'

'Not really,' Ilona commented, placing a steaming mug of coffee in front of him and pulling a cake tin from the shelf above the fridge.

'Cake,' he grinned, helping himself to a large slice. 'You've come well prepared.'

'As a matter of fact, I made it this morning,' she replied, reaching for a smaller piece.

'Very domestic, I must say. But then I seem to recall a certain little girl who was always ready to help Mattie on baking days. Must have rubbed off. This is as good as any Mattie ever made,' he teased, wiping crumbs from his lips.

'And so it should be,' she replied drily. 'It's Mattie's recipe.'

Alistair looked her full in the face and smiled a lopsided grin when he saw the crimson stain her cheeks. 'I thought it tasted familiar! Not that I get much of Mattie's cooking these days.'

'I was wondering. . . .' Ilona hesitated. 'Well, really, what I don't understand is why your mother didn't tell you I was here.'

'That's something that's been puzzling me a bit too,' he answered. 'But then I only spoke to her on the phone, and she seemed a bit worried about something. I was in a hurry at the time. Perhaps I didn't give her enough time,' he replied apologetically. 'Still, she's been a bit forgetful lately. Maybe it just slipped her mind.'

Ilona looked up in surprise. 'Mattie didn't strike me as being forgetful—in fact, quite the opposite. You're talking as though she's a candidate for an old people's home!'

'Hold on now,' he retorted hotly. 'It *is* my mother we're talking about here, and I certainly didn't intend to give *that* impression.'

'Well, you did,' Ilona broke in angrily. 'And I won't have you talk about *my* Aunt Mattie like that, even if you are her son!'

'Let's get something straight right now, young lady,' Alistair replied in a hard, flat voice. 'She is *not* your aunt. That would make us cousins, and that's the last thing I want. And furthermore, how I talk about my mother is strictly my business.'

Fury made Ilona's green eyes flash. How dared he talk to her like that! No blood ties could have made her closer to Mattie than she already was, and for this great pompous oaf to deny her right to call his mother 'aunt' was just too much. 'She is my aunt, and nothing you say or do will make me think of her as anything else!' Ilona spat, her voice low and husky.

'You forgot the "so there" and the tongue out,' Alistair laughed at her. 'That was always what you did when you were little, as I recall.'

Her fury melted at the absurd picture he'd conjured up and they both broke into spontaneous merriment. 'What a silly thing to get heated about,' she smiled. 'Still, if I recall, you didn't seem to mind people thinking we were cousins then.'

'That was then, this is now.' Ilona wasn't quite sure what he meant by that cryptic remark, but refused to be drawn and ignored it.

Alistair put his coffee cup down with a distinct thud, resolve and determination written all over his face. 'I'd better get my gear in from the car,' he said. 'Then we can make some decisions about who's sleeping where.'

The sudden change in his tone took Ilona by surprise. She hadn't thought about sleeping arrangements or that they would both be staying. In fact, she had been half expecting him to suggest she leave and had been mentally preparing for the long drive back to Adelaide.

'Does that mean I can stay?' she asked, a note of gentle teasing in her voice. She wasn't quite prepared for the look of astonishment that crossed his rugged features. Somehow her words had an effect on him that she hadn't expected, and she was overcome with embarrassment when she realised that the huskiness in her voice due to her throat problems had added a quality to it that she hadn't intended.

His eyebrows raised quizzically. 'My, my,' he said softly. 'You certainly have grown up over the past few years—or is that voice part of the star image?'

Ilona stroked her throat absently and turned away to hide her confusion. That she was flirting with him was not the impression she had intended to give, and she was completely at a loss on how to correct it. 'Just force of habit,' she whispered, still with her back to him. 'Doesn't mean a thing,' she added, a little louder, hoping to sound flip. 'You'd better get your gear. I'll see about starting dinner. You must be starving.'

Alistair threw her a look that smacked of bewilderment then shrugged and left the shack to comply.

'Hope you haven't filled the fridge too much.' His voice from behind her gave her a start, and she spun round to see him laden down with two of the largest coolers she'd ever seen.

'My goodness! What have you got there? It looks as though you're planning to stay for a month.'

Alistair laughed. 'Only a couple of days. But I always bring a bit of extra ice, just in case I catch any fish.'

Ilona was surprised. Surely he didn't mean that? There certainly wasn't room in the fridge's tiny freezer for much ice, and it looked as though he'd brought enough to fill it three or four times over. 'But it will melt,' she said in dismay.

'Oh, obviously you haven't found my ice box, then,' he grinned. 'Follow me, child. Your education on shack living is about to begin.' He grabbed her by the hand and virtually dragged her behind him, down the stairs and round the side of the shack to what she had assumed was a spare door left lying on the ground. He heaved it up on to its side with an effort. Underneath, Ilona was amazed to find a hole had been excavated and filled with straw. The sides of the hole were lined with zinc.

Alistair looked as pleased as a small boy who had discovered how to open the cookie jar. 'See! An icebox,' he said smugly. 'All you have to do is bury the ice in the straw and it keeps for a couple of days—sometimes longer. Depends on the weather.' His words came out in short bursts from the effort of pulling all the straw from the makeshift refrigerator in preparation for packing it with ice.

The years slipped away, as if by magic, while they packed the ice into its straw bed. Though they had never been close because of the difference in their ages, when she was a child, Alistair would sometimes look after her while her parents went out, and it was then that he would act the way she had always imagined a big brother would.

She found the shyness she felt with him disappear and melt as quick as the small pieces of ice that broke from the blocks and dropped to the hot sand. Even Alistair's initial reserve melted and he dropped back into the habit that he had ten years before of calling her 'Loney'. But somehow, even though she felt comfortable with him now, she could not bring herself to use the childhood name she had called him then. For he was no longer 'Al', but definitely Alistair—still full of fun and teasing and treating her as if she were still the schoolgirl he had helped with her homework, but somehow changed.

Changed, she knew, much more than she. Even after the years she had spent building up her career and dealing with producers and financial backers, her hard-headed attitude was a sham—a sham she kept carefully hidden even from her manager. She had built up the image of a tough professional, purely to survive, and no one, except perhaps Aunt Mattie, knew how hard it had been for her to live up to her own carefully cultivated role.

Alistair, she felt, was a different kettle of fish. She smiled to herself at the metaphor. Fish! When they were organising a way to keep the kettle of fish he hoped to catch from spoiling.

'Hey, what are you smiling about? This is serious work, my girl.' He grinned his familiar eye-crinkling grin that had been one of the reasons ten years before that she had developed a teenage crush on him—a crush she remembered that had disappeared quickly when they'd moved away. Or almost!

'Nothing,' she replied, smiling to herself. 'Just happy.'

'Well, see how happy this makes you, squirt,' he laughed, and threw a piece of ice at her.

It landed on her neck and before she could brush it off, slipped, leaving a trail of goosebumps behind it, straight down between her breasts and lodged in her bra. She squealed with feigned outrage, 'Beast!' then, before he could catch her, she dropped another lump of ice down his back and ran.

Even though she had been barefoot for most of her time at the shack, her feet were still not hard enough for her to run over the pebbles that edged the sand, and she heard his shouts of hilarity at the sight she made trying to escape. Throwing a look over her shoulder, she saw him standing watching her and his laughter echoed with the call of the gulls.

'I'm only giving you a head start,' he shouted breathlessly, laughing. 'You won't get far!'

But by then she was on the sand and she could run without fearing for her feet. 'Catch me now!' Her voice was hoarse and throaty, but for once she refused to worry about the effect shouting would have on it. For once in she couldn't remember how long, she was having fun, real fun. Not the manufactured plastic fun that seemed to be the norm with the people she met as Ilona Craig, star.

As she ran across the sand, she turned to taunt him with his tardiness. But he had already started to run after her and was too close for comfort. Hair flying in the evening breeze, she flew across the beach, kicking up spray from the waves that lapped at her feet and soaked the bottom of her jeans. She heard his feet pounding behind her and her heart began to pound in rhythm.

Long tapered fingers caught her shoulder and she gasped. Bringing her to an abrupt stop, Alistair pulled her round to face him. 'Caught you, you little devil!' he exclaimed. No sign of distress marred his even breathing. It was almost normal, and Ilona knew at once that he was superbly fit. Her heart was pounding painfully and for some reason she couldn't bring herself to look into his eyes. Unaware of her breathlessness, he caught her up in his arms, spinning her round as he had years before.

Familiar—that was how his arms felt. Strong, hard and familiar. For the first time since her parents had died, she felt safe. She knew without being told that with Alistair, there would never be any reason to fear anything. A voice deep inside her told her that with him, she would be safe, always, and she tucked her blonde head into his shoulder and revelled in the unfamiliar feeling.

'Oh, no, you don't! You're not going to get out

of it by playing possum like you used to!' he grinned.

'I'm not playing possum.' Her voice came out a throaty groan.

'Doesn't matter what you're playing at, Loney, you asked for this, cheeky child. Putting ice down my neck—it isn't done, you know.' His voice was light and teasing and full of laughter.

Ilona's spirits rose to match his and instinctively she joined in the game. 'Don't! Please don't, Alistair. I'll be good—I promise.'

'Too late,' he gurgled, choking back mirth, and dumped her unceremoniously, screaming and squirming, into the surf.

Her hair was plastered to her head as she surfaced spluttering. The soaking shirt emphasised the full roundness of her bosom as it clung to her like a second skin and the wet jeans moulded her hips. It surprised her that she wasn't angry. If anyone else had done this to her she would have been furious, she knew. But she was far from angry. She was happy, alive, bursting with joy, and she wanted to shout it to the world. But her voice was gone.

All she wanted now was to stay, at least for a short while, back in her childhood with him. Back in the times when everything was simple and nothing mattered except having fun. Away from the conflicts and problems she had come to believe were part of life.

Something had changed in Alistair's face. A look she couldn't decipher was in his eyes. His soft brown, laughing eyes changed to hard black stones as they raked her figure.

He scooped her up in his arms again, oblivious

to the water that soaked his clothes and ruined his shoes. Ilona's breath caught in her throat as the rays of the setting sun turned his hair to molten copper.

'It's getting late, child,' he said gruffly. 'The wind's getting up too. You'd better get inside and dry off or you'll catch your death of cold.'

Depositing her roughly on her feet, he took her hand and pulled her, unprotesting, back to the shack. 'Get changed,' he commanded. 'I'm going to get the rest of my gear from the car.' He looked at her intensely, before spinning on his heel and hurrying away.

Ilona stood at the foot of the small steps that led to the cottage, wordless and confused. He had changed—changed back, so suddenly to the man who had abused her before he knew who she was. Her heart ached for the Alistair of old. The Alistair who made her feel alive. The Alistair who made her happy and content. Oh, please, show me how to bring him back, she begged the night air, then slowly turned to trail dejected up the stairs.

A beach coat hung on a nail outside the front door, and she hastily shed her sopping clothes and shrugged into it, throwing her wet garments over the rail to dry. Then, dispirited, she wandered unseeing into her room to change.

In the little unpainted room, there was no mirror. No way she could see how she looked. It seemed for the first time since she had come here that it was important how she looked. She had been pleased to be able to ignore that aspect of her life for a while and had revelled in the unfamiliar feeling of no make-up and windswept, uncombed hair. Now it seemed imperative that Alistair see her looking her best. But how could she do that with her hair salt-filled and stringy, needing shampooing badly and no facilities to bathe and groom herself properly.

She did the best she could, in the circumstances, pulling her hair back into a plait and pinning it up out of the way, then adding perfume and a bright lip gloss that she hoped would brighten her pale features. It was almost dark outside now, and she wondered what Alistair was planning to do. The other bedroom was full of fishing gear, including a small aluminium dinghy, complete with outboard motor. If he planned to sleep in there, he would have to move that at least. Ilona had been surprised when she first looked in there on her arrival. But on reflection, it was a sensible place to store movable objects while the shack was empty. The only thing she was unsure of was how he had managed to get it in there in the first place and, more to the point, how he intended to get it out. But that was to soon be made perfectly plain.

'You ready yet?' His deep, resonant voice drifted through the door to break off her reflections. 'You'll have to help me get the boat out. Unless, of course, we're sharing tonight! I refuse to sleep in the car for you or anyone else.'

Ilona's heart leaped. This was the voice of the Alistair of old, teasing, fun-filled and cherished, and she almost ran out to help, unreasonably pleased that he was treating her in the old childlike way once more.

Like a child offered a treat by a well loved

older brother, she hurried to dress, pulling clean shorts and shirt on regardless of whether they matched or clashed, and danced out excitedly to help him. She found him standing, hands on hips, tapping a bare foot impatiently. He had discarded his sodden shoes and she noticed them neatly placed in a corner of the kitchen recess packed with newspapers. Whether his slacks would be salvageable after their rough treatment was a moot point, for now they were rolled up to his knees and creased, she imagined, beyond repair.

He brushed past her and began to drag the dinghy from the bedroom and across the floor to the door. 'How do you get it out when you're here by yourself?' she asked, eyes wide in amazement as the unwieldy thing seemed to scrape past obstacles by magic.

'Oh, I manage. But it's easier with two. Just hold it steady while I lift it over the rails,' Alistair ordered.

To her surprise, the boat was more bulky than heavy and once out of the shack and over the rails, they were able to carry it across the rocks to the sea with ease. Now she found an explanation for the stake that had been driven into the sand some yards from the shack's front door. It was to moor the dinghy to and no longer looked so incongruous.

Satisfied that the small craft was secure, Alistair stomped up the stairs, shaking sand from his feet as he did. 'Now I can get out of these and into something more suitable,' he said, indicating his ruined slacks with a nod. 'Especially if there are going to be any more of the high jinks you seem so fond of. But first, I have to invade your boudoir.' A gleam entered his eyes and his eyebrows lifted in a way that set Ilona's heart racing. He grinned at her reaction. 'Only to get a bed,' he teased. 'The spare one is stowed under yours and the spare mattress is under the one on your bed. So I'm afraid I'll have to pull your very neatly made bed to pieces. Unless, of course, you'd like to leave it till tomorrow and let me share yours.' The gleam was back in his eyes again, and Ilona laughed.

'I don't share my bed with just anyone,' she quipped—then immediately realised she'd said the wrong thing.

'So you do share it sometimes?' His tone held a hard edge of reproof.

'No, as it happens, I don't. But even if I did I don't think it would be any of your business.' Ilona's reply was a stock one that she'd given to many men over the years who had tried to find out if she gave her favours lightly as did some of her colleagues. But somehow it wasn't the answer she really wanted to give to Alistair. She wanted to tell him she had never slept with a man. That until now, she had never really even been tempted. Oh, she had been asked, many times, and even had a few try to coerce her. But she had always managed to keep men at a distance and for the first time in her life she found herself wanting to defer to a man, to be soft and gentle with him and to be close to him. Yes, even to sleep with him and to wake in the morning safe in his arms.

The teasing light was gone now from his hard black eyes, and Ilona despaired of ever getting it back. She damned the profession she had chosen for herself for making her into a wisecracking fool. Damned it for taking the quiet innocence she had possessed once and replacing it with a shell of hard sophistication that had now become almost second nature. Damned it for making her into something she really wasn't and deep down would never want to be. Cursed it while knowing that it was the only career she wanted and would ever want. Not for her a home and babies while she could bask in the adulation of her audiences. But she saw the look of disgust in Alistair's eyes and her heart pounded wildly. Why, when she knew so well what she wanted from life, did a little voice deep down inside insist that what this man felt about her was so important?

If he had been a director or a critic, she would have understood. Or would she? She was established enough now, to be able to make her own rules. The only person she really had to please now was herself. Until today that had been enough. But now? She pushed aside that uneasy feeling. Damn him anyway. If he didn't like it, he could jolly well lump it!

Still, it hurt to think that he would have such a low opinion of her. She had thought from his conversation that he had kept up with her through her letters to Aunt Mattie. Ilona had told *her* everything. Perhaps Alistair felt she had neglected to tell her some of the more personal things. But she hadn't. Aunt Mattie was her lifeline to sanity in a world that thrived on the outlandish and bizarre and Ilona had poured out her hopes and fears to the older woman while presenting a hard outer shell to the people in her world.

'Is there something wrong, Loney?' Alistair's voice broke the silence and interrupted her reverie. The teasing tone was gone now, from his voice too, and in its place was a hint of flirtation—encouraged, she knew, by his suspicions about her relationships with men. She looked him full in the face, trying to gauge his mood by the look in his stormy black eyes.

It seemed to Ilona that he was confused about her, as though he still wanted to think of her as the child he had known while seeing her as the woman she now was. Poor Alistair, she thought. It must be hard for him suddenly to find his little next-door neighbour all grown up and living a life he couldn't possibly understand. Her annoyance disappeared instantly. She desperately wanted to reassure him, to tell him that she wasn't what he thought she might be. But she couldn't seem to find the words. It seemed to her that if she brought her world into this magical time, it would shatter the illusion and peace and timelessness. But the illusion was cracking, because she couldn't.

She continued with her interrupted preparations for dinner in silence—a silence due more to her whirling thoughts than to the pain that was back in her throat.

'Is something wrong?' Alistair asked again, over the remnants of the dinner that she had placed mutely before them. 'You've said nothing all evening. I suppose my company must be pretty tame compared with what you're used to.'

'It's not that, Alistair. Honestly.' Her voice broke and he looked at her sharply. 'I've got a sore throat and I've been trying to rest it.'

'Why on earth didn't you tell me, child?' he asked anxiously. 'Have you seen a doctor? Have you anything to take for it?' His concern, she knew, was genuine and it seemed to bring back their childhood relationship. 'I'll get you something for it,' he said abruptly, and rising, went to the kitchenette.

Ilona watched him, feasting on the deft movements that seemed so incongruous in a man of his size. Presently he returned with a steaming mug. 'Drink this,' he ordered.

The smell was faintly familiar and Ilona wrinkled her nose in distaste. 'What is it?'

'Honey, rum and butter. Careful, it's hot. It's very good for sore throats. It may not cure what's wrong, but it should ease the pain.' He watched her sip it and smiled wryly at the face she made. 'Come on, it isn't that bad. In fact it's quite nice.'

'I don't like rum.' Ilona was surprised that her voice sounded almost normal. 'I've been using a spray,' she told him huskily. 'But it only seems to work for a little while and I can't use it as often as I'd like. The instructions say it could be dangerous to use it too often.' Her voice was nearly normal again from the hot, soothing drink.

'See, it's getting better already,' he said, a smug smile on his face. 'But if it doesn't improve drastically in the next day or so, you're going to see a doctor, whether you like it or not.'

Ilona smiled. He was taking things into his own hands again, just as he'd done when things went wrong when she was a child and had taken her troubles to him.

'Come on, drink it up. Then we might take a walk before bed.' His eyes as well as his lips were smiling now and she felt a surging sense of relief. He seemed to have forgotten the tension that had been between them, and she was glad he had. Perhaps now they could continue as they'd started.

CHAPTER TWO

ILONA looked up through her thick gold lashes to watch Alistair cross the room to their table. The sunlight caught his hair, and once more she marvelled at its ability to shine copper in the sun. He really hadn't changed much over the years, she realised. He was still tall and craggily handsome, broad of shoulder and slim-waisted. But what had changed—and, she mused, the reason that it had taken her so long to recognise him yesterday—was his manner.

Gone was the gangly immaturity of post-adolescence and in its place was the air of a man completely in control. From his arrogant stance to the almost cruel set of his full sensual mouth. Even his walk gave the impression of command. Only his hair, unruly and untamed in the wind, hinted at a softening in him.

Ilona had woken late. The rum and honey that he had made her drink once more before bed had been enough to send her, for the first time in weeks, into a sound, dreamless sleep. Her nostrils had crinkled at the faint aroma of frying fish and the sound of a deep masculine voice singing softly had made her jump, unsure where she was until the memory of yesterday had flooded back to leave her with a feeling of peace.

Alistair had been fishing, long before she had even looked like waking, and the smell of fish was the result of his catch. Two huge King George

whiting were browning happily in the pan and
Alistair's voice broke into her reverie, calling her
to rise and shine.

Stretching luxuriously, she had pulled on a
gown and flip-flopped into the kitchen on her
ridiculous mules. High-heeled, fluffy blue mules
that were so absurd in the setting of a fishing
shack that even Ilona found it hard to take
offence at the derisive laughter that rolled out of
Alistair at the sight. But she was strangely
attached to these silly things. They were not what
she would have chosen for herself, but they had
been a birthday present from her manager's niece
who had picked them as being suitable for a
'star'.

That a child would take the trouble to pick
something so personal and go to so much trouble
to find something that she felt fitted with the
personality she knew as Ilona Craig had touched
her deeply. So these silly slippers meant more to
her than anything she could have bought for
herself, and somehow they had become a sort of
good luck charm.

She smiled to herself as she remembered telling
Alistair about the slippers that morning and the
hilarity of their fresh fish breakfast.

He placed a glass of fresh orange juice in front
of her and smiled. 'It's nice to see you looking so
bright,' he commented, sitting next to her and
taking a sip of an ice-cold beer. 'Does that mean
your throat doesn't hurt so much?'

They were in the lounge of the Wallaroo Hotel.
Alistair had been overly anxious about her throat
that morning and had insisted that they take a
trip to the township so that the local doctor could

take a look at it. He seemed to be well known in the little town and had no difficulty in getting an appointment for her. But they had some time to kill before the doctor could see her, so they were sitting in the hotel while they waited.

'You know, I really don't know very much about you,' Ilona commented, glancing sideways at the tanned face of her companion. 'Mattie didn't go into much detail about what you'd been doing over the years.'

Alistair stiffened. 'Oh, I thought you two swapped stories every time you met like a couple of long-lost sisters. I'd have thought she kept you very much up to date.'

Ilona flinched at his tone. Sarcasm wasn't a trait she remembered him having and he hadn't used that tone with her before. Why what his mother told her about him should trouble him was a puzzle. Perhaps it wasn't sarcasm. Maybe she was just overreacting to a tone. She looked up from her drink to see that she hadn't been mistaken, and coloured from the sharp look in his eyes.

'Mattie told me very little about you,' Ilona snapped. 'She always said you were too busy to tell her much, and what you did tell her she didn't understand anyway.'

'What makes you think you'd understand any better than Mattie?' he asked pointedly.

'Does it matter?' Ilona retorted. 'I was only trying to make conversation. But I can see that whatever it is you do for a living is taboo as far as I'm concerned, so let's drop it, shall we?'

'Suits me,' was the guarded reply. 'Anyway, we don't have time to go into anything in depth and you shouldn't be using your voice too much at the moment.'

'I suppose not. But it's hard not too. You don't realise how important a voice is until you have to do without it. I. . .' Ilona broke off abruptly as his hand covered her mouth.

'Shut up!' he ordered. 'Until told otherwise, keep it to a bare minimum.'

She began to chuckle, but stopped herself with difficulty when she saw the look in his eyes. He must keep his secretary on her toes, she thought, if this is his reaction to disobedience. No wonder he isn't married yet! No self-respecting woman would put up with much of that kind of treatment!

Alistair glanced at his watch. 'Time to go,' he said, rising as he did and drawing her up from her chair by the elbow. 'Now we might find out what's wrong with that throat of yours.'

Ilona was touched somehow by the obvious concern in his voice and the bitter thoughts that had been running through her mind after their disagreement vanished.

It wasn't far to walk to the doctor's surgery, and they strolled amiably the few blocks in the hot mid-morning sun.

The place was empty when they arrived and the doctor was able to see her immediately. She entered his consulting room with trepidation. Now that she had been forced to seek professional help she knew that things were worse than she had been willing to admit, and her heart started pounding with fear. Fear of all the unknown and terrifying possibilities that had raced through her mind since her throat had first begun to hurt.

The doctor was a youngish man who gave the impression of quiet competence and his soft mild-mannered attitude began almost at once to put her fears to rest. He took her history quickly and efficiently, phrasing his questions so that little more than a yes or no was required as answer and after only a few minutes was ready to examine her throat.

At the long-expected and feared 'Say Ah!' she closed her eyes and mind and sat tense and blank while he did all the things she had been dreading for so long.

'Finished now,' he said at last. 'You can relax,' and the wide beam on his face helped her to do just that. 'I suppose now,' he continued, 'you'll be expecting an instant diagnosis and a bottle of pills that will fix this up overnight.' His tone was humorous with an underlying hint of seriousness.

'That would help a lot,' Ilona smiled. 'But I gather that's not what I'm going to get, is it?' she asked.

'Certainly isn't, Miss Craig. In fact, the first thing you're going to get is a good talking to. Anyone in your profession who neglects the sort of symptoms that you've had needs a good spanking. So consider yourself well and truly spanked!'

Ilona appreciated his friendly manner and the fact that he hadn't lectured her. But his words, humorous though they were, hit home harder than a lecture.

'What I'm going to suggest now,' the doctor continued, after a moment of silence when he seemed to be studying her face intently, 'is that you see a colleague of mine in Adelaide.'

Ilona was surprised. She had thought from his manner that he would be able to fix everything himself. 'Why?' she asked huskily.

'Well, to tell you the truth, I don't have the facilities to do what's necessary in this case, so it's imperative—and I must emphasise that—imperative, for you to see a specialist immediately.'

'So there is something very seriously wrong?' Ilona asked. She felt relieved in a way that her fears had been realised.

'That really depends on your interpretation of "serious". What I think you have is a benign growth on your vocal chords. Warts, if you like. There is a chance, a slight chance in this case, of the growth being malignant, but I would be extremely surprised if it was. What needs to be done is the growth sliced off. Once that's done, then all your huskiness will disappear and the pain you've been feeling will go too. The pain has nothing to do with the growth, by the way, it's just from straining to speak and sing.'

'How long would it be before I could sing again?' Ilona queried uncertainly.

'That's the main reason why I want you to see this particular man in Adelaide. He's one of Australia's leading E.N.T. specialists and he'll know more about that than I would.'

The doctor pulled a telephone directory over to him and looked up a number. 'I'll phone him now and arrange for you to see him as soon as possible. This should be your top priority at the moment. So I don't expect any argument.'

Ilona was stunned—too stunned to argue. But in a strange way she was prepared. She had known for some time, deep down, that things were serious, but had not been able to bring herself to meet the challenge. Now her subconscious was in turmoil, blaming herself for being a coward and perversely blaming Alistair for bringing things to a head. Immersed in her misery and confusion, she missed the conversation between the two doctors until she was pulled back into the present by the click of the telephone receiver being placed back in its cradle.

'Well, my dear, that's settled. Dr Anderson will see you tomorrow at two. He suggested you go to see him prepared for a trip to hospital. If it's what I think, he wants to operate without delay.'

Ilona was surprised that she felt no fear once the dreaded word 'operation' was said. It felt as though her brain had gone into neutral and that nothing the doctor could say would jar her into action. She sat motionless and withdrawn, hearing nothing and staring at a spot above the doctor's head. She didn't hear him rise and open the door, summoning Alistair with a peremptory wave of his hand. She was unaware of the two men's conversation. She only knew that Alistair was there when he put an arm around her shoulders and patted her gently.

'Come on, Loney,' he said gently, 'we have to go and make some arrangements about getting you back to Adelaide.'

Ilona looked up then and her mind snapped back into focus. 'Of course,' she said with a smile. 'There's a lot to be taken care of before tomorrow, and there isn't much time.'

The startled look that passed between the two men escaped her, for she was still in a sort of trance. Her mind concentrating on what had to be done before she saw the specialist the next day.

'Now, Miss Craig,' the doctor said formally, 'I don't want you trying to do too much in such a short time. If you could leave things be until you've seen Dr Anderson, it would be better for you in the long run. I've given Alistair a script for you and I want you to get it filled and start on the pills straight away.'

'Of course, Doctor,' Ilona said absently, as she took the referral he had written for her and rose to leave.

'I'd be much happier if I knew you had some family here to help you through this,' he said worriedly.

'Don't worry about that, Doctor,' Alistair broke in. 'My mother and I will see that Ilona is well looked after.' And he took her lifeless arm and guided her out.

Outside in the brilliant November sunshine, Ilona began to feel more composed. The terrified thoughts that had been spinning round inside her head gave way to more sensible ideas. Modern medicine was safe and painless, she knew. But the old horror of hospitals that had been with her from the days when her parents had lingered after their tragic accident was uncomfortably near the surface, and she knew it would take all her strength and willpower to avoid a nervous collapse if she were forced to go into hospital herself.

Alistair seemed to know without being told that her strange behaviour was more than just the fear of what might happen to her, and much to her relief he didn't question her or try to reassure her. Somehow he seemed to know that what she needed now, more than anything, was to continue as though nothing were wrong.

Without consulting her or even mentioning it, he drove through the bushland, pointing out places of interest and rambling on in his deep comforting voice about the history of the area.

'They used to call this area the copper triangle, you know,' his voice broke through Ilona's reverie, bringing her abruptly back to reality.

'No, I didn't,' she said, starting to take an interest in her surroundings.

He smiled at her when he realised that she was at last listening to him. 'Yes, before the mines shut down, this was one of the largest copper areas in the world. But it's been mined out. Most of the miners were Cornish, and in a minute or two we'll see some of the original Cornish cottages.'

Ilona looked at him quizzically. 'Do you think we have time to sight-see?' she asked. 'I do have rather a lot to sort out before tomorrow.'

Alistair breathed a sigh of relief. 'Thank goodness you've snapped out of your trance,' he commented. 'I thought I was going to be burdened by an hysterical female!'

'Well, if you thought that,' she snapped, 'you should have just taken me back to the shack so I could have packed and left. I'd hate to have been a burden.' Her tone was sarcastic with a hint of self-pity.

'Come off it, girl, I knew you'd snap back pretty quick. I was just having a dig at you,' he chuckled.

'Well, I'm in no mood for your kind of humour. So it might be wise if you turned this car around and took me back.' Ilona was angry— not really with him, but with herself. Angry because she'd let her guard down and allowed this man to see the vulnerable side of her that she kept hidden from everyone. Everyone, that was, but Mattie. How she needed Mattie now! Needed her strength and understanding. Mattie wouldn't laugh at her; Mattie would understand.

Ilona hadn't been taking a great deal of notice of the passing scenery and she was taken aback when Alistair pulled the car into a parking space outside an extremely picturesque cottage. 'We're here,' he said flatly. 'But if you really are in such a hurry to get back, I'll turn round and head back.'

'I'm sorry,' Ilona said contritely. 'It's just been a bit of a shock, that's all. It really is very nice of you to have thought of this. We may as well look at it now we're here.'

As soon as the words were out of her mouth, she knew they were wrong. His eyes became flinty and he glared at her. 'Don't do me any favours!' he snarled, starting the car and revving the engine furiously.

She reached over and touched his arm. 'Alistair, please don't be angry with me,' she said huskily. 'I really didn't mean that the way it sounded.'

He turned to face her, his eyes burning into hers with a look almost of disgust. 'That doesn't work with me,' he stormed. 'It may with the sort of hangers-on you have in your line of work, but I've been wheedled by experts, and you certainly don't fit into that category!' His voice softened as the tears welled in her eyes and she turned away to hide them. 'But then maybe you are an expert.'

The hastily wiped tears clung to her eyelashes like rain droplets and her voice was shaky when she answered. 'I wasn't trying to do anything. I was just trying to apologise for my rudeness. But if you won't accept an apology there isn't much I can do about it, is there?'

A look of puzzlement crossed his face and his eyes softened with concern. He leaned over and touched her cheek. 'Who could refuse an apology like that, especially from someone with eyes that particular colour green? I should really be the one apologising, I suppose,' he mumbled, switching off the car motor. 'I'm just not used to dealing with girls like you.' His voice dropped so that Ilona had to strain to hear his words. She thought she heard him say that he could get used to being wheedled by emerald eyes, but she didn't ask him to repeat them, because she was sure they hadn't been meant for her.

'Come on,' he said aloud. 'We might as well play tourist while we're here,' and he got out of the car and opened her door for her.

The cottage was magic, like walking into the past. All the furniture was original and the curtains and bedspreads had been handmade in another time. Ilona was particularly taken by the crocheted spread on the double bed and would have liked to have touched it. But ropes prevented people from getting too close, and she supposed that was sensible in this day and age of disregard for other people's property.

The garden of the cottage had been set out like

an English garden, with many of the plants having been brought there by the Cornish miners years before, and they spent some time wandering happily through it.

It was with regret that she realised they would have to leave, and she was silent most of the way back to the shack. Her thoughts still caught up in the memories of a bygone era, and she was jerked back to the present abruptly by Alistair's words as they arrived at the shack.

'If we made an early start, we could stay over till tomorrow morning. It's only four hours' drive to Adelaide and your appointment isn't till the afternoon.'

Surprise registered in her voice. She hadn't really thought he would be coming back with her, and that he should assume he was was comforting. 'You don't have to come.'

'Why not?' he asked.

'Well, you're here for a break, aren't you? It would be a shame to spoil it just because I have to return.'

Ilona felt drowsy and jaded. There seemed to be no reason for her lethargy, and she stifled a yawn.

'I wondered when those tablets were going to take effect,' Alistair said nonchalantly. 'I've been expecting some sort of reaction for a while now. The chemist said they'd take an hour or two to work, but you must have been fighting them.'

The doctor *had* said for her to start the medication he had prescribed straight away, and she had taken two of the tablets at the chemist's shop. But Ilona hadn't realised that he had prescribed sedatives. She had been too numbed to really think what they were, and now she was angry that her faculties would be numbed even more by drugs. Drugs were something she avoided. She had seen the results of them on some of the people she worked with in the music business, and they frightened her.

She had seen colleagues become 'hooked' on drugs legally obtained from doctors and having to resort to illegal means to acquire enough for their habits. So she had another reason for refraining from obtaining medical help. A stupid reason to most people, but with her already entrenched fear of hospitals and doctors a perfectly valid excuse to her.

'Why didn't you tell me what they were?' she cried. 'If I'd known, I would never have taken them!'

'Exactly,' was his smug rejoinder. 'And I didn't want to have to hold your nose, pretty though it is, and force them down your throat in public. Think what the gutter press would have made of that.'

'Think what they'd make of this,' she retorted, nodding at the cabin, a spark of her old spirit surfacing. 'What well-known songbird is having a rest in a well-concealed hide-away with some unknown redheaded Lothario?'

'I'm not redheaded!' Alistair threw back angrily.

'Oh, then you admit to being a Lothario?' she quipped.

'Well . . . .' Her laughter cut off his reply and he was forced by its infectiousness to join in.

'That's much better,' he said, when the

laughter subsided. 'It's nice to see the sparkle back in your eyes again.'

'The big question now, of course, is what we're to do with your car,' Alistair mused, after a few minutes' silence.

Ilona looked at him in surprise. 'What about my car? It will go back with me, of course.'

'It certainly won't,' was his sharp reply. 'You won't be in any fit state to drive while you're taking those tablets, and there's no way I'd allow you to, anyway.'

'But I've got to take it back. It's a hire car and I can't just abandon it here miles from anywhere. I'll just have to stop taking the tablets until later. Unless of course you insist on coming back with me and want to leave your own car here.' Her voice was mocking.

Alistair gave her a sharp look. 'Why don't you just stop all this liberated nonsense and leave everything to me?'

'Why should I? You can't just come wandering into my life and take over as though I were a schoolgirl! I've managed perfectly well for a long time now and I'm sure I can manage now if you'd just shut up and let me think about things without making facetious remarks.'

'Come on, Loney,' he almost pleaded. 'I was only trying to point out that you're in no fit state at the moment to handle things alone, and since I'm here you may as well let me sort things out for you.'

This was too much for her, and it suddenly struck home that she was miles from anywhere, certainly not her usual robust self and, she had to admit, afraid. Afraid of what would happen the next day and unsure of her ability to cope with this situation alone. All her objections crumbled and she deflated like a punctured balloon. Later, thinking back on her sudden submission and feeling guilty at her lack of what she had always thought of to herself as backbone, she put the blame on the sedatives. But a sneaking suspicion still lingered that it was something more, something tied irrevocably to her burgeoning feelings for Alistair. But she pushed the thought away. There was no place in her life now for a man. Any man!

There was silence in the little room, as both withdrew into their own thoughts and Alistair wandered aimlessly round the tiny kitchenette, waiting for the kettle to boil. Suddenly, as though he had reached a decision, he blurted, without looking at her, 'Look, I didn't think you'd take things like this. I mean. . . . Oh, hell, I don't know what I mean! Anyway, I made some arrangements while you were at the doctor's. I was pretty sure he'd send you back to the city, so I arranged for Dave at the service station to take your car. He's going to Adelaide in a couple of days to pick up some parts and he's taking his mechanic with him. So they've agreed to take your car back with them. They'll be here in a couple of hours to pick it up.'

Nothing surprised Ilona any more, but she felt she had to say something. 'That was pretty high-handed of you, wasn't it?'

'I suppose it was,' he agreed, 'but I felt it was necessary. And I'm damned if I'm going to apologise!' he added defensively.

'I suppose I'd better think about packing,' Ilona murmured, stifling another yawn.

Immediately his tone became concerned. 'Don't bother about that now. Just go in and have a sleep. You'll feel better after a nap, I'm sure, and there are a few things I have to see to before we leave.'

She just nodded and trailed dejectedly into the bedroom, where she stretched out on the bed and almost at once drifted off into a light, drug-induced, dream-filled sleep.

The trip back to Adelaide passed, for Ilona, in a sort of dream. Against her objections, Alistair had insisted that she take the sedatives prescribed for her and she dozed most of the way.

Dave from the service station had arrived at the shack the evening before as Alistair had planned and she told him where to deliver the car, giving him a cheque to cover the rental with some misgivings. But he appeared an honest sort and Alistair vouched for him so she seemed to have no alternative. She had refused categorically to allow Alistair to pay for the car and he hadn't made an issue of it, much to her surprise.

When she had woken from her fitful nap, she found that Alistair had done most of what was needed to close the place and only the boat had to be loaded into the bedroom again before they left. He wouldn't let her help with it, and she watched him manoeuvre the bulky dinghy into the shack with ease and wondered why he had insisted on her helping to get it out. But the thought flitted away quickly like so many of her thoughts since she had been taking her tablets, and she decided then that she would take no more.

By the time they entered the outskirts of Adelaide, the effects of the early morning tablet had almost worn off and she sat up to take notice of her surroundings. She had always felt that Adelaide was one of the most beautiful cities she had ever seen, and she sat back to enjoy again the sights she loved so much. After all, this place had been her home for a long time and in her heart she still felt it was.

The old buildings, so well preserved, fascinated her and the churches were more beautiful than any she had seen anywhere else, especially the Greek Orthodox ones with their Eastern influence and beautiful lilac stained glass that caught the eye and the sun.

So wrapped up in her own misery and fear was she that it hadn't occurred to her that she had nowhere, in this city she loved, to go, except to Mattie's. She had given up her hotel room when she decided to go to the shack and her permanent home was a flat in Sydney, close to her recording studio and the places where she performed. She realised that she didn't even have the necessities for a trip into hospital, as she had come prepared for a quiet holiday and had only brought one suitcase with her.

'Where are we going?' she asked, half expecting him to say they were going to his mother's.

'I thought we'd better go to my place,' he answered. 'That way, you won't be bothered by people recognising you.'

That was an eventuality that had completely escaped her and she mentally chastised herself for letting go so completely. It was the mention of her fans that really brought Ilona out of her shocked condition, and from then on he began to function almost completely normally again. The fear that had stunned her into a half dream world, she pushed firmly to the back of her mind and began to plan what would need to be done if surgery were called for.

'I'll have to get in touch with Simon,' she said, and Alistair glanced around at her, surprised. Her voice was no longer meek and wilting, but although still husky it had the strong, self-sufficient ring that he had noticed when they met again at the shack. He smiled to himself. But Ilona was so caught up in her own plans and mental arrangements that she missed it.

'Who's this Simon?' he asked. 'You didn't tell me about him.'

Ilona thought she caught a hint of jealousy in his tone, but ignored it. Typical man, she thought—mention someone else when you're with them and they get their backs up immediately!

'He's my manager, and he'll have to know what's going on. He's due here in Adelaide in the next day or so. I'll have to ring him as soon as possible.'

'Wouldn't it be better to ring him after you've seen the specialist?' he queried. 'Then at least you'd be able to tell him exactly what's going on.'

Ilona saw the sense in that suggestion and agreed. But somehow she felt that she should have insisted on her own plan. Why Alistair should make her feel so defensive troubled her. After all, she told herself, all he's trying to do is help out. I really should be thankful for that. But she wasn't! He was taking over her life, and one part of her objected strongly. The part that had kept her going in her career determined to reach the top, and to hold on to her own values in the process. But another tiny part of her, the part that wrote long letters to Mattie pouring out her troubles and fears, *wanted* him to take control and to carry all her burdens for her.

Navigating the mid-morning traffic with the ease of familiarity, Alistair manoeuvred the powerful Ford through the busy city centre, and Ilona wondered where 'his place' was. Feeling that perhaps it was somewhere on the other side of the city, perhaps in the foothills, she sat back to watch the passers by, expecting to leave the city. But she was shocked, almost, when the big car suddenly turned into a narrow driveway beside two of the towering business houses and descended to an underground car-park.

An attendant hurried over as they drifted to a stop beside a lift door. 'How you doing, Mr McLean?' he asked in a friendly way. 'Haven't seen you for a while.'

'I've been away again, Fred,' Alistair replied. 'Can you get her serviced and cleaned?' he asked, indicating the car with a nod.

'Sure thing. When do you want her back?'

'Tomorrow will do fine. If I need transport, I'll take a cab.'

'No worries,' Fred replied, taking the proffered keys and helping Alistair with the bags from the boot.

Ilona noticed that Fred made no comment about her being along. In fact, he seemed to take it for granted that Alistair would be accompanied by a woman, and she wondered how many he had brought here.

She made no comment as the lift shot them up

to the top floor. But she did wonder how he had managed to acquire such an unusual place to live.

The top floor consisted of a flat taking up the complete floor space. The lift, she had noticed, had a security key to operate the controls to the top floor, and now she knew why. The lift doors opened directly into a huge, open living space. Ultra-modern, almost austere, its charm lay in the unusual furniture placements and vivid use of colour.

Instead of separate rooms for living, dining and study, the furniture had been arranged so that there was ample space for each. But the areas were separated by ingenious use of bookcases and occasional furniture, and in one case, a lush tropical display of indoor plants.

The kitchen had been divided from the rest of the living area. But instead of a normal bench type divider, a semi-circular bench-high fish tank, stocked with a myriad brilliantly coloured tropical fish, served as the base for the tiled top.

The floor was polished, with scatter rugs placed strategically to blend with the furnishings and with the areas in which they were placed.

The whole apartment was bathed in the brilliant morning sunshine flooding through picture windows at opposite sides of the room.

Alistair dropped the luggage at the lift door and strode across to one of the windows to adjust the slatted blinds that dropped from beneath a pelmet at ceiling level, a pelmet that had been so cleverly installed to be almost invisible.

'That's a bit better,' he commented, adjusting the opposite side. 'Now you won't need to wear your sunglasses inside.'

Ilona just smiled and drifted over to a chair, taking in her surroundings as she did so.

'I take it you aren't impressed with the accommodation?' Alistair said with a hard edge to his voice. 'But then people in your business are used to more opulent surroundings.'

Ilona looked sideways at him to see if he were joking, but to her complete surprise he seemed to be serious.

'Of course I'm impressed! It's absolutely stunning. I've never seen anything like it. I'm just speechless, that's all.'

He disappeared into the kitchen before she could see whether her answer had pleased him or not and the sounds of running water broke the strained silence. She felt that something needed to be said. 'It's just that you seemed so at home at the shack that I didn't imagine. . . .'

'You didn't imagine what?' he broke in. 'That I could live like a human being?'

Ilona bridled. What gave him the right to needle her like that? Just because she was in show business it didn't put her on a par with Mae West, or any of the other notorious females who had their plush houses and apartments splashed all over the women's magazines. But before she could think of a remark cutting enough to throw at him, he appeared with a steaming mug of coffee.

'Never mind,' he commented, 'I think the guest room will be more to your liking—all pink and fluffy.'

'Decorated no doubt by one of your many live-in women friends!' Now what had made her say that? It must have been the look that the man downstairs had given her. But she didn't care. He'd been asking for it.

'That's better,' he said, to her surprise. 'At last I've got a bite out of you. You've been like a robot since last night, and that sort of attitude isn't going to get you through what's ahead. It's time you started to face what's coming and began behaving like the girl I once knew. The girl I met at the shack,' he added quietly.

The tears welled and began to spill over on to Ilona's honey-coloured lashes. I won't cry, she told herself, I won't. But somehow she couldn't control them.

'Look, through that door,' he pointed. 'Go and wash your face, you'll feel better. In fact it probably would help if you had a shower,' he added, striding to pick up her bag and head off in the direction he had indicated.

'Well, come on. While you're getting yourself together, I'll call Mattie and tell her what's going on.'

CHAPTER THREE

NAKED, Ilona stood in front of the mirror in the huge bedroom of Alistair's flat. She peered at herself critically. The events of the past couple of days had certainly left their mark! The dark circles under her eyes pointed to nights of interrupted sleep and her hair, falling in lank strands, made her skin look sallow instead of healthily tanned. It was time now, she thought, to do something drastic.

She examined herself in the glass. At least her figure was still the same, she told herself with a rueful smile. Slender, but with curves in all the right places and a waist that seemed incredibly small for someone of her height and build. For she wasn't exactly a small girl—five foot six with broad shoulders that sloped enticingly to a heavy, full bosom. A bosom that caught most men's eyes. Her hips flared from her tiny waist to broad but shapely hips, tapering to long, well-shaped legs.

All in all, she thought, not bad. In fact, much better than average. Now, what to do to make herself feel human again? A long, hot bath was definitely called for and a shampoo to shock her hair back to its normal gleaming honey mane. A face-pack while she soaked to take the sallow look from her face and eye-drops to bring the sparkle back to her lustreless eyes.

She turned and added a generous dose of

perfumed bath salts to the steaming bath water,
then slid tentatively in. Lowering herself gingerly,
for the water was scalding, she stretched out in
the steaming water and began to relax. In her
head, she planned what to wear for her
appointment with the doctor. But she was more
concerned with how she would look to Alistair
than the impression she would make on her
medical adviser.

Perhaps it was a good sign, she told herself
wryly. After all these years worrying about how
to handle her career, now was the time to handle
Ilona Craig, person. But why did it have to be
Alistair McLean who brought on this sudden
attack of the 'romances'? It was just because he
came along at the time when she needed someone
and perhaps there was still a little bit of her
adolescent crush left, Ilona justified. Still, she
thought, it won't hurt to indulge yourself a little
and enjoy the attention while he's around. It isn't
as though you're in love with him. He's just nice
to have around.

Still musing to herself, she applied her
favourite face mask and settled back to indulge in
the luxury that she had been denied while at the
beach shack.

It was quite some time later that she
appeared in the living room of the apartment,
not quite Ilona Craig—star, but a much more
sophisticated version of the beachcombing Ilona
that Alistair had first seen barely two days
before.

Her shining, honey-coloured mane had been
washed and blown into a long, sleek bob and her
emerald eyes highlighted by a hint of eyeshadow.

The jersey dress and matching jacket were in a pale apple green shade that picked up the colour of her eyes and surprisingly brought out the golden lights in her hair. She knew she looked good. It was why she had bought the outfit. Apart from the fact that it was uncrushable and travelled well, she loved the way the skirt flared from her hips to swish almost seductively around her knees and set off her well rounded calves to perfection.

She was surprised to see Alistair sitting relaxed and obviously showered and shaved in one of the armchairs, reading the morning paper. She guessed that he must have an *ensuite* off his own room, and smiled to herself as she remembered thinking she would be accused of being a typical female and hogging the bathroom.

'Something funny?' he asked, looking up and catching her smile.

'No, not really,' she replied enigmatically.

'Well, I must say that's a distinct improvement,' he said dryly.

'I do have a certain image to maintain, you know,' she answered huskily. 'Can't have the doctor think I'm one of those *strange* showbiz types.'

'Heaven forbid!' he said, giving her an odd look. 'I had heard that you didn't mix much with your fellow entertainers. In fact, it seems that you're considered somewhat of an oddity yourself by your peers.'

Ilona was stunned. She knew that many people in her profession considered her a little standoffish, but how did Alistair know that? It wasn't common knowledge. It had never made the papers and had only just recently become known to her.

'You seem to be very well informed about my entertainment business,' she said tartly.

'It's my business to know things like that,' he replied.

'Oh? And what is your business?'

'Just this and that,' he replied—rudely, Ilona thought. 'We'll just have time for some lunch before you're due at the doctor's,' he added, changing the subject.

'I'm not really very hungry,' she said flatly.

Somehow she felt rejected, and she mentally shook herself. If he wanted to keep his business interests secret that was his prerogative. 'Anyway, I was going to call Mattie.'

'No need,' he broke in. 'I've already called her. She's away at the moment, but she'll be back later tonight. I just caught her before she left. She *was* going to cancel her plans, but, I persuaded her not to. I told her you'd be busy seeing the doctor and that tomorrow would be a better time for her to come over.'

Ilona was flabbergasted. She had been counting on Mattie's support to get her through this afternoon. In fact she had hoped that Mattie would come with her to the doctor's office, and now Alistair had taken it into his own hands to plan everything for her.

'It would have been nice if you'd allowed me to speak to her,' she complained, a cutting edge to her voice.

Alistair looked at her in surprise. 'That was hardly feasible. You were in the bath. Did you want me to come in and hand you the phone while you were scrubbing that pretty little body of yours? Or would you rather I'd called you out here so you could drip bubble bath all over the carpet?' he asked wryly. 'I must be slipping,' he added with a distinct leer. 'That, my dear, could have been *quite* interesting!'

'Oh, do behave, Alistair,' Ilona shot back at him, ignoring the lecherous look in his eyes. 'You should have known I'd want to speak to her.'

'You can chatter all you want to her tomorrow,' he said, 'she'll be here first thing in the morning. Now, stop pouting because you've had your plans upset and come on or we won't have time to eat.'

They ate a hasty snack of sandwiches and coffee in a small restuarant nearby, that appeared to Ilona to cater for the people who worked in and around the area of Alistair's flat. And it seemed he was well known there, for he spent most of the time nodding acknowledgement to the greeting from the other diners.

She glanced at the clock on the wall as they finished their coffee. 'Well, I suppose I can get a taxi from outside,' she said. 'It's time I found that doctor's office.'

'Time *we* found that doctor's office, you mean. You don't think I'd let you go by yourself do you?'

'Well, I thought you'd have business to attend to. I'm quite capable of going by myself, you know, now that I've got over the initial shock.'

Alistair rose and as he pulled out her chair, dropped a fleeting peck on the back of her neck. 'Don't argue with *me*, young lady! I'm coming with you and that's an end to it.'

Ilona smiled and brushed his cheek in a gesture of thanks as she did. A gesture that was at once both friendly and intimate. A gesture that caught the eye of a grey-haired middle-aged lady at the next table and caused her to smile, the sort of smile that made it plain she was recalling her own youth and perhaps a similar incident.

Neither Ilona nor Alistair noticed the man who was standing at the cashier's desk until he spoke, and they both spun round at the sound of his voice. 'Well, well, Alistair! I thought you were out of town—a fishing trip, I think your secretary said. Of course, I'd return from a fishing trip too, if Miss Craig were the reason.'

Alistair looked angry. 'Look, Harry, this is a personal matter,' he snapped.

'I've no doubt it is,' Harry interrupted. 'But you really didn't think you could keep something like this quiet for long, did you?' His smile was suggestive and Ilona thought Alistair might hit him.

'When I said personal, Harry, I didn't mean it the way you obviously did,' Alistair grated. 'Miss Craig is a very old personal friend. In fact, a family friend, and at the moment she'd like her privacy.'

'I'll bet she does!' Harry leered.

It was obvious to Ilona that Alistair was trying hard to keep his temper in check, by the twitch of his set jaw.

'Look, Harry,' he said very calmly, but with an undertone of anger, 'Miss Craig is here on private, personal business, and until it's resolved, I'd *personally* appreciate it if you were to leave it alone. If you do, I guarantee that I'll give you an exclusive interview next week some time. Will you do that for me?' His eyes were hard and Ilona felt he had the power to manipulate this man.

'Guaranteed?' Harry asked.

'Guaranteed!' Alistair agreed. 'But only if you keep this meeting out of that rag you call a paper.'

'That's hardly a nice way of asking,' Harry shrugged, 'but if it gets me an exclusive with you, who am I to argue?'

'Ring my secretary in the morning,' Alistair shot over his shoulder as they left, 'and she'll set it up.'

In the taxi that Alistair hailed it was obvious he was fuming. 'I didn't think Harry and his sort frequented that district,' he muttered angrily. 'I wonder what brought him out from under his rock?'

'Who is he?' Ilona asked, knowing full well what the answer would be.

'He's a reporter on one of the local papers and he supplies gossip about well-known people to one of the syndicated columns that appears nationally.'

'I should have known, I suppose,' Ilona replied. 'But I didn't think anyone would be looking for me here.'

Alistair patted her hand. 'That was a plus for him. He's been trying to interview me for weeks now, and I think he was as surprised to see you as I was to see him. Don't worry about it, I'll fix it up when I speak to him later.'

The taxi pulled up outside an old sandstone building that had a number of brass plates prominently displayed outside. Ilona put thoughts of Harry and his kind deliberately to the back of her mind to concentrate on the more important matter of the doctor. After all, she thought, if things don't go well here, I'll be finished as a singer, and people like Harry won't want to know me then.

Doctor Anderson was a surprise to Ilona when she was shown into his office. Young, she thought, for the position he held, he looked in his early thirties and his calm competent manner complemented his suave, fair good looks. His piercing china-blue eyes could twinkle with laughter too, for she noticed the tiny laugh-lines that radiated from them and gave his otherwise bland good looks character. His voice was soft, with a hint of an accent that Ilona couldn't place and found intriguing. The image of a Viking chieftain flitted through her mind, and she chided herself for being fanciful.

'Do sit down, Miss Craig, or may I call you Ilona? I see by the card you filled in for my receptionist that it *is* your real name. Sorry,' he said, seeing the look of dismay on Ilona's drawn face, 'I didn't mean to be tactless. But I've been a fan of yours for some time now, and I suppose I'm a little overawed.'

It really hadn't occurred to Ilona that someone like Doctor Anderson would fit into the fan category and could be affected by meeting someone like her. For her, doctors were somewhere between Royalty and superstars, and to find that he was human enough to behave like any normal mortal was very reassuring. It made her now want to put him at ease, and she relaxed visibly. 'That's perfectly all right,' she smiled, 'and I'd be happy if you called me Ilona. I suppose we'll be seeing a lot of each other over the next few days, so it would be nice if we were on some sort of friendly footing.' She knew she was waffling. But she couldn't stop herself and he smiled at her as if he knew exactly how she felt.

'Well, in that case,' he smiled, 'you'd better call me Ian—much more civilised, I feel, than Doctor, don't you agree?'

Ilona sighed. This was going to be much easier than she'd thought, and she felt she could trust Ian to tell her the truth, no matter how bad it might be.

She missed the satisfied look that briefly crossed the doctor's face, a look that said he had achieved his objective—the objective of getting his patient to relax and trust him. 'Now, I'll tell you what we're going to do this afternoon, and after that we'll decide between us what's the best method of approach for this particular problem.'

Ilona caught a look of surprise on Alistair's face when she finally returned to the waiting room. Ian's arm was round her waist and she was smiling confidently at him. Alistair rose, dropping the magazine he had been leafing idly through as they entered, prepared, it seemed, to take charge of a distraught Ilona. Instead, he found a laughing, relaxed girl who seemed to be flirting with the handsome doctor. His rugged face clouded and he glared at them both.

'Mr McLean, isn't it?' Ian asked calmly, extending his hand. 'Ilona has all the details and I'm sure she'll fill you in on the arrangements we've made. I'm very pleased she has someone here to see her through this. I'm sure I'll be seeing you in the next few days. If anything crops up that you would like explained, don't hesitate to call me. I'll be only too pleased to help in any way.'

Alistair, to Ilona's surprise, looked unbalanced. He shook the doctor's hand in silence, and mumbled some sort of reply to the friendly overtures, while glaring at him from under drawn eyebrows.

The atmosphere between the two men was icy and Alistair continued to glare until Ian withdrew his arm from around her waist and almost pushed her into Alistair's arms.

The silence in the taxi on their way back to Alistair's apartment was intense, broken only by the sounds of the late afternoon traffic. Ilona tried to think of a way to lighten the atmosphere, but because she really didn't know what had caused Alistair's sudden change of mood, she was at a loss.

As they pulled up in front of his building, Alistair broke the silence himself. 'You certainly managed to charm the good doctor,' he snapped. 'What did you do? Turn the legendary Craig sex appeal on so he'd be eating out of your hand? You sure know when to use your stagecraft to its best advantage, don't you?'

'I don't know what you're talking about,' Ilona replied, angry and sad at his attack. She was bewildered. What on earth had brought this on? He was behaving like a jealous lover. The thought brought a smile to her pale face. She really didn't know how a jealous lover would behave. She'd never had one!

'I might have known you'd think it was funny,' Alistair grated between clenched teeth. 'From what I've read about you, you never keep a man for too long anyway. Now I'm not in the least surprised!'

They were standing on the pavement in front of the building, and their angry exchange was beginning to draw the startled attention of passersby.

'Alistair,' Ilona said, as calmly as she could, 'if you have something to say, it would be better if you saved it till we get inside. People are beginning to stare.'

'We can't have that now, can we?' he snarled. 'It might get into the papers and ruin the image!'

A withering glare was all that she could manage before she stormed off into the building. She was speechless. At no time had he given her any indication that his feelings were more than just platonic, and now he was behaving as though he had a proprietorial interest in her. It was too much! With everything else she had on her mind, she was in no position at the moment to deal with an emotional problem like this. It was just as well that she'd be out of his way and he'd have no reason to get upset with her.

He caught up with her at the lift and stood silent and brooding beside her. His arm went around her waist as he guided her into the lift, and as the doors closed on them he pulled her into his arms to kiss her with an intensity that took her breath away. His lips were hard and fiery, burning and bruising, his arms steely hard, moulding her to him so that she felt his long, hard frame along the full length of her body.

She tried to resist, angry at his audacity, afraid of the passion that his lips portrayed, aware that he was fully aroused, confused by the uncalled-for reaction of her own emotions. Her lips parted, partly by the force of his, and partly of their own volition, and as they did, his lips became gentle, savouring the sweetness and femininity of her soft moist mouth.

His lips left hers, to trail lazily, sensually across her cheeks till she could feel his hot passionate breath in her ear. His tongue traced the shell-like curve, sending ripples of pounding desire through her whole being. Her heart raced and pounded to the rhythm of a phantom band, and she felt instinctively that she now knew the meaning of the songs of love that she had sung before. They weren't sweet and soft as she had always imagined. No, love songs had a hidden, passionate, driving rhythm that only someone who had been kissed like this could understand.

She broke away, breathless and hot, as the lift doors opened and gazed into his stormy black eyes. 'What did you do that for?' she asked, turning from his sardonic stare to hurry to the relative safety of the apartment's living area.

'Why not?' his deep, throaty voice came from behind her. 'Since you seem to be dispensing your favours freely today, I thought I might as well find out what it is you have that can keep the men panting around you.'

She turned to see him leaning lazily against the wall watching her intently. 'You, you. . . .' She was lost for words. He could he treat her like this? How could think she was like that? What gave him the right, with just one kiss, to send her heart spinning into a spiral of hope and despair?

'I don't know why you're carrying on like that,' he said silkily. 'It was fairly obvious that was what you were after, and you can hardly say you didn't enjoy it.' He moved then, smoothly and like a panther towards her. 'How about an encore? I certainly enjoyed it. In fact, I could say that with a little more practice, we could be very good together.'

'How dare you!' Ilona fumed. Her voice deep and husky. 'How dare you treat me like some *thing*? I'm not something to be used by you or anyone else,' she cried, absently stroking her throat, more to soothe the lump that threatened to well up and make her cry than to alleviate any pain.

Alistair's eyes travelled to her hand and his eyes softened. 'Is your throat playing up again?' he asked softly.

Ilona looked at him in amazement. How could he suddenly become solicitous of her wellbeing after what he'd just said and done? 'Of course it's sore! What did you expect? That the McLean treatment for female patients would be a miracle cure?' She hated herself immediately she had said it. But he deserved it! And she wouldn't take it back. She couldn't. She would never let him know that something that meant so little to him had affected her so profoundly.

'I deserved that,' he said, subdued. 'I really don't know what came over me.' He smiled, a slow, bashful grin that tore at Ilona's heartstrings and began the pounding in her veins once more. 'If I say I'm truly sorry and that I have no excuse other than that I was worried about you, will you forgive me?'

Ilona wasn't convinced that he was sorry and she felt in her heart that he was humouring her. But she couldn't bring herself to refuse him and she didn't really want to be angry with him. All she wanted, or so she kept telling herself, was for them to be as they had been before. She refused to accept that what she really wanted was for Alistair to kiss her again just as he had in the lift and to take her to the same giddy heights and beyond. But she stifled the thought and smiled. 'All right,' she said. 'If you promise not to let that happen again.'

His grin was infectious and they both laughed in unison. 'Of course I won't let it *happen* again. Next time it will be well and truly planned!'

'Alistair!' she laughed, not taking him seriously. But her heartbeat quickened at the look in his eyes.

'Now, young lady,' he said, as they sat down to a cup of coffee a few minutes later, 'you'd better tell me what the charming Doctor Anderson had to say. I seems that the main reason for your trip this afternoon got sidetracked somewhat.'

Ilona looked at him carefully to see if he was angry again. Somehow she felt that he disliked her doctor, but he seemed only to be keeping things in a light vein. 'I'm glad you think he's charming,' she replied, unable to stop herself from teasing him. 'I think he is too—very charming. In fact I think he's rather dishy.' She watched his eyes cloud and smiled to herself when she saw him deliberately control himself. So he's a bit jealous, she thought. And her heart sang.

'Never mind how charming he is,' said Alistair, his voice dark with restraint. 'Just tell me what he said.'

'He took some tests, to see if the growth is malignant. . . .'

'So it could be?' Alistair broke in, his voice full of obvious concern.

'He doesn't think so, but he wanted to leave nothing to chance. He said he'd have those results by tomorrow before he operates to slice it off.'

'When does he plan to do that?' Alistair's tone was worried.

'The day after tomorrow. But he wants me to go into hospital tomorrow, so that the anaesthetist can look at me before the op. And he also wants to organise some sort of pathology testing during the operation, something called a frozen section. It seems that they can find out while I'm still in theatre whether it's malignant or not, and if it is they can go further if necessary.'

'I thought you said that he'd know tomorrow before the operation from the test he took today.'

'Well, it seems that the swab he took today would confirm a malignancy if it is one. But it wouldn't necessarily be positive. Although Ian said. . . .'

'On very friendly terms with him, aren't you? Ian, even!' Alistair got up to refill the coffee cups and Ilona couldn't see his expression.

'He's very nice and I trust him,' she threw at his retreating figure. 'Anyway,' she continued, '*Ian* said that he's seen quite a few cases similar to this and that none of them were malignant. But he doesn't want to take any chances. So he'll have one of these frozen section things done just in case.'

'You don't seem to be too worried now,' Alistair commented, putting her refilled coffee cup in front of her.

'No, he showed me all the stuff in books about it and explained what was going to happen. But most of all, he emphasised what would happen if it goes untreated. So it seemed to me that I have no alternative.'

Alistair raised his eyebrows. 'What do you mean, no alternative?'

'Well, if I don't have this done the chances of my ever singing again are zero. . . .' Ilona's voice trailed off.

'And if you have it done?' It hardly seemed necessary for him to verbalise the question.

'He doesn't know. He's never had a case where the patient was a singer before.'

Alistair broke in before she could finish. 'And you're just going to let him chop your throat around without knowing the outcome?'

'If you'd let me finish. Another reason he wants me to go into hospital tomorrow is that he's going to get in touch with a couple of other specialists overseas who've had some experience with things like this to see if he can find out all that sort of thing. He's even suggested that he send me to one of them if it looks as though they could save my voice. But we won't know for sure until tomorrow.'

'Well, I'll give him one thing,' Alistair said softly, 'he's certainly got you into a much better frame of mind about all this than you were yesterday.'

'He showed me that having something done is inevitable and I might as well accept it. Now, if it's all right with you, I'd like to ring Sydney and speak to Simon. He's going to have to cancel engagements and things for me.'

'Go ahead. Phone's on the desk.'

As Ilona dialled the Sydney number of her manager's office, she watched Alistair clear away the coffee cups and surreptitiously admired the hard, masculine lines of his body, and her own body ached to feel it pressed against her once more.

CHAPTER FOUR

ILONA put the telephone receiver into its cradle with a thoughtful expression on her face. 'Alistair,' she called, 'Simon's already here in Adelaide. He got here yesterday. Apparently something has come up about a recording contract with another recording company and his secretary said he wants to see me as soon as possible. He left a message with her in case I called, for me to ring him at his hotel.'

Alistair appeared from the kitchen to give her an enquiring look. 'If you think it's *that* important, ring him now.'

'Yes, I will,' she replied, picking up the phone and dialling the number she had jotted down on the pad beside it. 'Mr Cantrell's room, please.' Her face lit up with pleasure when she heard the familiar voice of her manager and friend. 'Simon! Seems you've been looking for me!' she laughed into the phone. 'Now, don't say that. You know I told you where to find me if it was important. No, no, not now, something much more vital's come up. We can talk about it when I see you. If he can make it, I'll bring a friend. Yes, a *man* friend!' Her laugh rang out full-throated, for the first time in days, and Alistair frowned, concerned.

'You'll just have to wait till tonight to decide. If he comes, that is! See you later. 'Bye, Simon.' With that she replaced the receiver and turned smiling to Alistair.

'That all sounded very cryptic,' he commented drily.

'Not really! He's just invited me to dinner at the Ayers House. Well, us really, if you'd like to go.'

Alistair frowned again. 'I had planned to take you to dinner myself, but I suppose this will have to take precedence over pure pleasure.'

'Don't be like that, Alistair, please. You'll like Simon. Apart from being a very shrewd business-man, he's really very good fun.'

'Well, I suppose I can cope with an old love as well as a new one in one day. I must say you're a glutton for punishment. How do you manage to keep them all sorted out?'

Mirth bubbled over and Ilona giggled un-controllably.

'What's so funny?' Alistair demanded.

'Nothing . . . nothing.' But to his annoyance, she continued to giggle without telling him why.

She dressed with care for dinner. Wearing the only suitable dress she had brought with her, she found she had to rely more on careful and skilled make-up to highlight her brilliant green eyes than on her dress. For she had only packed a very plain though elegant black jersey sheath. Cut high at the front but low and cowled to the waist at the back, it really needed some sort of ornament to lift it, but she hadn't felt it necessary to pack any jewellery, and now she was forced to make the best of things.

She piled her long honey-coloured hair loosely on top of her head, leaving the smooth column of her neck bare.

She carefully disguised the dark smudges of

worry that had begun to appear beneath her eyes and smoothed slightly more blusher than she would normally use across her high sculptured cheekbones to give her more colour. Her eyelids she coloured with a soft matte-silver powder that made her eyes shine greener than normal and glossed her lips with a deep rose lip-gloss. Many blondes would not have been able to wear that particular colour, but somehow Ilona's skin tanned a soft molten-honey shade that, with her green eyes, called out for bright-coloured lips.

Satisfied, she picked up her clutch purse and went to the kitchen to get a cool drink while she waited for Alistair to appear. He was already dressed, looking almost dashing in a raw-silk suit in oatmeal tones. His shirt was open at the neck where a zodiac disc of heavy gold hung on a very masculine chain. He smiled in appreciation at the sight of her. 'Black is definitely your colour,' he commented, raising his glass in mock salute. 'Like a drink before we go? We've got time.'

'Mmm, love one! Something long and cool, please.'

Alistair turned to prepare her drink. 'Does this Simon character organise your publicity along with everything else?' he asked drily.

Ilona's green eyes widened and her delicately plucked brows lifted. 'Yes, I suppose you could say that.'

'That's not exactly a direct answer. Don't you know?'

'Of course I know. But it depends on what it's about. If it's a concert he has very little to do with it—the people organising the concert do that. If it's a record, then the record company controls the publicity. He usually deals with the publicity for personal appearances. But he does have the final word on things. A sort of veto, you might say.'

'I see. . . . You mean he decides whether the sort of publicity others are arranging will be good for the image?'

'You could say that. I've never had any worries about that sort of thing. Simon always makes sure it's in good taste.' Ilona sipped the drink he handed her.

She couldn't see where the conversation was taking them. But she was prepared to let him continue to question her about the details of her career if it meant they could keep this amiable mood going.

'Do you know why he's in Adelaide?' he asked.

'Not really. He said before he left Sydney that he would be over here some time soon to deal with some business. But it seems that the business came up quicker than he'd anticipated. Why do you ask?'

'No reason really. I just wondered how much you really know about the business side of your career. Not much, it seems!' Ilona looked at him sharply. His tone somehow was smug, as if it suited him for her to be kept in ignorance. But she shrugged it off as fanciful.

Alistair glanced at his watch. 'Time we were going. I hope that tonight's little dinner party isn't one of your faithful Simon's publicity stunts. I don't want my name in the papers. Nothing personal, you understand,' he gave her a mocking grin. 'I just like my privacy.'

'I'm sure,' Ilona told him, as they entered the

lift, 'that Simon would have warned me if there were going to be anything like that. Of course one can't always avoid being recognised in public,' she added slyly, watching his face intently.

'I suppose not,' he replied, his face setting into deep thought.

The evening was warm and Alistair had chosen to take his own car instead of a taxi. Ilona settled down into the plush seat and happily watched the bright city lights as he carefully navigated the evening traffic. They said very little on the way to the restaurant, but she was pleased that the silence was not a heavy one and she felt that they had put that afternoon's incident into the background. Although they still hadn't been able to return to the easy familiarity of the days spent at the shack, the electric crackle of the afternoon was gone and just a faint trace of a tingle was left. Ilona felt it most when he touched her, however fleeting the touch, and she wondered, indeed hoped, that he felt it too.

She studied him surreptitiously as he drove. His face set in concentration. He really was a handsome devil, she smiled to herself. Not the classic handsomeness of a Greek statue, more the unorthodox ruggedness that was appreciated in Australia. It was really, she mused, more a feeling than a look, a feeling that the beholder sensed, a feeling that the man could take all the worst that this rugged, barbaric country could throw at him, cyclones, floods and droughts, and singlehandedly conquer, yet still have a softness about the eyes that bespoke tenderness and a gentleness with anything weaker.

Alistair had them all, with something else that

had been missing with other men she had met over the years, some of whom had been extremely attractive and in some cases would have been considered better looking than Alistair. But she had felt that something had been missing. She had never known quite what it was, but she had always known she had seen it before. Where, she could never remember, and she had sometimes thought it was something to do with her dead father. She had often wondered if she had been searching for someone to take his place. She knew better. What she had been searching for was that look of determination that Alistair had—a look that said he knew what he wanted from life and knew exactly how to get it, a look that sometimes said, 'Get out of my way or I'll run right over you', yet hid a tenderness that could be touched and hurt by people he cared for.

She had seen it years before, but childishly hadn't recognised it, and she hugged the knowledge close to her like a prized possession.

Alistair helped her from the car and they entered the restaurant only a couple of minutes later, and Ilona immediately began to search amongst the other diners to find Simon. She spotted him seated in a dimly lit corner with a rather attractive redhead, and wondered who it was.

'There they are,' she said, pointing them out to Alistair. 'I wonder who that is with him?'

Alistair looked surprised and Ilona laughed, imagining that his surprise was due to Simon. For Simon was a middle-aged man, short and rotund with hardly any hair, with a jolly happy face that belied his shrewd business brain. He was adept at using his innocuous looks to achieve an advantage in his dealings with people who claimed to be good at bargaining, and many of them were surprised at the end of negotiations to find that the amiable little man had outfoxed them without their being aware of it.

Alistair paused, as if unsure whether to go in. 'Loney,' he said softly, turning her to face him so that he could speak to her in an undertone, 'I've forgotten to make an important phone call. Would you mind going over by yourself and I'll join you in a few minutes?'

Ilona smiled. 'No, that's fine. I can keep Simon guessing about you a little longer that way. He's not used to me bringing a man friend along anywhere and I know he's dying of curiosity, so I can keep him in suspense a little longer.' She smiled, savouring the teasing she would be able to give her friend and manager, and missed the little sigh of relief that escaped from Alistair's set lips.

'I won't be long,' he murmured, and hurried off.

Ilona made her way over to the table and Simon spotted her, giving her a friendly wave as she approached. 'Where's your boy-friend?' he asked, rising to draw out her chair. 'Don't tell me he's decided not come. Too shy?' The question was followed by a hearty laugh and Ilona joined in. Simon was always laughing, and that was one thing Ilona liked so much about him. No matter what the problem, he could always find something to laugh about.

'He's here,' she replied happily. 'He's just had to make a phone call.'

'Good,' Simon smiled. 'Want a drink while we're waiting? Oh, sorry,' he added hastily, 'naughty of me. Ilona, this is the lovely and talented Megan Reynolds. Miss Reynolds is the publicity director for Fame records. She's been trying to entice us to sign with them.'

Ilona looked at the redhead—a classic redhead with the thick creamy skin that only a few redheads are blessed with, and a slight scattering of freckles across her shapely nose that bespoke a love of sunshine. 'How do you do, Miss Reynolds?' she said, her voice sure and in command. For this was business, and Ilona had automatically reverted to the role she played in her working life.

Megan Reynolds smiled, a dazzling smile that lit up her grey eyes. 'I'm so pleased to meet you. We've been trying to arrange for a meeting like this for some time now, but you're a very hard lady to pin down.'

'Only when I want to be. Or should I say when Simon wants me to be?' There was no warmth in Ilona's smile; she had become wary. This was business, and she couldn't afford to let her feelings intrude. She couldn't afford, just now, to let the feeling of friendship that sprang from Megan take over, in case it would affect any bargaining that might ensue from the meeting.

A waiter approached and unobtrusively whispered into Megan's ear. 'You'll have to excuse me for a moment,' she said, as the waiter left. 'It seems that someone is trying to contact me and it's important. Do excuse me.' Gracefully she rose and left them, wending her way across the room to the appreciative stares of some of the male diners.

Simon watched her go, before turning to Ilona with a blank expression on his face that she knew from past experience meant he was mulling something over. 'Seems both our companions can't be kept away from their respective business even to have a friendly dinner.'

'You could hardly call this a friendly dinner for Megan, you old shark,' Ilona told him humorously. 'You known darned well that this is the first step in your campaign to get the best of Miss Reynolds. That is of course if she has a proposition that meets with your approval.'

'Now, now, Ilona! You know I'm always perfectly fair in *all* my dealings! But of course it would depend on the *proposition* where the lovely Megan is concerned,' Simon laughed.

'Simon, you old devil!' Ilona teased. 'You just behave yourself or I'll tell Ruth all about your carryings on!'

They both laughed happily, Ilona knew that Simon was devoted to his wife, Ruth. Married for twenty years, they were as devoted as when they had first married. Although they were childless there always seemed to be a continual string of children passing through the comfortable terrace house they owned in Paddington, Sydney. Ruth was the epitome of the mother image, and although disappointed that she could never have her own, she lavished her maternal feelings on the children of her many friends and relatives, always, it seemed, to have one or two with her for holidays or during family crises. The welfare department even used her on occasions to take children of complete strangers in emergencies.

All the children loved both Ruth and Simon and one or two who had been helped at some time in the past still found time to visit them, bringing their families and babies to be petted and spoiled and generally loved as they had been.

'My, my,' Simon broke into Ilona's reflections, 'seems Megan has found a friend!'

Ilona looked up. 'Goodness, that's Alistair,' she said, in surprise, as she watched the two wend their way though the tables to their own. She saw Simon's eyebrows raised in an unspoken question, but said nothing. But her heart leapt at the sight of the two who came towards her. It was obvious that they knew one another well. But how well?

'Ilona,' said Alistair, as he and Megan approached, 'it seems that Simon's dinner partner is an acquaintance of mine.'

'So I see,' Ilona said blandly. 'You haven't met Simon yet. Alistair, this is Simon Cantrell. Simon, a friend of mine, Alistair McLean.'

The two men shook hands and Ilona watched their faces. Alistair's face was guarded and Simon's closed. Their reaction to one another surprised her. She had thought that they would get on well together, but something was making them react badly to one another, and she didn't know what.

Surely it wasn't the remark Alistair had made about Simon being an old lover? He must realise now that there was nothing like that between them. But what was causing that strange look from Simon? Could Simon be worried that there was more to her relationship with Alistair than there was? But that wouldn't be a problem. Simon would be happy for her if there was. He and Ruth had always said that she needed to fall in love, that she'd never really know what life was all about until she did.

She looked at them both again. Perhaps she was just imagining things. They seemed to be talking fairly amicably now. Come on now, she told herself, stop seeing things that aren't there. She gave herself a mental shake and smiled at her table companions. 'How about ordering now?' she said. 'I'm starving, and I'm sure Megan won't mind talking business over dinner. Will you, Megan?'

Megan flushed slightly. 'I was hoping you wouldn't say anything about that, as a matter of fact. You see, Simon told me just before you arrived that he hadn't had time to discuss it with you yet, and that puts me in a bit of a spot. I'd really planned just to talk to him at this stage and then meet with you later. I hadn't really expected to see you tonight.'

The waiter handed them the menus and Ilona took the opportunity to mull this over behind hers. For a businesswomen it seemed pretty lame. In her position, Ilona would have felt that she were killing two birds with one stone.

'I wouldn't worry too much about that if you both just give me some idea of what's involved,' she said. 'I can listen in and give you my thoughts on things. We should be that much further advanced by the end of this evening. It will save a deal of time. Don't you think so, Alistair?' she asked, hoping to make him feel involved.

'I pass,' he said grimly. 'I'm just here to see that you get home safely.'

Ilona was stunned. What was going on? There was an undercurrent at the table that she couldn't fathom. Everyone was studiously avoiding each other's eyes, and she felt like an outsider breaking into a private conversation.

Simon was the one to break the tension. 'I think we should just forget business for tonight and have a nice dinner,' he said, looking directly at Ilona. 'After all, we shouldn't expect Megan to talk business with an outsider present, even if she does know him. Sorry, Alistair,' he added, smiling in Alistair's direction. 'We'll just have to make arrangements for the three of us to get together tomorrow some time and sort things out then.'

The waiter brought their entrees and it was a few moments before Ilona could drop her bombshell. 'Sorry, Simon, tomorrow is out of the question. I'm afraid I'm going into hospital.'

Simon was stunned. His mouth gaped like a fish out of water and he spluttered as something went down the wrong way. 'You're going *where*?' he gasped.

'To hospital, Simon dear. That throat problem of mine is a little more serious than I led you to believe, I'm afraid,' Ilona said, rather too calmly.

Simon put down his fork and looked hard at her. 'You'd better tell me all about this. It's going to make a few problems, by the look of things.'

Alistair broke into the conversation, much to Simon's impatient disgust, and Ilona was shocked at the look Simon gave him. 'I think it would be a good idea if I took Megan to the bar for a while and let you two sort things out on your own. I'll just tell the waiter to hold the rest of the dinner for a while. Come along, Megan,' he commanded imperiously, helping her out of her chair. 'Just let us know when you're finished, won't you,' he added, brushing Ilona's shoulder as he passed.

She reached up and touched his hand in thanks, pleased that he had taken control of the situation and come up with such a sensible solution. It had never occurred to her when she spoke to Simon earlier that there would be any problems talking business over dinner. But then she hadn't expected anyone else to be there, and she certainly hadn't expected the antipathy that would spring up between the two men who were now the most important people in her life. Apart from Mattie, that was. But then Mattie held a place in her life that was unique and no *man* could ever affect.

'Now, Ilona,' Simon broke into her musings, 'you'd better tell me what this is all about.'

'It's simple really, love,' Ilona told him, patting reassuringly at his outstretched hand. 'Alistair made me see a doctor and it seems I have some sort of growth on my vocal chords. If it isn't removed I'll end up not being able to sing at all.'

'And if it is?' The question almost went without asking.

Ilona lifted her shoulders in a delicate shrug. 'Who knows?'

Simon's eyes widened. 'You don't seem too concerned,' he said, amazed.

'At this stage,' Ilona replied, her voice resigned, 'there hardly seems to be much I can do, so I've decided to just take it as it comes. Tomorrow we may know a great deal more. Dr

Anderson is doing some research today and hopes to be able to tell me my chances then. We'll just have to wait and see . . .'

'There doesn't seem to be anything else we can do. Still, I must say I'm relieved that you've taken the trouble to get help now. It could have been a great deal worse. And if the worst comes to the worst . . .' Simon broke off. 'I didn't mean it to come out like that, Ilona. I just hope that everything works out. But in the meantime I'll just cancel everything till further notice. It really won't be worth talking to Megan now, will it?'

Ilona knew that Simon had her best interests at heart and that his coldblooded-sounding words were more shock than anything and they didn't worry her, for he was a friend and no matter the outcome, she knew she could rely on him and Ruth to stand by her. 'Don't worry about things just now. Wait until I've seen Dr Anderson tomorrow. Then we can make any decisions that need to be made.'

'By the way,' Simon asked, 'how did Alistair get involved in all this?'

'Oh, I'm sorry,' Ilona explained, 'I thought you realised. Alistair is Mattie's son. I was using his fishing shack and he came down unexpectedly. It was a nice surprise after all these years.'

Simon's eyes clouded. 'Yes,' he mused, 'it must have been . . . quite a surprise!'

Ilona was too wrapped up in her own thoughts to catch the edge in his voice and she sipped her wine before asking, 'What exactly was this deal with Megan? Not that it's likely to come to anything at the moment, I suppose. But I'm still interested to know.'

'Well, you know that your contract with the record company expires soon. It seems that Fame records somehow got wind of it and want you to sign with them.'

'I thought Fame was just about out of business?' Ilona asked.

'It was. But it's been bought by a wealthy type who's trying to diversify and, I might add, prefers to remain anonymous. It seems that he has a new direction for the company to go and is prepared to back his own judgment with cold hard cash,' Simon explained.

Ilona's face lit up with interest. This was her business and she loved every facet of it. She loved the wheeling and dealing almost as much as she loved to sing and could listen for hours while Simon explained the behind-the-scenes manoeuvrings that went on. 'He must have a pretty high opinion of his theory to back it under the present economic conditions.'

'Well, basically,' Simon expanded, 'that's exactly what his theory is based on—present economic conditions. You see, with unemployment highest amongst the young, which is the record companies' biggest market, he's decided that unless he can somehow give them what they want at a price they can afford, then the record companies will fold completely, and that will ultimately affect the performers.'

Ilona was all ears. 'That sounds fine, in theory. But how does he hope to achieve it?'

'Two ways. One, cost-cutting, obviously. And that means moving out of the major cities to less expensive recording studios, ones that aren't getting the work and will *therefore* charge less. Here . . .'

'Here?' Ilona queried.

'Yes, here,' Simon continued. 'They have the best recording facilities in Australia right here in Adelaide.'

'What's number two?' she asked.

Simon's eyes lit up and Ilona knew the look well. This obviously had appealed to him and he had decided that it was good business for all concerned. 'Two is not putting out long-plays with just one artist.'

'What do you mean?' Ilona broke in, giving Simon time to gulp his wine.

'It's really very simple. The youngsters won't be able to buy one album of all the artists they like, so he plans to give them composites—two, three, maybe four well-known artists on each album. In some cases, albums made up of a variety of artists, each with one number per album. What it basically amounts to is that you, for example, would record the same number of songs over a one-year period as you would for the two or three albums a year that you're doing now, but they would be distributed between maybe twenty. Just think, Ilona, that would mean that you would be getting that much more exposure. I think it's a terrific idea. And the kids would be getting what they want.'

'It does sound good. But how does he know it will work?'

'The man's not just a financier, it seems. He's taken the trouble to get a market research team on the job and they've had questionnaires out to thousands of record shops around the country trying to find out what the customers think. If the results that Megan has shown me are anything to go by it's going to be a winner.' Simon sat back, beaming. Then his face dropped. 'But I suppose we can hardly consider Fame's offer at this stage, can we?'

'No, we certainly can't,' Ilona's face was thoughtful. 'Still, if everything goes well with this operation we could.'

'Well, I guess we'll just have to wait and see. Won't we?' Simon was obviously disappointed, and she couldn't help feeling sorry for him. He'd worked so hard over the years to help establish her as a name in the entertainment business, and now to be faced with the prospect of everything he'd, they'd, worked for disappearing overnight must be a daunting prospect. She felt sorry for him. She knew that she should be feeling as he did. But the fact of what was happening to her physically and what she must undergo was still uppermost in her mind and she couldn't bear to face the future. Not yet! She just wanted to live in the present until she knew the outcome.

But somehow she needed to help Simon overcome his distress. No amount of words, she knew, would help. But actions could. And a thought entered her mind that might possibly, just possibly, do the trick.

'Simon, do you remember those tapes I made earlier this year? The ones that we were going to use on the last album but didn't. Do we own the rights to them or does the company?'

Simon's eyes lit up. He didn't need to be told what was going through her mind. 'We do,' he said triumphantly.

'Well then,' she said happily, 'it seems we

might just have something to offer Fame records now, after all. There must be ten or a dozen numbers on those tapes that we've never used.'

'Ten or a dozen at least,' Simon crowed. 'That could give us about six months' breathing space if Fame are prepared to take a chance. And somehow,' he grinned, 'I think I can persuade them that it will be a chance worth taking. It seems, my dear, devious little songbird, that I've trained you well. It should have been me that thought of that.'

'Never mind who thought of it,' Ilona beamed. 'Just be thankful someone did, and get in there and do your stuff!'

CHAPTER FIVE

APART from a feeling that Megan and Alistair knew each other better than they were prepared to admit, that niggled at the back of Ilona's mind and made her feel uneasy, the evening turned out to be a mild success.

Simon insisted that no more business was to be discussed when they returned to the table, and the conversation was general, with Simon imparting his zany sense of fun to things and keeping the atmosphere light. It was Alistair who insisted on breaking things up early, with the comment that it would be a big day tomorrow for Ilona and she really should have an early night.

The drive back to the apartment was completed almost in silence. But it was the silence of easy friendship, and the feeling of unease that had worried Ilona all evening was missing. She replayed the evening in her mind and decided that what she had found incongruous in everyone's behaviour had really just been her imagination. She put it down to being emotionally on edge about tomorrow and mentally called herself a fool for even thinking that Simon and Alistair could be keeping something from her. That was the phrase she'd been looking for all night! It had felt that everyone had been keeping something from her. But now, on reflection, it was all in her mind. Or was it?

Even though she could rationalise her feelings

about Simon and Alistair, nothing, she told herself, could bring her to accept that the beautiful redhead Megan had been completely honest. But then why should she be? After all, she was a business woman and surely she had every reason to withhold information that would put her proposition in a bad light. That must be it, Ilona decided. That feeling had to be something to do with Megan's proposition, and she would have to make Simon check it out more fully before they committed themselves.

Alistair turned to smile at her as they pulled into the underground car park, and her heart leapt. Things were going too fast for her. In that moment she realised that she had fallen in love!— irretrievably, irrevocably in love with this man who had suddenly reappeared in her life at such a time. A time when she could well do without this sort of emotional upheaval. Could that be what had made her so wary of Megan Reynolds? Was it jealousy? Megan was certainly a woman to be afraid of, beautiful, intelligent, and Alistair knew her—knew her better than he had let everyone think, Ilona was sure of that. All the uneasy feelings returned and all her rationalisations went out of the window and she frowned as they stepped out of the lift into the apartment that she had become so fond of.

'Coffee?' Alistair asked as they entered.

'Yes, I'd like that,' she replied. 'But let me make it.'

'No, I'll do it. You find some music, then sit down and relax. I won't be long.' He disappeared into the kitchen.

Ilona went to the stereo to see how it operated

and began to sort through the records that were carefully stored in racks on shelves beside it. One rack, she found to her surprise, consisted of almost every record she had ever made, even down to the first single, and she smiled happily to herself. So he hadn't forgotten her over the years. She chose a Frank Sinatra record and put it on, and the mellow tones of the master flooded the apartment.

'Did you and Simon get your business sorted out?' Alistair's voice was muffled as it drifted to her from the kitchen.

Ilona glanced up and saw him appear with a tray. 'Sort of. There are a few things that still have to be sorted out.'

'It seems a shame that you couldn't fix everything up tonight,' he mused, sitting down and pouring the coffee. 'You aren't going to get much time in the next few days.'

'That's true,' she replied slowly, wondering whether Simon would be able to sort everything out without her. The last thing she would need would be for Simon to be bringing business problems to the hospital.

She glanced at him from under her lashes and was surprised to see that he was concerned.

That's nice of him, she thought, to be *worried* about things like that.

'I think Simon can cope,' she reassured him. 'We've got a plan up our sleeves. It will just depend if the new owner of Fame Records is prepared to take a bit of a chance.'

'Oh!' It was the expression of someone fishing for more information, and Ilona was surprised. Alistair had shown no interest over dinner, why should he be interested now? He's probably just trying to talk about something I'm interested in, she mused. It shouldn't do any harm to tell him, after all, he'll know that it isn't something to be bandied about.

'Well . . .' she began hesitantly. Then Alistair's crooked grin made her heart turn over and she plunged on unable to keep anything from him. 'You see, we've got quite a few songs on tape that have never been released and they belong to us, not the record company. Simon thinks that if Fame is prepared to use them, instead of me live, it would give me at least six months before we'd run out of material. Perhaps even a year.'

'What about concerts?' asked Alistair, turning to pour out more coffee so that she missed the look in his eyes.

Ilona smiled. 'We hadn't planned any for the next few months anyway, and Simon has managed to cancel the couple of guest spots I had coming up in the next week or so, so there are no problems there.'

'Don't you plan to tell anyone about your throat problem?' he asked quietly.

Ilona shrugged. 'If it's bad news, I suppose we'll have to. But if the doctors think things will get back to normal, we thought we'd keep it quiet until we know for sure what's happening. And if Fame accept our proposition, I can't see why we can't. Can you?'

'I suppose not.' Alistair's voice was thoughtful. 'How will Fame be able to use tapes?' he asked.

'That's no problem really, they'll just have to do a bit of technical stuff with the background to make it commercial, and if they have good enough people it shouldn't cause any problems. It's done all the time.'

She thought Alistair looked smug, but she pushed the thought aside hastily. You're letting the feelings that you had over dinner cloud your judgment, she told herself sharply.

'Well,' Alistair broke into her musings, 'it looks as though you and Simon have thought of everything. Now we'll just have to hope that things go the way you want tomorrow.'

'Yes, we will, won't we,' Ilona replied quietly, happy that he had included himself in her plans.

The music stopped and the silence was stark for a moment. She rose and went to the stereo, turning the record over, then she returned to the living area and sat on the floor at his feet.

'Don't you like chairs?' he laughed.

Ilona looked up at him through her lashes. 'I love listening to music like this—I always have. Don't ask me why, I don't know. It just seems right somehow.'

'It certainly seems right at this moment,' he answered, stroking her head gently.

She leaned back and felt him remove the pins that held her hair. She shook her head to let it tumble down in a molten flood when the last pin had been removed. 'That's nice. Do you do that for all your girls?'

'Not for girls,' his voice was husky. 'Only for women. And then only for women with honey-coloured hair and green eyes—and you know there aren't many of them about.'

Ilona's voice caught in her throat. There wasn't anything to say. If she did, she would break the mood, and that was the last thing she wanted to do.

This feeling of closeness was what she had always dreamed of, and now it was happening just as she had imagined, she didn't know quite what to do. But she had no need to do anything; Alistair did it all.

Fluidly he rose to his feet, pulling her with him, pulling her into the warm circle of his arms. His lips were close to her ear and she felt the hot breath tingling against her cheek. 'I've wondered lately what it would be like to dance with you,' he murmured, as they swayed to the music.

He pulled her closer, until she could feel his hard frame against every part of her. His hands went to her hair and he held her face away from him to look deep into her clouded eyes. 'You really have grown into something special,' he whispered, showering her eyes with tiny kisses.

His lips were hot and possessive, sending currents of electricity through her. She felt hot and flushed. An aching need to be closer flowed through her and she wound her arms around his neck, tugging gently at the crisp curls that lay on his collar. She buried her face in the crook of his neck. 'You promised me once that you'd kiss me on my sixteenth birthday,' she whispered. 'But you'd gone by then.' Her voice was plaintive. His nearness brought all the memories of that time when she had loved him to distraction flooding back. A time when every word he had uttered had the power to make her quiver, when a casual remark could send her into a tearful mood for days on end, a time when not to see him made life intolerable. That time had only lasted for a few brief months, passing quickly when he left and she grew up, taking up all the activities of a normal teenager.

'Did I really promise that?' he asked softly.

Disappointment flooded through her veins, but passed like magic when he tilted her head. 'Maybe it isn't too late to keep that promise,' he moaned, his lips covered hers.

This was different from the kiss he had almost forced on her earlier. This kiss was gentle, seeking, lingering and so very sweet. 'That was for your sixteenth. Now, I think, I've got a few more years to make up for,' he smiled into her eyes, then took control of her lips once again, this time with a passion that left her breathless.

His hands moved from her hair to trail across her shoulders and down her spine, moulding her against him and moving her body until the gentle motion made her nerve ends tingle and a cry of desire escaped. She'd never felt like this before, never felt the need to become part of another human being, never wanted to give herself to a man as she wanted to give herself to *this* man.

His lips left hers to trail across her cheeks, and a sense of loss overcame her. She wanted his lips on hers, to feel his breath mingle with hers. No one had ever made her feel like this before, and she knew instinctively that no one else ever would. Her hands moved into his hair, tugging frantically at his head to bring his mouth once more to hers.

'Greedy little green eyes,' he muttered as he took possession of her lips again and his hand moved to cover her breast, searching through the soft material of her dress for her nipple.

A contentment flowed over her. This was right. The time was right. The man was right. There was no niggling doubt, none at all. No mattter the outcome, she wanted to give herself to him now.

The music stopped, and Alistair let out a soft moan. 'Damn!' he whispered as he pushed her gently away from him. 'Mr Sinatra has a very bad sense of timing,' he laughed throatily as he strode over to switch off the stereo.

Ilona stood for a moment, unsure and bewildered. She felt abandoned. But she knew that it hadn't been deliberate, and she sat down on the armchair and took a calming sip of her brandy. Her body was still alive with mysterious feelings that she wasn't sure she could control— that she wasn't sure she wanted to control. Her lips and body felt hypersensitive, and only with Alistair's withdrawal did any doubts surface, doubts that she knew would be dissipated like snow in the sun the moment he took her in his arms again.

Her breathing returned slowly to normal and her body began to stop shaking, only to return again to its peak of tactile awareness as he moved behind her to lean over and plant a kiss on the soft vulnerable spot at the nape of her neck.

She glanced up over her shoulder and found him smiling down at his jacket mysteriously gone and his silk shirt open to the waist. The heavy gold zodiac disc glowed dully amongst the crisp red hair that curled across his muscular suntanned chest.

Catlike, he glided around her chair, to lean down both hands on the arms of the chair and kiss her lightly on the brandy-flavoured lips. His lips moved, tracing fire across her cheek to nuzzle a spot just below her ear. He stood up and looked down at her smiling, his hand outstretched. She took it instinctively and he drew her gently to her feet.

'You didn't pick that dress with seduction in mind,' he whispered in her ear, his fingers trailing across the high neckline of her dress, pushing the soft jersey away to kiss the pulse that throbbed at the base of her throat.

Ilona clung to him, her knees weak, and his lips descended to hers to plunder the softness of her mouth, hard and passionate, with an intensity that matched the hardness of his body. He picked her up effortlessly in his arms, and carried her unprotesting to his bedroom—a room that Ilona had not until this moment entered. Sightless with desire and ecstasy, she was unaware of the surroundings. She felt only his touch as he unfastened her dress, allowing it to drop from her shoulders to the floor to spread like a dark pool beside the bed.

Delicately, with the ease of practice, he unfastened her bra, drawing it from her trembling body to free her heavy tender breasts.

His lips seared across her neck and down to burn and scald across her body until tenderly they took her aching nipple as he lifted her and laid her unprotesting on the bed.

She lay trembling with an aching need she had never felt before, a need she knew he could satisfy. But with a strange feeling of apprehension. She wanted to stay, to know what it was like to be loved completely by this man. But she wanted to run too, to jump from the bed and run to some place of safety. A part of her didn't want to take the plunge into the unknown, the unknown realms of physical delight that she knew it would be with Alistair.

Her eyes flickered open as she felt the bed move with Alistair's weight and she turned towards him, groping blindly for the reassurance of his arms.

The dull, pale rosy light of sunrise woke her and she stirred restlessly, wondering where she was. Then the memory of the night before flooded back and she blushed, realising she was naked—naked in someone else's bed. Carefully she reached for the sheet to cover herself.

'No need for that, my love,' Alistair's voice came from the direction of the window. 'I've been standing here admiring you for quite a while now.'

The voice brought her to full wakefulness and she grabbed the sheet convulsively, dragging it up to her chin, her face aflame, the colour deepening as his laugh boomed out when he saw her embarrassment.

'Get out and let me get back to my own room,' she almost pleaded.

'Why? I thought you enjoyed last night,' he smiled as he moved towards the bed.

Ilona cowered beneath the sheets. Nothing in her life had prepared her for this, and she realised just how naïve she was in sexual matters. Megan, she could bet, would have no problems handling this sort of situation.

Alistair sat on the side of the bed and she huddled away from him. 'Are you frightened of me, Loney dear, or just of yourself?' he asked quietly, reaching out to stroke her arm. 'I won't hurt you.'

'How do I know you won't? How do I know you don't go round boasting about your conquests?' Tears sprang to her eyes. She really didn't think he would. But she could think of nothing else to say that might make him go so that she could come to terms with what had happened to her and what was still happening inside her head. She'd never been so confused before.

'Don't be a fool, Loney. Do you think I'm as juvenile as all that? I'm a grown man, not some teenager who has to prove he's a man. I know that last night was the first time for you—and I must admit it came as rather a shock. After all, you'd led me to believe you had some experience . . .'

'I did not!' Ilona broke in. 'You just assumed that.'

'Well, maybe I did. But you did nothing to make me believe otherwise. And do you know something, sweetheart?' Ilona's heart leapt at the endearment. 'I was flattered that you chose me. More than flattered, really,' he added. 'I think proud would be more the word. But that doesn't really explain it either.' He leant over, gently turned her face towards him and kissed her. 'Let's just say that we both had a unique experience last night, one so precious that I want to keep it as our secret until we know if it will build into anything more.'

Ilona heard the words, but they didn't really register, for his lips were taking her back to the heights of pleasure that she had known the night before and her body was responding in a way she couldn't control. She turned towards him and wrapped her arms around his neck, letting her body respond to the tantalising tingle of his skin.

CHAPTER SIX

TIME had slipped away from Ilona and Alistair in the huge king-sized bed, and now they were both in a hurry. Mattie was due any time now and there was so much to be done before Ilona had to present herself at the hospital. But no matter how hard she tried, she could not seem to bring herself back to the present. Her mind kept returning to the feel of Alistair's lips and the satiny smoothness of his skin.

As she dressed and smoothed the skirt of her dress over her hips, she smiled, remembering how his hands felt as he undressed her. Snap out of it, she told herself, or people will think you're a fool, going round with that smug look like the cat that got the cream! She looked at herself in the mirror and smiled at the soft contented look in her eyes and realised that her face had changed. Not dramatically, but subtly—a change that would be obvious to anyone who knew her really well, and she thanked her stars that the only ones who did were Mattie and Simon, and somehow she knew that if they did guess, they wouldn't condemn her.

The coffee was ready when Ilona stepped into the kitchen and Alistair was reading the paper over his toast. He hadn't changed, she thought as she scrutinised his face. But then why should he? This wasn't a new experience for him. Oh, she cried to herself, I wish it were! I wish it had been the first time for him too. But then it might not have been so wonderful, and she silently thanked all the women who had gone before her while resenting them at the same time.

'What would you like to eat, my love?' Alistair asked, and Ilona looked at him intently, trying to analyse his tone. I must stop this, she told herself, or I'll drive myself crazy. Accept the fact that you love him and that he doesn't love you— not now, at least. Why she was sure he didn't love her wasn't clear. But something in the back of her mind made her wary when he wasn't touching her. When he was, good sense went out the window and she determined that she would have to take a great deal of care what she said to him while she was under his spell. My God, she thought, I never knew love could be so complicated!

'Toast will be fine. I'm not really very hungry,' she said, putting bread in the toaster. 'What time's Mattie coming?'

Alistair looked up from his paper and smiled. 'Any time now, so if you don't want her to guess what you've been up to, you'd better get that look out of your eyes.'

'What look?' Ilona asked, concentrating hard on the toaster.

'The one that's changed your eyes from emerald to old jade,' he murmured, coming up behind her and encircling her with his arms.

'Alistair, no!' she gasped as his lips slid down her neck.

'No what?' he asked, turning her around to kiss her soundly. 'What a lovely way to start the day,' he murmured against her lips.

'Am I intruding?' Mattie's voice was amused. 'If you like, I'll go out and come in again.'

Alistair laughed. 'Sit down, Mother, and pour yourself a cup of coffee. Let Loney get time to stop blushing!'

Ilona crossed the kitchen in two hurried strides, to take Mattie into her arms and hide her blazing face in the older woman's shoulder.

'I'm so glad to see you,' she whispered.

'Well, I'm glad to see you too,' Mattie answered, patting her on the shoulder. 'And I'm delighted that you two are getting on so well. Not that I had any doubts about that. Now enough of this,' she said, pushing Ilona away. 'Let me have my coffee, we've got a million things to attend to before this afternoon. And you, my lad,' she said to Alistair, 'had better go and do whatever it is you do to make a living. You'll only get in the way here.'

Alistair laughed. 'Sure, Ma!'

'Enough of the Ma!' Mattie threw at him. 'Just be on your way. Ilona and I have girl talk to do and we don't want a big hulking man around eavesdropping!'

Alistair picked up his jacket from the back of a kitchen chair and pecking them both lightly on the cheek, threw a cheery, 'See you both later,' over his shoulder as he sauntered out.

Ilona didn't know what to say to Mattie and she sat over her coffee, silent. Had it been anyone else but Alistair she would have been bubbling out all her innermost feelings to the woman who had taken her mother's place. But Alistair was Mattie's son and it didn't seem right somehow to talk to his mother the way she would like to.

'You love him, don't you?' Mattie asked at last.

'Do you mind?' Ilona replied. She didn't need to confirm Mattie's question.

'Mind? Goose ... did you think I'd sent you down to the shack for the good of your health?'

'Mattie, you planned that!'

'Of course I did. It's time that great lump of a son of mine settled down and did something about presenting me with a few grandchildren. Besides, you're ready now to take the plunge, and he's loved you since you were a child. He just hasn't admitted it to himself yet.'

'He hasn't seen me for years. How could you know that he still felt anything after all this time?'

Mattie looked hard at her. 'When he's always asking if I've heard from you. When he buys every record you've ever made. When he keeps looking for girls with emerald green eyes. It wasn't hard.'

'Mattie, you're a romantic!' laughed Ilona. 'How would you know that I'd still feel the same as I did years ago? It was only a crush.'

'If you'd ever had a halfway serious romance in all the time you've been away, I might have had my doubts, but. . . . Anyway, I'm allowed to try a bit of matchmaking, aren't I? If nothing had come of it, at least I would have tried.'

'I hope Alistair never finds out what a conniving mother he has. He might just resent it, and then what would happen?'

'You aren't going to tell him, are you?'

'Of course not,' Ilona smiled.

'Well, then, there's no need for him to ever find out, is there? Now, finish your toast, we've got some shopping to do.'

Shopping with Mattie had always been a delight for Ilona, and today was no exception. Mattie seemed to know all the small out-of-the-way boutiques, which meant that they were able to bypass the major department stores and avoid recognition. Although one or two of the boutiques' staff knew her it was easier to cope with individuals than crowds, and Ilona was pleased with the success of their shopping expedition.

At Mattie's insistence, she bought a number of delightfully frivolous nighties and négligés, to keep her spirits up if she were in hospital longer than she had planned. But she refused to replace her ridiculous blue mules, grasping at them as the good luck charms they were.

Ilona suspected that Mattie's insistence on seductive bedwear had something to do with Alistair. But she was happy to go along with things and put away her rather prim pyjamas and stark dressing gown.

Mattie also insisted she restock her beauty case, making sure that she had everything she would need to keep up the 'image', as Ilona put it.

Their shopping was a happy friendly affair and Ilona was relaxed for the first time in days. But Mattie always had that effect on her. She was a relaxing type of person and seemed to know instinctively how to put people at their ease. She never questioned people, but they would tell her their troubles anyway and always found a sympathetic ear and some good down-to-earth advice.

Over coffee and cake in a small coffee lounge not far from the apartment, Ilona decided to probe Mattie about Alistair's business interests. It had become important to her to know, and whenever she had raised the matter with him he'd avoided it. Why? was the question that continued to nag at the back of her mind, and this was the only thing that she felt was spoiling their relationship.

It was a difficult subject to drop into the conversation casually, so she decided to take the bull by the horns, and when they were comfortably settled with their coffee she put the matter to Mattie directly. 'What exactly does Alistair do for a living, Mattie? He seems to be very secretive about it.'

'Oh, I wouldn't say that, love,' her friend replied. 'He just doesn't like talking about it, that's all. He's always telling me I wouldn't understand it anyway.'

'But do you?' Ilona's eyes sparkled.

'Of course I do. But I'd never tell him that. He still likes to think that women can't cope with business and should be kept behind the kitchen sink. Still,' Mattie mused, 'maybe he's changing his ideas. I've noticed lately that he seems to be doing business with a few women.'

Ilona's mind slipped back to the dinner at the Ayers House and the beautiful Megan. Although Alistair had not said he knew her Ilona was still sure that they had some thing in common and she was almost certain that it had something to do with his business. She really didn't want to believe it was anything more personal. 'What exactly does he do, Mattie?' she asked at last.

'Well, he was left the controlling interest in my brother's business when Robert died a few years ago, and he decided to take an active interest. He'd been involved with public relations for a while before that, and using his contacts and know-how from that field he built the business up to a fairly large manufacturing concern. They make components for electronic equipment now. I think he's been diversifying lately. But I must admit he's kept whatever it is very quiet.'

Ilona was surprised. 'Doesn't he tell you what he's doing?'

'I don't really see that much of him these days, he's so busy. And when I do we don't seem to get round to that sort of thing. He'll tell me when he's ready.'

Ilona sipped her coffee thoughtfully. None of what Mattie had told her explained the nagging feeling of concern that had plagued her for the past couple of days about Alistair's business interests, and she decided that she must be just imagining things.

She looked up sharply when a faintly familiar voice addressed her. 'Well, well, Miss Craig! It looks as though you have quite a few friends here in Adelaide.'

The face was familiar, but it took a few moments before she realised who it was. Harry, Alistair had called him, and he was some sort of reporter.

'I have many friends here,' Ilona snapped. She disliked him instinctively. 'Not that it's any of your business.'

'Anything you do or say is my business. You're well enough known to be news, and news is my business,' the slightly decrepit little man sneered.

'If this is the way you get your news,' Mattie broke in, 'then I don't expect you do too well.'

Harry had the grace to flush at Mattie's remark, but chose to ignore it. 'I don't suppose you'd like to comment about your relationship with Alistair McLean. Still, the old standby, "We're just good friends", would be enough. You are good friends, aren't you?'

'Don't answer that, Ilona,' Mattie said flatly. 'It's time we were leaving anyway.'

'Your friend here obviously hasn't had a great deal to do with reporters,' Harry sneered. ' "Ilona Craig refused to comment about her relationship with Alistair McLean" will make a much better story than "Just good friends!" Thanks a lot. I'll see you around, no doubt—that is unless you plan to leave town because of media harassment about your new friend.' He laughed slyly and left.

'The nerve of the man!' Mattie exploded. 'Do you have to put up with much of that sort of thing?' she asked, gathering up her bag and parcels.

'No,' Ilona replied. 'Most of the reporters are very nice. But now and again you strike one like him, and he gives the rest of them a bad name.'

The encounter with Harry had spoiled Ilona's morning and they returned to Alistair's flat in almost total silence.

To Ilona's surprise, Alistair was waiting for them, and she felt embarrassed that she'd been questioning his mother about him such a short time before. But he didn't seem to notice her abstracted manner, or if he did he must have put it down to worry over her hospitalisation, she thought.

'Had a nice time?' he asked, kissing them both on the cheek.

'Apart from a rather unsavoury run in with a newspaper man, we had a very nice time,' Mattie told him.

Alistair's face clouded. 'Was it that little weasel of a fellow who spoke to us the other day?' he asked Ilona.

'Yes, it was.'

'Damn the man! I told him to leave you alone. I'll speak to his editor. Though what good that will do. . . .'

Ilona touched his arm. 'Don't do anything, please. It could only make matters worse. They'll think there really is something we're trying to hide and keep hounding and digging until they find out about my going into hospital, and I'd rather not have anyone know about that until things have decided themselves one way or another.'

'What do you mean, something we're trying to hide?' Alistair was angry.

'He suggested that you two had what I believe is referred to as "a thing going",' Mattie laughed in an effort to lighten the mood. 'I hope you'll let me know if you have. I'd hate to find out from the papers!'

Alistair smiled wryly and Ilona looked sheepish, causing Mattie to burst into genuine laughter at their embarrassment.

'I suppose the best thing to do is just forget it,' Alistair smiled. 'Let's think about lunch instead. We should go somewhere nice before you get incarcerated in that hospital, my love.'

Mattie smiled at Alistair's endearment and the

flush that came to Ilona's cheeks when she heard it. 'I really don't think that would be such a good idea, you know,' she commented. 'You could run into that man again. Besides, I'd already planned a nice quiet lunch for the three of us here, so I suggest the two of you sit down and relax while I get busy in the kitchen.'

Ilona wandered over to the window. Somehow she felt unsure of Alistair with Mattie there and didn't know quite what to say to him. But her problem was solved for her.

'Come over and sit down here with me, darling,' Alistair called softly. 'I've missed you.'

'But it's only been a couple of hours,' she smiled, sitting beside him.

'Is that all? Seems a lot longer,' he murmured, nibbling at her ear.

'Alistair, don't do that!' she protested. 'Mattie could come in any minute.'

'She won't mind. Besides, I thought you liked it.'

'Oh, I do,' Ilona moaned as he turned her towards him to nibble at the corner of her mouth.

She melted into his arms, all doubts dissolved. Near him like this, nothing mattered, only his arms. Only him. Whatever he was, she could forgive him anything while he kissed her.

All too soon the time came for her to leave and she began to shake a little. Alistair and Mattie both noticed her agitation and tried to calm her. But nothing worked until Alistair told her he would stay with her in the hospital until she settled in. The soothing strength of his hand holding hers in the taxi they took did much to settle her nerves.

Mattie's motherliness helped too. But Ilona's fear and trepidation didn't stop completely until she was settled into her room and the deep soothing voice of Dr Anderson, almost hypnotic in its tone, began to explain all over again what they planned to do. He gave her the news that he had been in touch with his colleagues overseas and that the prognosis was good. He felt that there was no need for her to worry and that he had every hope of her getting her voice back. Although, he stressed, it might take some time.

Because he could see her agitation, he ordered a sedative, and Alistair stayed with her until it took effect and she dozed. The last thing she heard was his voice in her ear telling her to relax and that he would be back later in the evening.

Ilona woke to the clatter of dishes outside her room. The door opened and a woman in a pink uniform entered carrying a dinner tray.

'Dinner, dear. I hope you enjoy it. You're going to theatre tomorrow, aren't you?' she asked kindly. It was more a statement than a question and she went on, giving Ilona no opportunity to reply, 'So this will be the last meal you'll have for a while. You were asleep when I came before to see what you'd like, so I hope you like steak and salad. I thought that would be best.'

Ilona nodded as the little woman rambled on, setting out the tray on her bed table and adjusting it so that she could reach everything easily. 'You just press the bell, now, dear, if you would like anything else or you don't like what's here and the nurse will get me. Then I'll get you something you would like.' She bustled out smiling.

Ilona wondered if she had recognised her and that this was V.I.P. treatment, but decided that this was the way she treated all the patients and was pleased that even the kitchen staff were concerned with her wellbeing.

She really didn't feel too hungry, she decided. But the steak was delicious and the salad fresh and enticing, and she found she was hungrier than she'd thought, and she finished it all, to the delight of the domestic, who seemed very pleased when she came back for the tray. 'Well,' she said, looking at the empty plate, 'that's lovely. I'm glad you enjoyed it, dear. My name's Rose, and if there's anything you want later on, you just let me know. I'll be looking after your meals while you're in here, and if there's anything you particularly fancy I'll see what I can do. I'll see you at supper time. 'Bye for now!' And she was gone in a whirl of pink starched efficiency.

The sedative had all but worn off, but Ilona still felt relaxed and drowsy and, after her meal, much more calm. She went into the little bathroom attached to her suite and brushed her teeth, then settled back into bed with one of the books she had bought that morning.

She was surprised when Dr Anderson reappeared. She hadn't expected to see him until the next morning. But she was pleased none the less.

'How are you getting on, my dear?' he asked. 'I was just seeing another patient and I thought I'd drop in.' His tone was fatherly and comforting and Ilona wondered why he was taking that tone with her. He certainly wasn't old enough to be her father, and had things been different, she might have considered him for a much different role.

She smiled to herself at her musings and his eyes widened in an unspoken question. 'I was just thinking,' she commented, 'you're much too young to take that tone with me. Or do you always treat your patients like small children?'

To her surprise, he burst out into infectious laughter. 'Caught!' he laughed. 'I'll tell you a secret, if you promise not to tell anyone else,' he said, sitting on the edge of her bed. 'I'm really shy.'

'I'll bet!' Ilona giggled.

'I am,' he insisted, 'and "that tone", as you call it, is my way of covering it up. But if you can remember to go on calling me Ian, we'll keep things on a friendly basis. How's that?'

'Perfect, Ian.' Ilona smiled, and they both laughed as he took her hand and patted it.

'I'm sorry,' Alistair's voice interrupted, 'I didn't know the doctor was with you. I'll come back later.'

'No, that's all right, Mr McLean, I was just leaving. I'll see you tomorrow, beautiful. Bright and early,' Ian Anderson quipped, rising from the bed and waving as he left.

Ilona waved back and turned to smile at Alistair, who was standing at the bottom of the bed. His eyes were hard and flinty and his lips set in a line. ' "Beautiful"!' he scoffed sarcastically. 'Not very professional!'

'Come on, Alistair, he was just being nice, he probably treats all his patients like that.'

'If he does,' Alistair grunted, 'it certainly isn't with that particular look in his eyes!'

Ilona was astounded. He sounded jealous. She looked closely at him, wondering if he were teasing or serious and realised that he really was serious. 'Don't be silly, Alistair, Ian was only being kind.'

'So it's Ian now, is it?' Alistair said with a hard edge to his voice.

'Yes, it is,' Ilona snapped angrily. 'And if you're going to behave like some petulant teenager, I think I'd rather you left. I've got more to worry about at the moment than dealing with that sort of thing!'

Alistair stared at her in surprise. She'd never spoken to him like that before and she was pleased somehow that she had the power to break through his self-assured exterior. At that moment she caught a glimpse of the little boy that she knew had been there all along.

'I'm sorry, darling, really I am,' he apologised. 'But I'm worried about tomorrow and I suppose Dr Anderson seemed like a good person to take my frustration out on. Forgive me?' he asked with that heart-stopping, lopsided grin that always had the power to make her heart jump.

'Well, you let Ian worry about tomorrow and come here and help me to stop worrying,' she smiled, reaching out for his hand and drawing him down on to the side of the bed.

He sat down and drew her into his arms, holding her close and kissing her face with small tender kisses, until she turned her face up for him to claim her lips in a kiss that blotted out all fear and left her breathless and giddy.

'This is becoming a habit,' Mattie's voice said from the doorway, and they broke hastily apart.

'But don't let me interrupt. I can still remember how it feels and I'd hate to get the reputation of a party-pooper!' She laughed delightedly and started towards the door.

'You'd better stay, Ma,' Alistair said wryly. 'I think you're going to have to get used to this sort of thing from now on, if I have anything to do with it!'

'That would be very easy,' Mattie replied happily. 'Just as long as you don't teach Ilona to call me "Ma"!' She turned to Ilona, who was staring round-eyed at Alistair. 'I've been trying for years to make him stop calling me that. It makes me feel a hundred years old.'

'All right, then,' Alistair interrupted, putting his arm around his mother's shoulders. 'But I can still remember Dad calling you that. And at the time I thought you liked it.'

Mattie's eyes clouded and tears were very near the surface. 'Your father did call me that,' she agreed, her voice shaking a little. 'But it was short for Mattie, and no one else ever called me that.'

'Why didn't you tell me that before?' Alistair asked, bewildered.

'Because, you great lummox, you wouldn't have understood before.' Mattie's voice was almost normal.

'Well, I don't really think I understand now.'

'You will,' Mattie smiled. 'You will. Now, enough of this. We're here to cheer Ilona up and all we've managed to do is confuse her, by the looks of things. How are you, dear?'

Ilona had been watching them both in total bewilderment. The only thing that had really made any sense to her had been Alistair's words implying that he planned to be around for some time, and she wondered if he'd meant it or if it was just something he had said to explain his actions to his mother. But she thrust it aside and revelled in his closeness and the tender way he held her hand while they chatted about nothing and everything.

Too soon it seemed visiting time was over and Mattie, diplomatic as ever, left them with a cheery 'Goodbye' so that they could have a few moments alone.

'Well, my love,' Alistair murmured against her hair, 'I suppose this will be the last time I'll hear your voice for a while. Tomorrow when I see you, you won't be feeling much like talking, even if it's allowed, which I doubt. I don't suppose there's anything special you'd like to say?'

It was definitely a question and Ilona longed to tell him she loved him. But something held her back. Something told her that this was not the time. The time would come when she wouldn't be able to deny it.

But it wasn't now. Perhaps if he were to tell her he loved her it would be different. But she wasn't prepared to commit herself when she was still unsure of how he felt about her, no matter how many hints he threw out.

Alistair shrugged, giving his lovingly familiar lopsided grin before gathering her in his arms again and kissing her all over her face. 'That will have to do me for a while, I suppose. I'd better go now before some old dragon of a Sister comes in and throws me out. Take care, darling, I'll see you tomorrow.' And with that he was gone, and Ilona was alone with her thoughts. Confused thoughts, niggling doubts and also dreams of what *could* be. What she hoped *would* be.

CHAPTER SEVEN

EVERYTHING was fuzzy and she couldn't see who was talking, but she could hear the voices. They sounded familiar, but she didn't know why. She couldn't speak and her body wouldn't obey her brain, so that she could tell whoever it was that she was there and they could help her.

The voices came again, more distinct now. 'Why didn't you tell her? You didn't have to keep that from her, she would have understood and probably gone along anyway. But to do it this way! You're a right bastard, and if I find out that you've hurt her in any way ... so help me, I'll ruin you! I've enough contacts to do it too.'

'Simon, I didn't do it deliberately, it just happened.'

Simon! That name was familiar. Why can't I put a face to it? Ilona moaned silently to herself. She could hear the voices again and tried desperately to understand.

'You didn't do it deliberately!' The tone was sarcastic. 'From what I've heard about you, everything you do is deliberate and well planned!'

What were they talking about? Why couldn't she open her eyes to see who it was? But her brain gave up and the clouds she'd been fighting enveloped her again and she drifted off.

The clouds were breaking up, just enough for her to push through to consciousness, and once more she heard voices. Familiar voices. Only this time someone was holding her hand and patting it distractedly.

'Oh, God, Mother, she's taking so long to come out of it! What am I going to do if she doesn't? I don't think I could live now, without her!'

'Don't be foolish, Alistair. The doctor said she's fine. She'll wake up soon, you'll see.'

Ilona squeezed the hand that held hers and opened her emerald eyes, cloudy now from the anaesthetic, and tried to smile.

'Don't try to talk, darling, just nod your head. Are you in pain?'

Ilona shook her head almost imperceptibly. She tried to smile at him. He looked so lost and his hair, that was normally so tidy, was awry, just as if had been in the wind at the shack. He ran his hand through it in agitation and she realised why. Poor dear, she thought, he really is worried. But she had no way to comfort him except to squeeze his hand again. And that seemed to work, for the haunted look left his eyes and he smiled.

She looked past him to see Mattie's plump comforting figure coming towards the bed. 'How are you, sweetheart?' she asked, kissing Ilona on her damp forehead. 'I'm so glad it's over, and the doctor says, successful. But he'll tell you all about that later. You'd better just go back to sleep for a while. We'll leave you alone to rest.'

Alistair rose to leave with his mother, but Ilona clung to his hand. 'Do you want me to stay?' he asked.

Ilona nodded and he sat down again, and thankfully she drifted back into her clouds.

Ilona sat up in bed, happily applying her make-up. The operation on her throat had been, according to Ian Anderson, a complete success—medically, that was. But the crunch would come when he allowed her to start speaking again. He had, until now, made no mention of her singing, and she hadn't asked him. Somehow it had lost a great deal of its importance in her life now that she had Alistair. And she was sure she had him. He had been so wonderful in the last few days, never missing an opportunity to visit her, bringing flowers and ridiculous, but sentimental gifts like the great green frog that sat staring at her from across the room.

That she hadn't been able to talk to him hadn't seemed to be a problem, for they had spent a great deal of time just sitting together holding hands and there hadn't seemed to be a need for words. But today she had a surprise for him. Ian had just told her that she could speak a little—just a whisper, and only if it didn't hurt. And she was planning to keep all her words just for Alistair.

She finished her make-up and reached for the papers. One of her joys in life was to read the Sunday papers in bed, and she had been looking forward to this since she realised that today was Sunday.

She loved to read the gossippy columns about people she knew or had heard of, trying to match innuendoes to people. Although she was not a gossip at heart this was something she could do without anyone knowing, and it gave her a feeling of secret knowledge about some of her colleagues, when she had put two and two together from the papers and later found her theories had been right. There was nothing vicious about this pastime, for she never spoke to anyone about it, just kept it to herself and enjoyed the outcome.

Skipping quickly through all the hard news in the front of the paper, she finally came to the section she wanted and settled down to enjoy it. There were a lot of snippets about people in Adelaide and South Australia that she didn't know, and she skimmed through them looking for parts about the entertainment industry.

Her eyebrows raised and her intake of breath was audible when she spotted a short paragraph at the bottom of the page.

'What well-known local young business man was seen dining with one of Australia's budding superstar singers? The lovely chanteuse wasn't booked in to appear anywhere locally and it appears she's just taking a break. Could she have picked our fair city just to see her escort?'

Ilona knew immediately that this referred to herself and Alistair and although annoyed, she realised that this sort of thing was inevitable. But what had made her gasp so audibly was the paragraph almost next to it.

'Rumour has it that Alistair McLean, the young business man who has made such an impact in financial circles over the past few months, is the power behind the takeover of the almost defunct Fame Records. It seems he's trying to diversify into other fields. A reputable source says that he's attempting to woo another company's best money-making singer for Fame. Seems they're friends from way back. Still, friendship doesn't necessarily mean she'll sign.

Asked recently about their relationship, she offered a "No Comment".'

Ilona was appalled. Everything clicked into place. All the questions that had been going round in her head before she went into hospital were now answered, the hesitation on Alistair's part when she asked him about his work now explained. He had been using her! How could she have been so naïve? She'd even given him all the ammunition he needed. She'd told him about the tapes that she and Simon still had and about her plan to use them.

The paper shook in her hands. That had been the night he made love to her—after she had let him know that this operation wouldn't affect her record-making abilities for the next year.

A year would be all he needed, she knew, to pull a company like Fame back on to the rails. That was if he had an established star working for him.

Ilona couldn't believe her eyes! Someone was making it all up—they had to be! How could those kisses, those caresses have been faked?

Her heavy lashes drooped languidly over her emerald eyes as she remembered that night, and the perspiration broke out on her brow as her mind drifted back.

Alistair's hands had been so gentle, so loving, bringing her to a peak of desire that she could hardly believe possible. His lips had touched her gently like a butterfly's wings at first, in places she had never dreamed a man would kiss her, and as their joint passion rose had become hard and demanding and almost bruising in their intensity.

As she remembered, her heart began to pound

as it had then and she could feel again that heart-stopping moment when he had finally taken her. It had been like the culmination of a torture—a sweet torture, a torture that she wanted to beg for again and again, a torture that she wanted desperately to learn how to inflict on him. Only on him!

And he had taught her how. Slowly and gently he had taught her when he realised how little she knew, guiding her with care, showing her with skill how to please him as he pleased her. And it had seemed so natural, so right that they could play one another's bodies like fine-tuned instruments until that final driving, pounding crescendo that was born from the rhythm of love.

Ilona's heart was pounding again as it had then and her breath was coming in short gasps, so real had her imagination and memory been. I'll make you pay for that night, Mr Alistair McLean! she screamed to herself. I'll make you roll over and pay . . . in spades! And tears of rage and a kind of loss she couldn't explain coursed down her cheeks.

Revenge! That was now the name of the game! Revenge for using her. Revenge for taking advantage of her naïvety. She had to admit deep down that she'd led him to believe that she'd been experienced. But that was no excuse! Not now! He could have told her at the very start that he *was* Fame Records. Things would have been different. She would have willingly signed, just for old times' sake if for nothing else. But to make her want him and damn him to hell, need him, just so that he would have an advantage in a business deal was too much! Too much!

It was irrational, she knew, to think like this. There *could* be a perfectly good reason for what he had done. Perhaps he even did love her a little. . . . No! Ilona was too well versed in the intricacies of her own world to believe that. She had seen it all before and kept herself apart from it. Only now, like a fool, to have fallen into the trap that she had pitied so many others from falling into. A trap she had so carefully avoided for so many lonely years.

That was what galled so much! The lonely years—years she had begun to hope were over. The future to be filled with Alistair. What a laugh! Ilona Craig—ice maiden! That was what she was known as to many of the men in her industry, she knew. Behind her back, of course, never to her face. Till now, it had only amused her. Now it hurt.

The ice had been melted and turned into rivers of fire that could only be quenched by one man— a man she felt had used and betrayed her just as he had melted the ice. Now she had to make him pay. But how? was the question. Could she make him love her, then laugh in his face? No, he was too experienced for that, and she was far too naïve.

What would hurt him the most? His business! If he failed to make Fame Records into the success he planned, would that do it? Maybe. . . He could still do it without her voice, she knew, because the contract was signed and the tapes were on their way to Simon now, and a publicity campaign was even now being mapped out to advertise the release of the first record with four other artists and Ilona Craig.

The idea came in a flash. All she had to do was get her hands on those tapes! Then Alistair would look a fool when his first release couldn't match the promised publicity. How to get them was another matter. But she wasn't a complete fool and if she couldn't manage *that* at least, then she had no business calling herself a woman!

Ilona brushed away the tears angrily. He wasn't worth it. No man was. Not now, not ever again. Once she'd shown him what she thought of him and made him suffer, she would use men in the future when and if it suited her. She vowed never to let any man get to her as Alistair had. And if she ever entered into a relationship with a man again, it would be on *her* terms, and the price would be high.

She was drowsing fitfully in the humid afternoon sunshine that poured through her window, her honey-gold hair spread over the propped-up pillows, when Ian Anderson made his daily visit. She was aware of someone in the room and she wakened with a start to find him just looking at her.

He appeared worried, and Ilona's heart lurched. Surely nothing had gone wrong at this late stage! She reached for the paper and pencil that she now kept beside her until she had been given permission to speak again, not wanting to trust her voice still, but he anticipated her.

'Nothing's wrong with you, my dear. But we do have a problem. The press have somehow found out you're here and they're jamming the switchboard with their calls. A few have even arrived claiming to be relatives come to visit. So far your admirable Mr Cantrell has managed to fob them off with some waffle about a mild infection and needing a good rest, but I think for your own good and the good of the poor staff here, we're going to have to move you to another hospital.'

Ilona made a face. But before she could start to write anything on her pad Alistair's voice broke the silence from outside her room.

'My good woman,' he grated, 'I don't care if you're the Matron or the Queen of Sheba! I *am* a friend of Miss Craig's, and if you were literate enough to read you'd have seen it splashed all over the morning paper. And if you don't step aside, I'll walk right over you!'

Ilona grinned at Ian, then for the first time since the operation, gave her voice a trial run.

'I'd have given anything to have seen *that* exchange!' Although the voice was a husky whisper there was no pain, and her eyes sparkled excitedly.

She had deliberately whispered, and now she tried again and found that she could speak in a normal tone quite easily. 'That Matron of yours must be a gem to be able to handle the famous, or should I say infamous, Mr McLean like that!'

Ian grinned. 'She is! And what's more, not only is she extremely capable and competent, but attractive too. Which could have something to do with the ominous silence from outside your door.'

'Are you fishing to see if I'm jealous?' Ilona bantered, flashing her jade eyes at him.

'Could be! After all, I'm sure the nurses have made it quite clear that I'm single, eligible and halfway in love with my favourite star patient.'

Ian's tone had been decidedly humorous, but Ilona thought she caught a faint undertone of wistfulness and she became aware that he was almost serious.

Almost hating herself for the thought that crossed her mind that to use his feelings for her would be bitchy and unworthy, she pushed them aside. After all, men had been trying to use *her* for years now. Women's Liberation was now the name of the game, and she'd have to learn the rules fast. Use men, any man, no matter who or what the consequences!

'Perhaps,' she said, giving him most bewitching smile, 'it might be a good idea to let Alistair in. He's obviously upset, and he might even have a solution to the problem.'

'You're probably right,' Ian agreed reluctantly, but added firmly, 'I'll do all the talking—you've used that voice enough for the time being. We don't want to push things along too fast just yet.'

'You're the boss,' she quipped, smiling brightly, and Ian rang her bell to summon a nurse.

'Nurse, I believe a Mr McLean is lurking somewhere outside waiting to see Miss Craig. You can show him in now.'

The nurse grinned at his phraseology but just nodded and opened the door. 'You may come in now, Mr McLean.'

Alistair burst into the room, obviously agitated and angry, almost bowling over the nurse in his hurry.

Ilona, to the delighted Dr Anderson's surprise, reached out and took his hand, holding it intimately between both her own, imperceptibly moving sideways till she was leaning against his shoulder, her honey-gold hair brushing his neck.

He looked at her quizzically and she smiled into his questioning eyes while sensing behind them the fury building in Alistair at what appeared to be a very intimate and more than professional scene.

She was delighted at the result of her deliberate deception and just smiled sweetly at the furious Alistair.

'I suppose you've seen the papers,' he burst out angrily, striding determinedly to the other side of the bed and pulling Ilona's hands away from Ian.

'He's behaving like a dog that's lost his bone to another mut,' Ilona thought. 'Well, it serves him right!'

But she couldn't take her hand away, and the old familiar tingle crept up her spine and she flushed more in anger with herself than embarrassment.

Ian glared at Alistair. 'I don't know what the papers have to do with anything. But we certainly have a problem.'

Alistair looked up at him in surprise. 'What problem?' he demanded. 'The only problem I'm aware of is personal between Ilona and myself.' It was obvious to Ilona that he wanted the doctor to leave. But Ian ignored the hint.

'The media have found out that Ilona is here and we're having problems keeping them at bay. I've just been telling her that we'll have to do something drastic. I would suggest moving her to another hospital under an assumed name, but she thinks you might have another solution.'

Ilona sat in the bed watching the exchange

between the two men and feeling something like an inanimate package that had become a bone of contention, and her anger at their treatment began to simmer.

'I suppose you've already picked out another hospital and name,' Alistair grunted.

'Well, as a matter of fact. . . .'

'Hold everything!' Ilona could stand no more and broke into the conversation, taking them both by surprise. 'I know you said no more talking, Ian, but I am here, and I do have some say in all this! In fact, I should have *all* the say. And it seems to me that none of you have thought about getting hold of Simon to see if he can do anything.' She closed her mouth tightly as if to say wordlessly that she would say no more until Simon arrived.

Alistair was stunned. He hadn't heard her voice for what seemed like an eternity and he just looked at her mutely. Then as if by magic, all his anger, jealousy and frustration disappeared. 'My God, you can speak!' he grinned, bending over to kiss her lightly. 'You've no idea what a relief *that* is!'

Oh, haven't I? Ilona thought. Now you know that I'm going to be able to talk again, I wonder how long it will be before you want me to sing? Now that it looks as though your investment might just pay off after all, let's see how you plan to protect it!

'Well, if you want to speak to Simon before making any decisions,' Ian said quietly, 'I'll leave now, and we'll discuss things later. But I must warn you, Ilona . . . not too much talking. Hear?'

'I hear.' She gave him her brightest smile, much to Alistair's annoyance.

As Ian left, Alistair perched on the side of her bed. 'I suppose you've read the papers? No, you shouldn't answer that—I can see you have. I hope you'll let me explain.'

'Explain what?' Ilona's voice was husky, more with emotion than pain.

Alistair's face was set. It was clear he had trouble explaining any of his actions to anyone, she thought.

'Explained about my owning "Fame",' he almost whispered, gazing fixedly into her eyes.

Ilona broke the stare by looking down at the hand that she had pulled from his. 'Do you have something to explain? I thought the papers made everything very clear.' Her voice was icy.

'I know it looks bad, darling.' Alistair sighed. 'But somehow the subject just didn't come up at first . . .'

'You've got a very convenient memory,' she broke in 'I seem to remember a discussion about your business interests at the shack which you seemed loath to go into at the time.'

Alistair's mahogany-tanned face darkened as he flushed. 'Well, at that time, I didn't know Megan had made any overtures to Simon, so. . . .'

'So,' Ilona snapped, 'it was none of my business what you did—even were I stupid enough to accept *that*. What about later? What about dinner with Megan, and afterwards . . . what about then?' She was on the verge of tears and she held herself stiffly as he put his arms around her.

'Darling, by then it was too late. I didn't want

to have you think badly of me. Damn it, I couldn't think straight about anything to do with you by then!'

Ilona pushed him away. 'Someone told me that you know exactly what you're doing all the time. And I'm prepared now, to believe that. It's too late to reverse any business dealings we might have. But in future that's all it will be ... business.'

She saw that her words had stung, and she was pleased—pleased in her head. But her heart ached—ached to hold him, ached to go back and start again, ached to tell him she didn't care and she'd forgive him anything. But her head wouldn't let her tongue speak, and she watched him in desolation as he rose and stalked to the door.

At the door he turned, his dark eyes black with rage and frustration and a shaft of sunlight making his copper hair burn like fire. 'If that's the way you want it, so be it. But don't think I wanted to disappear. I have every intention of staying around to see that my investment is secure. So you'll just have to get used to seeing me every day, Loney darling!'

Ilona cringed at the way he said her name. With hate and loathing, it seemed, and her heart felt as if it had shattered like a hot glass that someone had plunged into ice-cold water.

She could feel the cracks and the cold, a bitter, soul-freezing cold, and she wanted to die until her anger took over and her mind once more took control of her heart.

Now she knew about broken hearts. When her voice came back properly and she could sing again . . . in the summer when she could sing . . . she'd be able to really sing about broken hearts.

She thought of all the books she'd read about famous writers who claimed that they had to experience emotions before they could really write about them. Now she knew it was true for singers too. Those who had experienced what they were singing about would of necessity do it better. Now she could really sing about love and heartbreak, and she consoled herself with that.

As she dried the tears from her lashes and carefully disguised her heavy eyes with make-up in the bathroom, she heard people enter her room. She was pleased when she found Mattie and Simon there together.

'Have you and Alistair been quarrelling?' Mattie asked as Ilona tiredly climbed back into bed. 'He's like a bear with a sore head—hardly spoke to his poor old mother a minute ago in the corridor!'

'Yes,' Simon added, 'he did seem upset, and in somewhat of a hurry.'

Ilona's throat was beginning to ache and her voice was husky as she replied. 'More like a difference of opinion on business matters,' she whispered.

'So you know?' Simon's tone was questioning.

'Know what?' Mattie looked at them both in dismay.

'It doesn't matter, Mattie,' Ilona whispered. 'Let's forget it for now. We have to do something about these press people.'

Simon shook his head and Ilona knew the look in his eyes well. He rarely became angry, but when he did his eyes became hard and a white line appeared across his upper lips as he pressed his lips together to hold back his rage. And he was angry now, angrier than she'd ever seen him.

'Simon, don't worry about it. It doesn't matter any more. Just make sure everything goes as we'd planned. The rest doesn't matter.'

Both Mattie and Simon could tell from her voice that she should stop speaking and rest her throat, and Mattie broke in. 'You stop talking, my girl. In fact I'm going to make sure you do!' And she bustled out of the room with a look of angry resolve on her kindly face.

Simon waited till the door closed, then took Ilona's hand. 'I warned him. I told him that if he hurt you, I'd break him—and I meant it. He's going to wish he'd never laid eyes, never mind a hand on you!'

'Simon, please don't do anything, just forget it! I can take care of Alistair myself and I don't want you or anyone else involved. It was my own fault, and if it hadn't been him it would have been someone else. I just had to learn the hard way.'

'If you say so,' Simon conceded reluctantly. 'But you only have to give the word and I'll have the bastard black balled all through the industry.'

'That would be going a bit far, darling.' Ilona was pleased none the less that Simon would go to such lengths on her behalf. 'All I want you to do is to make sure when you get those tapes from Sydney that you send them to Alistair at his home address. Here it is.' She wrote it on a piece of paper for him. 'I'll take things from there.'

'What are you planning?' asked Simon, bemused.

'I don't really know yet,' she replied. 'But

something is beginning to take shape, and I'd rather do it myself.'

'Whatever you say, but remember, if you need any help. . . .'

Simon's voice broke off as Mattie returned with Ian Anderson.

'It seems you've been taking liberties with that voice, young lady,' he said, 'so Mattie here has suggested, and I agree, that this discussion should come to a halt, at least for now, and you can both come back later to sort things out.'

Simon and Mattie agreed readily, and both kissed Ilona and left with the promise to return after lunch.

'Meanwhile, young lady,' said Ian, turning to his patient as the visitors left,' you're going to take this capsule and have a nap.'

Ilona accepted the medication gratefully and within minutes was drifting off into blissful, soul-refreshing, heart-mending sleep, to waken hours later refreshed and better able to cope with everything.

She had slept through lunch and Rose, the friendly little domestic, appeared with coffee and sandwiches.

'I didn't want to wake you for your lunch, dear, and Nurse said it would be all right if you slept. But I thought you might be hungry and this would keep you going till dinner time.'

'Rose,' smiled Ilona, 'you're a darling!'

Rose blushed with delight and left singing happily to herself, a song that Ilona recognised as being from her last record.

After her coffee and sandwiches she felt better and prepared to take on the problems of the press, and she looked rested and happier when Simon and Mattie appeared to discuss it.

'Simon and I have talked things over with Ian and we've come to the conclusion that the best thing for you is to be with me for a few days at Alistair's flat. He's going away on business in a couple of days, so we wouldn't have to worry about him,' said Mattie.

Ilona was pleased when she heard that. She didn't think she could cope with seeing him every day as he had threatened, especially outside the hospital atmosphere.

'You see,' Simon broke into her reverie, 'his place is close by in case anything goes wrong. And Ian will be able to call in daily. The only problem is getting you out of here and to the flat without the press following.'

Ilona's eyes brightened. She had always loved a challenge, and this would be one that would brighten her existence and take her mind of Alistair.

'Can you stall the press for another day?' she asked Simon.

'Sure, but that's about all, without letting the cat out of the bag about your voice,' he replied.

'Well,' Ilona drawled, her mind racing, 'I think we're going to have to tell them. I can't see any way round *that*. But I'd sooner leave it a day longer while we sort this disappearing act out.' Simon was puzzled.

'What do you mean?' he queried.

'Simple,' Ilona smiled, an idea taking shape. 'If we give them *that* before I go to ground, then they might just be happy and let things go for a while.'

Simon beamed. 'I see what you mean. If they can't find you, they can still write about you not being able to sing. "Will she or won't she ever again" sort of things. And that should give us some breathing space.'

'Right,' Ilona agreed. 'Now I have the germ of an idea. But it will take a while to sort out, so what I'd like you both to do is have everyone, Ian, Alistair,' Simon's eyebrows rose at the name, but Ilona just smiled and confirmed, 'and you and Mattie here tomorrow about lunchtime. I should have everything thought out by then.'

'Meanwhile,' Simon smiled, 'I'll just keep handing out the "no visitors, no comment" routine to the boys outside till then.'

'Fine,' Ilona grinned. 'So off you both go while I play games on paper.'

'I must say,' said Mattie, kissing her goodbye, 'you certainly have picked up since this morning. I hope Alistair has too.'

Ilona kissed her gently. 'Don't worry about him, Mattie. He can take care of himself,' she said cryptically, and Mattie frowned in consternation as she left.

CHAPTER EIGHT

ILONA watched, with a wry smile on her face, as all the people she had summoned came in. They all looked slightly apprehensive, except Alistair, who looked downright annoyed, and that in itself added to her enjoyment.

'Now you all know I can't talk very much, so I've written out a list of instructions for each of you . . . No, Alistair,' she smiled, seeing him start to interrupt. 'Just read those, then you'll understand.' She handed each their envelopes, Alistair, Simon, Ian, Mattie and the young nurse, who was completely bewildered at the whole thing. But Ilona noticed the smile and sparkle in her eyes as she read her instructions and knew she had chosen well. The girl had intelligence and a sense of humour, and from what she had seen of her and the few conversations they had had during her stay in the hospital, Ilona knew she could be trusted.

'I don't like it,' Alistair stated defiantly. 'It won't work.'

Mattie smiled at her son. 'You've no sense of adventure, my dear. I think it's quite clever and really quite simple. Simple plans usually work best.'

'We can only try,' Simon butted in with a grin. 'And after all, I'll be the one left holding the baby at the other end. It shouldn't affect any of the rest of you if it doesn't.'

A babble of comments broke out, that Ilona stopped quickly.

'It's really up to us, and that's how I want it handled, so if any of you don't want to help, you'd better say so now, so I can get something else. . . . No one? Good! Then I suggest you all follow instructions and I'll see you all later.'

'I think a rest is in order for you right now,' Ian said in a very professional manner, but with a most unprofessional grin on his face. 'So I suggest we all leave.'

There was a flurry of goodbyes and Ilona was left on her own, happy that things had gone so well and rather pleased that she had taken over, much to Alistair's annoyance. Well, she thought, he's going to be a damn sight more annoyed by the time I'm finished!

Mattie called in later that evening with an armful of packages. 'There you are, my dear. I hope they're all right.'

'Bound to be,' Ilona smiled. 'I trust your judgment.'

'I'm glad you said that,' said Mattie, a look of concern in her motherly eyes. 'I know you and Alistair have quarrelled over something and I really don't want to know about it. But I wish you two would patch it up. I was so pleased when I thought you two were such good friends, and now you're both snapping and snarling at one another like two dogs fighting over a bone. I *do* wish you'd both sort out the problem—it can't be very serious, surely?'

'Mattie, I'm sorry, I can't tell you what the problem is. But it will all sort itself out one way or the other in the next few days. So don't worry about it.' Ilona sighed. She hated telling untruths to Mattie. But she couldn't bring herself to tell her friend now badly Alistair had hurt her.

She couldn't tell her about this as she'd told her about other things in the past, because Alistair *was* her son and for once Mattie couldn't be objective. Ilona felt very alone. For the first time in her life she had no one to talk to. Not even Simon, who for some reason refused to discuss Alistair with her. And for some reason seemed to dislike him and had from their first meeting.

Mattie rose. 'It's time I left, dear, tomorrow is going to be a big day. I'm glad we'll have some time together before you go back to Sydney, and I *do* hope you and Alistair sort it out.'

She leant over and gave Ilona a hug. 'I hope everything goes well tomorrow. I wish I could be there,' she laughed. 'I'd love to see it. Still, you can tell me all about it later. Sleep well, darling.'

At six-thirty the following morning, Ilona and Nurse Dean were busy packing Ilona's small overnight bag as breakfast arrived.

'Have your breakfast, Miss Craig,' Nurse Dean urged. 'You'll need it, and I can finish this. Everything is about ready and Dr Anderson will be here in a few minutes.'

Ilona agreed readily and sat down to her breakfast. She was strangely happy—even after what had happened, for she was now taking matters into her own hands, and she always felt good when she was in control of her own life.

Not long after, Ian arrived and whistled in appreciation. Ilona was carefully adjusting a bright red straw hat on to her lovely head—a hat that matched exactly the vibrant red of the jacket that fitted snugly over her plain white linen dress. The whole ensemble was finished with matching belt, bag and pumps.

She finished tucking her hair under the crown of her hat as Ian remarked, 'Very striking! You'll stand out a mile.'

'That's exactly the idea,' Ilona replied, and all three smiled happily.

Nurse Dean adjusted her cap over her light brown, blonde-streaked hair, pushing a stray wisp under the cap and fastening it securely with a pin. 'I'm ready,' she grinned, adjusting her blue nurse's cape over her snowy white uniform.

'Good,' Ilona replied, 'time to face the wolves. That is, if they're there.'

'You bet they're there,' Ian interjected. 'There's about a dozen already. Simon must have told everyone who puts out any sort of paper at all. It wouldn't surprise me if there was someone from the *Medical Journal* out there too!'

Ilona raised a quizzical eyebrow and then smiled when she realised he was joking. But she flushed slightly. She still wasn't in full control, she realised, to have been taken in by a remark like that, and she chided herself silently. It was going to take longer than she'd thought to get back to her old self. Perhaps, she mused, I never will. Damn Alistair McLean for making such a change in her life!

The three conspirators filed out of the room, to be met by the Matron, who guided them to the front door, where in full view of the media, she shook hands with Ilona and ushered them out.

Cries of, 'Over here, Miss Craig,' and, 'Ilona, Ilona!' came from all sides, and newspaper men and photographers and TV interviewers pushed and shoved to get close.

Ian raised a hand for silence and raising his voice over the din almost shouted, 'If you'd all quiet down, Miss Craig has a prepared statement for you!'

The babble dropped to a muted murmur as Nurse Dean drew a paper from under her cape and nervously began to read.

'Miss Craig would like you all to know that she has undergone minor surgery on her throat. For the present she is, by order of her doctor, not allowed to speak, but she has asked me to tell you that she hopes to be back on stage in the near future. Meanwhile, as you are aware, she has signed a contract with Fame Records. In order that Fame can continue its operations she has supplied them with material that was taped a few weeks ago before her throat problems, and the record company will be using this until such times as she can record again. In the meantime, Miss Craig will be returning to her home in Sydney, to recuperate.'

There was a babble of noise and voices till one broke through.

'Will Miss Craig give us some information on her friendship with the owner of Fame, Mr McLean?'

Ilona's eyes clouded, but she smiled nevertheless and nodded at Nurse Dean.

'Miss Craig has instructed me to say, "no comment".'

Another voice broke in, 'Nurse, are you going to Sydney with Miss Craig?'

Nurse Dean smiled brightly, pleased that the one question they had been hoping would be asked had been. 'Unfortunately, no. I've been Miss Craig's personal nurse for the past few days, but because of family commitments I'm unable to do so. However, Miss Craig has professional help waiting for her in Sydney and I'll be accompanying her to the airport, where she'll be met at the plane by her manager. Miss Craig's doctor has approved these arrangements. Now, unfortunately, we must bring this news conference to a close or Miss Craig will miss her plane.'

At these words Ian took Ilona firmly by the arm and all three pushed their way through the crowd of reporters to his car, which was parked at the entrance to the hospital.

After helping both women into the back seat he climbed behind the wheel, and in a blaze of flashing bulbs they raced off in the direction of the airport.

The newsmen scattered to their waiting cars and took off in hot pursuit.

Simon had made arrangements for Ilona to board the plane to Sydney without going through the usual routine of the airport and Ian was allowed to drive his car on to the tarmac in front of the waiting plane.

The two women stepped calmly from the back of the car and Simon, who had been waiting at the foot of the boarding steps with the hostess, hurried towards them to kiss the one in the striking red and white outfit.

She shook hands demurely with the hostess, kissed the nurse briefly and shook hands warmly with Dr Ian Anderson. Then with a regal wave at the reporters who were craning their necks at the barrier, she boarded the plane with Simon.

The nurse and Dr Anderson climbed into the waiting car and drove carefully to the gates and away.

'Well, my dear, it seems to have worked!' Ian grinned at Ilona, who was sitting calmly beside him in Nurse Dean's cap, cape and flat white shoes. 'I hope Nurse Dean won't have too much trouble at the other end!'

'She shouldn't,' Ilona smiled. 'She's only going as far as Melbourne and returning tonight. And Simon has a change of clothes for her on board.'

'But what's going to happen in Sydney when Simon gets off the plane without you?'

'Well, it seems that my dear Simon has decided that he needs a holiday. He's meeting his wife in Melbourne and they were flying to Tasmania for a week or so. So you see, Ilona Craig and manager are going to manage to disappear between here and Sydney!'

'But won't the airline people say anything?' Ian was genuinely worried.

'Not if they want to keep my business and a lot more well known people as well! If the newspapers want to check, they'll find that Miss Dean boarded in Adelaide and got off in Melbourne, as did Simon, but that Simon and Miss Dean then travelled to Tasmania and by the time they sort all that out I should have well and truly disappeared—at least for now.'

'But what about Nurse Dean?'

'She's flying back here as Miss Jones, just to confuse things a little more!'

Ian seemed satisfied. 'You really have a streak

of the criminal in you, you know. The way you worked all that out, you'd think you'd practised hiding from the law!'

'Not really,' Ilona replied quietly. 'I just read a lot of mysteries.'

They both laughed as Ian pulled up in Alistair's underground car park.

'What really bothers me, though,' he mused aloud, as they entered the lift, 'is that you should be coming here. I thought from the way you've been acting towards Alistair in the past few days that this would be the last place you'd want to come to.'

'Well, this is stage two in my plan,' Ilona said cryptically as the lift doors opened to reveal Alistair and Mattie waiting for them. 'You see, darling,' she continued, touching his hand in an intimate gesture, 'Alistair is leaving town for a few days. Aren't you?' she asked, smiling sweetly at him, and her heart leapt at the scowl that crossed his face as she continued to hold Ian's hand.

Ian and Mattie were both confused and it showed on their faces. But neither was prepared to comment, and neither Alistair nor Ilona noticed, because they were too busy watching one another.

'Well,' Alistair broke the silence, 'it seems that everything is under control and that I'm no longer needed, so I'll be off.' He picked up a suitcase that was standing next to the lift and prepared to leave. 'I don't suppose you'll be needed either,' he said to Ian with a sting in his voice, 'so we'll leave together, shall we?'

Ian looked more confused at Alistair's tone. 'I

had thought of staying for a little while to make sure that Ilona settled in. But if you insist. . . .'

'Yes, I damn well *do* insist!' Alistair glared. 'My mother is quite capable of seeing to *Miss Craig*, so I can't see any need for you to stay. I suppose you'll be visiting daily?' His voice was harsh.

'Well. . . .' Ian began.

'Don't worry, Ian dear,' Ilona broke in. 'I'll see you this evening, won't I?' she smiled sweetly.

'If you two want to make dates you can do it over the telephone,' Alistair grated, almost pushing Ian into the lift.

Mattie spun round to face Ilona as the lift doors closed. 'What was all that about?' she asked, a hint of anger in her voice. 'I know you don't feel romantically inclined towards Ian, so why the display?'

'Why not?' Ilona asked, her face deliberately blank.

'You're playing with fire, my dear. Alistair won't put up with that.'

Ilona's eyes widened. 'Why not? He doesn't own me.'

'No, he doesn't,' Mattie admitted, 'but knowing my son, I think he would like to, and he's never been very good at losing. He takes a loss very personally.'

'Well, he's just going to have to accept it, isn't he?' Ilona was getting cross, because she could see what Mattie was thinking and she *did* feel guilty.

'No matter what you've got in your head, you shouldn't use Ian Anderson. He could be hurt, and that's not fair,' Mattie scolded. 'Not fair at all!'

'I know, Mattie, I know. But I couldn't help it. He just happened to be there. But I promise I won't hurt him.'

'It may be too late for that,' Mattie commented quietly.

Ilona started. 'Oh, Mattie, I hope not!'

'Well, it's too late now, I suppose. We'd better forget it for the time being and get you settled in.'

Later that afternoon Ian rang to see how she was and Ilona was happy to tell him she was fine. But she was worried when he didn't mention coming round to see her in the evening, and only said he'd see her some time the next day.

After she had rung off, she breathed a sigh of relief. He obviously hadn't taken her seriously and she was relieved that she wouldn't have to go into details about her behaviour. With luck their friendship would slip back to the easy patient–doctor relationship that had existed before.

Ilona and Mattie's life settled into a quiet placid routine interspersed with visits from Ian, who seemed a little withdrawn but not unfriendly, until a few days after she had arrived from the hospital, and then everything seemed to happen at once.

The day started normally until Mattie went out as usual to collect Alistair's mail. The package that Ilona had been waiting for arrived, addressed to Alistair in Simon's handwriting, and she knew it contained the tapes that they had promised him. She had given Simon instructions to send them to the flat and not direct to Fame Records, telling him she wanted to listen to them again before they were whisked away. Simon had accepted her explanation with raised eyebrows, but had agreed reluctantly.

Shortly after the package arrived, Alistair had phoned to say that he would be driving home the next day around lunchtime, and Ilona's heart skipped a beat when Mattie told her.

She knew it didn't give her much time to complete her plans, but she still intended to continue with her present course—regardless.

The one bright spot in the day was Ian's visit. He came as usual but brought a visitor, Nurse Dean.

'I thought you might like to see your co-conspirator again, so I've brought Margaret with me,' he smiled in explanation.

'I'm so glad to see you again,' said Ilona. And she was. From the way Ian and Margaret behaved it was obvious to Ilona that they were more than friends, and she was glad—glad that Ian had found someone and that she didn't have to worry about hurting him.

As he examined her throat and told her that there was very little more he could do for her, Ilona's heart lightened. At least now she could start to continue with her life without worrying about her health.

'You mean I can try to sing again?' she asked excitedly.

'No, I don't think that would be a good idea,' he frowned. 'In a few weeks, perhaps. But I think when the time is right, you'll know. I'll still drop by now and then and if anything happens or you need to see us, you only have to phone and leave a message at my rooms, with Margaret.'

Ilona's eyebrows rose slightly in enquiry, and Ian and Margaret both laughed.

'I've got a new job,' Margaret blushed. 'I'm Ian's receptionist now.'

'And I've got hopes of having her take charge of more than my patient's records,' he grinned.

Ilona felt she should tell Ian of her plans, but she couldn't bring herself to let anyone into her secret. She felt vulnerable still and her ability to put her faith and trust in anyone was now sadly lacking. She'd tell him the whole story one day, she promised herself.

After they had left, Mattie told her she had some shopping and business to attend to and left her alone in the flat with the package. Ilona knew what she was planning wasn't quite ethical, but her heart cried that what Alistair had done to her hadn't been ethical either, and she pushed the guilt to the back of her mind.

The package was a padded Jiffy postal bag, rather like a large padded envelope that was fastened securely by staples. Ilona examined it carefully, then went to Alistair's desk that took up the whole of one corner of the living area. Feeling somewhat like a spy, she searched the drawers till she found what she was looking for, and was pleased that his stapler was the same size as the one used to close the package.

Using his ornamental stiletto paper knife, she carefully opened and removed the staples and poured the contents, two cassettes, on to the desk. They both had adhesive paper labels on them with the contents of the tapes written by hand on to the labels.

She searched the drawers of the desk once more

and drew a sigh of relief when she found a batch of labels almost the same size as those on the cassette. With her nail scissors and a razor blade that she found in Alistair's bathroom, she carefully cut the label to the same size as the one on the cassette and wrote exactly what was on it on to her dummy label.

Then she went to Alistair's collection of pre-recorded cassettes and picked two at random. She smiled to herself when she found that one of them was an old tape of her own, one of the first recordings she had ever made, entitled 'Ilona Craig—Song for Hurting Hearts.' Her mind flew back to the time she had recorded it and the fun she had had finding songs for it. But she pulled herself reluctantly back to the present and covered the printed label with her own false one. It would pass at a glance, she thought, but careful inspection would show it had been tampered with. It didn't matter. Once Alistair played it he would know anyway. She just needed him to know that she had substituted the tapes.

She replaced the tampered tapes into the cassette cover and very carefully restapled the bag, so that it wasn't obvious that it had been opened. Now that had been taken care of, she replaced the paper knife, stapler and labels exactly where she had found them. Then she realised she had two tapes to dispose of.

She thought of putting them through his tape recorder and wiping them clean, then on closer inspection found that Simon had broken off the tabs that allowed this so that they couldn't be wiped accidentally, and in a way she was glad. It seemed a shame to wipe out all that work, no matter what the reason.

Behind her, she heard the lift and knew that Mattie was returning, so hastily she put the tapes into the covers of the one she had substituted and replaced them in the cassette rack.

When Mattie stepped out of the lift, Ilona was in the kitchen putting on the kettle and smiling softly to herself. 'Song for Hurting Hearts', Ilona mused—very apt, almost poetic justice. But she doubted that Alistair would recognise that. Still, *she* would know, and that in itself was a kind of reward.

Mattie had been shopping in anticipation of Alistair's return, and she chatted happily about the dinner she planned for the following evening, and Ilona was tempted to tell her she wouldn't be there.

She hated hurting Mattie after so many years of friendship and confidences. But Mattie *was* his mother, and Ilona couldn't bring herself to put her old friend into such an unenviable position. She knew in her heart that Mattie would understand how she felt.

But she also knew that Mattie would have to find an excuse for her son and would try to persuade her to stay and hear his explanations.

Ilona didn't want explanations. Not now. She wanted everything to be as it had been, and that was clearly impossible. She couldn't forgive Alistair, not now, perhaps not ever. No, she told herself, *not ever*. No 'perhaps'—that would be leaving a way out for him, and she didn't want to give him one.

It was hard for her, knowing that Mattie was going to be hurt, to continue as if everything was all right, and she found it more and more difficult as the day went on. Mattie seemed to sense her unease, and eventually, putting it down to excitement over Alistair's return, insisted that Ilona have an early night. Ilona agreed with relief and took herself to bed, where she tried to still the nervous flutterings of her heart in the pages of a book, till at last she fell into an uneasy sleep—a sleep broken by vivid dreams of Alistair's lips on hers and his arms holding her tight.

She woke in the morning, still tired and drawn, her nerves stretched tight as bowstrings that hummed at the slightest touch.

Over breakfast, she carefully prepared Mattie for what was to come. 'I've got to go to my bank today, Mattie,' she commented quietly over her coffee. 'There are a few things I have to make sure are taken care of back in Sydney.'

'Oh, I can do that for you, dear,' Mattie replied. 'You only have to tell me what to do.'

Ilona floundered, 'No, it will need my signature. There's an insurance premium to be paid and the rates on my flat are due soon. I have to organise for my bank to pay them, in case I'm here longer than I expected.'

Mattie smiled brightly. 'Oh, I'm so glad! You must have decided to sort things out with Alistair if you're thinking of staying.'

Ilona allowed her to continue thinking like that. She knew it was wrong, and when Mattie found out she would be very hurt. But at the moment it was for the best. Or so she told herself, hastily.

'But how,' Mattie broke her train of thought,

'will you be able to get to the bank without being recognised?'

'I've thought of that,' Ilona answered quietly. 'I thought I'd just go in a pair of jeans with dark glasses on and my hair covered by a scarf. I'll only need to be gone a short while, and as long as I get my business done in the manager's office I shouldn't have any trouble.'

'I suppose not.' Mattie didn't sound too sure. 'Shouldn't I come with you?'

'No!' Ilona almost shouted, then carefully modulated her voice so that her nervousness didn't show. 'I know you've got a lot you want to do here this morning, so I'll go by myself. It will be nice to get out for a while,' she smiled, trying to put Mattie at ease.

'Well, if you're sure——' Mattie left it at that, happy to be able to start planning for Alistair's return.

A little later Ilona returned to the kitchen looking decidedly unrecognisable in her jeans and sandals, a plain scarf covering her hair and large black sunglasses masking her face and covering her well-known emerald eyes.

'How's that?' she asked.

'Oh, that's fine, dear,' Mattie smiled. 'No one should recognise you like that—I hope!'

'So do I,' replied Ilona, kissing Mattie on the cheek. 'I've rung for a taxi. It should be here soon, so I'll be off now.' She gave her friend a fierce hug, much to the older woman's astonishment. 'I love you, Mattie,' she added, before picking up her bag and hurrying towards the lift.

As the doors closed, Ilona saw Mattie watching her with a strange, puzzled look on her face that wrung her heart, and she determined to let her friend know why she had been forced to take the action she had as soon as possible.

Please don't hate me, Mattie, she begged silently, brushing a tear away from beneath her glasses. You'll understand one day. Oh! I hope you will!

CHAPTER NINE

ILONA climbed into her waiting taxi with a sigh of relief—relief that she hadn't really lied to Mattie. She really did have to go to her bank, and she gave the driver the address of its main Adelaide branch. Her rates were due soon and the premium on her household insurance policy, and she wanted to arrange payment of them since she certainly didn't plan on returning to Sydney for a while yet.

She had planned to—that was until last night. Before going to bed, she had been sure that to return to Sydney would have been the best plan. She had friends there, and she could have settled back into her flat and had Simon, on his return from Tasmania, not to mention Simon's wife Ruth, to turn to. But she had changed her mind.

While going through her handbag to sort out what she would need, she had found the key to Alistair's shack. In all the confusion surrounding her hospitalisation, she had forgotten to return it and apparently he had forgotten she had it. Now the shack seemed the best place for her. She would be on her own, able to sort out her tangled emotions in quiet solitude.

It seemed like cheating somehow to use it without permission from either Alistair or Mattie. But he had cheated her, hadn't he? Her voice came out in a whisper, making the taxi driver give her a strange look in his rear-view mirror.

Ilona covered her mouth in a feigned cough.

'Here you are, lady,' the driver said, pulling up his cab in front of the bank building. 'Don't I know you from somewhere?' he asked as Ilona paid him.

'No, I'm sure we've never met,' she replied.

'You just look a bit familiar,' he added, giving her a wave as he left.

Ilona was used to that sort of recognition and had found over the years that her truthful if slightly ambiguous reply, usually worked, as it had this time. Perhaps later the driver would realise who she was, but she doubted it.

She took a deep breath to calm her nerves and went into the cool, high-ceilinged bank. She was a little unsure of how she would be treated here, but she knew that to set her plans in motion she had to take the risk.

She steeled herself to act as she would if things were normal as she approached the information desk. She realised then how much the events of the previous days had affected her, knew that it would take all her will power to return to the person she had been before Alistair had broken down her defences.

The girl at the desk was pleasant enough, but rather surprised when Ilona insisted that she see the manager without first giving her name. However, Ilona's tone was assured enough to force the issue and within minutes she was ushered into the manager's office.

He was more than helpful when Ilona produced her papers and he had recovered from his surprise. He arranged for her payments to be made without hesitation and returned to the office with the cash that she had requested from her account. In fact he couldn't have been more helpful, and she found herself explaining to him her need for anonymity. He seemed to understand, and assured her that her visit to his bank would be completely confidential.

'In fact,' he told her conspiratorially 'if there is any other way I can help, Miss Craig, I'd be only too glad.'

'Well——' Ilona wondered if she should ask him, then decided she should. 'I need to rent a car, and I don't want to advertise the fact.'

'That will be no problem,' the manager assured her. 'One of our clients runs a car rental business and I'm sure if I explained the situation, he'll be only too willing to help.' So saying, he looked up his telephone index and dialled a number.

Ilona looked around the office as he spoke into the phone, then turned towards him as she heard the receiver being replaced in its cradle.

'That's been sorted out for you. If you can find your way to this address,' he handed her a card, 'your car will be ready for you. I've taken the liberty of arranging payment for it on a weekly basis directly from your account. So if you'd care to sign these forms, you won't have to worry about that.'

'That's very kind of you.' Ilona really was pleased and signed with alacrity.

'Would you like me to arrange a taxi for you?' the manager asked, the phone already in his hand.

Ilona agreed, and a few minutes later was in the cab heading towards the rental agency, where without fuss she signed the documents and took possession of a medium-sized inconspicuous station wagon.

Now that her plans were working to her satisfaction, she drove through the city towards the road to Wallaroo, her eyes searching for a shopping complex. She found one without difficulty and parked in the car park close to a bank of public telephones. She knew she had to tell Mattie not to worry, and that was something she wasn't relishing.

Mattie answered immediately, and before she could speak, Ilona told her she was going away and not to worry. 'I'll be in contact with you, Mattie, very soon. Please don't worry—I just have to be by myself for a while,' she finished, then hung up before Mattie could reply.

She found a small, dark coffee shop in the complex and taking a seat well in the rear of the shop, ordered coffee and sandwiches. Then over her lunch she carefully made a list of what she would need in the way of clothes and provisions.

List in hand, she spent a surprisingly happy two hours, shopping like any normal suburban housewife. It had been so long since she'd been able to do so that she had forgotten how enjoyable it could be.

But her pleasure came to an abrupt end when she found herself drawn to a music shop. She had had to leave her guitar at the apartment and had decided to buy another—nothing special, just a cheap acoustic guitar that she could strum and pick out tunes on.

Unfortunately the proprietor was a youngish man who obviously kept up with his business, and he watched her intently as she examined the instrument she wanted. When she took it to the counter to pay, he surprised her by calling her by name. His reaction was such that it was impossible to deny her identity, but by agreeing to autograph some records for him and explaining that she was on holiday incognito, she managed to convince him to keep her visit quiet. Whether or not he would was another story, Ilona thought, as she piled her purchases into the station wagon and, checking her map, set off for Spencer Gulf.

She arrived at the shack close to sunset and after unpacking and turning on and stacking the fridge, made her bed and ate a meal of cold meat and tinned vegetables. Then she cleaned up the kitchen and with her coffee in her hand went to sit, in the growing darkness, on her favourite rock to see the last of the sunset and watch the moon come up.

It was so peaceful, so relaxing, so far from her troubles that at last, for the first time in as long as she could remember, she took herself to bed and slept content and dreamless till the sun woke her next morning.

The next day was spent making the shack as comfortable as possible. She even managed to move the dinghy from Alistair's room out on to the beach. It took her longer than it had Alistair, but she refused to be beaten, and by dint of much manoeuvring and quiet cursing under her breath, she managed it.

In the process of tidying up she found a cache of paints and brushes. She looked them over carefully and reached the conclusion that they had been intended for the inside of the cabin and, delighted, she decided to use them, and started in

Alistair's room. She was happy that the colours were bright—lemon, apple-green, violet and plenty of white, and she spent the next week happily painting everything in sight, until her clothes, face, legs and hair were paint-spotted and her body was healthily exhausted.

Between bouts of painting, she ate hugely and took long walks along the beach, feeding the gulls till they followed her every time she appeared begging in raucous caws for titbits. Her evenings were spent reading, listening to the transistor radio she had bought and strumming quietly but happily on her new guitar.

The day that the painting was finished, she surveyed her handiwork. The kitchen sparkled, apple-green walls and stark white woodwork, the cupboards white with green trim. Alistair's room she had painted lemon with a bright white trim and she had painted the old wardrobe, dressing table and bedhead white too. She had used the violet for her room and the whole shack had taken on an air of being cared for. But something was missing, and she decided that it needed curtains—bright, bold prints to tone with the new colour schemes and perhaps even bedspreads and a couple of washable tableclothes.

She hadn't really thought what Alistair would say about the changes, but when she did she decided she didn't care much. If he didn't like it, he could re-do it all. She was just glad that the painting had given her something to do, something else to think about besides herself and her problems. And she was going to finish it with the touches she had decided on. At least then she would be able to tell herself that she had finished a job she had started from scratch with no help at all. It felt good to be working like this. It had been too long since she had done anything like it and she had forgotten how much fun it could be. Maybe that was one of her problems. It had been too long since she'd been able to decide to do something and then do it. For too long she had had to ask Simon whether she could do this or that. For too long she had had other people do things for her. Now that she had had a taste of really taking care of herself again she wondered if she would be able to slip back into the pampered existence she had known. Maybe this problem with her throat had been a blessing in disguise, giving her the time and the way to sit back and really look at what she'd become. And more important—what was ahead.

More years of being someone she really wasn't. More years of having to lead a life in the limelight. More years of having to hide if she wanted to do something like this. And most of all, more years of having to decide if new friends were interested in her or what she could do for them. Only a month ago that had seemed like the sort of life she was cut out for, and she had thought of no other. Now she wasn't sure, and she knew that she had much more soul-searching ahead of her before she would be able to drop back into her old identity.

Pushing those thoughts aside, she pulled out a notepad and pencil and over a coffee made a list of what she felt was needed to finish her redecoration of the shack. She hoped she would be able to buy them all in Wallaroo or Kadina and decided she would set out early the next day to shop in the small towns close by.

Tired but happy, she climbed into bed, closing her eyes after surveying the bright cleanness of her room, and slept like a baby.

The next day was Friday, she noticed when she checked the date, and she realised then how time had slipped away. With no TV and only the radio now and then, she had completely lost track of the days and she laughed aloud to think that Ilona Craig, star, didn't know what day it was. She laughed because it was one of Simon's favourite sayings when he was being derogatory about someone—someone whom Simon thought wasn't too bright. 'You know that Bill Smith?' he would ask. 'I bet he wouldn't even know what day it was!'

She wondered to herself, as she threw her toilet gear and a change of clothes into a bag she had bought, how Simon would react to her not knowing what day it was, and the thought buoyed her mood no end. The first thing she planned on her outing was a stop at the Wallaroo Hotel where she planned on booking a room for the day and having a hot bath and washing the paint from her hair. She had taken showers under the outside bush shower every day, but the thought of a hot bath was tempting and she decided that after all her hard work she deserved it.

She had no trouble booking into the hotel under an assumed name, and she spent an hour soaking in the old-fashioned bathtub that was deep enough to let her sit in water up to her neck. She hummed to herself as she lathered her hair and was surprised as she looked in the mirror to

see that her skin had taken on a healthy golden
glow. Her hair had lightened in the sun in streaks
that women paid dearly for to achieve at the
hairdresser's, and her tan, she thought, put a ray-
lamp tan to shame.

After her bath, Ilona pulled her damp hair
back in a ponytail, noticing as she did so that it
really needed styling again. But somehow it
didn't matter. She was more interested at the
moment in using the laundry facilities at the
hotel. She had thrown her laundry into the back
of the station wagon in the hopes that she would
find a laundromat, but the proprietor had said
she could use the hotel's laundry facilities and she
accepted happily.

It had been so long since she had actually done
her own laundry that it was an experience for her,
and she revelled in the role of housewife as, pegs
in mouth, she pegged her sheets and clothes on
the lines at the back of the hotel. More articles for
her list, she thought, a clothes line, pegs and
detergent. She smiled as she realised that she was
setting herself up for quite a long stay. But her
eyes clouded as she thought that Alistair could
decide to drop in and spoil it all. Still, she told
herself, he seemed to have been too busy to worry
about fishing for a while, so perhaps she would
be able to stay for quite a while yet.

After she had done her chores, Ilona decided
that time had come to try to fill her shopping list
and to phone Mattie to let her know that she was
all right. She wondered if Mattie would be able
to tell where the phone call was coming from. But
was happy when she found an STD telephone
and didn't have to put through a normal trunk

call. At least that was one hurdle jumped. Mattie would only know that she was calling long distance—nothing else.

Ilona fed her coins into the telephone and dialled the number.

'Is that you, Mattie?' she asked as the line cleared of beeps.

'I'm sorry, Mattie is back at her own home.' Alistair's voice made her heart flutter guiltily. What was he doing at the apartment at that time of day? And why hadn't she realised that Mattie would have gone home?

'Are you still there? I can give you her home number if you want it.' He sounded annoyed, as if he had been interrupted.

'I'm sorry to trouble you,' Ilona said quietly. 'I have her number—I'll call her there.'

She took the receiver from her ear to hang up and heard an angry shout. 'Ilona, is that you? Don't hang up, damn you! I want to speak to you.'

She couldn't speak to him. She was amazed that his voice still had the power to affect her like this. She thought she had come to terms with that. But it was clear she hadn't, and she hung up on his exasperated, angry words with shaking hands.

She was shaking so badly that she had trouble feeding more coins into the telephone to call Mattie. But she knew she had to.

Mattie answered promptly and her voice was obviously worried, but the ring of relief in it when she heard Ilona's voice was enough for Ilona to know that she was doing the right thing, and she calmed considerably.

'Mattie, I'm just ringing to let you know I'm fine,' she said.

'Where are you? Simon's worried sick and Alistair's threatening to call in the police!'

Ilona was shocked. He had no right to do that, and her indignation was enough to drive the shaking feelings away completely. 'He has no right to do that, Mattie. I'm not missing, just on holiday, and I want to be by myself for a while.'

'Ian's worried too. You know,' Mattie's tone was more normal now, 'he said to tell you to check with a doctor soon, if you haven't already. I wish you'd speak to Alistair, dear. I don't really understand what happened between you two. I know it was some sort of business problem, but I'm sure if you spoke to him, Alistair could explain. He's not eating and I'm really worried about him.'

Ilona sighed. It was his own fault. He should have told her about Fame at the beginning instead of hiding his interest. 'I'm sorry about that, Mattie. But there's nothing to say. He'll just have to work out his own salvation—that's what I'm trying to do. Will you call Simon and tell him I'll be in touch?'

'Of course I will. But can't you tell me where you are? I promise I'll keep it to myself. But I could come to you if you needed me. No one need know . . . not even Alistair, if that's what you want,' Mattie finished reluctantly.

'No, Mattie dear, it's better this way. When I've sorted myself out, I'll come back to Adelaide to see you and perhaps you can come to Sydney with me for a holiday.'

'So you're in Sydney?' Mattie jumped to a conclusion that Ilona hadn't wanted to imply.

'No, I'm not. If I was, Simon would have found me, wouldn't he?' Ilona hoped Mattie would accept that. But she knew, somehow, that Mattie had decided she was in Sydney and nothing Ilona could say would change her mind.

There was silence for a moment, and Ilona could hear the older woman's breathing. She could almost feel the concern coming through the telephone and she cut the conversation off hurriedly before she broke down and told her friend everything.

'I must go now, Mattie. Don't worry—and take care. I'll see you soon,' and she hung up, shaken.

It took a few minutes for her to pull herself together. She almost went back to the hotel to get her car so that she could flee back to the shack and safety, then her mind took over again from her heart and she was able to convince herself that what she had done and was doing was best for *her*. She knew deep down that it was selfish in a way. But she consoled herself with the thought that she could be no use to anyone else until she had got herself sorted out.

Calmer, if still a little guilty, she continued her shopping spree, surprised at the range of goods available to her in such a small community. She had little problem in acquiring the curtains and bedspreads, and even found a bright washable rug to place inside the kitchen door as well as some gaily coloured kitchen canisters to sit on top of the fridge and add the final touch to her redecoration.

It was past lunch time when she had finished, but still early enough for her to order a meal at the hotel, and she returned there thankfully to eat and review her list.

She had just finished putting away her purchases and was taking her seat at a table in the lounge while her lunch was prepared when she noticed the man at the bar. She had felt that someone was watching her and had glanced round surreptitiously to see if she was right. She was.

The man at the bar looked faintly familiar, and Ilona racked her brains to try to remember where she had met him before. As he approached her, bent on speaking, his friendly smile brought it back. The local doctor! Damn, why did I have to run into him? Ilona cursed silently, while smiling at his greeting.

'Well, well, I didn't dare to hope we'd meet again,' he smiled, pulling out a chair opposite her. 'Mind if I join you for a moment?'

'Not at all,' Ilona replied. She certainly did, but she felt she couldn't tell him so directly.

All sorts of questions flashed through her mind. Shall I tell him I don't want anyone to know I'm here? Will he tell all the locals? What am I going to do?

'I didn't think I'd have the pleasure of seeing you again,' the doctor said pleasantly. 'Ian Anderson contacted me and told me that the operation was a success, though there's still some doubt about your singing.'

'Oh, I didn't know Ian would have contacted you!'

'Professional courtesy. I *did* refer you, and as I'm the referring doctor it's courtesy to give me a report.'

'I see. When did you speak to him?' Ilona queried.

'Only last week. He seemed worried—seems you disappeared without a trace. Want to tell me about it?'

'It's personal really. I felt I needed some time to myself and this seemed like a good place to be. You aren't going to get on the phone as soon as you leave here and tell, are you?' she added anxiously.

'No, I won't do that. As long as you drop into my office after lunch and let me check your throat. That way we can keep it confidential between doctor and patient, and I'll know you're all right.'

'Thank you, Doctor—I appreciate that. You've no idea how much!'

'Well, I'll be off. See you shortly.'

'Yes, fine—and thank you.'

Ilona ate her lunch in a dream almost. Should I go and see him? she thought. Maybe if I just don't bother he'll still keep quiet. But she wasn't sure, so she finally decided that it would be best to do as he had asked, and before driving back to the shack with her shopping, she called in for her check-up.

He was pleased to see her and quite pleased with his examination. Everything was as it should be, and he agreed with her comment that being alone and talking to no one for as long as she had had speeded the recovery. But he gave her his home address in case anything should go wrong, so that she could contact him at any time of the day or night.

In a way, Ilona was pleased that she had run

into him. Now she could tell Mattie when next she phoned her that she'd seen a doctor and perhaps then Mattie would stop worrying. She was almost happy when she arrived back at the shack, and she set about hanging the curtains she had bought and putting her clean laundry away with a new zest. She had overcome the trepidation she had felt at making contact with Adelaide and was once more convinced that she was doing the right thing.

She spent the next day cleaning up the shack. Sorting out cupboards and generally putting everything into order. Only when she had finished and put all the rubbish that had accumulated over the years into garbage bags ready to go to the Wallaroo tip did she realise that things would quickly get back to the chaos she had found before her clean-up once she had to bring the dinghy back inside. Still, once she left, she probably would never return, so she would never see it degenerate again. It wouldn't be her problem, though she felt that what was needed was the lean-to rebuilt and made into a lock-up. That way, the boat could be left there in relative safety.

She was inspecting the shed, wondering to herself how much time, money and effort it would take to carry out her idea when she pulled herself up with a jerk. Painting Alistair's shack, was one thing, major rebuilding something else. Still, it would have been nice to finish the job. The thought crossed her mind that maybe when she returned to Sydney, she could get her solicitor to approach Alistair to sell. Approach him without revealing who the prospective buyer was.

The more she thought about it, the more she liked the idea. But she was sure he wouldn't sell. Still, it would be fun to try and much more fun to tell him who he'd sold to if he did! Then a nagging doubt crossed her mind. It would be much nicer if they *both* owned it! How can you think that, Ilona Craig? she asked herself. After everything he's put you through! She couldn't really tell why she had become so attached to this place, why it meant so much to her, but she knew that when she finally left—never to return—something special would be missing from her life.

It was dusk by the time she had finished her inspection of the lean-to, and she checked the dinner that was cooking slowly in the oven. It wasn't quite ready, so she picked up her guitar and sat on the steps strumming softly and watching the sea. She felt very much at peace with herself. But somehow that wasn't quite enough, and she wondered why she felt something was missing. She had everything she had ever dreamed of—money, fame, friends who loved her. What more could she want? The thought that perhaps a husband and children was what were missing had just crossed her mind. And she was prepared for the first time in her life to think seriously about that when the roar of a motor car interrupted her.

It wasn't coming here, but taking the road that passed above the shack, and her heart left her mouth, only to jump back into it when she heard the shouts and screams of drunken revelry and the sound of the car stopping.

For the first time since she had come here, she was afraid. No one had come near her for almost two weeks, and now that someone had it brought fear. Not the fear of being recognised, but the fear that was to be found in the city at night, because the shouts and laughter hadn't stopped. Instinctively she ran headlong inside and locked the door. She hadn't switched on any lights, so the shack was in darkness, and she hurried round making sure all the windows were closed.

She cowered in fear at the kitchen table, waiting for the voices to come closer. But they didn't, and the fear began to recede. Then they were quiet for a while and she wondered if they had left. They couldn't have, she told herself, she hadn't heard the car leave—and the fear took hold of her again and her throat constricted. Perhaps they were creeping up on her. What was she to do?

Then she remembered the rifle. She had found it in the wardrobe in Alistair's room and had wrapped it in a towel and replaced it, sure that she would have no need of it. She had wondered at the time why it was here; Alistair didn't seem the type to use a gun and there didn't seem to be any need for one in this solitude.

Shaking, she unwrapped it, and found to her dismay that she had no idea how to use it. But perhaps the sight of it would be enough. She wondered if she should go out with it and confront the people. Perhaps they would leave if they knew someone was here, and she wondered if she should turn on the lights. God, why isn't Alistair here? she found herself asking the darkness. Alistair would know what to do.

The silence was unnerving, more unnerving than the drunken shouts, and she stood in the kitchen holding the rifle to her like a lifebelt, wondering how she could get help. She had just decided to try to reach her car and drive to town or to the nearest house when she heard a rattle on the roof.

My God, they're throwing stones! she screamed silently. But the sound wasn't like stones and she realised that they were shots when the bedroom window exploded and the glass shattered all over the floor. She couldn't leave now! But what could she do?

Any courage she had had almost left her, until she realised that all the shots were coming from the back of the shack, and she crept under the kitchen table for protection. It seemed like hours before the firing stopped and the sound of a car engine impinged on her shaken ears. They were leaving! Vandals, that was all they were. They must have thought the place was deserted.

Ilona crept into the bedroom and peering fearfully through the broken window, saw the headlights and tail-lights of the car disappear into the darkness. Still clinging to the rifle, she switched on the lights and with shaking hands began to make herself a cup of coffee—liberally laced with the rum that Alistair kept in the kitchen.

She was calm after that, but it was more the calm of shock—shock and horror, shock that this could happen to her. She ate her dinner mechanically, unable to think or plan, and went to bed fully clothed, cradling the rifle in her arms. The rifle had become her life support even though it wasn't loaded, and she didn't know how to load it.

She lay in bed sleepless, shocked and bewildered. Nothing like this had ever happened to her before and she realised how vulnerable she was alone. Alone, that was the problem! For the first time in her life she really felt alone, and the thought of the years ahead without someone, someone to cling to, to love, to call her own, became more than she could bear. For the first time in her life, she saw the years stretch in front of her, not as the glittering future she had always pictured, but as lonely, bitter years.

She saw the years ahead when Mattie would be gone, and Simon, and her future for once looked bleak. Everything that had happened to her over the past few weeks, crowded in on her and she wept bitter tears. She had lost Alistair because she had been too proud to let him give her an explanation. Simon would be angry with her because she'd gone off by herself, too full of her own self-interest to take him into her confidence. She had even put Mattie through a bad time. Dear Mattie, almost like a mother to her, and she hadn't bothered to think how Mattie would feel—not really. She'd been too full of herself. Ilona Craig—star! Ilona Craig—selfish, unthinking coward!

Too much of a coward to face what had happened. Too much of a coward to let her friends help her through. Even too much of a coward to face a couple of drunken louts who would probably have run for their lives if someone had walked out of the shack and confronted them.

Well, maybe it wasn't too late. Maybe if she went back tomorrow and apologised to Mattie and Simon she'd be able to salvage something. Maybe it was too late. But at least she could try, and she drifted into sleep, her courage returning.

CHAPTER TEN

ILONA woke with a start. It was pitch dark and she was still clutching feverishly at the rifle in her hands. Her hands had frozen on to the weapon and she stretched them tentatively to bring them back to ife. She wondered what had woken her. Then as if to answer her unspoken questions the sound of a car door slamming at the front of the shack broke the stillness.

Oh no, they can't be back! They can't be! The words shrieked in her head, as she sat bolt upright in the bed hugging the rifle to her chest as if it could magically protect her.

She strained her ears, listening intently for any sounds that might tell her how many there were, but there was no sound, and she relaxed slightly, beginning to believe she had been hearing things. Rising as quietly as she could, she crept into the kitchen to peer out of the window in the hope of seeing nothing. But as she pulled the new, bright curtain aside she was dazzled by the flashlight, and she drew back frantic and screaming.

The door burst open and she held up the rifle, sobbing, 'Don't come any closer or I'll shoot!'

The rifle was swept from her grasp and the light switched on almost at the same instant. 'And what, may I ask, did you think you were going to do with this?' Alistair's voice was half angry, half mocking. 'Apart from the fact that it isn't loaded, the safety catch in still on,' he added, examining the weapon. 'What had you planned to do? Club me to death?'

Never in her whole life had she been so pleased to see anyone. 'What are you doing here? You frightened me half to death!' Her voice was weak and shaky and her legs wouldn't hold her, so she sank down thankfully on to a chair.

'Never mind what I'm doing here. What are you doing here? And why the gun? You didn't seem to need it last time you were here!'

'I hadn't had anyone shoot out my bedroom window last time,' Ilona answered. There was no anger in her tone, only relief, and Alistair looked at her closely.

'What on earth do you mean?' he asked, as if he didn't quite catch what she'd said.

Ilona watched the puzzlement in his eyes. She might not want to see him, she might even hate him for what he had done. But she was glad he was there, glad *he* had the rifle, glad he'd come. 'Just take a look at the bedroom window,' she said quietly.

He stalked into the bedroom, switching the light on as he did and the sounds of his angry cursing floated back to Ilona. 'Damned vandals! I hope to God they come back while I'm here!' He strode angrily back to the kitchen. 'This happened earlier this evening, didn't it?'

'Yes,' Ilona replied, 'but how did you know?'

'The Wallaroo police phoned me earlier. They'd had reports of some young hoodlums playing havoc with the shacks along here and they thought I'd better come down and see if they'd done any damage here. They'll be out some time this morning and I wanted to be here when they did.'

'Oh! Why?' Ilona asked anxiously.

Alistair laughed at her expression. 'I thought it would be easier for me to explain your presence here than for you to. And besides, I didn't want to have to bail you out for trespassing.'

She was stunned. He'd known she was here! But how? Her courage was returning and she felt her legs would obey her, so she rose and put on the kettle for coffee, asking quietly over her shoulder, 'How did you know I was here?'

'You'd better put a lot of rum in mine—that is if you're planning to make one for me! Or are you planning to throw it over me?'

She ignored the remark. 'You didn't answer my question!'

'That's right, I didn't!'

'Well, are you going to tell me?' Ilona's hands began to shake with anger and frustration. She turned with both mugs of coffee in her hands to see Alistair surveying the room with a quizzical expression on his face.

'My, my, you *have* been busy! Don't tell me you did *all* this with your own fair hands. I must say you didn't do a bad job! Or did you get a painter in to keep you company?'

Ilona refused to rise to his baiting. 'I did it myself,' she said, slamming his coffee in front of him so that half of it spilled on to the new tablecloth.

'Temper, temper! Now you've ruined this nice tablecloth. And there's no one but you to wash it!'

She sat down at the opposite end of the table,

ignoring him and sipping her own rum-laced coffee. 'I suppose you'd like me to play twenty questions to find out how you knew?'

Alistair grinned. 'No! But I think there's more important things to talk about than how I knew you were here. But just to set the record straight, since it seems to be the most important thing for you, I'll tell you.'

Ilona's temper flared. 'Don't do me any favours,' she snapped.

'Oh, I won't! I stopped doing you any favours about a fortnight ago when you walked out and left my mother worried sick about you. You're a selfish little bitch, Ilona Craig—selfish to the last. Not a word about how Simon *or* Mattie are. Just how did you know I was here?' Alistair imitated her throaty voice sarcastically. 'Well, that was easy! I got an electricity bill a couple of days ago, and it was fairly obvious from that that someone was here!'

'It didn't have to be me,' Ilona threw at him helplessly.

'I didn't know anyone else who had a key,' Alistair snapped, glaring at her. 'In fact I had my suspicions earlier that you were here, but the electricity bill confirmed them.'

'If you thought that, why didn't you do anything about it,' Ilona retorted, 'since you were *so* upset about Mattie.'

Alistair half rose from his chair, a look of fury on his face, then sank back breathing hard. 'What the hell would have been the use?' he snarled. 'You'd made up your mind to disappear. It wasn't any of my business!'

'Then why did you come racing down here tonight?' she asked in a quiet voice.

'Not for your benefit,' he snapped.

'Oh?' she asked.

'I came to save myself the trouble of having to come to the Wallaroo police station after they'd charged you with breaking and entering. I didn't want to have one of my recording stars mixed up with the police!'

Ilona's hard-won control snapped. 'You—you rotten . . .!' she spluttered, lost for words. 'That's all you think of! You don't give a damn about me or Mattie or anyone else. Just your bloody business! Everything you do is directed towards furthering your interests, and you have the gall, the unmitigating gall,' she shouted, pushing her chair back and rising to her feet in fury, 'to call me selfish! It's you—you who's selfish! Not only selfish but a user! You used me and Simon, and I wouldn't be surprised if you used Megan as well!'

'Megan has nothing to do with this.' Alistair's voice was flat, hard and menacing. But Ilona was too angry to notice.

'Megan has nothing to do with this,' she mocked. 'But you do! You do, Alistair McLean, and I hate you for it!' Her hand, still holding the coffee mug, came up as if of its own accord and the contents flew across the table into his face.

She stood for a second, stunned, then whirled past him and out of the door while he wiped the coffee from his eyes with her already ruined tablecloth'.

'That's right—run!' she heard as she fled. 'Run away again! But there isn't anywhere you can run to. You've left your car keys here,' and she heard his bitter laughter as she ran towards the sand.

Ilona fled along the beach in the moonlight, breathless and tearful, until she could run no more. Then, using the lights of the shack as a guide, she trailed dejectedly back to sit again, lost and alone, on her favourite rock, staring fixedly out at the moonlit sea.

She had been so pleased to see him at first, glad that someone had come to dispel the fears of the previous evening. Glad, she had to admit, that it had been him. Why, oh, why had she allowed things to get to this state? She'd promised herself that today, because it was today, four a.m. by her watch, that today she'd go back and quietly sort everything out. Perhaps she would never get back the mindless joy that Alistair had brought to her before. But maybe, just maybe, they could have started again.

She had wanted to let him explain his actions to her, wanted to accept his explanations, but five minutes in his company and they were spitting at one another like wildcats. He knew she was here and hadn't come. If he'd felt anything for her he would have. Her mind was a whirl of conflicting emotions. One part of her wanted to run back and throw herself into his arms—forgive him everything and beg him to forget the past weeks. The other part hated him—hated him for his arrogance and selfish pride, hated him for using her, for making love to her to bind her to him so that she'd sign his contract. Hated him for breaking down her defences and making her vulnerable.

The night breeze blew silently round her, soothing her aching head and drying the tears that fell from her sea-green eyes. What was she to do now? It was four o'clock in the morning and she could hardly go back to the shack to pack her things. She couldn't face him—not yet! But she knew she would have to. Have to pull herself together and walk into that cabin, collect her belongings and with as much dignity as she could muster, leave. Leave Spencer Gulf, Adelaide and South Australia, never to return. Not while Alistair lived here. Go back to Sydney and pick up her life again. But not as a singer—not yet. Even if it meant giving up a career she had spent so many years in building, she would never sing again if it meant that Alistair McLean would benefit in any way.

Perhaps Simon could somehow get her out of that damned contract. But why bother? She had enough money and investments to start in some other business. Over the past few days the idea of standing on stage again had lost its old attraction. Perhaps now was the time to think of building a new future, a future without the problems of her present career. A future where her life would be her own and not hemmed in by fans and managers, agents and contracts, records and public appearances. But most of all, a future without Alistair McLean.

The idea of a new future was appealing, but frightening too. How could she organise a future without him? It would mean without Mattie too! God, what a mess, what a rotten, rotten mess! And it's all been your own fault, Ilona told herself. You walked in and fell without once thinking what the outcome would be!

Fell like a lovesick schoolgirl for a pair of brown eyes, a lopsided grin and hair that gleams copper in the sun. Fell like a child for a man who couldn't in a million years want you for ever when he could have his pick of the most beautiful girls around. Why would he pick someone like me? she asked herself. If I'd been thinking straight I would only have to take a good look at Megan to know that he wanted me for more than just myself!

What a fool I've been! But everyone's entitled to make a fool of themselves once in their life. What I have to do now is put it behind me. Chalk it up to experience! It only happened because he was there when I was down and needed someone. I'll know to be on my guard in future when I'm vulnerable, and it won't happen again. And that's a promise—never again!

It's bound to hurt for a while, hurt more because I was stupid than because he meant anything. I can live without him—I've proved it over the last couple of weeks, and if he hadn't turned up now I probably would have managed for the rest of my life. So why should I let him affect me like this? He isn't anything special, just a man, and a not-too-honest one at that!

The more Ilona thought the stronger her convictions became and the more her courage returned. I can go back and get my things and leave. I don't have to let him goad me. I'll just ignore him. It's nearly five o'clock and the sun will be up soon—just the right time to pack up and leave. I can be back in Adelaide before it gets too hot and Mr McLean can shut up the shack by himself or stay here till he rots for all I care!

Ilona was pleased she had reached a decision. It would make it easier for her now that she knew exactly what she was going to do. She would go back now to Adelaide, say goodbye to Mattie and head back home to Sydney, home to her flat and the idea of a new life. She had plenty of time to decide what she would like to do and even where she wanted to live—it didn't have to be Sydney. Perhaps it would even be for the best if it wasn't. The only things keeping her there were her flat and Simon, and once Simon knew of her decision, she was sure he would help her no matter how disappointed he was.

Determined to take matters into her own hands and to resolve her problems as quickly as humanly possible, Ilona set about the task. Her first problem was to face Alistair, and white-faced with determination, she went back into the shack.

'I'm glad you're back,' said Alistair as she strode into the room. 'I was just about to call you. Breakfast's ready.'

Ilona was unprepared for his greeting. She'd been prepared for anger, abuse or even silence, but certainly not for this. 'I'm not hungry,' she responded defiantly.

Alistair pushed her into the nearest chair. 'I don't want any arguments. Eat it, or else!'

'Or else what?' she asked belligerently.

'Or else you'll wear it like I wore the coffee,' he answered with a stony smile, slapping a plate of scrambled eggs in front of her.

Ilona ate in silence. There seemed no reason not to, and she had a long drive ahead of her. At least she wouldn't leave hungry. She left the table as soon as she had finished and retired to her room to gather her belongings together.

She could hear Alistair clattering dishes in the

sink and then a silence. She wondered what he was doing, but couldn't bring herself to investigate. Finally, changed from the shorts and top she had slept in into jeans and a blouse, her hair plaited and pinned under a scarf, she emerged with her luggage.

Alistair was sitting at the table with a pile of papers that had obviously come from the open briefcase that sat on the floor beside his chair. 'Ready to go?' he asked. His voice was almost friendly, she noted.

'Yes, so I suppose this is goodbye!'

'Not yet! There's a few things we have to get straight before you fly the coop.'

'I was under the impression that we'd said all we had to say.' Ilona was near to tears and had difficulty in keeping her voice level.

'*You* might have. But I have a lot more to say, so you'd better sit down, because you're not leaving here till I've said them.' His voice was level, but Ilona caught a hint of determination bordering on menace and she sat down, more to keep her legs from shaking than in response to his order.

'Well, you'd better get on with it,' she told him shakily. 'I've got a long drive ahead of me.'

He just looked at her, raising one eyebrow in an unspoken question, and her heart began to flutter as it had before. 'Read these,' he commanded, tossing the bundle of papers across the table to her.

'What are they?' she asked, picking them up and beginning to scan them against all common sense. Her curiosity was awakened and got the better of her.

She flipped through the pages and found that they were business contracts and papers relating to Alistair's business interests and more specifically to his interests in Fame Records. 'Why should I be interested in these?' she asked, indicating the papers with a disdainful gesture.

'Because, my love,' he told her, and Ilona's cheeks reddened at the endearment, 'they'll explain a few things if you take the trouble to read them. But perhaps it would be simpler if I explained, then you can verify my explanation from those papers.'

'If you insist.' Ilona refused to give him any hint of her feelings, confused as they were.

'It seems I'll have to start at the beginning,' Alistair began.

'That's always a good place.' Her voice was facetious, and Alistair glared at her.

'First, you know that Mattie set us up to meet here. She told me so and I believe she also hinted as much to you. True?' The last was a question.

'Yes,' Ilona had to admit, 'that's true, and little good it did her.'

'Oh, I don't know,' Alistair mused, smiling. 'I enjoyed it. I thought you did too!'

'If all you've got to say is a rehash of the fool I made of myself, I'm leaving now!'

'Sit down and listen. You owe me that much,' he ordered.

'I owe you nothing!' Ilona snapped, her anger surfacing.

Alistair sighed. 'I knew this wasn't going to be easy, but you aren't helping. Please,' he asked softly, 'please, just listen.'

Ilona's eyes gazed into his and she called

herself every type of fool to be taken in again. But nothing on earth could have made her leave now. She had to hear his story, had to give him this chance—had to give *herself* this chance.

'I was as surprised to find you here as you were when I arrived. But I must say I was happy to see you again after so many years. I didn't know that you'd affect me the way you did, and in the beginning I felt it had nothing to do with *us* what I did for a living. In fact, I didn't even know that you were negotiating with Fame!'

Ilona couldn't help herself. All the pain she had felt at what she had believed was his betrayal surfaced. 'I'll bet!' she snapped.

'It's true! I didn't know that till we had dinner with Simon and Megan. I was extremely surprised to find her there. The phone call was from me—just to get her away from the table to find out what was going on.'

Ilona looked at him in disbelief. 'You really expect me to believe that?'

'Well, that's where those papers come in,' Alistair nodded at the bundle that she was fiddling with in her anxiety.

'If you take the trouble to read them, you'll find that what my company bought was another one that manufactured audio equipment. Part of their set-up was Fame. It was a sideline that tested their new equipment and made a few records to offset costs. We'd planned to close it down. But Megan, who was employed by the previous owners to try to make it pay, put a suggestion to the Board that seemed to have merit, and we decided to let her have a year to prove it was feasible. She had complete control and a budget separate from the rest of the business. If she couldn't start showing a profit after a year, Fame was to be closed down.' Alistair rose, still talking and began to make coffee.

'So, you see, I had no idea what she was up to, and when I found out at dinner that night and afterwards from you, I was between the devil and the deep blue sea! If I'd told you in the beginning about my connections with Fame it wouldn't have mattered. But I didn't think. I haven't thought straight since the first time I set eyes on you again down on the beach!'

Ilona's eyes widened and she riffled through the papers in her hands to hide their shaking. 'You could have told me then. I would have understood.'

'Would you?' asked Alistair, turning to face her and their eyes locked across the kitchen.

Ilona broke the contact. 'I think so—at that stage, I would have believed anything you told me. I'm not quite as naïve now.'

'Loney, I was *so* worried about you. Worried about your throat. Worried that you'd think I had a hand in the negotiations. I wanted to tell you, Simon wanted me to tell you . . .'

'Simon knew?' Ilona broke in.

'Yes, he knew, that's why he was so cool to me. He threatened to do all sorts of drastic things if I hurt you . . .'

'I know that,' Ilona said slowly. 'I heard him, I think, while I was coming out of the anaesthetic.'

'I didn't want to hurt you. But everything happened so fast and I convinced myself that once you were out of hospital I'd be able to let you see those papers and explain everything. But those damned newspaper men beat me to it, and by then it was too late!'

'That's easy to say now. As I recall, you only seemed to be interested in whether I'd be able to sing again!'

Alistair stared in disbelief. 'I didn't give a damn for myself if you'd sing again or not!' he told her angrily. 'But I was worried about you! I didn't know if you'd survive if you couldn't sing. I knew how much your career meant to you and I just wanted to see you happy!' He sat down opposite her again, wearily pushing a mug of coffee towards her. 'There, that one's boiling, if it helps any you can throw that one over me too. But I'd sooner you drank it!'

Ilona laughed harshly. 'You, worried about whether I'd sing again for my benefit? It's ironic really!'

'What's ironic?' Alistair was obviously confused.

'Well, I've just spent an hour sitting on a rock thinking about all this, and came to the conclusion that what's happened was a blessing in disguise.' Ilona paused to gather her thoughts together, for things were taking shape in her mind that had only been niggling in the background before. 'I came to the conclusion that singing didn't really mean as much to me as I'd thought. In fact I'd decided that I was going to give it up and start in some other business.' The words came out slowly and hesitantly as the aimless thoughts congealed into solid decisions. She began to formulate in words what had been swimming around in her mind. Putting into words, more for her own benefit than Alistair's, ideas that she had suppressed deliberately.

'You see, I'm nearly twenty-six now, and for years I've worked, worked hard, to make a name for myself. But I've missed out on so much.' Tears filled her eyes as she spoke the words held inside for so long. 'You were the first love that I've ever had, the first man I've ever thought seriously about, and I realised, subconsciously I suppose, that if I continue in the life I've been leading, there really isn't any place for a husband and family. I wouldn't admit that to myself. But I decided this morning to get out, find a life where I'd have time for myself and to let other people in.'

She was crying hard now, crying because she'd thrown away a chance at happiness with Alistair.

She told herself that she had never seriously thought that she and Alistair could have made a life together, regardless of Mattie's hints, but she had thought that perhaps they could have been happy together for a while. But as she sobbed she knew how much she loved him and how long it would take to get over the hurt. For ever! No matter what she did with her life from now on, she would never get over him. She knew now that she never had. She had loved him as a child, and as a teenager, and now she loved him as woman, and she sobbed the harder.

'Loney, you're getting all those papers wet. There's no need to cry, darling.' His hands were on her shoulders, caressing and tender, and she had no idea how he came to be standing behind her. 'Come on, sweetheart, don't cry—it's all right, everything is all right.'

He bent and kissed the back of her neck, whispering as he did, 'Everything's going to be all right, honey, trust me.' It was the worst thing he could have said, and she rose slashing the tears from her eyes.

'How can I trust you? You couldn't trust me!' She knew she was being hysterical and emotional, but she couldn't help herself, and she ran to the bedroom and threw herself on to the bed, sobbing once more.

She felt his presence rather than saw it and she sat up in the bed watching him. His eyes were tired and a look of concern and bewilderment was there. But Ilona was only concerned about herself. If he touches me I'll scream, she told herself. But as he sat on the bed and began to stroke her cheek gently, she didn't.

'Don't fight me, Loney,' he murmured, sitting down on the edge of the bed. 'Please don't fight me. I'm sorry for anything I've done to hurt you. I've been callous and unfeeling and all kinds of a fool. But I didn't want to hurt you.'

Ilona cowered away from him as he leant towards her to kiss her and turned her head away from his lips.

Something in Alistair snapped and he grabbed her chin in an iron grasp, turning her head so that she was forced to look at him. 'God damn it, woman, what do I have to do? Do I have to get down on my knees and crawl?' His voice was low and angry and his eyes were flinty with passion.

His lips found hers in an angry kiss, a hard, defiant kiss that branded her as his woman more than any words ever could, burning and controlling until finally all her anger and hurt disappeared and her lips opened to the taunting demands of his, and she melted into his arms, home at last.

The kiss seemed to last an eternity—an eternity, but only a moment. And Ilona clung to him, wanting it never to end.

'You, foolish, foolish woman,' he moaned, fumbling with the buttons of her blouse to release her breasts. 'Didn't you know how much I loved you? Couldn't you tell?' His words muffled as his kiss trailed down between her breasts sending shivers of desire through her entire body.

Ilona's fingers stroked his hair and neck, weak with desire and an all-consuming need. He wanted her, he loved her. It was too much to take in!

Later, she couldn't remember how they shed their clothes, how they ended together naked in the tiny single bed. All she knew was that she had cried, 'I love you—oh, I love you!' as his fingers had brought her to the peak of passion and his body had carried her over it to the calmer waters of contentment.

She lay beside him, watching his face as he slept, wondering why he should have this hold over her and wondering if it could last. He had said he loved her—but he had mentioned nothing of marriage. Then with a sigh she closed her eyes and drifted off to sleep again.

When she woke, the sun was streaming into the little room and she was alone. She could hear voices outside—Alistair's well-loved deep growl and another voice she didn't recognise. She wondered whether she ought to go outside to investigate. But she was too peaceful and contented to move, so she lay listening until the voices stopped and she heard a car drive off.

'So you've finally woken up?' Alistair asked a few minutes later when he came in with coffee. 'I was going to have to wake you if you weren't.'

'Who was that outside?' asked Ilona, pulling the sheet over her nakedness and accepting the steaming brew.

He grinned and pulled a chair up to the bedside. 'The police, you saucy wench. Just as well he didn't want to question you straight away,' he added, nodding at her bare shoulders. 'I don't think the local constabulary would have been prepared for you like that!'

She blushed, and he laughed at her embarrassment. 'Anyway, I said we'd go to the station later and you can make a statement about last night! Now, before we do anything there's a few points we still haven't cleared up.' His voice was firm, but his eyes were twinkling, and Ilona wondered what he meant.

'I thought we'd sorted *everything* out,' she whispered, looking down at her coffee.

'Most things, and *very* satisfactorily,' Alistair agreed, making her blush again. 'But now that you know all about my connection with Fame, there's the small matter of your contract with poor Megan! You've certainly made life difficult for her.'

Ilona squirmed with guilt as she remembered the tapes. 'Oh?' she asked quietly.

'Yes—Oh! I really was surprised when I found Simon had sent those tapes to me and not Megan, even more surprised when I played them. That wasn't nice, my love. Not very nice at all!' He was lecturing her, and Ilona began to feel like a schoolgirl being dressed down for some minor infraction.

'Well, I was angry—very angry,' she admitted. 'Anyway, I didn't destroy them, I can tell you where they are. But I won't say I'm sorry!' she told him, a hint of defiance creeping in.

'You'd never make a criminal, you know,' Alistair laughed. 'It wasn't hard to find them once I'd played those dud ones. If you'd been serious, you should have taken them out of the flat all together.'

'I was going to,' she admitted, 'but Mattie came back too soon and I forgot to collect them before I left. To be honest,' she laughed, relieved that he didn't seem to be upset about it, 'I forgot which covers I'd put them in, and it would have looked odd to Mattie if she'd found me scrambling round among your cassettes.'

'Still, it took me a while to find them. I was so angry. If you'd been there at the time you wouldn't have been able to sit down for a week,' Alistair said quite calmly.

'You wouldn't have hit me, would you?' she asked surprised.

'Better not tempt me. I warn you now, I've got a rotten temper. So the best thing you could do,' he warned, 'is not to provoke me. Or if you do, get out quick!'

Ilona wondered if he were joking and she smiled as he bent over and gave her a kiss. 'I'll try not to,' she murmured happily. 'But I suppose now I won't be able to give up my career completely, if those records are still going to be made. I *had* begun to think of myself as a star in decline,' she laughed to show that her words were facetious.

'A star in decline,' he repeated thoughtfully. 'More like a falling star.'

Ilona grinned. 'I like that—a falling star!' In more ways than one, she mused happily. It's really more a fallen star, she thought, and began to laugh.

Alistair rose and took her in his arms. 'I hope you're going to let me catch *this* falling star and take it home for ever.'

Ilona's heart began to flutter wildly and she could feel his beating in rhythm against hers. She wondered if she had heard correctly.

'Well?' he asked in her ear.

'Well what?' she whispered excitedly.

'Can I catch my falling star?'

'That depends on how you plan to keep it,' she answered.

'Safe, warm and very much for myself,' Alistair answered against her lips.

'No singing?' she asked, pulling her lips from his reluctantly.

'Only if you want to, and only when you have time.'

'What do you mean, time?' she moaned as his hands pushed the sheets from her breasts and his hands took possession of them.

'I think,' he murmured against her skin, 'that you might be too busy, for a while, raising a couple of other stars.'

'Oh!' she moaned as his lips burned fire over her rosy peaks, then nuzzled them into burning excitement.

His lips left her skin and his head rose till he

could look into her glazed eyes. 'That was a proposal, in case you hadn't realised,' he whispered.

'I had,' she breathed. 'But I didn't know what kind.'

'What do you mean, what kind?' he asked, stroking her hair.

'Decent or indecent?' Ilona smiled.

'Decidedly indecent at the moment, wench,' he laughed. 'But I have no intention of letting anyone else make any sort of proposal indecent or otherwise to you—not while I've got breath in my body!' And he pushed her back against the pillow and took her once more to paradise.

Begin a long love affair with

HARLEQUIN SUPERROMANCE. ™·

Accept LOVE BEYOND DESIRE **FREE**.

Complete and mail the coupon below today!

- -

FREE! Mail to: Harlequin Reader Service

In the U.S.
2504 West Southern Avenue
Tempe, AZ 85282

In Canada
P.O. Box 2800, Postal Station "A"
5170 Yonge St., Willowdale, Ont. M2N 5T5

YES, please send me FREE and without any obligation my
HARLEQUIN SUPERROMANCE novel, LOVE BEYOND DESIRE. If you do
not hear from me after I have examined my FREE book, please send me
the 4 new **HARLEQUIN SUPERROMANCE** books every month as soon
as they come off the press. I understand that I will be billed only $2.50 for
each book (total $10.00). There are no shipping and handling or any
other hidden charges. There is no minimum number of books that I have
to purchase. In fact, I may cancel this arrangement at any time.
LOVE BEYOND DESIRE is mine to keep as a FREE gift, even if I do not
buy any additional books.   134 BPS KAP2

NAME _____ (Please Print)

ADDRESS _____ APT. NO. _____

CITY _____

STATE/PROV. _____ ZIP/POSTAL CODE _____

SIGNATURE (If under 18, parent or guardian must sign.)

SUP-SUB-22

This offer is limited to one order per household and not valid to present
subscribers. Prices subject to change without notice.
Offer expires January 31, 1985